The Exploiters

The Exploiters

SAMUEL EDWARDS

PRAEGER PUBLISHERS
New York · Washington

Published in the United States of America in 1974
by Praeger Publishers, Inc.
111 Fourth Avenue, New York, N.Y. 10003

Library of Congress Cataloging in Publication Data

The exploiters.

I. Title.
PZ3.G323Ex [PS3513.E8679]   813'.5'2   73-19435
ISBN 0-275-05140-4

Printed in the United States of America

For
John L. Hochmann

◆◆

He who loves God and shows courage is valorous;
he who loves not God and shows courage is foolhardy.

—Mohammed

◆◆

One

"I love going to bed with you, Turk. Everything else stinks."
Bobbie Kenyon stood at the kitchen counter and hugged her
dressing gown tighter.

Dale Kenyon grinned as he leaned against the door frame,
and after hitching his trousers higher, jammed his hands into
his pockets, which hauled them lower. He made no comment.

There was no need for Bobbie to glance in his direction.
She knew he was admiring her rear end, that his dark eyes
were gleaming and that the mustache that had given him his
nickname was probably quivering. Now, as in the past, he
didn't hear a word she said. "I'm due at the office at nine,"
she said, her voice becoming strident. "After breakfast you
can clear out."

"You know me better than that," Dale said in his deep
voice. "I'll clean up the dishes, and then I'll give you a lift
to work. Just the way I always did when we were married."

"Always? Ha! You were away for three and a half of the five years we were together."

He turned and walked into the living room, and returned with the vase containing the three dozen long-stemmed roses he had brought when he appeared out of nowhere the night before.

Bobbie knew without looking that he placed the vase on the kitchen table with a flourish. And, just as she anticipated, he held her chair for her when she brought their scrambled eggs and toast to the table. Not until she sat down did she force herself to study him. There were a few flecks of gray in his black hair, perhaps a line or two at the corners of his eyes and mouth; otherwise he was unchanged. At thirty-four he was still a magnificent specimen, and she hated herself for succumbing without a struggle, which was precisely what his women always did.

"No toast for me, thanks," he said. "I'm three pounds over my limit."

Bobbie had no appetite, and sipped her steaming coffee. "Okay, Turk. What's the pitch?"

Dale's eyes widened. "What's that supposed to mean?"

"You pop out of the blue after eighteen months, pretty posies in hand. You feed me the fanciest dinner in New York, and enough champagne to make certain you'll wind up in the sack with me. I know you, Turk, and I know you don't go to all that trouble unless you want something."

"I told you last night, honey," he protested. "I just got back after prospecting for a year and a half in Indonesia—"

"I happen to know the Djakarta Oil Corporation didn't get its lease from the Indonesian government, so you're out of a job. Again."

His smile was as candid as it was charming. "Hardly my fault."

"Getting fired is never your fault. Like the time you landed in a jam in Kuwait—"

"Saudi Arabia. Because they thought I was playing favorites in Dubai. Which is exactly what I was doing, following the orders of the Aapco front office."

"We won't go into all that again," Bobbie said, and passed him the sugar bowl. "Why look me up when there must be dozens of New York names in your little black book? Is it because I'm still executive secretary to the president of the American-Arabian Petroleum Company—and there's something you want from us?"

Dale lit two cigarettes and handed one to his former wife. "I had a tip that McIntosh is looking for somebody with my qualifications, and although I couldn't find out any details, he knows me, and he knows I produce."

Bobbie sat back in her chair and examined him at length. "Your name never came up," she said thoughtfully, "but it just could."

"What's the job?"

"I'm not at liberty to say."

Dale put his hand on her bare forearm.

Bobbie jerked away, almost upsetting her coffee. "Don't start that again."

He withdrew, but remained confident. "Meet me for lunch."

"No way. I've got to make a verbatim record of an executive committee meeting that will last through the lunch hour."

"You really are on the inside at Aapco, baby. What's hot these days?"

"The price of crude. By the barrel or the tanker load. Take your choice."

Dale grimaced. "Very funny."

"I recovered my sense of humor after the divorce. After forgetting I'd ever had a sense of humor."

He managed to look hurt.

"I know your act." Bobbie gestured impatiently, her mouth hardening. "See here, Turk—I'll make you a deal."

Dale brightened.

3

"Stay out of my life for good. In return, I'll put in a word for you with Mr. McIntosh. Call me at two this afternoon, and I'll let you know if and when he can see you. In the meantime, pack your bag, get out of here—and don't leave your dirty laundry behind!'"

Dugald McIntosh, like so many of the top-ranking men in the oil industry, didn't look like a $275,000 per year executive. He had bought his conservative suit off the rack, his necktie and shirt were modest, and his steel-rimmed glasses were self-effacing. But his manner was incisive and his gaze was sharp as he looked in turn at each of the five members of the executive committee gathered in the paneled board room on the fifty-sixth floor of the Aapco Building.

"Gentlemen," he said, "our troubles, like Job's, are still multiplying. The public still can't understand that this business is subjected to the basic laws of supply and demand, and that we can control neither oil shortages nor prices. The information department is still struggling to overcome resentment, but there is no real cure until we achieve Nirvana. Unlimited quantities of oil and mid-sixties prices."

The other members of the committee laughed dutifully.

"The building of the shale oil converter plant in Wyoming is ahead of schedule, but it will be another eighteen months before it becomes operable, as you know. Meanwhile the new refinery in Maine is progressing at a snail's pace—"

"And the cost continues to escalate," the finance chairman interrupted. "We budgeted five hundred million for the project, and it appears it will cost us an additional one hundred million, at the least."

"I hardly need tell you what that does to our budget, gentlemen," Dugald McIntosh said. "Our operations for the year will still be profitable, but we'll have to slash our dividend by fifteen to twenty cents a share, so we're sure to get a lot of flak at the annual stockholders' meeting. Which

4

can't be helped. Am I going too fast for you, Mrs. Kenyon?"

"No, sir." Bobbie continued to punch the keys to her shorthand machine.

"All of you have copies of our operations projection. Look at the last paragraph on page eleven, and you'll see our situation. Until the Alaskan crude begins to flow and the Wyoming shale processing is completed—not to mention the beginning of operations at all three of the new refineries under construction, we'll be at the continued mercy of our friends in the Arabian Gulf."

"I'm not necessarily opposed to shortages," the finance chairman said, rubbing his chin. "I can think of worse predicaments for Aapco than too little gasoline, too little heating oil, too few byproducts for petrochemical manufacture."

"Provided," the operations vice-president added with a smile, "we can persuade the other major companies to develop similar shortages. Our stockholders' chief interest is that profit-and-loss line on our annual statements, and as long as our dividends keep rising, we're doing okay. There is no such thing as consumer resistance in this industry. Oil is a necessity of life."

The head of research and development, a scientist with little interest in business affairs, raised an eyebrow. "It seems to me you're asking a great deal of the other major companies if you expect them to join us in creating an artificial shortage."

The others laughed.

"According to rumors that haven't been kept secret from the American public," the finance chairman said, still chuckling, "it wouldn't be the first time we've used sleight-of-hand to raise prices."

"Not that Aapco would be a party to such a conspiracy." McIntosh glanced at Bobbie to make certain she was entering his remarks on the record.

The head of research and development looked duly chastised. "What concerns me is our dependence on the

Persian Gulf producers. There's nothing in the operations projection on how much longer we'll have to mark time, Dugald. What's your estimate?"

"I have none. I can only guess, and pulling a figure out of the air, I'm reasonably sure we'll be forced to walk a tightrope for at least three more years. Possibly longer. So we're totally dependent on our Arabian partners, especially the emirate of Abu Bakr."

The others, already aware of the situation, nodded.

"It must be obvious to you that our situation there is complicated by the palace coup that took place six days ago. The new ruler, Shaikh Suleiman ben Yosef, moved faster than the jet he's just ordered from Boeing. He's consolidated his position in no time, and we'll have to deal with him, whether we like him or not."

"Why shouldn't we like him?" the finance chairman asked.

McIntosh shrugged. "I'm afraid we know too little about him to make any judgments. He's one of the deposed Shaikh's seventeen half brothers, and the Middle East intelligence department has very little data on him." The president of American-Arabian Petroleum consulted a sheet of paper on which he had scribbled a few notes. "He's forty-one years old. Likes blondes and Bourbon, in that order, but lives a puritanical Muslim life in Abu Bakr."

The executive vice-president gestured impatiently. "What are his politics?"

"Unknown."

"Will he honor our agreement with his half brother, or will he manufacture a loophole that will reduce our percentage again? We can't afford many more cuts."

"We know literally nothing about the policies of Suleiman ben Yosef," McIntosh said. "He's the last of the Abu Bakr princes we expected to ascend the throne, and we've been caught unprepared."

The group turned to the head of operations, and the executive vice-president frowned. "How come?"

6

The operations chief chewed on an unlit cigar. "I've been turning the Abu Bakr office upside down the past few days, but it isn't their fault. They've tried for years to romance Suleiman, just as they have the other princes, but he's kept his distance. I've seen a teletype facsimile of the record. They've invited him to lunches, dinners, gazelle hunts, visits to our field installations, inspection tours in a chopper, even weekends in Rome and Vienna, but he's turned them down every time."

"Is he chummy with the Russians?" the research and development head asked.

McIntosh's laugh was sour. "Hell, no. The very few public statements he's made indicate that he's even more anti-Red than Faisal of Saudi. He sees Communists under his bed."

"Who are his friends?"

"We don't know." The executive vice-president slapped the table. "Goddammit, let's find out!"

"I'm putting as much heat on Red Hamilton as I can, Fred. He's a good man. He's spent more than twenty-five years in the Gulf states, and he knows the Arab mind better than he understands the West."

"Why the hell isn't he producing?" the executive vice-president remained belligerent.

Dugald McIntosh intervened. "We promoted Red to his job as general manager of the Abu Bakr operations nine years ago because he was friendly with the shaikh who's been deposed. So it may take him a little time to win the confidence of Suleiman."

"Meanwhile," the finance chairman said, "the new Shaikh can reduce our share from fifty-one percent to twenty-five, or even less. He can cut back production, or even close down the wells. The discovery of the new fields—which no one knows about yet; no one, mind you—combined with our current production flow in Abu Bakr, will keep Aapco afloat until Alaska and the shale converters begin to produce. Without them we may as well cut our throats."

"There's no doubt we're in a spot," McIntosh said. "But we can't afford to panic. We don't want to make Suleiman aware of our weakness."

"As if he didn't know," the executive vice-president said. "Show me one Arab ruler who doesn't know the score these days—or who can't find it out from the Harvard Business School graduates on his staff."

The president took command. "I've called you here, gentlemen, because I want to propose a temporary plan of action. It would be premature to replace Red Hamilton, I think. Later, maybe, but not until we learn a great deal more about the new Shaikh. For the immediate present, I propose that we send a special emissary to Abu Bakr. A personal representative of this group, who will express our pleasure at the new eminence Suleiman has achieved, and who will present him with several gifts on our behalf. I've spoken to London this morning, and Rolls-Royce is holding a new Silver Cloud sedan for us. Our emissary can fly it to Abu Bakr. Along with a blonde or two, and anything else that will win us Suleiman's good will."

"Suppose he sees through bribes? He may be pretty shrewd. And he's come into a royal treasury worth billions, so he doesn't need us to supply him with automobiles. Or blondes." The finance chairman was contemptuous.

McIntosh's smile was cold. "You miss the point. I want to send someone who can take Suleiman's measure. Someone who will test the temperature of the Abu Bakr throne. Someone whose judgment we can trust, a man who can establish a relationship with the new Shaikh in a hurry, and who can come back with a report on him. We can't make long-range plans until we form a personality profile on Suleiman."

"I don't know that we'll gain much," the executive vice-president said, "but we have nothing to lose. Who do you have in mind?"

The president nodded, then turned to Bobbie. "We'll need

no further transcription for the moment, Mrs. Kenyon. I'd like an off-the-record discussion."

Bobbie sat back in her chair.

"Ordinarily," McIntosh said, "I'd ask Mrs. Kenyon to leave, but I believe she can be of help to us. Ever since yesterday afternoon I've been drawing up a tentative list of prospects, and this morning Mrs. Kenyon suggested another. Dale Kenyon, her former husband."

The finance chairman made a wry face.

"That son of a bitch," the operations head said.

"Turk Kenyon isn't one of my favorite people in this world," McIntosh said, "but he may be made to order for this particular assignment. Mrs. Kenyon, I wonder if you'd care to tell the committee why you recommended him."

"I'll be glad to, sir," Bobbie said, "but first of all I'd like to make it clear that I have no personal ax to grind. I want nothing more to do with Turk myself. Ever. But I do think he'd be the perfect emissary to send to Abu Bakr. He knows the oil business. He's spent most of his adult life in the Gulf states, and he can be as much of an Arab as Suleiman himself. He's shrewd and tough and ruthless, you can rely on his judgments—and he's loaded with charm. In fact," she added bitterly, "it drips off him. I despise him, but if anyone can become Suleiman's buddy overnight— and bring an accurate personality profile back to this com- mittee—Turk's the man. And may the Lord help us all."

The oldest of the Abu Bakr oil fields, discovered in 1944 and commencing production in 1950, were located a short distance west of the Persian Gulf, and extended over an area of about forty thousand acres. Their stainless steel rigs broke the monotony of an otherwise unrelieved landscape, a region of low, rolling hills and shallow valleys, an expanse of brownish-gray sand and boulders. The land was one of the most inhospitable known to man.

On the Gulf, due north of the fields, surrounded by a six-

9

foot wall of mud and brick, was the original American settlement, where the dwellings of foremen, supervisors, and
clerks were located. To the south of the fields, about twenty
miles from the Abu Bakr capital, El Ain, was another
American community, also surrounded by a wall, and here
the executives of Aapco, the company physicians, and the
department heads made their homes.

No part of the American complex bore an official name,
as its existence had never been recognized by the ruling
Shaikhs or their government. But the region of the wells
was called Roosevelt Fields, the "suburb" of the foremen
was known as Truman, and that of the executives as Eisenhower. The combined population of the two towns was
8,547; without exception the inhabitants were Aapco employees and their dependents. An Abu Bakr decree prohibited subjects of the ruling Shaikh from living in either
community, and most natives who worked as servants
arrived soon after sunrise and left before sundown.

Visitors, who usually arrived at the El Ain airport, were
obliged to drive to the American towns by way of the
capital, whose fifty thousand permanent inhabitants were
crowded into mud dwellings erected on narrow lanes that
hugged the cliffs facing the sea. The only buildings of
consequence in the Old Town were the Grand Mosque and
two lesser mosques, the royal palace, and a rickety hotel. In
the New Town were the hospital, elementary and secondary
schools, and the other modern structures built with Abu
Bakr's share of oil profits.

One of the most conservative of the Arab emirates, the
tiny nation clung to the ways of antiquity. The Word of the
Prophet was law, Bedouins from the interior rode their
camels through the winding streets, and all women were
veiled. The total population of slightly less than three million
persons, spread over a land the size of New Hampshire,
Vermont, and Rhode Island, enjoyed one of the highest rates
of per capita wealth in the world, thanks to black gold

that was carried to the seaport in pipes that never ran dry. But commoners did not share in these riches. Although there was a free medical program, which had been instituted by the deposed Shaikh Muhammad, most of the oil profits were invested by the ruling family in American stocks or reposed in Swiss banks, and it was rumored that one billion dollars in gold rested in the palace vaults.

After traveling backward in time to the sixth and seventh centuries, any visitor was astonished by the first glimpse of suburban Eisenhower. There the streets were broad, the substantial pastel-colored houses, each with large, screened porches and many with swimming pools, were done in the best pseudo-Spanish California style. There were two cars in every garage, homes boasted air conditioning and every household gadget known to American manufacturers, and the clipped lawns were a deep, luxurious shade of green. Thanks to the most efficient of desalinization plants, Eisenhower, like Truman, suffered no lack of water.

This was a blessing to the company wives, who grew vegetable gardens to supplement the produce from Egypt and Lebanon available at the Aapco-owned supermarket. These plots were tended by local gardeners, and most newcomers could not understand why the natives grew only tomatoes in their El Ain backyards. The veterans alone realized that water was plentiful only in Eisenhower and Truman.

On the surface the two American communities were transplanted Middle Western small towns. Their weekly newspaper was devoted to local affairs. Their amateur theatrical group was presenting Thornton Wilder's *Our Town*. Their church auxiliary was rehearsing a production of a musical revue. Their women wore bikinis as they sunned beside swimming pools, and went to the supermarket in shorts. They bought their liquor at the Aapco package store, and saw American films at two local theaters.

· But Western civilization was strictly confined within the

walls of Truman and Eisenhower. Women who left the suburbs were required to appear in voluminous robes and veils. A man who carried liquor from either suburb—at any time and for any purpose—was subject to instant dismissal and deportation. If he was lucky, and wasn't arrested by the Abu Bakr constabulary. As an occasional culprit learned to his infinite sorrow, few prisons anywhere offered accommodations as miserable as a cramped cell of the El Ain mud jail.

The largest and most imposing house in Eisenhower was that of Lyman Hamilton, Aapco vice-president and Abu Bakr resident manager. The place belonged to the company, to be sure, but Red Hamilton had lived there for years, and was inclined to regard it as his personal property. He came home, hot and dusty, after an inspection trip that had taken him eighty miles into the interior, where the new northwest fields were located, and subsequently he had spent a frustrating hour listening to the complaints of the Minister of Oil.

Now, however, refreshed after a swim in his pool, and clad in sport shirt, sandals, and shorts, he wandered through the air-conditioned house to the kitchen. A burly man who had never known an employer other than Aapco, he was permanently tanned after spending a quarter of a century in the Arabian sun, and only a few streaks of red remained in his faded hair.

The oven door was open, and Ruth Hamilton, wearing a strapless tube top and white shorts, was poking at sizzling meat with a long fork. After twenty years of marriage, the entire time spent in the Arabian peninsula, except for an occasional trip home to see relatives, she still had the figure of a girl, her husband thought. In fact, from the rear she was indistinguishable from their daughter, Judy, who was nineteen. Her husband picked up her martini glass on the table. "I'll refill this for you if you'll come into the living room."

"As soon as I put on the potatoes. Real potatoes, imported from Maine."

He lingered in the kitchen, waiting until she finished her chores. "How did it go today?"

"Life was far more peaceful," Ruth said, "when Judy was off at school in Switzerland."

"Now what?"

"She told me she and the Watrous boy were going into El Ain to shop at the *suq*. I didn't think anything of it, but I happened to see her just as they were leaving. She wasn't wearing a *feredezah* or a veil."

Red was stunned. "She knows better than that!"

"Of course she does. She said she meant no harm, and it's high time Abu Bakr joins the modern world."

"I might have been able to protect her if Muhammad was still on the throne. But Suleiman is an unknown quantity, and if the stories about him are true, he's fanatically puritanical. He'd have packed her off to Cairo on the next plane!"

His bikini-clad daughter appeared behind him. "Oh, Daddy, I wasn't going to start a revolution. Don't make a big deal out of nothing." She went to the refrigerator for a Coke. "I know dozens and dozens of people in El Ain, and they know me—"

"All the more reason not to defy local conventions. Damn it, Judy, you're not an ignorant foreigner. You grew up here!"

The girl faced him defiantly. "Billy Watrous and I went to the Sheraton for lunch. There must have been ten Egyptian and Lebanese women around the pool—dressed the way I am right now."

"The hotel is private property. Besides, as you well know, a ten-foot wall cuts it off from the outside world. There would have been hell to pay if you'd gone to the bazaar in a short skirt. You've seen Arab mobs in action, and you know it doesn't take much to spark a riot. A tradesman who recognized you might have jumped to the conclusion that you were thumbing your nose at his standards—and he'd have been right. Young Watrous could have been hurt, even stoned to death, and God knows what might have happened to you."

"I'm sorry." Judy's contrition appeared genuine for an instant. "Anyway, I've heard the same lecture from Mother, so you can save your breath."

"Judy," Red said slowly, "this is the first time young Watrous has visited Abu Bakr, so I hold you responsible. My offer of a job and a year off from school was contingent on your behavior. Act up once more and you're at USC. We won't even wait until the fall semester."

Judy returned his angry look, then turned away. "If nobody minds, I'm going for a swim."

Ruth did not speak until her daughter had gone. "I'm ready for that refill now. A stiff one."

Red walked beside her to a glass-enclosed patio, its shuttered jalousies shielding it from the glare of the desert. "Maybe we're asking for trouble. A year's a long time for a kid."

"But we promised," Ruth said. "For the past eight years she's been off at one school or another, never visiting us for more than a few weeks at a time. We've got to be fair to her, Lyman."

"In case you haven't noticed, she's ripe. Her figure is like yours."

"Better."

"A gross exaggeration." Red smiled, then sobered. "It's tough enough for an adult woman to maintain her balance in an artificial town stuck in the middle of nowhere. It must be doubly difficult for a child."

"Judy is no child, as you just observed," his wife said. "She's a woman, and she'll have to accept responsibility for what she does. Just as I've had to do." She drank her new martini quickly.

14

They were careful not to look at each other. "It was easier back in the forties, when we were still exploring and getting production of crude organized," Red said at last. "Old Spindletop Blake used to say that oil and family life didn't mix, at least in this part of the world. I'm afraid he was right."

"Your precious Mr. Blake was hopelessly old-fashioned," Ruth said. "When a man's job is here, whether by choice or out of necessity, his wife and children make the best of it. And things work out fine, provided there's enough good will all around."

"Yeah," Red said, and mixed himself a highball. "What's on the schedule for tonight?"

"I turned down two invitations. You're always tired and scratchy after an inspection trip."

"You make me sound old," he said with a grin. "Come to think of it, the thermometer hit one hundred thirty in the Great Wadi this noon. A trifle warm, even for me."

The telephone rang, and Ruth crossed the room to answer the call. "Hello. Yes, Mrs. Brown. Red, a cable from New York, in code."

He continued to sprawl in his easy chair. "Copy it for me, will you, Ruthie?"

She took the message, then brought it and his code book to him.

Red worked in silence, flipping back and forth through the pages as he deciphered the message.

Ruth wandered to a side window that looked out on the pool and idly watched Judy practice her backstroke. When she glanced at her husband, she saw his face was grim. "Problems, Lyman?"

"We'll have to open Guest House Three next week. The front office is sending a special ambassador with gifts for Suleiman."

Ruth forced herself to guess. "Turk Kenyon?"

Red nodded, averting his gaze.

"It was inevitable that we'd see him again," she said.

He remained silent.

Ruth went to him and placed a hand on his shoulder. "Lyman."

Red neither replied nor looked up at her.

"I'm a big girl," she said, speaking slowly and distinctly. "I don't make the same mistake twice."

He knew a response of some sort was required, so he reached up and patted her hand.

The gesture was feeble, but she supposed that, under the circumstances, it was the most she could expect.

Paul-Pierre Gautier, French Minister and Envoy Plenipotentiary to Abu Bakr, sipped the thick, sweet coffee, then balanced the cup and saucer on top of the pile beside him. Even an experienced diplomat found Arab protocol endlessly boring. "If Your Excellency intends to visit Paris this summer, my government will be delighted to place a guest house at your disposal."

It amused Shaikh Ahmed al-Husayn, Abu Bakr Foreign Minister, half brother of the deposed ruler and of his successor, holder of degrees from the Sorbonne, Cambridge, and Harvard, to reply in French. He reached inside his *agal* for an Indian case of inlaid ivory and removed an American cigarette; then, flicking aside his *ghutra,* or head cloth, he produced a flame with an English lighter. "You're very kind, but I keep my regular suite at the Ritz."

"Of course," Gautier murmured.

"More coffee?" Behind the horn-rimmed glasses a hint of humor appeared in Husayn's eyes. As other foreign diplomats and representatives of Aapco, particularly Red Hamilton, could testify, His Excellency was known to produce tiny cups of coffee for hours on end, especially when he suspected that a visitor had an ax to grind.

Gautier knew he would have to take bicarbonate of soda,

in any event, after he returned to his legation. "As Your Excellency pleases."

Husayn's manner changed, and he became crisp, in the style of the Americans he had admired for the better part of his thirty-five years. "You've come to see me for a purpose. What is it?" A sudden attack sometimes threw a visitor off guard.

But the French envoy easily shifted gears. "It has come to the attention of my government that His Highness would like to possess some of the new generation of Mirage fighter-bombers whose export has been forbidden."

"I am neither His Highness nor the Minister of Defense," Husayn said.

"To be sure, Your Excellency, but it has occurred to me that you might wish to be informed of a new development. My government is prepared—privately, of course—to make a full squadron of the new aircraft available to Abu Bakr."

"At a bargain price, no doubt." The Foreign Minister fingered his full beard.

"I'm confident a price can be arranged that will be satisfactory to everyone concerned, Your Excellency."

Husayn switched to Arabic. "And what is it that the Republic of France wishes in return?"

The envoy's expression indicated that no such idea had crossed his mind. "Nothing, Your Excellency. My government merely wishes to recognize—in a tangible way—the accession of His Highness to the throne. And to express our hope that he reigns for many years."

"*In sha'a 'llah*," Husayn said piously.

"*Al-hamdu li-'llah*," the French Minister replied, himself praising God.

"I dare say you've heard rumors about our explorations in the Great Wadi."

"In El Ain," Gautier replied, "one hears fresh rumors daily. One rarely believes all one hears."

"This rumor has persisted," Husayn said, his humor fading. "But I do not know if it is accurate."

The diplomat cleared his throat. "It has also been said—without verification—that His Highness took the throne because His former Highness was disposed to permit the Americans to develop and exploit the Great Wadi."

Husayn's face remained blank. "When a government changes hands the diplomat, like the student, searches for reasons. This has been true throughout history."

"As Your Excellency knows from your own studies at the University of Paris, the logic of power is unlike any other. It is said that His Highness, although the friend of all people and all nations, is less inclined to be partial toward the Americans."

"I would be insolent if I dared to interpret the mind of His Highness. Suleiman ben Yosef will speak for himself when he deems the time appropriate."

"No one in the diplomatic corps more eagerly awaits that occasion than I." Gautier inclined his head. "I hope His Highness will receive the Ministers in the near future."

"He is putting his house in order, but you will be notified by the Ministry of Foreign Affairs when he finds the time to schedule a reception."

The French Minister accepted the rebuke with a steady smile. "It will be a splendid occasion. Meanwhile I shall notify the Defense Minister of my government's decision to make the most advanced Mirage fighter-bombers exclusively available to the Abu Bakr air force. I know, certainly, that Your Excellency will regard it as a gesture of friendship on the part of France, and that you realize no strings are attached to the offer."

Husayn took another cigarette from his case and lit it. "You may rest assured," he said, "that I am aware of the spirit that motivates the Republic of France. You won't resent it if I remind you that American-Arabian Petroleum has an agreement with the emirate of Abu Bakr that has been in force for many years. Under its terms Aapco has the right to make the initial bid on any new oil fields discovered in the realm."

"I've not forgotten the existence of that agreement," Gautier said, "and I respect the sanctity of contracts, as does my government. But it has been known to happen that a great prince sometimes makes adjustments in his alliances after he comes to power, and France always thinks in terms of the future."

"Very wise," Husayn said. "Perhaps you have heard the old Arab proverb that he who plans for tomorrow feels today's hunger pangs less acutely."

Few Romans, other than the scantily clad prostitutes, were frequenting the Via Veneto, but the tourists were out in force. Although it was not yet noon, Americans, Japanese, and Germans filled the street, jostling one another as they photographed everything in sight. Priests from a hundred countries and nuns from fifty rubbed elbows with handsome, well-groomed young men who held hands as they sauntered in pairs. A party of English schoolgirls in uniform filled one sidewalk, their high sopranos sounding like starlings, and an American film star was almost mobbed as he bought a packet of pipe tobacco in a small shop.

No one paid any attention to the woman who took a small table in a sidewalk café, in the third row from the sidewalk, and there was no reason why anyone in the open-air cage should have noticed her. Even the waiter barely acknowledged her request for a cup of espresso. She might have been a school teacher from Viterbo or Sheffield or San Francisco, a colorless person of indeterminate age, and the most that could be said in her favor was that she was unobtrusively neat.

Her dark hair, gathered in a small bun at the nape of her neck, was lackluster. She wore no makeup, and ordinary dark glasses protected her eyes from the late morning

Roman sun. Her inexpensive sandals shielded the soles of her feet from the hot pavement, but did nothing for her legs, and her loose-fitting summer dress of gray cotton effectively concealed her figure. She tapped a cigarette on an unpainted thumbnail, then lit it with a tiny wax match, and buried herself in an early edition of an afternoon newspaper as she sipped her coffee.

The man who entered the café and looked around uncertainly before taking an empty place at the table next to the woman was nondescript too. His suit was badly cut, his shirt and necktie were cheap, and his shoes were dusty. He was hawk-nosed, with black, neatly combed hair, and his eyes, behind steel-rimmed spectacles, were mild. He, too, ordered coffee, which he gulped, and he did not open the folded newspaper he carried under his arm.

He spent no more than seven or eight minutes in the café, and he left his newspaper on the table when he departed. Neither he nor the woman acknowledged each other's presence in any way.

Even as he left the table she picked up his newspaper, placed it inside her own, and asked for her bill.

A few moments later she moved off down the Via Veneto, walked several blocks, and then hailed a taxi. Settling herself in a corner, she looked out of the rear window from time to time, and was satisfied that no one followed her. The driver dropped her at the corner entrance of a large complex of modern, middle-class apartment buildings. She caused no stir as she made her way to the far side of the development.

Eventually she reached her apartment, a drab place consisting of an underfurnished living room, a Spartan bedroom, and a tiny kitchen. Locking herself in, she took a magnifying glass from a kitchen drawer, then concentrated on a long series of tiny pinholes in the margins of the newspaper the man in the café had left behind.

She worked steadily for an hour, and when she was done she allowed herself the luxury of a faint smile. That smile broadened when, momentarily removing her glasses, she glanced at her reflection in a small wall mirror. Her eyes, even without makeup, were extraordinary: they were luminous and huge, their color in the noon light that filtered in through the closed window a deep shade of sea green, and they were simultaneously sensual and intelligent, sleepy and alert.

Donning her glasses again, she went into the bedroom and threw a few inexpensive belongings into a cardboard suitcase. It was time to go to work, so she burned the newspapers in a small grate, settled her black wig more firmly on her head, and left the key to the apartment on the kitchen table when she departed.

Out of habit she walked several blocks, sometimes turning right and sometimes left, before she hailed a taxi and asked to be taken to Leonardo da Vinci international airport at Fiumicino. Again she checked the rear window repeatedly to make certain she wasn't being followed.

At the airport she bought a tourist-class ticket to London on British European Airways, producing a superbly forged Italian passport, and when she went to the waiting room she seemed to melt into the crowd of tourists.

Two

♦♦♦♦♦♦♦♦♦♦♦♦♦♦♦♦♦♦♦♦♦♦♦♦♦
♦♦♦♦♦♦♦♦♦♦♦♦♦♦♦♦♦♦♦♦♦♦♦♦

Most of the patrons had moved into the dining room for lunch, and the middle-aged, aristocratic-looking lady found Dale Kenyon alone at a corner table in the Hotel Connaught bar. He jumped to his feet when he saw her, kissed her hand, and immediately ordered her a dry sherry.

"Isabel," he said, "You look the same as ever. Marvelous."

She ignored the compliment. "When did you get to London, Turk?"

"Several days ago. I've been busy."

"You didn't call me until last night." There was gentle reproof in her voice.

"I had to rent an airplane big enough to hold a Rolls," Turk said. "That and a few other odd chores have kept me on the go. Besides, it didn't occur to me I might run into trouble in the other department. What's happened to all the beautiful women in England?"

22

"You're slipping, old boy," Isabel said. "No one stays in London at this time of year."

"It wasn't that way the last time we did business."

"It is now," she said, and then relented. "But I told you there was no need for worry. I've never yet failed you."

They were silent while the waiter served her drink.

Turk raised his half-consumed Bourbon on the rocks. "Here's to you, Isabel. Long may you prosper."

"So I shall. As long as I have clients like you."

He reached into an inner pocket, then handed her a sealed envelope. "Your fee. As agreed, two thousand pounds."

She placed the envelope in her handbag without checking the contents. "I enjoy doing business with you, Turk. As always. And if my client isn't quite right for the assignment, do let me know and I'll find you another. Although I'm confident you'll be delighted. She's really extraordinary."

"Don't sell me a bill of goods, Isabel."

"I wouldn't dream of trying, my dear. You'll see for yourself. At tea time. You're staying here?"

"No, at the new Berkeley, in Knightsbridge."

"Then I'll ring her and tell her where to go. She'll use my name. The customary routine."

"What's she like, Isabel?"

The woman laughed. "You *are* in a state. I've never seen you so jittery."

"The stakes are pretty high this round. She's a natural blonde, I hope."

Isabel's gaze was severe. "Have you ever known me not to meet specifications?"

"Okay, I apologize," Turk said. "I wish I'd been around twenty-five years ago, when you were active in the business yourself."

A speculative gleam appeared in the woman's eyes for an instant. "So do I, my dear."

He crossed and uncrossed his legs, drumming on the table. "At least fill me in on a few details. She's English?"

"The young lady could be English or American, but I don't believe she's either. Occasionally she speaks with a slight trace of an accent, but it didn't sound Scandinavian to me."

"Then you don't know her yourself."

"We've just met, which is why I was a little late."

"Dammit, she'd better come through," Turk said.

"Her credentials are impeccable," Isabel said, "and I'm willing to grant you a complete refund if she falls short."

"Speaking of which, what's the tariff?"

Isabel smiled. "I'd rather you settle the details with her yourself, my dear. Her fee will seem less outrageous after you've met her."

He grimaced.

"Whatever is wrong with you?"

"Isabel," Turk said, "not only is this job important to my bosses, but it's make or break for me. I've been out of the mainstream for the past couple of years, and people forget past accomplishments. A guy in my line makes a lot of enemies, so I know the knives are being sharpened for me. If I pay off I'll be in clover, but if there's a foul-up I'll be out on my tail, lucky to wind up with a gang of two-bit prospectors in the Andes or on the upper reaches of the Blue Nile. I'm not all that young any more, so it's a question of produce—or else."

For a few weeks each year, after the rains came, a mighty torrent poured down from the Mountains of the Prophet, transforming the Great Wadi into a green bed three quarters of a mile wide. The Bedouin tribes gathered there from all parts of Abu Bakr to graze their flocks, and knowing no international borders, they came from Saudi Arabia and Kuwait too, as well as from Yemen to the south.

By summer, however, the Wadi was dry again, transformed into a vast trough, its sand packed hard, its boulders bleak, the mountain heights to the west forbidding. No permanent roads had been built here, and automobiles that came into the area were forced to depend on balloon-like, double-width tires for traction. The Abu Bakrian preferred his camel. Red Hamilton couldn't blame him.

The natives were right when they called the Great Wadi the land God had forgotten. The temperature was over 140°, and the furnace-like heat was so intense that Red wished he had worn a *ghutra* instead of the smaller *burnoose*. Long heat waves danced and jiggled everywhere above the surface of the parched earth, and it was possible to see two or even three mirages in the distance. At least the *shamal* wasn't blowing today, and the foreigner could share the joy of the native that reddish-brown clouds of stinging sand weren't choking him while they obscured the sun.

The blistering sands seemed to burn holes in Red's sandals, and he shuddered every time his companion, Shaikh Ahmed al-Husayn, offered him a swallow of water from the skin made of a sheep's bladder. Even after all these years the contents of a water bag still tasted like mutton tallow to him. He'd been walking steadily for the better part of two hours, moving on foot from one experimental rig to the next, and he was ready to admit he was tired. His clothes were plastered to his body, and the sun seemed to be drilling through his skull.

But the experimental rigs were proving the contention of the geologists that the Great Wadi would produce as much oil as the northwest fields. No one could seriously doubt the extent of the new discovery, which would double or even treble the wealth of Abu Bakr. The new field would be Red's swan song, and he'd be ready to go back to the States and stay there. Except.

What would he do in the New York office? Wear a tie and

jacket every day, play office politics and wish he were back here, where a man could escape from his desk? Ruth would enjoy living in a Connecticut or New Jersey suburb, of course, and it would be far better for Judy to be transplanted permanently to a place where her own cultural standards predominated. He was wrong to be thinking only of himself. Besides, he was burned out, like the bald, jagged boulder off to his left. It had absorbed so much desert heat by day and such numbing cold by night that it would shatter if struck with a mallet. Some days he had the feeling that his nerves were on the verge of shattering too.

The helicopter in the blue and white of the Royal Abu Bakrian air force stood directly ahead behind yet another boulder, the pilot dozing in its shade, and Red breathed a trifle more easily. Another physical ordeal was about to end.

"Red," Husayn said, addressing him in English, "we will tell no one what we've seen today."

Red gaped at him. "The sun has made you dizzy, Ahmed. We'd better discuss this after we get back to El Ain."

The Arab shook his head. "For six months we've had the idea that we've got something important here, and now we know it. But I want to keep the actual existence of a new oil field secret for a while longer."

"How is that possible?" Red was irritated. "I've alternated two crews out here, which means sixteen Americans and about forty Abu Bakrians know about the discovery. Plus your pilot. And my two assistants at Eisenhower, and—"

"You keep your people's mouths shut, and I'll take care of mine." The Foreign Minister was firm. "Stall your New York office on actual statistics for a few weeks more." He stopped, unplugged the water bag, and offered it to the American.

Red accepted a swallow, and stood silent for a moment. "What's the advantage?"

"One might call it the lack of a disadvantage. New York will order you to prepare a contract extension for Abu Bakr to sign, or will send out some high official with a contract. But I can't sign anything these days, between you and me."

"You've got to be kidding."

"I don't know where Suleiman stands, and I'm afraid he'll balk if I push him. Let him grow accustomed to the throne, and he'll become more malleable."

"*Bismi 'llah*, Ahmed! Aapco has an iron-clad contract with Abu Bakr—"

"Red, you are not naive. If Suleiman feels like tearing up his agreement with Aapco, that's precisely what he'll do. Your New York office can sue him in World Court, and even get a judgment against him. But there's no way to enforce it. The oil-producing countries have the whip hand these days."

"Suleiman has never been chummy with us, but he hasn't been particularly friendly with anyone. Surely he'll honor his legal obligations, Ahmed." Red was too angry to think clearly.

"Suleiman will honor obligations he feels like honoring. Muhammad delegated a great deal of his authority and was the first ruling shaikh of Abu Bakr ever to go Western. Suleiman won't repeat the mistake. In case you don't know it yet, my friend, the clock has been set back precisely thirteen hundred years. This country is an absolute monarchy."

"Its wealth is based exclusively on oil." Red tugged at his *burnoose* to shield his face from the sun.

"The royal family must be worth three billion dollars. None of us knows for sure, and it doesn't really matter. Even if we blew up every oil well in the country, we'd still be rich."

"What the devil does Suleiman want?"

Husayn gestured toward the helicopter. "We'll talk on the way back to town. Better than getting sunstroke in the Great Wadi."

They awakened the pilot, strapped themselves into their seats, and soon were flying above the limitless expanse of desert.

Red removed his sunglasses and wiped his bloodshot eyes. "If it weren't for Aapco, Suleiman would be living in a mud palace."

Husayn stared out the window, then turned to Red. "You've lived with us for a long time, but even you don't understand us. No outsider does. It adds up to something very simple, Red. Eleven hundred years ago we conquered the civilized world. Allah was in his heaven, and the Koran was the penultimate Word of Truth on earth. You've forgotten all that, but the Arab remembers. Especially Suleiman. Some of us in the family have had exposure to the outside world, but his non-Arab contacts have been limited. Even when he's gone abroad he's taken his own world with him."

"What does he want?" Red demanded.

The Foreign Minister was amused as well as exasperated. "In a single world—respect."

"Does he think he'll get it by tearing up legally binding contracts?"

"Pieces of useless paper. Did you ever see our Bedouins, the proudest men on earth, prostrate themselves before Muhammad? Suleiman—just as those like him—wants the whole world on its collective knees before him. That's his idea of respect. You Americans *think* you're masters of the universe, but Suleiman *knows* he is, so he's got to prove it. To you more than to anybody else."

"I realize some of the Gulf states have been gobbling up bigger and bigger shares of oil profits in recent years. But Suleiman wouldn't throw Aapco out of Abu Bakr! That's unthinkable, Ahmed."

"Only because you refuse to think in those terms. Believe me, I know my brother. That's why I'm urging you to keep quiet about what we've learned."

"Where do you stand in all this?" Red demanded.

The Foreign Minister smiled. "I, too, am a member of the brotherhood of Arabs. I am an Abu Bakrian and a defender of Islam. I may have only two wives, so I'm more modern than some of my relatives. So modern, in fact, that I don't believe oil sitting in the ground will do much for my country, any more than stashing boxes of gold in underground vaults will help my people. I want Abu Bakr to have a balanced economy, with our own steel mills and petrochemical plants. We can say what we please about the Israelis, but they've made the desert bloom, and what they can do we can do. I want to see citrus groves and farms. A diversified economy. And a healthy, literate people whose dignity has some solid substance behind it."

"Now you're talking sense," Red said.

"The best way to achieve those goals, I happen to believe, is through friendship with the United States. A partnership, which doesn't mean letting you walk all over us, you know. If I had my way, I'd ask you to pay for the development of the Great Wadi oil fields, and I'd keep sixty percent. Oh, I know, you'd scream if I restricted you to forty percent, but in the end you'd accept."

Red nodded. "I'm afraid that's exactly what we'd do."

"However," Husayn said, "I'm not my own master. I'm the subject of Suleiman ben Yosef, as much his subject as the thief whose right hand is chopped off by royal decree. I won't like it if Suleiman commands me to expel Aapco, but I'll still obey his orders. History is like the tides, as an old Arab saying has it. We may draw back in the wrong direction for a time, but we'll surge forward again. And after a thousand years of waiting, we can afford to be patient a little longer."

"I've got to warn my headquarters."

"That's strictly up to you," Husayn said. "All I ask—for your sake and your company's, as well as my own dream of the future for Abu Bakr—is that you say nothing at present about the potential of the Great Wadi field. Give Suleiman a chance to leave the imprint of his own hind end on the cushion that rests on the seat of his throne!"

Dugald McIntosh studied the decoded cable from El Ain, then stared out of his windows, rolling an unlit cigar between thumb and forefinger. An Aapco tanker was unloading oil onto barges in the East River far below, a scene that ordinarily would have delighted him, but today he took no pleasure in anything. He even glowered at Bobbie Kenyon when she brought a pile of letters in for his signature, but he did manage to admire her legs and the trim figure beneath her snug-fitting sweater and skirt. He was rarely in too sour a mood for that.

"Why is it," he demanded as she stood beside him, handing him one letter at a time, "that even the best men eventually go to seed in overseas assignments? For years Red Hamilton was the most dependable executive we had in the Middle East. Now he's useless!"

Bobbie was accustomed to her employer's diatribes, but didn't know what he meant. "Communications brought you a cable a few minutes ago, didn't they?"

"That's right. You haven't seen it." He gave her the message.

It was succinct: STILL AWAITING GREAT WADI TEST RESULTS. IMPOSSIBLE TO INITIATE CONTRACT EXTENSION UNTIL FINAL FIGURES ARE RECEIVED. WILL CABLE DATA SOONEST. REGARDS. HAMILTON.

"How the hell long does it take those jokers to drill a half dozen experimental wells? I could do the job myself in forty-eight hours!"

"You know nothing in Arabia happens overnight. And the Great Wadi is difficult to reach from the Gulf coast." Bobbie saw her attempt to soothe him failed, so she opened a bar on the far side of the room, shook two pills from a bottle and gave them to him.

McIntosh took his medication without complaint, swallowing it with a small quantity of ice water. "Sit down, Bobbie."

She took the leather chair beside his desk, and knew that, as usual, he was staring at her legs.

"I want your advice," he said.

She indicated surprise.

"I'm thinking of asking Turk to look into the status of the Great Wadi tests while he's in Abu Bakr. It won't take him weeks to send me the score."

"If you're asking me, don't do it," she said.

"Why the hell not?"

Bobbie refused to be intimidated. "Turk will ride roughshod over Hamilton. There's bad blood between them anyway, and when they start clobbering each other, there'll be hell to pay."

McIntosh's laugh was flat. "Good! May the better man win." He paused. "Strictly between us, if Kenyon is able to establish a relationship with the new Shaikh, I might give him Hamilton's job."

Bobbie smoothed her linen skirt and spoke with great care. "I'm in favor of it personally, because it would get him out of my hair. But I think it would be a mistake."

"Reasons?"

"The men in Abu Bakr are loyal to Hamilton, and so are their wives."

"How come I don't know about this feud?"

"It isn't the sort of thing that's reported to you, Mr. McIntosh. Several years ago, the last time Turk was in El Ain, he had a fling with Hamilton's wife. Everybody there knew about it, and there was a lot of talk. The Hamiltons managed to stay together, which is more than I can say for Turk and me, although I must admit the incident was just one of many that turned me off. Nothing is ever Turk's fault." Bobbie forced a smile. "That isn't fair. Until he showed up the other night I hadn't seen or heard from him in a year and a half. Maybe he's steadier now. We'll find out when we see how he handles the job you've just given him. What I do know is that Hamilton is reliable. If he says the data isn't ready, you can bet Aapco's last dollar that it isn't."

"You know, of course, Mrs. Kenyon, that a productive field in the Great Wadi can increase our annual net by millions of dollars."

"I do know it. I also know Hamilton never fails to follow an order. If it were up to me—and you asked for this, Mr. McIntosh—I wouldn't upset any barrels of oil just yet. See how Turk makes out with Shaikh Suleiman, and by then maybe Hamilton will have cabled the test figures. We have a few days' leeway. Let's take advantage of them."

"My problem is that I'm as cantankerous as Turk, and never should have been made an executive. You're probably right, and I owe you a dinner for it."

He had been building up to the invitation for weeks, but Bobbie was still unprepared for it, and hesitated.

"My daughter-in-law has invited me to Oyster Bay tonight, but I'm too damn restless for a dinner party. I'd rather stay here in town and go to some comfortable place with you. And I promise not to discuss business."

She took a deep breath. "In some circles you're the most eligible widower around. I don't happen to travel in those circles."

"What's that supposed to mean?"

"Our situation is classical, Mr. McIntosh. You figure it out."

"If you're afraid I'll make a pass at you—"

"It wouldn't do you any good if you did," Bobbie interrupted.

"If I'm not old enough to be your father," he said, "I could at least qualify as his younger brother."

"I don't want to lose either my standards or my job," she

said, "and I'd hate to be placed in a spot where I'd be forced to make a choice. That's honest, Mr. McIntosh."

His smile was rueful. "I've never known you to be anything else, which is one of the qualities I like best in you. Look here, Bobbie. All three of my sons talk Aapco business when we're together. My daughters-in-law see dollar signs in front of their eyes when they look at me. I find society stupid, and a guy who started life as an independent wildcatter will never know which fork to use. Sure I'm rich, but I can be as lonely as a poor man."

He, too, was honest. She nodded.

McIntosh regarded her response as promising. "If you want me to take an oath that I won't try to paw you or proposition you, I won't do it. I've been living alone for a long time, and you don't need me to tell you that you're an attractive young woman. On the other hand, I know a lady when I see one, and I'm still enough of a Texan to prove it."

A quick smile lit up Bobbie's face. "Mrs. Kenyon," she said, "accepts with pleasure Mr. McIntosh's kind invitation to dinner. Provided Mr. McIntosh will let her turn her desk and phone over to someone else a half hour before closing time, so she can go home to change."

"Hell," he said, "go now. I'll pick you up at seven."

"Fine. I live—"

His roar of laughter drowned her words. "I've fought runaway fires in the fields, and I've been in more free-for-all scraps than I can remember. In more recent years I've battled the Wall Street wolves on their own ground, and I've won. But it took me a month to work up the courage to ask you to sit down at the dinner table with me. Do you suppose for one damn minute that I don't know where you live? I reckon you don't know me as well as you think you do!"

The house was like scores of others in the old El Ain casbah. Made of mud with a flat roof and surrounded by a wall, it clung to the side of a cliff that overlooked the sea. Its windows were open to the heat of day and the cool of evening as well as to the countless mosquitoes and flies that the recently organized Royal Abu Bakrian Health Service had not yet eradicated. It was completely lacking in modern conveniences, including electricity, and the only furniture in the central chamber, which opened onto a miniature court-yard, were two dilapidated chests of drawers and several large, stained cushions of faded silk. Two students from the Royal College, both in traditional robes and headdresses, were seated on the cushions. A third man, wearing a Western-style sport shirt and trousers, but bearded like the other two, paced the room.

He was only a few years older than his companions, but his manner intimidated them, and they watched him in silence as he moved back and forth across the chamber, the soles of his sandals slapping on the hard-packed dirt floor. Occasionally he glanced at his cheap wristwatch, muttered, and shook his head.

Eventually a shrouded woman slipped into the room, and the man stopped pacing. "You are late, Farima," he said, pointing an accusing finger.

As she removed her veil and robe the college students sat upright. In her early twenties, she wore a skimpy blouse that emphasized her large, full breasts and tiny waist, and her short skirt revealed shapely legs. The pacing man did not intimidate her. "*Allahu akbar*, Ali," she said. "When will you learn the Bedouin virtue of patience? I was followed by a member of the secret police, and had to give him the slip or we'd have been forced to move our headquarters again."

"My sister," Ali Nasar Jalal told the students, "is never at a loss for reasons to excuse her lateness."

She laughed as she seated herself on a cushion, and made no attempt to pull down her skirt when it rode high on her thighs. "It is enough that I am here. Begin."

Ali moved to a vacant cushion. "The old-fashioned of this

34

country would say that Allah frowned on our great enterprise. But I call it bad luck that Shaikh Muhammad was deposed just as we completed our plan to assassinate him. We must start again, so the people of Abu Bakr must wait a little longer before we throw off the chains of our oppressors."

"I hear no clamor in the streets for our revolution," Farima said, her voice mocking. "Oh, I know. The people must be led, as Lenin wrote. But our situation is not healthy. Our numbers have dwindled, and our treasury is empty."

"Hamid and I," one of the students said, "offer ourselves as volunteers. We will hijack an aircraft of the imperialists, and will demand a large ransom."

"No," Ali said. "I forbid it. Our Arab brothers throughout Islam seek respectability at almost any price these days, and they condemn the capture of airplanes. We'll need the support of the more radical regimes when we take power, and we can't afford to antagonize them now."

The student was petulant. "All the members of my cell voted in favor of the hijacking."

"As did mine," his companion added. "What choice are we offered?"

Ali raised a hand for silence. "Before we can remove Shaikh Suleiman from the throne we must learn more about his habits, his day-to-day way of life. A hijacking would alert him and his secret police, and we'd be lucky to escape from the country with our lives. And where would we go? The Saudis would give us no refuge, and neither would Kuwait. Or any of the emirates. No, comrades, we shall succeed only if we continue to work secretly."

"But for that, as for anything else, we need money," the student said.

"True," Ali said, "but we must be careful. There's a chance I can obtain funds in Syria or Iraq, but some of the brotherhood in those countries have forgotten the Bedouin virtue of keeping their mouths shut. We must assume that Suleiman is not disbanding Muhammad's corps of foreign agents, and we'd be in great danger the moment the new Shaikh learned we had obtained money from another country."

"Then we and our movement will rot," the student said.

"Never," Farima said cheerfully. "It takes a woman to develop a plan that will work."

The men looked at her.

"It is not accidental," the girl said, "that I have found a job in the American compound. In the house of the chief of all Aapco in Abu Bakr."

Ali raised an eyebrow. "Be careful, Farima. The man Hamilton has lived here for a long time, and knows the ways of Abu Bakr very well."

"But his daughter doesn't," Farima said. "She lived here as a child, but now she goes to schools in Europe and she has forgotten what little she knows of the Arabs. I am her teacher. Soon she will make me her personal maid, and we will become friends."

Ali grimaced. "What of it?"

"At the right time," Farima said, "we will kidnap her. The Americans who rob us of our oil are richer than any shaikh, and her father will pay a huge ransom for her return. Then we'll have enough money for our immediate plans."

The students were enthusiastic.

Ali sat still and pondered. "The idea is not lacking in merit, but there are holes in it. What if Hamilton asks Suleiman for help? Then the regime will learn of our existence."

"I've thought of that, too," a triumphant Farima said. "We will instruct Hamilton to tell no one of his dilemma and to pay the ransom quickly if he hopes to see his daughter alive again."

"Arabs," Ali said, "have a reputation for impulsiveness, but Americans are worse. I'm not going to rush into this scheme. I want to think about it."

"You'll come around to my plan," Farima said, "because you won't be able to invent a better one."

Dale Kenyon's guest was announced by the desk, and he waited for her in the living room of his hotel suite. She was on time to the minute, he noted with approval.

The girl who arrived a few moments later was stunning—she had a full mouth, oval face, and wavy, honey-colored hair that fell below her shoulders. She was tall and slender, perhaps somewhat thinner than most Arabs liked, but no man could fail to admire her high, firm breasts and rounded thighs. Her legs were good, and she carried herself with grace, her air elegant.

Her eyes were her most startling feature. They were exceptionally large and an almost liquid green, and their intensity made Turk slightly uncomfortable. The girl gave him only a glimpse of her eyes, however, before donning a huge pair of sunglasses.

Her handshake was cool, nothing more, and her manner was crisp. "I hope I haven't kept you waiting, Mr. Kenyon." She spoke perfect English with just a trace of an indefinable accent.

"Not at all. Will you have a drink?"

"I prefer tea, thank you." Her voice had a faintly husky quality.

When he finished calling room service he saw she had made herself at home in an easy chair, and was lighting a cigarette with a gold lighter she took from her shoulderbag. The choice was perfect, he thought; certainly she didn't look like a call girl.

"Shall we discuss business first?" she asked.

Turk found it disconcerting that she took the lead. "Sure. What can you tell me about yourself?"

"That depends on what you want to know." Her smile was contained. "As a beginning, you may call me Lee."

"Your nationality?"

"I shall carry a British passport on this assignment," she said. "I assure you it's genuine, and in order. There will be no border hitches that will embarrass you or your company."

"I suppose you know the nature of the assignment."

She crossed her legs, absently tugging at the hem of her Shantung dress. "I am to become well acquainted with the new ruler of the emirate of Abu Bakr. Presumably I'll be given a propaganda message of some sort to be delivered on behalf of your company."

"No message," Turk said. "You'll fill the bill completely by becoming chummy with Suleiman ben Yosef."

Lee nodded approvingly. "Very wise. I find punching across a message comparable to gilding the lily."

A room service waiter arrived with tea and sandwiches.

Lee moved to a sofa and did the honors, the tray having been deposited on the coffee table in front of her. "Cream or lemon?"

"Just sugar, thanks. One lump." Her self-assurance, her ability to take charge were impressive. "Obviously," he said, "you feel you can handle this job."

"I know my business." She sounded curt.

He accepted a cup of tea from her and retreated to the easy chair she had vacated. He had wanted to sit on the sofa beside her, but there were important details to be settled before their relationship became more personal.

"As I understand it from our mutual friend," Lee said, "I'll be expected to spend approximately one week in Abu Bakr."

"The visit could be extended to about ten days, depending on how you and Suleiman hit it off. I'll escort you in and out of the country. And while I think of it, I hope you won't be upset by the local customs. You'll have to wear a robe and veil entering and leaving the country."

"I'm familiar with Arab traditions," she said.

"I have no idea what customs may be observed at the palace, but I suspect you'll find it less formal there."

"I dare say." She sipped her tea and took a bite of a tiny cucumber and watercress sandwich. "Now, if I've satisfied your curiosity about me—"

38

"You haven't." He realized she had told him almost nothing.

"Well, it's my turn. First, what can you tell me about Shaikh Suleiman?"

"Very little. He's about forty-two, and stood fifth or sixth in the line of succession before he pulled off his coup. His mother was the daughter of a Bedouin chieftain, and he's proud of his desert ancestry."

"What languages does he speak?"

"Only Arabic and a limited English. He and some of his half brothers were educated by tutors at the palace in El Ain. He was sent to school in the United States, but attended college there for only a year. I have a sketchy report on that year—"

"May I see it?" Lee interrupted.

"Of course." She was as thorough as a business executive, he thought as he went into the bedroom and removed a single sheet of paper from his attaché case.

The girl scanned the document. "He attended few of his classes, took no examinations, and wrote no papers," she said. "His one accomplishment was learning English. What I find significant is that he had no known friends in his dormitory, and that what most of those who knew him remember best is that he preferred to eat his meals alone."

"This was the best the company could supply, I'm sorry to say. All it adds up to is that Suleiman—twenty years ago, at least—was a loner."

"Not necessarily," she said. "He may have been shy, and was probably handicapped because he didn't know colloquial English. His lack of interest in his studies needn't be particularly significant, either. Recent events have demonstrated that he's very ambitious and has something of a genius for detail."

The sharpness of her analysis surprised him.

"Let's just say the job will be something of a challenge." Lee removed her sunglasses.

Again he was struck by her unusual eyes.

"One more question, Mr. Kenyon. Do you happen to know whether Suleiman's personal tastes are kinky?"

Her crisp, impersonal air was unsettling. "I'm afraid I have no idea. All I can tell you is that we've been informed on good authority that His Highness enjoys the company of blondes."

"Fair enough, but I place a condition on my acceptance of this assignment. If his tastes are kinky, all bets are off, and I reserve the right to cancel the deal."

He tried to hide his dismay. "The whole thing depends on what you regard as kinky."

The girl's manner did not change. "I'm being hired to establish a private relationship with Suleiman, and anything that develops naturally—and privately—is fine. But if he's one of those jaded Arab princes who wants to call in his harem or whoop it up with his pals, that's not for me."

"Fair enough."

"Then we understand each other, Mr. Kenyon."

"Turk."

"All right, Turk, all that we still have to settle is my fee. Twenty-five thousand dollars in cash, half payable now and the other half before we board the airplane to leave Abu Bakr."

"Isn't that a little high?"

"With an extra seventy-five hundred if the visit is extended for three days."

"Ever rob a bank?"

"Take it or leave it," she said.

He didn't want to admit in so many words that he had no real choice. "You'd better produce."

"I always produce. But I'm no robber. If Suleiman and I don't hit it off, which isn't likely, you won't have to pay me anything beyond the original installment."

"Generous of you, I'm sure." He saw that her eyes had turned to green ice.

Lee shrugged.

"Okay, lady. We've made the deal on your terms. But the banks are closed for the day, so I'll have to give you a check for the initial twelve thousand five hundred."

Lee made no objection, so he wrote the check and handed it to her. "We'll leave in the morning."

"Not too early in the morning," she said. "I'll want to make certain this clears through my bank before I leave London."

"You're very trusting."

"There's no reason I should trust you, or vice versa. We've come to a professional understanding."

Turk moved to a place beside her on the sofa. "Since we're going to be in this deal together, I suggest we start to build a little rapport."

His intent was obvious, but the girl made no move.

He slid his arm across the back of the sofa, then let it drop around her shoulders.

Lee gently placed her hand around his wrist.

Suddenly an excruciating pain shot up the inside of Turk's arm, rendering him helpless, and he realized she was exerting pressure with a finger.

Lee released him, her expression still bland.

He removed his arm and rubbed it, thinking for a moment that she had broken it.

"You'll be all right in a minute or two," she said. "Don't panic."

The pain subsided, and Turk found he could move his arm with ease again. "Where did you learn that cute little trick?"

"Someone in my kind of work must be able to protect herself," Lee said.

"Nobody told me you're a woman wrestler."

She laughed, and her amusement was genuine. "It was helpful to clear the air, Turk."

"I heard your message."

"Good. We're making progress. I believe in defining the terms of a partnership agreement at the outset."

Turk's arm still tingled. "I'd have been better off if I'd gone into partnership with a rattlesnake."

"That," Lee said, "would depend on the rattlesnake's reliability, and whether it could perform the task you assigned it."

Three

His Highness, Shaikh Suleiman ben Yosef al-Husayn, Emir of Abu Bakr and the Sayeh Islands off its coast, bore a strong resemblance to the hawk that perched on his wrist. His dark eyes were small, penetrating, and hooded, his mouth was a thin line between his mustache and beard, and his nose was long and thin. Something else in his manner also suggested the hawk: he was in repose yet alert and ready for instant action.

A cup of untasted coffee sat beside him on the low table. The curved sword that was the symbol of his high office rested in its scabbard, conveniently within arm's reach; near it was the bell rope that would summon members of his household staff. Gold drapes bearing an Arabic geometric design framed the windows, and the same motif appeared on the cushions that covered the low-slung throne of gold and inlaid ivory. The room had remained virtually unchanged through the centuries, and the only touch of modernity was the gold and white telephone with its five push-button lines.

Suleiman's tension was so great that he generated a similar feeling in others, and the members of his government, official entourage, and household staff, few of whom had known him well before his coup, were discovering it was almost impossible to relax in his presence. Certainly Shaikh Ahmed al-Husayn felt less comfortable with him than with any of his other half brothers. But members of the family stood on no ceremony with one another in private, and Husayn lit a cigarette without asking permission.

His Highness indicated with a gesture that he wanted one too.

"I didn't know you smoked," Husayn said.

"I am learning. Many things." Suleiman looked at the cigarette before leaning forward to the flame of his brother's lighter. "American."

"The best made."

"There must be English and French cigarettes equally good. Also Canadian."

"The Russians make cigarettes too," Husayn said pointedly, "but I don't care for their taste."

Suleiman bared his teeth in a smile. "I've always said you were shrewd, Ahmed."

The younger prince returned the smile.

"But not too shrewd, I hope, or too ambitious."

"I am often reminded of the proverb that he who tends his own garden will gather more figs than he who covets the larger garden of his neighbor."

"Allah has given you wisdom," His Highness observed.

"Allah also opens my eyes to the world around me. Not a half hour ago, as I stood at a window of my house on the cliff, I saw an aircraft carrier flying the hammer and sickle of the Soviet Union."

Suleiman's eyes seemed to become smaller. "Sailing inside my territorial waters?"

"No, I watched it through my binoculars. The Russian

admirals are careful not to violate the rules governing such matters. Just as their air marshals permit no flights over our land."

"But they show a new interest in Abu Bakr since the throne became mine."

"Naturally," Husayn said. "They knew Muhammad would not recognize them, but now their hopes have risen."

"Has no one told them I believe the Russians and the Israelis are the infidel scum of the world?"

"Oh, they've heard. But they've also picked up rumors that you aren't fond of the United States, either, so they hope you'll establish diplomatic relations with them. Soon. And they send an aircraft carrier to cruise off your shores as a way of reminding you that they exist."

Suleiman glared. "I need no reminders."

"Your position will become clear when you receive the diplomatic corps and let your feelings be known openly."

"I refuse to be rushed." His Highness sounded petulant.

"If the discovery of a new field in the Great Wadi proves to be extensive, your hand will be forced," Husayn said.

"I don't see why."

"I've already explained to you, Suleiman, that Aapco will demand an extension of its contract, which it has every right to do. And the American government will also exert pressure."

"And if I let them wait, neither accepting nor refusing, what then?"

"Other countries and their oil companies will clamor for the right to develop the new fields."

Again Suleiman bared his teeth. "The French are already talking about giving us fighter-bombers at ridiculously low prices. Soon it will be the turn of the English. Then the Japanese will offer to build us supertankers of our own, and will make us gifts of cash. One nation will inform us it will develop the fields in return for a twenty-five percent interest. Another will go into partnership with us for only twenty percent. You will be a principal player in a rare comedy, my brother."

"And how will that comedy end?" Husayn asked.

"We shall accept the bid most favorable to Abu Bakr, of course."

"We'll be short-sighted if we break our agreement with the Americans," Husayn said.

Suleiman rang for his falconer and had the hawk taken away. Then, his manner chilly, he looked hard at his brother. "Are French and English warplanes less effective than American aircraft?"

"Abu Bakr needs many things the Americans can supply in greater number and quality than anyone else. Computers, tractors, desalinization plants. Steel mills. Foods of many kinds that will improve the living standard of our people."

"We've been in bondage to the Americans long enough."

"The coin has another side, too," Husayn said. "Our capital accumulates rapidly, and there is no investment anywhere superior to the blue chip stocks of American industry. Or the bonds issued by the American government."

"You've been talking to our brother Habib at the Finance Ministry. You and Habid offer me identical advice."

"I have neither seen nor spoken to Habib al-Husayn since Allah called you to the throne, Suleiman. My own common sense tells me the Americans, who offer us the best protection against the Communists, are our natural partners. This has been proved in our long relationship with Aapco. They would be the deadliest of enemies as well."

"As Allah is my witness, I have the courage of a Bedouin, and I fear no man, no nation!" Suleiman raised his voice for the first time.

Husayn quickly realized his tactical blunder. "No one questions your courage."

Suleiman was somewhat mollified. "My enemies press

46

against me on every side, but they are learning I am not another Muhammad."

A clock chimed in an anteroom, and in the distance, above the low hum of the air conditioner, they could hear the *muezzin* calling the faithful to prayer.

"Ride with me to pray at the Great Mosque," His Highness said. "To prove I take no offense, Ahmed, you shall command my escort."

Husayn rose and walked to the windows that overlooked the large central courtyard below. There, dressed in *ghutras* and flowing robes, a cavalry squadron of one hundred men, all armed with automatic rifles, waited for the ruling Shaikh.

The younger man knew better than to laugh. "We're at peace with the world," he said. "Surely you don't need the protection of a full troop when you go to prayers."

Suleiman's lean face became animated. "This very morning, while I prayed to Allah in the Omar Mosque, my men made six arrests outside the building. Two have confessed they are agents of Israel, sworn to murder me, and three admit they are in the pay of Moscow. The sixth died before he could tell us the identity of his masters."

Husayn knew better than to reply, but he was alarmed. The people of Abu Bakr had been docile for centuries, but they no longer lived in total isolation, and the random apprehension and torture of innocents, if it continued, would threaten the roots of the monarchy itself.

"Will you come with me?" Suleiman demanded.

Husayn swallowed a sigh. "It will be an honor," he said.

Judy Hamilton looked at her reflection in her bedroom mirror, and there was a hint of desperation in her giggle. From neck to toe she was concealed by the voluminous black *feredezah,* and her head was hidden under a cumbersome *yashmak,* a hood with narrow slits for her eyes. "Just ghastly," she said. "Absolutely nobody would even know me.

47

But," she added to her similarly attired companion, "it doesn't look as silly on you as it does on me."

"That is because I have worn the *feredezah* and the *yashmak* all my life," Farima Jalal said.

"You don't mean you like this outfit?"

"I despise it!" There was loathing in Farima's voice.

Judy could not see her face, but the intensity of her feeling was evident. "Let's get out of here before we expire."

They walked to a convertible parked in the driveway, and Judy hauled the skirt of her robe up to her waist as she slid behind the wheel. "They didn't make this thing for driving, that's for sure," she said as the car quickly gathered speed.

"Arab women don't drive." Farima spoke quietly now.

"You mean you don't know how to drive?" Judy was incredulous.

"Where would I learn? The wages I will earn in my whole life will not buy even an old automobile."

"That settles what we're going to do this afternoon." The convertible shot out of the compound and headed north. "We'll go out to the desert, and you'll have a lesson from one of the best drivers around."

"Your father will be very angry when he hears what you have done," Farima said. "And I will be discharged."

"He won't hear."

"But he will ask where you have been."

"There are ways to get around him. I'll tell him I went to Roosevelt. That will make him happy. It always gives him a jolt when I pay attention to his precious wells."

"But he will know you weren't there!"

"That's where you're wrong, honey," Judy said. "We'll pay a little visit to the field to establish our alibi, and Daddy won't be able to say a word. Not only am I wearing this ridiculous costume, but I've got you along as my chaperone."

A concrete road had been built between Eisenhower and Roosevelt. Judy pressed the accelerator to the floor, and since there were no other cars on the road, in a few minutes the towering steel derricks of the oil field loomed ahead.

The car screeched to a halt at an open gate, where two Abu Bakrian armed guards, both in Aapco uniforms, stood sentry duty. Both men gaped at the girls who were wearing native attire.

Judy reached inside her robe, found her identification card, and handed it to the guards.

They examined it at length, handing it back and forth, and finally returned it to her, waving her inside.

She drove more carefully now, knowing that any violation of the speed limit would be reported to her father. "What a farce!" she said. "What a security system! We show up looking like a couple of refugee Halloween witches, and they let us through. How did they know I look like the picture on my ID card?"

"They don't, of course," Farima said.

"And they didn't have the guts to tell me to take off my *yashmak* so they could make sure I'm me."

"They wouldn't dare," Farima said. "They are Abu Bakrians, and like all traditionalist Arabs they know that such an insult to your honor would be avenged by the male members of your family. Soon the sentries and all the men of their families would be dead."

"How primitive can you get? The law—"

"The law of Islam would uphold them," Farima said. "I want—very much—to see Abu Bakr give up her old ways and become part of today's world. But there are some things that won't be changed for many years, and there is nothing in Islam more sacred than the honor of an Arab woman."

"All I know is that we could have been a couple of terrorists in disguise. We could start fires, even blow up this whole oil field—and get away again before anybody would even guess who we might be."

"Such disguises have been used for many purposes and for many hundreds of years," Farima said.

"I can't wait to tell Daddy there's a great big hole in his precious security system."

The nearest of the wells loomed ahead, and Farima stared at the masses of steel and concrete. What puzzled her, as it did all those who were unfamiliar with the operations of an oil field, was the silence. There was no clanking of machinery, and even the pumps worked quietly, sucking the crude oil from reservoirs deep below the earth's surface and sending it through huge pipes to the coast, where it would be loaded on tankers.

"What's wrong?" Judy asked.

"Nothing. I'm fascinated."

"By the wells?"

"I have never seen a well," Farima said. "Your company and our rulers have banded together in a conspiracy. They keep the ordinary Arab at arm's length while they rob us of our heritage and share the profits between them."

"That isn't fair!"

"The world is unfair."

"The least I can do is show you around, although there isn't much to see. First of all, most people think the oil comes from huge underground pools, but that isn't so. It collects in the pores of underground sandstone and limestone, and in the cracks between rocks. In this part of the world most of the reservoirs are dome-shaped, which is the simplest kind."

Judy went on to explain that the oil was drawn to the surface through layers of salt water and gas found in the upper part of the reservoir, and that Persian Gulf oil was particularly valuable because it was relatively pure, having remained separated from both the gas and the salt water.

The oil drained naturally through the reservoir rock under its own gravity, and the process was aided by the gas cap and by the water-bearing portion of the reservoir. Some reservoirs were regarded as "closed" because they contained no gas or salt water, and Judy explained that the Gulf states were fortunate because there were more of these "pure" wells in the area than anywhere else in the world.

Ultimately, in the life of most oil fields, the time came when the natural pressures no longer sufficed to bring the oil to the surface. This happened, more often than not, when the greater part of the oil in a reservoir still remained there. Thereafter man-induced pressure was applied, either by injecting water into the reservoir rock, which was the simpler method, or by injecting gas into the rock. Such methods were used infrequently in the Middle East, and in Abu Bakr, as elsewhere in the area, the crude had sufficient potential energy to flow to the surface without artificial help.

As the original well had been bored, a variety of drill bits having been used to cut through different kinds of underground rock, the cavity had been lined with concrete to prevent the sides from caving in. The wellhead itself was fashioned of concrete, and was capped in steel, and the tap was opened or closed by a large steel wheel.

"The derricks," Judy said, "were built for the boring machinery, and aren't used any more after the well begins to flow. Some of them have been removed for drilling elsewhere."

"Why do the others still stand?" Farima asked.

"My father says Aapco finds it less expensive than it would be to haul them away or dismantle them. Besides, they look impressive to people who know nothing about oil."

"Expensive window dressing. And a terrible waste!"

"I wouldn't know about that."

"Of course not. You're an American." Farima softened. "Anyway, you're right about one thing. The wellheads are very simple. They look like nothing."

"The next stage is separating the oil from the salt water and gas, and that's complicated because they do it in stages and have to know the precise chemical composition of what the flow contains. There are four separators in Abu Bakr—or is it five?—and the closest is about ten miles from here, right on the seacoast, so the oil and gas can be placed in storage tanks until they're sent overseas. Would you like to visit a separator?"

"I've lived twenty-three years without seeing one, so I can survive a little longer." Farima's voice was dry.

A jeep with balloon tires raced across the desert toward the girls. The man behind the wheel was a Westerner in short-sleeved shirt and trousers, but he wore a *burnoose* to protect his head from the sun, and his expression indicated that he was annoyed. Calvin Hodges was the superintendent of the Roosevelt field wells, a post he had held for a decade. He allowed no interlopers to trespass in his domain.

"What are you doing here?" he called in Arabic as he pulled to a halt and walked to the car.

Judy answered in the same language. "If it pleases Allah and your worship, we need a quart of oil for our automobile."

He peered at her, his eyes narrow, but was unable to identify her beneath her *yashmak*. "Who are you?"

She could control her laughter no longer. "I never dreamed you were so cheap, Cal. Refusing a couple of hardworking girls a quart of oil. You must have a half million barrels a day running through that pipe."

He recognized her voice, and his craggy features relaxed. "I haven't spanked you in years, Judy Hamilton!"

"It might be more fun now than it was years ago."

He reddened beneath his tan and retreated.

"Don't get in anyone's way. And behave yourself."

Judy continued to laugh as she watched him drive off.

Farima, who had understood little of the English portion of the conversation, was thoughtful. "That man is important here?"

"He's the boss."

52

"He did not ask you to identify me." There was wonder in the Arabian girl's voice.

"Of course not. It was enough for him that you're my friend."

Farima's look of cunning was hidden by her *yashmak*. "I have changed my mind. Another day I will learn to drive. This afternoon I would like to visit the oil separators. I want to see everything in the oil fields."

The country club was one of the most expensive, and exclusive, on Long Island's North Shore. The members enjoyed their own yacht basin, tennis courts, and two championship eighteen-hole golf courses. Youngsters had their own swimming pool, so adults enjoyed the quiet of the Olympic-sized pool. There were umbrellaed tables on two sides, so that those in bathing suits could eat lunch at the edge of the pool rather than on the terrace or in the dining room.

Even at poolside the menu was varied, the service impeccable, and the food superbly prepared. What a way to spend a Saturday! Bobbie Kenyon picked at her chicken salad, made small talk with Dugald McIntosh, and counted her blessings. A sixth sense had told her to wear a maillot rather than a bikini, and she had been right; her bathing suit showed off every line of her figure to the appreciative McIntosh, but she was seemingly conforming to the club's conservative standards.

This was her third date with him in a week, and she knew she was walking a tightrope. He would proposition her, but she intended to sidestep, neither accepting nor rejecting his advances. The game she was playing was dangerous, she knew, but she had no intention of slipping into an affair with her boss. The job of office wife didn't appeal to her, and there was too little to gain by stopping work altogether and living as his mistress.

In spite of his great wealth and power he was a lonely man, so Bobbie had the natural advantage, provided she weighed every move—and luck was on her side. It was too early to think of becoming Mrs. Dugald McIntosh, yet it wasn't. His growing personal interest in her was obvious, and the stakes were so high that just thinking about them made her dizzy. A self-made oil magnate wasn't like other wealthy men, and he put on no airs. Many of the top-ranking people in the business were married to women who had been nobodies, like themselves, and no stigma was attached to a wife's lack of social standing. To hell with what the McIntosh sons and their blue-blooded wives might think. The old man would make up his own mind, and when that happened he'd take no advice from them—or anyone else.

Their conversation was interrupted by the approach of a gray-haired man in matching trunks and robe. "Dug, you rascal, it took a lady to get you out here!"

McIntosh stood and shook the man's hand. "Mrs. Kenyon, Mr. Bell."

As Bobbie accepted the introduction she wondered how Bell would react if he knew that on many occasions she had spoken to him on the telephone. He was one of McIntosh's closest friends and business associates, and as board chairman of International Consolidated Oil he was one of the major powers in the industry.

"Sit down, Hector!"

"Just for a minute." Bell looked hard at Bobbie and approved. "You got him out here, Mrs. Kenyon, and that's something. The next miracle will be to persuade him to change for a swim."

"Have a drink, Hector," McIntosh said.

"No, I don't want to disturb you while you're eating. But I'm glad I ran into you. Before the afternoon is over I'd like to have a little talk with you."

"We can talk now. Bobbie knows all of my professional secrets."

She was amused because he didn't identify her as his secretary, so his provocative remark undoubtedly led his friend to jump to unwarranted conclusions.

Bell eyed her again, then sat back in his chair and summoned a waiter. "A glass of iced coffee, very black. Mind if I smoke a cigar, Mrs. Kenyon?"

"Not at all."

"Dug, I've been hearing all sorts of rumors about Abu Bakr the past few days, and I don't like them. Your explorations in the Great Wadi were a bust. You've discovered the richest new field in the Middle East. Shaikh Suleiman is throwing Aapco out of his country. Suleiman is even more in your pocket than Muhammad was. What the hell goes on out there?"

McIntosh glanced at Bobbie. "I wish I knew, Hector. We're doing our damnedest to find out."

"Frankly, I'm worried about ICO's twenty-five percent stake in your Abu Bakr interest."

"How could I forget it? You came to our help when we were overextended."

Bell turned to Bobbie. "We shoot for the moon, Mrs. Kenyon, and sometimes we land there. We're a private club in the oil business."

"So I've heard." Her manner was demure.

McIntosh appreciated her delicacy and grinned at her before turning back to his friend. "My Abu Bakr manager tells me he doesn't have definitive test results yet. I don't believe him, but I can't imagine why he'd lie to me. We should know where we stand by the beginning of the week, no matter what. I've sent a special emissary to sound out Suleiman."

"Who is he?"

"Turk Kenyon."

"Nobody better, if he stays out of trouble." Suddenly Bell looked again at Bobbie. "Any relation, Mrs. Kenyon?"

"My former husband."

"Ah. Then you're no stranger to the oil business."

"Not completely," she said.

Bell sipped his iced coffee. "There's a big 'if' in what I want to propose to you, Dug. Assuming you make a real strike in the Great Wadi, we can hogtie Suleiman. We can build our Persian Gulf refinery in Abu Bakr."

"Most of the boys seem to favor Kuwait or Saudi," McIntosh said.

"If you and I put up a solid front, they'll go along with us. ICO is willing to put up two hundred million."

"Leaving Aapco to foot the bill for the remaining four hundred million. Not bad at all."

In spite of her experience in the business Bobbie was impressed. The cost of erecting a new refinery in the Middle East was staggering, yet these two, playing a game of international oil chess on a mammoth scale, were completely calm.

"We can give Suleiman a small cut," Bell said. "He won't demand a big slice, I'm sure. The prestige will dazzle him. He'll have the only refinery on the entire Persian Gulf."

"Will your board sit still for this?" McIntosh asked.

"Sure. They've already voted the money, and the only question is where to situate the refinery. It makes sense to anyone. Mrs. Kenyon, I gather you know a little something about our industry. What do you say?"

Bobbie knew she had to be careful. "I can't even think in terms of that much money."

"Go ahead," McIntosh said. "Give him an honest opinion, Bobbie."

"All right, then. I think you're risking a huge sum on a shaikh who may prove unreliable. We—I should say you—don't have much protection. Suleiman could wait until you build the refinery—and then throw you out."

"Wrong." Bell chuckled and blew a cloud of cigar smoke at the beach umbrella over their heads. "It'll take three years to put up the refinery, and long before then we'll know if Suleiman is a double-crosser, like Quaddafi of Libya. And there's another angle. Distribution."

"Precisely," McIntosh said. "We own the tankers. So the gasoline and heating oil refined in Abu Bakr will just sit there if Suleiman gets nasty. The Japanese own quite a few tankers, and so do some other countries, but they wouldn't take a drop out of Abu Bakr if we put the heat on them. They wouldn't dare. We own too much crude and too many refineries in other places, and we could starve them if they refused to join our team."

"I'm afraid, Mrs. Kenyon," Bell said, "that we're in a real cutthroat business, where we slug without using boxing gloves. I hope you won't think any the worse of us."

"Oh, I won't!" Bobbie said. "Some women admire a ruthless streak in a man, and I happen to be that type."

"An extraordinary young woman," McIntosh said, pleased to be able to show her off.

"Don't let her out of your sight," Bell said as he rose and shook hands.

"I have no intention of it," McIntosh said.

"Call me when you get a report from Abu Bakr, and we'll get down to the details of the refinery."

McIntosh waited until his friend was out of earshot. "That was great, Bobbie."

"I meant what I said, Mr. McIntosh."

"First names, please, on social occasions."

"Dugald, then." The pace was quickening, and she felt a little uneasy.

"I've known for a long time that you're efficient, but I'm just beginning to realize your talents are being wasted."

The critical moment was at hand before she was ready to face it. "I love my job!"

McIntosh sensed her panic, and backed off. "Well, I have some ideas, but I want to think about them a little longer, before I spring them on you. All I'll tell you right now is that you have a bright future."

"I have complete faith in Aapco," Bobbie said, forcing herself to add, "and in you, Dugald."

Christopher E. Trevenian, the United States Minister to Abu Bakr, hated the Gulf coast in general and his appointment in particular. He had made his fortune in real estate and had contributed heavily to the campaign fund of the President of the United States. He'd hoped to be awarded a major European embassy. Instead he had been sent to the middle of nowhere, and he hadn't even been given the rank of ambassador. His legation was cramped, the heat was unbearable, the social life was so dull that his wife spent most of her time in Rome, and the protocol was impossible.

Worst of all, he was little more than an errand boy for Aapco. The real Minister to Abu Bakr—Red Hamilton—sat across the desk from him. Trevenian was irritated and hostile. "What makes you think I can set up an appointment for this new man of yours on such short notice? I've met Suleiman only once since he took the throne, so I can't just call him like an old chum."

Red had been handling political appointees in the American Legation for a long time, and thought it indiscreet to mention that he had known the Shaikh for years. "Turk Kenyon's cable was delayed, which often happens here. So I just found out this morning—only an hour ago—that he's arriving today. In a chartered plane." Red added the last for effect.

"He must be a mighty big wheel if he's hired his own airplane."

"He had to. He's bringing Suleiman a rather bulky gift. An automobile. And he wants to drive it straight from the airport to the palace, so the Shaikh doesn't learn of the gift in advance." Red made no mention of the blonde Kenyon was bringing with him. "My front office is vitally interested in this mission, Chris."

58

Trevenian knew another complaint would be lodged with State Department if he failed to comply with Dugald McIntosh's wishes. He was heartily sick of that Aapco phrase, "My front office," but Hamilton and his associates recognized no other authority. "Okay, Red," he said wearily, "I'll see what I can do."

The sun was directly overhead when Kenyon's plane rolled down the runway and came to a halt in front of the one-story building of corrugated iron that served as the terminal at the so-called international airport. Two passengers alighted, Dale Kenyon and a woman wearing the customary *feredezah* and *yashmak*. The windsock on the terminal roof was hanging limply, the sun's reflection on the desert was dazzling, and the pair halted abruptly, jerked to a stop by invisible forces.

Red Hamilton approached the aircraft. He and Kenyon greeted each other with a civility that in no way mitigated their mutual lack of cordiality. Hamilton was not presented to the woman, and pretended she did not exist; all he could see behind her *yashmak* were her amused green eyes.

"I suggest you wait inside the terminal while I supervise the unloading of the car," Turk told her. "It won't be much cooler there, but at least you'll be out of the sun."

Lee went off without a word.

"All set, Red?"

"The car will be filled with gas and oil right here, so you can drive it into town yourself. I had to pressure the legation, but they've made the arrangements at the palace, and His Highness will see you whenever you arrive."

"What's he like?"

"I wish I knew," Red said. "He's been playing it cool ever since he became top dog, but that seems to be his style. Even his cabinet ministers—most of them his half brothers—can't decipher him. They say he's always kept himself in a deep freeze."

Turk chuckled. "Lee will thaw him. I really lucked out when she showed up for this job. She's one cool chick."

"If you don't mind, I prefer to know nothing about her participation in your mission here."

Turk's smile faded. Red had lived in Abu Bakr so long that he had become as puritanical as the traditionalist Arabs, so it was no wonder he wasn't producing the results the home office wanted. A man in his position had to be malleable enough to take advantage of the breaks, and to create them when there were none.

They stood side by side, watching the Rolls Royce sedan being rolled out of the cargo hatch onto the runway. "We're putting you in Guest House Three," Red said, "and we've assigned you just one servant, who'll get your breakfast for you. All sorts of plans are being made for your entertainment, so I think it unlikely that you'll be eating any of your other meals in the guest house. But if you should, you're only a short walk from the bachelor mess. And before I forget it, Ruth is giving a little dinner party for you tonight."

"How is she?" Turk's manner was offhand.

"Completely recovered."

Turk merely nodded, finding it wiser not to pursue the subject. He wasn't surprised that Hamilton had learned the truth about what had happened a few years back.

"Our daughter is staying with us," Red said.

"That's nice."

"We intend to keep it that way, Kenyon. She's nineteen and very pretty." Red's voice was flat. "So this is just a friendly warning. Keep your distance. She may look sophisticated, but she's a kid, and I'll break your neck if you make a play for her."

"Relax," Turk said. "I don't attack children."

Neither spoke again as the car was being serviced.

Red broke the silence. "I'll have a car delivered to you at the palace so you can drive yourself to Eisenhower after you've seen Suleiman. You haven't forgotten the way?"

"I always know my way."

They parted without shaking hands.

Turk had his luggage and Lee's loaded in the trunk, then drove the Rolls to the terminal entrance. Lee was watching for him, and joined him in the car.

"This air conditioning is a lifesaver," she said, hauling up the skirt of her *feredezah* as she sat down. "I hadn't remembered how incredibly hot it could be on the Gulf."

"You've been here before?"

"Not in Abu Bakr."

He waited for her to continue, but she seemed to be lost in contemplation of the desert. "Don't take off your *yashmak*," he said, "or they'll throw you out of the country before we ever reach the palace."

"I know."

He wondered whether she had paid a previous visit to one of the other shaikhs of the Arabian peninsula. Apparently she knew her business, as she had indicated to him in their initial conversation, so he didn't pursue that line. "I asked our resident mogul for the lowdown on Suleiman, but he was as blank as the reports I showed you. We have very little to go on."

"That's why we're here, isn't it?" Lee's laugh was less husky than her voice.

Turk felt oddly stymied, and changed the subject. "I doubt if there are any telephones in the women's wing of the palace, so I'll make arrangements with the palace vizier to be notified when Suleiman has dismissed you."

"That will be a help, thank you. Just so the place is air-conditioned, I won't mind."

"Oh, it is. Shaikh Muhammad saw to that. I'm told the women's wing has its own swimming pool."

"You're assuming, I suppose," Lee said, "that Suleiman keeps a closed harem, the way his brother did."

"No ruler of Abu Bakr would last for a minute if he tried to abandon the old ways."

"I suspect," the girl said, "that no ruler of Abu Bakr would want to. Look at those miserable huts. No electricity, no running water, no toilets."

"They have plenty of sand," Turk said.

"I don't think that's funny," she said. "They live exactly as their ancestors did a thousand years ago."

He shrugged, then slowed the car as they approached the winding streets of El Ain. "They like it that way."

"Have they ever been offered better? Oh, I know they've used a tiny fraction of their oil wealth to build hospitals and roads and schools. But the ordinary Arab in this part of the world hasn't enjoyed many of the real benefits of their countries' sudden riches. So I can't accept the claim that he wants no change."

"Quite the crusader, aren't you?"

"Not at all. I'm trying to be sensible, and I believe the hatred of the Arab for the non-Islamic world will change as they themselves become industrialized and enjoy greater individual benefits and luxuries. Although these days I'd hardly call a bathroom a luxury."

Lee wasn't like any call girl he had ever known, Turk thought. She had displayed none of the self-fascination that was so often found in members of her profession; she was intelligent; and she did not hesitate to express her opinions. He had wanted to caution her to be careful of what she said in the palace, but decided it wasn't necessary: She seemed to know that Arabs, and princes in particular, did not appreciate feminine volubility.

The palace, a high-walled compound protected by machine-gun parapets every fifty feet, came into view opposite the Vizier's Pavilion, where many of the government's administrative offices were located. Two sentries, wearing *burnooses* and camouflage uniforms similar to those of the

British army, were on duty at the main gate. They carried scimitars in their belts as symbols of their membership in the royal guard, but both carried automatic rifles of American make.

Turk and his companion were expected, and admitted easily, a single telephone call to the vizier's office opening the gate for them. Turk drove a short distance, parked at the entrance to a courtyard where a fountain was playing, and snapped off the engine.

"Good luck, baby," he said. "If you get into a jam, don't hesitate to send word to me."

"I have no false pride," Lee said. "But I anticipate no trouble."

With no instruction from him she followed Turk at a distance of three paces, as was customary in the traditionalist Arab world. He was pleased, and felt increasingly certain that she was no stranger to the peninsula.

A chamberlain met them and conducted them to a small, inner chamber with a mosaic-tiled floor and inscriptions from the Koran on the tiled walls. Turk was offered a cushion and coffee, but the girl was expected to sit on the floor, which she did without hesitation. After a short wait another chamberlain conducted them to the informal audience chamber, a high-ceilinged room with grilled windows located about six feet above the floor. A number of robed courtiers stood in small groups, conversing in low tones, and a half dozen guards armed with automatic rifles were in attendance. Only Shaikh Suleiman ben Yosef was seated, perched on a high mound of silk cushions.

Turk bowed low, and Lee prostrated herself, her forehead touching the gold-and-silver tiled floor.

Suleiman allowed her to remain there for some moments before indicating, with a flick of a hand, that she had his permission to rise.

"I am delighted," Turk said, carefully speaking classical

Arabic, "to find Your Highness in good health. *Allahu yukaththir khayraka*," he added for good measure, requesting God to add to the ruler's well-being.

"*Al-hamdu li-'llah*," Suleiman replied piously. "Do you know of any reason my health should not be good?"

Turk was startled, but recovered quickly. "Not now, not ever. Your Highness is an ornament of Islam, and Allah will protect you to the end of your days." He wished he could see the eyes behind the sunglasses.

Suleiman's curt gesture made it plain that he had no intention of observing further amenities.

"The board of directors of the American-Arabian Petroleum Company rejoice over Your Highness's accession to the throne," Turk said, coming to the point of his visit. "As tokens of their esteem they send you two gifts." He motioned toward the girl, who again sank to the floor, and in a magician's manner, held up a set of automobile keys.

Suleiman's expression did not change. "Remove the female and have the women prepare her for a visit at my convenience."

Lee rose, and a chamberlain, careful not to touch her, moved beside her as she backed out of the chamber.

Turk found the ruler's abruptness disconcerting. He had shown no interest in the girl, which was fair enough, of course, since it was impossible to make out her face or figure beneath her robe and *yashmak*. But the keys failed to arouse his curiosity too, so it appeared necessary to become less subtle.

"Our directors," Turk said, "have made Your Highness a gift of a motor car."

"I have already seen it from an anteroom window, and I consent to its acceptance."

Only the ruler of an Arab Gulf emirate could be so cavalier in accepting a Rolls that cost more than forty thousand dollars. Turk placed the keys on the cushions in front of the

Shaikh, taking care to use his right hand and making certain the metal did not actually touch the prince's person.

Suleiman's nod was matter of fact.

The audience, it seemed, was at an end, and the disappointed Turk bowed low.

But Suleiman had not forgotten his manners. "It has been called to my attention that you are a hunter of note."

Turk took heart. "I am not lacking in limited skills," he said.

"At this season the wild *dalu* bird appears over our domain," the Shaikh said. "Do you intend to remain in Abu Bakr for a few days?"

"I do, Your Highness. I must escort the woman back to London." That was neat, Turk though; now the old goat knew that Lee was not intended as a permanent addition to his harem.

Suleiman's expression was unchanged. "Perhaps you will try your skill with me in a few days, and will come with me to hunt the *dalu* bird."

The invitation startled Turk, but he hid his elation. "I will be honored, Your Highness," he said, and after bowing again, he backed out of the chamber. He needed only a few minutes to arrange to be notified when Lee was released by Suleiman, and soon he was driving to Eisenhower in the air-conditioned American car that had been left at the palace for his use.

Clearly, Turk thought, someone had told the new ruler he was a sportsman, and he couldn't have asked for more than the hunting invitation. A day in the desert with the Shaikh and he would in a position to submit a comprehensive report, based on personal experience, to McIntosh and his board.

It wasn't too much to hope that his luck was turning. The years in Indonesia had been a total waste, and although no one could blame him for setting out with a group of partners in an attempt to find oil and establish a company of his own, he should have known better. The real action and the only road to the top lay through the major companies, most of them American, Canadian, British, and Dutch concerns. They still had the only clout worth mentioning in the industry, and a man who wanted to go places had to work for them. There was no alternative.

His problem, Turk knew, was that the major outfits no longer trusted him. When a man took risks and they turned sour on him, he became an outsider. Not that they'd blacklist him or even contemplate freezing him out, but he'd never be anything but a flunky unless he won the confidence of at least one of the dozen men at the top. The decision-makers in every business were members of a private club, and this was particularly true in an industry as closed as oil. If he came through now for Aapco, Exxon, Intercontinental, British Petroleum, and Shell would be clamoring for his services. Everything depended on his ability to predict how Suleiman would act.

For the immediate present he was satisfied. He had taken a giant step without extending himself, and he deserved a preliminary celebration. The guard on duty at the compound gate had been alerted, and waved him through, so he drove straight to the guest house that would be his home for the next few days. It was the smallest of the dwellings erected for the use of visitors, consisting of a living room, two bedrooms, and a small kitchen, but it was handsomely furnished in Scandinavian modern, and a large, comfortable terrace off the living room looked out on the green lawn.

The door was unlocked, so Turk deposited his luggage inside the entrance and wandered into the living room. The bar was still located in the far corner, precisely as he remembered it, and the ice-maker was full. He mixed himself a stiff Bourbon on the rocks, sank into an easy chair, and silently offered a toast to himself. Eventually he'd wander over to the bachelor mess for a cold curry soup, but he was in no hurry. The place stayed open all day, and the heat of Abu Bakr killed a man's appetite. Besides, experience had taught him to eat lightly for a couple of days after his arrival on the Gulf so his body could gradually acclimate itself to the change.

He finished his drink in several gulps, poured himself a refill, and lit a cigarette. Returning to his chair, he thought he heard someone moving around in one of the bedrooms, but dismissed the notion. The security in the compound was as foolproof as it was at Suleiman's palace.

But the feeling that he wasn't alone persisted, and Turk was surprised when he saw an Arab girl peering at him from the arch that led to the bedrooms. She was no ordinary Arab girl, either. She was in her early twenties and wore bright lipstick and heavy eye makeup; she was a trifle on the heavy side for his tastes, but was well-proportioned. Certainly her very short skirt and low-cut blouse did little to conceal her figure, and at first glance she seemed to be wearing no bra under her blouse. She was the type that frequented the nightclubs of Beirut and Cairo. Turk hadn't expected to find a modern native in Abu Bakr.

"Well, hello," he said, and raised his glass to her.

She turned and fled.

He had seen a feather duster in her hand, and concluded that she was the maid who had been assigned to look after him. "Come back," he called to her in Arabic. "I give you my word I won't kill you or eat you alive."

After a considerable wait the girl returned, moving with silent grace on bare feet, then halting again in the archway.

Turk concluded she was shy and ill at ease. "Come in and let's get acquainted. We're going to see a lot of each other in the next few days."

Her shyness vanished, and she advanced into the living room.

He held out his hand, even though he knew Arabs believed it improper for a man and woman to touch. "My name is Kenyon."

To his further surprise she accepted his handshake. "I am Farima. Your servant."

She was unlike any Arab woman he had ever seen in traditionalist Islam. Her mode of dress, her makeup, and, above all, her willingness to accept Western customs marked her as unique. "No one is a servant," he told her. "Let's just say we'll be working together. But there won't be much work to do around here, so you'll have plenty of time to take life easy when I'm not around. Join me in a drink?"

Farima glanced uncertainly at the bar. "The drinking of spirits is forbidden in Abu Bakr, but I would like to try. At the house of Hamilton many drink the martini."

Her spirit appealed to Turk, and her sensuality was all too evident. But there might be unwanted complications if she got loaded, and as he mixed her a martini he decided to warn her. "This has the strength of a gray shark in the Gulf."

Farima took the drink, and downed it in a single gulp. "It is good," she said, returning the glass to him. "It burns like the fire of Saracen, but I would like another."

"Here. But sip it this time." He illustrated with his own drink. "Or you'll become ill."

She laughed as she sat opposite him on a low couch. "I have seen many become ill in the house of Hamilton. Often the wife of Hamilton drinks spirits and must go to sleep. That I would not like."

So Ruth had become a lush. It happened to a great many American wives who lived in the artificial communities created for them in the Persian Gulf states. They couldn't adjust to the life here, but he hadn't thought Ruth would succumb; she had struck him as being one of those sensible New Englanders with a stiff backbone.

Farima sipped her drink, as he had indicated, and helped

herself to a cigarette from a box on the coffee table in front of her. "You do not object?"

"Certainly not! Help yourself whenever you feel like it."

"You have come from America?"

He nodded.

"You are one of the shaikhs of the oil company?"

"Not yet. Perhaps, if it is the will of Allah, I will become one someday."

"You are too modest, I think," Farima said. "You have already been received by Suleiman ben Yosef, and soon you will hunt with him."

She was well informed, which meant that the Abu Bakr underground telegraph was operating with its usual speed and efficiency. Less than an hour had passed since his audience at the palace.

"You are young to be a shaikh, and handsome."

Turk was conscious, as he always was in this part of the world, of the delicacy of the male-female relationship. The Arab believed that women were weak creatures so suffused with sexuality that the mere proximity of a man created in them an irresistible passion. He locked his wives, sisters, and daughters in his harem to protect them from their own desires and to preserve their honor, certain in his own mind that any woman would seduce or be seduced if let alone with a man for even a few minutes.

He was sure this girl had been reared on such myths, and it was probable that she believed them. So the days ahead, he told himself, wouldn't be dull.

Farima seemed to read his mind. Her lips parted as she gazed at him.

Turk was accustomed to taking the initiative, and found her attitude disconcerting.

"I, too, am considered handsome."

"You are," he assured her.

"But you do not like me?"

"What makes you think that?"

"You still sit in that chair, with the table between us." She was behaving in accordance with what she had been taught, and began to remove her blouse.

"Wait," he said. "Not so fast." He hurried to the door and bolted it.

In the moment he was out of the room Farima removed all of her clothes and stood before him naked when he returned.

He went to her, and as he caressed her she undressed him feverishly.

The girl's eagerness, her response to his touch, caused his own desire to increase. She was no novice in the arts of lovemaking, and as his caresses became more urgent she toyed with him expertly, her delicate hands roaming freely.

Turk gasped, and realized she was breathless too. He could not wait to take her into one of the bedrooms, and moved with her to the couch.

Farima pushed him onto it, then mounted him.

He could scarcely speak. "If this is the way you want it, that's fine with me."

She initiated a series of pelvic thrusts that became increasingly violent.

Turk saw her face above his, and her smile of triumph was an expression of sex incarnate.

Farima's thrusts became even more demanding.

He could hold back no longer, and the world seemed to explode. As nearly as he could tell, she also found release.

Five minutes later she was dressed again, sipping her drink, smoking a cigarette, and behaving as though nothing out of the ordinary had happened.

Turk discovered that his hands were trembling as he dressed. The Arab girl was almost too much, and his only regret was that the incident had been so short-lived.

"The young shaikh liked that which Farima offered him," she said.

70

"It was great, but it was over too soon."

"You will give me a key to this house, and when I come here tomorrow morning I will awaken you in a way that will make you think you have joined Allah in his Paradise. Make no appointments early in the day, because we will be together for a long time."

"That's a date," he said, marveling that she asked nothing in return. She was no trollop, but he had to recognize her generosity in some tangible way, so tomorrow he would make time to go into El Ain and buy her some jewelry in the *suq*. Arab women hoarded gold bangle bracelets, so he would purchase several for her.

Farima left silently, her smile enigmatic.

Later in the day, as Turk thought about her expression and tried to decipher it, a strange notion occurred to him. It had been she who had seduced him, and as he reconstructed their encounter he couldn't help wondering whether she had planned it.

Four

❖❖❖❖❖❖❖❖❖❖❖❖❖❖❖❖❖❖❖❖❖❖❖❖❖

The dinner party was successful, even though the hostess was unusually silent and the host appeared to be under a strain. Turk Kenyon rose to the occasion, as he always did when he had an appreciative audience, and the American and French Ministers laughed heartily throughout the meal, as did the former's wife. Judy Hamilton, who was the dinner partner of the bachelor Paul-Pierre Gautier, was captivated by the guest of honor, and eagerly sought his company when the party adjourned to the living room and terrace for coffee and liqueur. Those familiar with certain events that had taken place in the past noted that her father remained within earshot.

The diplomats gathered at one end of the living room, but when the British Minister went off, responding to a challenge to a game of billiards in the game room, Christopher Trevenian found himself alone with his French colleague.

"I have been waiting for the chance to speak privately with you, Monsieur," Gautier said.

Trevenian sipped his coffee.

"I congratulate you on the triumph of your oil company's special representative, Monsieur."

"He tells a pretty good story," Trevenian said, "but I wouldn't call what he's done a triumph."

"I refer to the Rolls-Royce he gave to Suleiman. I have been told on the best of the authority that His Highness spent the entire afternoon behind the wheel of the motor car, and that he is already planning a pleasure drive in it to the Oasis of Qar."

"I wouldn't be surprised if your information is accurate," Trevenian said, and grinned. "I heard the same thing, maybe from the same source."

The Frenchman's sense of humor was limited, and he did not return the other's smile. "This is the first time since Suleiman became Shaikh that he has indicated he is human."

"Maybe he is and maybe he isn't. My own impression of him is that he's a pretty cold fish."

"I have not yet had the privilege of being received by him," Gautier said, his manner becoming stiff. "Only you Americans have access to him."

"Don't you believe it," the U.S. Minister said. "I've had just one audience with him, and it lasted no more than a few minutes. He accepted the usual compliments—you know how the Arabs enjoy that flowery stuff. But when I tried getting down to brass tacks, he turned me off."

"The same happened to Sir David Hurst—he was telling me before dinner—on his one visit to the palace."

"It's my feeling that Suleiman is a tough man. But what he wants and where he's heading is beyond me."

"Me, also," Gautier said. "Perhaps, Monsieur, we should persuade our governments to provide us with large sums of money so we may purchase motor cars for Suleiman. And blondes."

"Maybe so."

"Who is the young woman this Kenyon delivered to the palace today?" The question was asked lightly.

Trevenian was not deceived. A call girl was available for a price, and after the blonde returned to Europe a representative of the Republic of France would offer her ample compensation in return for her impressions of the Shaikh. "Damned if I know, Monsieur Gautier. My government doesn't allow itself to admit there is such a thing as sex in the world, you know, so I can't even let myself know this girl exists."

"I am not bashful," the French Minister said, "so I went to Red Hamilton and asked him. But he is a straight-laced fellow, and knows nothing about the young woman."

The idea of a high-ranking diplomat having nothing better to do than investigate the identity of a prostitute struck Trevenian as ludicrous, but he choked back a laugh. "You could always go straight to Kenyon."

"Never, Monsieur. That one is too clever. Have you never heard about the time—about four years ago, I believe it was—how he won back the friendship of the Shaikh Muhammad, who had become angry with Aapco?"

"Yes, I'm familiar with the story." Trevenian refrained from saying that, in his opinion, the American industrial woods were full of shrewd young men like Dale Kenyon, all of them on the make, all of them lacking any sense of ethics. He himself had been naive when he had hoped to find a different atmosphere in diplomacy.

On the far side of the room Judy Hamilton was leaning toward Turk. "Is it really true that you appeared at a native religious ceremony on the island of Ceram wearing a loin cloth and a fake animal head?" Her giggle was infectious.

Turk laughed with her, then shook his head. "It's true,

and it sounds like quite a lark. But I should have known better. The government of Indonesia didn't think I was all that funny, and for a couple of weeks I thought they'd expel me from the country."

"But what actually happened at the ceremony?" the girl persisted.

"Nothing much."

"But there must have been—"

"Judy," Red Hamilton interrupted, taking his daughter's arm. "You're embarrassing Mr. Kenyon. There are some exploits in a man's past that aren't all that glorious in retrospect, and he'd rather not talk about them."

"Oh. I'm sorry, Turk."

Turk's smile was strained. "Not at all."

"Come along, honey," Red said. "You're my partner in the ping pong doubles tournament."

Turk watched father and daughter go off, his smile frozen.

Ruth Hamilton approached him, coffee cup in hand. "How have you been, Dale? Your appearance hasn't changed in the least."

"I try to keep fit, Ruthie. Which I couldn't if I ate many of your dinners."

She inclined her head.

"How are you making out?"

"I get along," she said, and took a deep breath. "My husband has known about us, Dale. For a long time."

"So I gathered today. He warned me to stay away from your daughter."

Ruth was surprised. "That wouldn't have occurred to me."

"To me, either. Apparently he thinks I'm a depraved lecher who'll chase anybody, even a kid."

"We never even mention you in private. In our domestic lives you're a non-person."

"Has it been as rough as all that?"

She met his gaze. "The worst I've ever known."

"I'm sorry, Ruthie," Turk said. "I never wanted to hurt you."

"It wasn't your fault. Can I give you another brandy, Dale?"

"Only if you'll join me."

She shook her head. "I've had my quota for the day. A cocktail before lunch, two before dinner and one glass of wine with dinner. I've seen too many wives turn into soaks out here. The boredom can do terrible things to you if you're not careful. I'm not including you when I say that, Dale. We had a ball together. The danger was that I might have turned to somebody else after you left, or else become a soak."

"Not a chance, Ruthie. Not with your conscience." He was relieved, and at the same time was annoyed with the Arab girl, who had lied to convince him that Ruth Hamilton had become an alcoholic. Maybe there had been no reason for the deception other than the habitual tendency of the Arab to denigrate anyone he or she disliked. On the off chance that there was more involved than he knew, however, he would weigh anything Farima told him with care.

The women's wing of the palace was large, labyrinthian, and isolated, with iron grilles over its high windows and sentries at the entrances. The doors that led to other portions of the complex were locked from the outside as well as the inside. No man other than the shaikh ever set foot in these precincts, and a large suite consisting of a reception hall, a bedroom and bath, a study and a dressing room was maintained for his exclusive use. Several gardens, tended by women, were surrounded by high walls, as was the swimming pool, where Lee was surprised to see some of the harem's residents sunning themselves in bikinis.

The ruler of the wing was Suleiman's first wife, a woman of about his own age, whose position was enhanced because she was also the mother of his eldest son. The entire household was under her supervision, and on rare occasions she made public appearances at her husband's side, always wearing a *feredezah* and *yashmak*.

The day when eunuchs acted as servants was long past, their places having been taken in the harem by women and in other parts of the palace by men. All were directed by Suleiman's second wife, who roamed where she pleased through the entire establishment, checking on the activities of her subordinates.

The Shaikh's third wife was in charge of the kitchens and of the buying of food. Each morning at dawn, dressed in her robes and veils, she went to the open-air produce market in El Ain to make her purchases. The fishmongers, butchers, and greengrocers saved the best of their wares for her.

Suleiman's eleven children lived in the wing, the boys and girls receiving separate educations; all of their tutors at this stage of their development were women. The eldest son, now twelve years old and heir to the throne, lived in a suite of his own, and would move to the men's wings when he reached puberty. In time his brothers would do the same, but his sisters would spend their entire lives in isolation, moving from the harem to the women's quarters in the homes of the men who would become their husbands.

Prior to his coup, Suleiman had also enjoyed connubial pleasures with a young, fourth wife, as Moslem custom permitted. Over the years he had rid himself of his fourth wife and taken another from time to time, accomplishing the legal process merely by saying, "I divorce thee" three times in the presence of two witnesses. Only the wealthy Abu Bakrians, like others of their class elsewhere in the Gulf states, could afford the luxury of keeping four wives. The ordinary Arab had to content himself with two.

Now that Suleiman had become the ruler of the principality it was no longer necessary for him to have a fourth wife. Custom permitted him to keep concubines instead, and if one of them were to give birth the Shaikh would marry her for a short time in order to legitimize their child.

Lee was given a room near those of the concubines, a small, utilitarian chamber that contained a low divan and a chest of drawers. She would sleep there, but during her stay at the palace she would be expected to spend most of her time with the other women. She would eat her meals in the dining hall, since only the first wife had the privilege of dining privately in her own suite.

The girl's time was her own, and she was free to wander where she pleased. Calling herself "Leila" because she knew the Arabs would be confused by her name, she soon discovered that the swimming pool was the gathering place. There the women gossiped, plucked their eyebrows, and filed their nails, spending their days in unrelieved indolence. The only books in the entire wing were to be found in the classrooms of the boys and girls.

There were four concubines in the harem, three of them Arabian and one a black from Nigeria, whose Muslim family had been pleased to sell her for a substantial price. The eldest of the quartet was about thirty and the youngest no more than fifteen or sixteen. Unlike the wives, they had no responsibilities and tended to band together; they were not snubbed by the wives, but they belonged to a different category and were aware of the distinction.

All four greeted Lee eagerly, and were delighted when they discovered they could converse with her in Arabic. They displayed no interest in her past, much less in anything that took place in the outside world. Their attitudes were childlike, and their one consuming interest was the gold jewelry the Shaikh occasionally gave them. Each spent approximately one night a week with Suleiman, and except when summoned by him could idle away the hours as she pleased. All were happy in their slothful existence, and without exception felt confident that, when the Shaikh tired of them, they would become the wives of members of his

78

court. Their place in the world was settled, and they aspired to nothing more.

What Lee found unusual was that all of the concubines bore deep, ugly scars on their left shoulders, the marks extending as far as their breasts in the front and down their backs in the rear. The scars on the body of the youngest were still livid. Lee tried to question each of the women in turn about these marks, but they refused to explain, and it was obvious they were frightened. She was determined to discover the meaning of those marks for the sake, if need be, of her own protection.

For the better part of twenty-four hours the visitor was left to her own devices. Then the first wife came to the poolside, saying there was no way of knowing when Suleiman might summon her. The concubines were directed to "prepare her," a task they accepted with a girlish zeal, and Lee forced herself to submit to their ministrations.

They plucked her eyebrows until only a thin, almost invisible line remained. Her blond hair fascinated them, and they washed it repeatedly, rinsed it in lemon juice, and perfumed it. She soaked in a marble tub for two hours, the combination of the heat and the perfume in the water making her fear she would faint. She thought the odor that suffused her was unbearable, but the concubines assured her that she was wearing the Shaikh's favorite scent.

Kohl was daubed on her lashes and smeared on her eyelids, and a thin line drawn with an indelible pencil replaced her eyebrows. Her lips were colored a deep purple, her cheeks were rouged, and a glittering paillete the shape of a crescent was pasted on one cheekbone. After considerable experimentation her fingernails and toenails were painted a shade of green that matched her eyes.

Then her nipples were tinted with henna, which was also painted on the palms of her hands and the soles of her feet. Finally they dressed her in a skimpy bra and low-cut harem pantaloons of gauzelike silk, and they advised her to wear no jewelry. Suleiman, they said, would notice that she was unadorned, and would remedy the deficiency.

At last they led her before a full-length mirror, and Lee didn't know whether to weep or laugh. She did neither, but stared at the reflection of the creature she had become. Only a day after her arrival in Abu Bakr she had been transported back through the centuries into an Arab world that now existed only on the Persian Gulf.

The first wife reappeared, and approved the transformation. "You are prepared to entertain His Highness?" she asked.

Lee misunderstood the question. "Of course."

"You can sing the ballads of Arabian conquests of old, and accompany yourself on the lyre-of-three-strings?"

The girl shook her head.

"What can you do?"

"Well," Lee said, "I'm told I can perform a passable belly dance."

The first wife raised an eyebrow. "We shall see."

She called the other wives and the concubines to her reception room, where they sat on cushions around the walls. Lee was handed a pair of tiny cymbals to attach to her fingers; she recognized them as primitive instruments, the precursors of the Spanish castanet. She wondered whether to start dancing without music, then smiled to herself as the second wife went to a stereo set located in a corner. It was one of the best and most expensive made in the United States, and its mere presence in this chamber changed the atmosphere of what might have been a scene out of the *Arabian Nights*.

In a moment the sounds of a plaintive Arabian song filled the room.

"Dance," the first wife said.

Lee moved to the center of the room, the tiles cool beneath her bare feet, and clicking her cymbals in time to the wailing tune, she took her first tentative steps, her hands over her head, her feet apart, her hips swaying and her belly rolling. Gradually the tempo increased, and her movements matched it, the faces of her feminine audience telling her that the women of Suleiman's household appreciated the ability of an outsider to perform a dance they considered their own.

The tune ended and another began. It was far more rapid, building quickly to a furious tempo, and Lee threw herself into the music. She was showing off, but she was determined to win the unstinting admiration of an audience far more critical than the Shaikh.

Suddenly one of the concubines joined her, then another came onto the floor. In a few moments all of the women with the exception of the first wife were dancing. All followed Lee's lead, and as her gyrations became more frenzied, they copied her movements. If they were engaging in a contest with her she was determined to win it, and every muscle in her body came into play as she plunged into the wild climax of the dance.

The Arab women were shrieking in breathless glee, the sounds of their voices almost drowning out the music. When the music finally ended they embraced each other and Lee, accepting her without reservation into their sisterhood.

She stood for some moments sucking in her breath, trying to recover her strength. Streaks of perspiration had caused her makeup to run, and she knew she would have to undergo the ordeal of another bath, another long session of face painting, but at the moment she did not care.

The first wife made her triumph complete. "His Highness," she said, "is certain to enjoy your dance."

"He will want you to stay here with us for all time," one of the concubines added.

The thought occurred to Lee that her victory might have been even more complete than she wished. If Suleiman's appreciation of her talents was so great that he wanted to keep her here permanently, it would be almost impossible for her to escape from the bondage of the harem into the modern world that was her own. For the first time since the start of her adventure into the past she felt a stirring of fear.

The so-called ICO Club, located on the thirty-seventh floor of the Intercontinental Oil Company's Manhattan headquarters, was actually a private dining room for the top-level echelon. A man's position determined his right to use the dining room, squash courts, sauna, and other facilities, and it was an unwritten rule that no one below the rank of assistant vice-president was admitted. Privacy and the food, in that order, were the principal attractions: the beef was flown to New York twice weekly from Texas, as was the frozen chili con carne, and the game birds came from Georgia.

Hector Bell's table was located in a corner near the picture windows, with a gap of ten feet separating it from other tables. No one else ever used it, even when the chairman was out of town. Bell was entertaining only one guest at lunch, and everyone in the room recognized Dugald McIntosh when he came into the room with Bell. Their orders were identical, and each of them drank two stiff Scotches before going on to shrimp cocktail, steak, salad, and side orders of chili. It was immediately apparent from their joviality that all was well in the relations of ICO and Aapco.

"You old rascal," Bell said, "that was a mighty pretty young woman you had out to the country club on Saturday."

"I think so myself." McIntosh was complacent.

"She lives in town, does she?"

The guest nodded, but volunteered no information.

"If she lives off her alimony from Turk Kenyon, she must have rough sledding."

McIntosh could be evasive no longer. "As a matter of

fact, Hector, she works for Aapco. For me. She's my secretary."

"Aha!" Bell beamed. "So that's the way it is!"

"I wish. Damned if I know how she does it, but she has a knack for holding me at arm's length."

"You? I've seen you bulldoze committees of the U.S. Senate and put a Secretary of the Interior or two in his place. Don't tell me a woman who doesn't weigh a hundred and twenty pounds has you hogtied."

"That's the way it is, Hector. I'm seeing her three or four nights a week, and most times I don't even think of making passes at her. She's good company."

"How good?"

"If I can't get her any other way, I might even marry her. My boys will raise the roof, but to hell with them. You can bet they won't shoot off their faces to me, not if they want to keep their jobs."

"No complications because she was married to the terrible Turk?"

"I don't see why. A lot of people, men as well as women, have been taken in by him. Bobbie sees him for what he is, which is all to the good. And the son of a bitch does produce, Hector. Just this morning I had a cable saying he's going hunting with Suleiman of Abu Bakr."

"I've got to hand it to him. Can he produce any data for us on the results of the Great Wadi explorations?"

"We included that in his original instructions before he left New York, and I reminded him of it just before he took off from London for Abu Bakr. I'm reluctant to prod him again by cable because Hamilton will see the message, and I don't want him to get the idea that we're going behind his back."

"If I know Kenyon, he won't need prodding, Dug. Ever wonder what sparks a guy like that?"

"The same thing that keeps us in harness. Money. A yen

for power, the desire to exercise control over people and events."

"But he lacks one quality. Self-discipline."

"I don't knock him for it, Hector. You and I need people like Turk Kenyon to do special jobs for us. The kind of jobs nobody else has the guts or cleverness to do. And they're especially valuable to us because they're expendable."

"I hadn't thought of it that way, Dug, but you're right. They know they're on their own when they go out on a limb, and that it's their funeral if we saw off the branch."

McIntosh chuckled. "I want to show you how smart Bobbie is. She set up one part of our current deal with Kenyon all on her own, without even checking with me first. He called from London one day, and she waded right in. Offered him an extra twenty-five thousand if he comes back to us with accurate, up-to-date figures on the Great Wadi."

"Couldn't be better," Bell said with a smile. "For twenty-five thousand Kenyon would choke his own mother to death, and then blow the whole wad on a couple of months with some broad."

A small oil lamp provided the only illumination in the mud dwelling, and Ali Nasar Jalal peered at his sister, who sat opposite him, complacently sipping thick, sweet coffee. "I tremble whenever you have that smug look on your face."

"I had no chance to get in touch with you," Farima said, "so I had to proceed on my own. Many things have happened, and all our plans must be changed."

"I make all the final plans and decisions for our committee. The regional agent for the party was very clear on that point when he visited us last month."

"Now," she said, "you sound like all other men. Hear me out."

"I'm listening," Ali said.

"We are not going to kidnap the daughter of Hamilton."

"Why not?" He glared at her.

"Because," Farima said, "there is a better use for her. She has automatic access to every imperialist oil facility in Abu Bakr. The men who work for her father treat her like a little princess."

"That is no surprise. What of it?"

"She is going to become one of us. Through her we can gain admission everywhere—the oil fields, the separator plants, even the tank farms where the oil is stored before it is taken away. We can set fire to every imperialist installation in the land."

Ali was incredulous. "Just how will you persuade the daughter of Hamilton to join the party?"

"Who says I'm going to recruit her?" Farima countered. "Perhaps she will help us without knowing what she is doing. I have become her friend, and can go anywhere with her. She is an innocent little puppet that can be manipulated at our will."

"Your thought is sound enough." Ali's agreement was grudging. "But the Palestine liberation forces will give us no more money, and I doubt that we can squeeze any more from Syria or Iraq. As for the Libyans, they may promise, but they won't keep their word. So we need funds."

"I intend to take care of that, too," Farima said. "One of the leading men of the oil company is here on a visit. He doesn't know it yet, but he'll pay us as much as we would have made from the kidnapping of Hamilton's daughter. The arrangements are already made."

Ali's expression in the flickering light was dubious. "The Americans have many faults, but they are not soft-headed, especially when money is involved. I can imagine no reason why an executive of the oil company would give funds to the committee."

"He won't give money to the committee. He will pay it to me," she said.

Ali took his time lighting a marijuana cigarette he had been rolling. "I can imagine no reason he would do that." Leaning forward, he lit the cigarette over the lamp.

The girl took the joint from him and helped herself to a drag. "Then you have no imagination."

He hauled himself to his feet, grasping the hilt of the knife in his belt. "If you're hinting what I think—"

"In Allah's name, sit down, Ali." Farima was calm. "What is the goal of our committee? To bring Abu Bakr into the modern world, a world in which all comrades, men and women alike, are equal. I want to hear no more of your old-fashioned morality."

"The honor of our family is not old-fashioned!"

"Now," she said with a deliberate laugh, "you sound like Suleiman ben Yosef and all the other members of the royal family. Honor indeed! Our family has been suppressed for centuries. We've lived in the gutter so long we know no other home. And just what is our family? I defy you to tell me the name of one—just one—of our great-grandfathers!"

He had to use all of his will power to force himself to sit again, and he sucked hard on the marijuana cigarette. "Islam," he said, "cannot be changed overnight."

"But isn't that what we're trying to do? Haven't we taken a solemn oath to foment a revolution and give the assets of this land to the people?"

Ali's nod of agreement was reluctant, and for a long time he pondered as he stared at the flame in the lamp. "If you are able to obtain the funds we need from this American," he said, "I want to know none of the details. Why he would give you the money is his business and your business. Just remember, please, that as chairman of the committee I must keep the respect of everyone, and not even the comrades share all of your advanced thinking. So I beg you not to tell anyone the details."

"I have no intention of revealing them," Farima said. "It will be enough that I will come back to you with the cash in my hand. And when I do, I will expect the regional agent to appoint me as co-chairman of the committee. Soon we shall see whether even the party is willing to admit that a woman is the equal of a man."

They left El Ain before dawn, the entire party mounted on some of the world's finest and most spirited horses. The twenty soldiers carried automatic rifles. The falcon handler, whose charges rested in wooden cages, carried no weapon other than his scimitar. Only Shaikh Suleiman ben Yosef and his American guest were armed with .38 caliber pistols, weapons that could barely reach the range of the elusive *dalu* birds. The servants who brought up the rear carried provisions for the outing; they were unarmed.

They took advantage of the cool of the morning, and with the Shaikh setting the pace they rode mostly at a brisk canter for an hour. Turk Kenyon sat his horse easily as he kept pace with Abu Bakr's ruler. It was difficult to converse, but he was content to wait.

They made their way across wadis, dry riverbeds, and headed into the limitless, rolling hills of sand and rock where there was no hint of vegetation. At this time of day, however, as the sky lightened, the desert was majestic, its grandeur enhanced by its loneliness. Turk loved the desolate landscape, and when he saw the Shaikh glance at him approvingly he realized he had shown his feelings. That was all to the good.

When the sun rose, the servants broke away from the rest of the party to establish a camp. Three quarters of an hour later Suleiman, relying only on his inner compass, led the group to the spot. A tent of silk, open on the bottom at all sides to admit any breeze that might be stirring, had been erected for him and his guest.

In a few minutes breakfast awaited them at the camp-fire the servants had made near the tent. The first dish was *couscous,* containing barley and semolina mixed with chunks of mutton, which had been prepared in the palace and was now being reheated.

The Shaikh, Turk, and the soldiers squatted around the fire, dipping into a huge iron bowl with their right hands and removing handfuls of the dish. Anywhere else, they would wipe their hands on damp cloths or dip them in bowls of water before repeating the gesture, but such refinements weren't followed in the desert, where water was saved for drinking.

Turk ate with relish, his appetite as sharp as that of his companions.

Suleiman had been watching him. "The lack of sanitation does not bother you. Most of your compatriots live in dread of germs."

"Allah will protect me from them," Turk said, and laughed.

A smile creased the Shaikh's thin mouth. "You are not like other Americans. You are more like an Arab."

"Had Allah willed it, I would have been content to live in this world," Turk said, and suddenly realized he was being sincere. He loved the Arab countries, and felt completely at home here, even more at ease than he did in the company of his Western peers. The Arabs might be illogical according to the standards of others, but he understood and admired these volatile people, who could rid themselves of their hostilities by making grandiose threats they did not intend to carry out. Above all, he thought, he admired their Bedouin ideal of courage, dignity, and hospitality. They were real men, and he thoroughly enjoyed living with them.

"You are not a convert to Islam?" Suleiman asked.

"I've considered it, but there are too few places in America where I could worship." It would not be diplomatic to admit he was a cynic who rejected all religion.

They ate the second dish, chopped dates held together with thick honey. By now Turk's appetite had lessened, so he ate sparingly, knowing the same meal would be served again early in the afternoon.

The ride was resumed, and they made their way across a series of dunes into the hills, where there was little sand and the horses picked their way with care over barren rock. The sun was merciless, but Turk felt comfortable beneath his *ghutra*, and he was pleased he had become reaccustomed to the climate so quickly, almost as though he had never gone elsewhere.

It was late in the morning before one of the soldiers shouted in triumph and pointed toward the cloudless sky. A small formation of about twenty *dalu* birds was approaching from the south.

Turk and the Shaikh quickly dismounted, checked their pistols, and squinted at the approaching birds, their dark glasses doing little to protect them from the glare. The American estimated the birds were flying at least five hundred feet overhead, and knew it would be foolhardy to try to bring them down with pistols. Skill was useless. Only blind luck would bag a *dalu*, but it was not his place to voice his objections. If the Shaikh wanted to trust to luck, he would do the same.

Suleiman broke the silence. "Release the hawks!" he commanded.

The handler opened the wooden cages, and two falcons soared upward. They flew above the *dalu* and then, diving and hovering around the terrified wild birds, drove them down to a level of about three hundred feet.

Both pistols spoke at the same moment, and within seconds the hunters, firing at different portions of the flock, emptied their chambers. Turk's six shots brought down two *dalu* and the Shaikh shot three.

"Well done, American," he said. "We will broil them as an appetizer for our lunch."

He could afford to be generous because he had shot the greater number, and Turk was pleased that the Arab had won the undeclared contest.

Suleiman chuckled, a dry, rasping sound. "My friends,"

he said, pointing upward, "can sense what we cannot yet see."

The falcons remained aloft, circling the area as they swooped lower, then rose higher. After a quarter of an hour they soared up out of sight.

"Soon," the Shaikh said, rubbing his hands together.

Turk could make out a few specks on the horizon to the south, and gradually realized that another formation of *dalu* birds, unaware of the impending danger, was approaching.

When they were almost directly overhead the falcons plummeted downward, their speed terrifying.

"It is their turn to hunt," Suleiman said.

Almost as he spoke the falcons struck, breaking up the formation and sending the *dalu* scattering in every direction.

Turk watched in astonishment as the hawks came to earth and settled on the outstretched palms of the handler. One carried a single *dalu* in his beak, while the other held two.

At Suleiman's command the hawks dropped their prey into his hands.

A feeble fluttering told Turk the tiny victims were not yet dead, the falcons having been trained not to destroy them.

Again the Shaikh chuckled, and tearing apart the still living creatures, he fed them to the hawks, his eyes gleaming behind his dark glasses as he watched them consume the meal they had earned.

Turk wanted to retch, but could not allow himself to avert his eyes. Unable to trust his voice after witnessing the brutal spectacle, he could only nod in seeming approval when Suleiman, the blood of the *dalu* covering his hands, turned to him in happy, almost innocent triumph and smiled.

Red Hamilton paced his office, and did not sit until Calvin Hodges came into the room. He waved the field supervisor to a chair. "How are things going?"

"We're on schedule, Mr. Hamilton. Well seventeen is beginning to slow down, of course, but she's confirming what we've known would be happening soon. Her rate of decrease is slow, and I wouldn't be surprised if she continues to produce for another year."

"Fine," Red said.

The supervisor brightened. "I hear Turk Kenyon is back, but I haven't seen him yet. I'm sure he'll pay me a visit."

"It won't be today. He's gone hunting with Suleiman."

"Trust the terrible Turk to combine pleasure with business." Hodges laughed loudly.

"Cal," Red said, "I've asked you to come here this morning to handle a confidential assignment for me. You're anticipating no problems at Roosevelt in the next week?"

"I'd be surprised if anything out of the ordinary happened in the field."

"Then your assistant could take charge?"

"Sure, Mr. Hamilton. He's pretty good—for an Arab." The supervisor had no idea he was being condescending. "What do you want me to do, boss?"

"I hate to ask this of you, Cal, particularly at this time of the year, but I want to send you out to the desert for about a week. A day or two longer, if necessary."

Hodges shrugged. "Hell, one hunk of desert is like another. That's how I see it."

"I'm sending you to the Great Wadi."

"Oh." The supervisor's smile faded. "I'll manage," he said. "I've lived in an oven before, and I can do it again. I don't even mind sleeping in a tent, provided I've got enough mosquito netting."

"I've already notified Murphy at supply to let you draw any equipment and provisions you want. Help yourself, and don't stint."

"Thanks, Mr. Hamilton. Ordinarily I don't drink gin, but it's the only liquor I can get down me without ice, so I guess I'll requisition a couple of bottles."

"Whatever you like."

"Are the experimental wells there starting to produce?"

"You'll have nothing to do with the experiments or the start of production there," Red said.

His subordinate blinked, but said nothing.

"I'm tripling the security guard there. I'm sending in reinforcements by helicopter this afternoon, and you'll go with them to take charge."

"I haven't handled security for a long time, Mr. Hamilton."

"They'll be under the command of their own officers, who will report to you. Even the security, as such, won't concern you. I've talked with the officer in charge by radio this morning, and his arrangements will be airtight after the reinforcements arrive."

"I don't get it," Hodges said.

"You'll be paid double overtime on a twenty-four hour per day basis, starting when you leave here and ending when you return. I'll also give you a two hundred and fifty dollar bonus."

"That will keep the old lady from yammering at me when she finds out I'm going to be away. But if you don't mind my saying so, Mr. Hamilton, you're handing me a lot of money for just sitting on my can."

"I'm sending you there for one purpose, Cal. I want someone with your authority there to prevent unauthorized visitors from even seeing the experimental field. You'll admit only those visitors who carry personal passes signed by me, and I expect to give my writing hand a vacation for the next week."

The supervisor leaned forward in his chair. "Who are you aiming to keep out of the Great Wadi, boss?"

"Anybody who might come snooping there. Most of all your pal, Turk Kenyon."

Five

◆◆◆◆◆◆◆◆◆◆◆◆◆◆◆◆◆◆◆◆◆◆◆◆◆◆◆◆

The house of Husayn claimed that its noble roots had originated at the time of the prophet in the sixth century, and no one in Abu Bakr was in a position to deny the ruling dynesty's myth. A few aristocratic families, however, privately knew better, even though they had no access to the records that proved the founder of the Husayn line had been a commercial upstart. Pearls had laid the foundation of the fortune, and the first of the line had himself been a diver in the seventeenth century, when European rulers had willingly paid vast sums for Persian Gulf pearls. As the industry flourished so had the house of Husayn, and it had become a family tradition, even after Selim Muhammad I had seized the throne of Abu Bakr late in the nineteenth century, for one of the senior branches to own and operate a small fleet of pearl diving boats. The modest profits were shared by all eleven of the senior branches.

Shaikh Ahmed al-Husayn, the Foreign Minister, had been

assigned the responsibility by his half brothers and cousins, principally because his country house, located on a cliff high above the sea and twenty miles south of El Ain, was located only a short distance from the coastal village the divers used as their home port. He was required to spend no more than half a day each month supervising their activities, and he enjoyed his traditional prerogatives, particularly the custom of accepting four white pearls and two black pearls from the divers as annual tribute.

The pearls studded the scabbard of a ceremonial scimitar hanging above the unused fireplace in Ahmed's study. The few foreigners who had ever been invited to this sanctum had been awed, and members of the family were impressed too, even though they themselves ranked among the wealthiest men on earth.

Shaikh Habib al-Husayn, the Finance Minister, after dining at the home of his full brother, went with him to the study. "The sultans of Turkey would have paid a handsome price for this little ornament," he said, taking down the scimitar and turning the scabbard over.

Ahmed closed the door behind them. "I wouldn't have sold it to them. Or to anyone else."

His brother held the scimitar closer to the light. "You should bring in an estimator from Beirut who will tell you its worth."

"I don't care about its worth," Ahmed said. "I like it for its sentimental value. By the way, if I should die before my eldest son reaches manhood, I'm leaving it to you."

"That's kind of you."

"Not at all, Habib. You've always liked it." Ahmed unlocked a wall safe and removed a bottle of French Cognac and two snifters. It was rumored that some of the more worldly members of the dynasty drank alcoholic beverages in the privacy of their homes, but no one, not even their servants, could prove it.

"Ah, *Cordon Bleu*."

"I know your tastes. If you like, I'll bring you a case when I go to Paris next week."

"I accept with pleasure, Ahmed. I ran out of it some time ago, and I wouldn't allow anyone else to do such an errand for me."

Ahmed switched to English, not because he feared his servants might be untrustworthy, but merely because it was wise to take no unnecessary chances in unsettled times. "After all, blood is thicker than half blood."

Habib smiled. "You'll be happy to hear I've enrolled my second son in the Harvard Business School, although he won't go there for another nine years."

Both brothers held M.B.A. degrees from Harvard, and Ahmed was pleased. "The coming generation must keep up the tradition if the country is to take and hold a place in modern society."

"If there's anything left of Abu Bakr," Habib said.

The Foreign Minister raised his bell glass in a silent toast.

The Finance Minister repeated the gesture. "What do you hear from the palace?"

"I had a brief audience early this evening, after he came back from a day's hunting with Turk Kenyon. He's impossible, Habib."

"What now?"

"Nothing specific. Government by whim. An inability to grasp anything beyond the most primitive concepts. I'm convinced he sees himself as the savior of Islam, and I wouldn't be surprised if he collects a huge arsenal and then declares a *jihad,* a holy war, on the infidels of the entire world."

"You haven't told him about the oil strike in the Great Wadi?"

"Do you think I'm mad?" Ahmed asked. "I've persuaded Red Hamilton to keep a lid on the news, but the secret is bound to leak out. In weeks, if not in days."

"There's no doubt in my mind what will happen when

word reaches the palace," the Finance Minister said. "He'll expropriate all foreign oil holdings, and he'll throw Aapco out."

"Correct. I can see him inching closer to that position each day."

"How will the United States react?"

"Slowly," Ahmed said. "Aapco will send some of its top brass here, men several cuts above the Turk Kenyon level. The State Department will protest. The palace will become stubborn, and then there'll be real hell to pay. All of our deals for the plants and factories the Americans are contracting to build for us will go down the drain."

"Let me write the rest of the scenario," Habib said. "Washington will persuade all of the Common Market countries—except France—to put us in a deep freeze too. The French will make us all sorts of offers, much bigger than they're making now, but they won't be big enough. The Russians will try to muscle in, and the palace will become hysterical."

"So far so good," Ahmed said. "What worries me is that the United States might become angry enough to send in the Marines. I'm not for one minute forgetting that America needs Abu Bakr oil, and will for several more years to come."

"There's no need for violence when there's a more effective way to bring us to our knees. Congress will pass a bill impounding Abu Bakrian bank accounts, bond holdings, and investments in the United States. Britain, West Germany, Scandinavia, and the Low Countries will follow the American example. Overnight, the family's investments in the industrialized nations will become worthless."

"Have you explained any of this to the palace?"

"Until I'm hoarse. He simply can't understand that money as such, even gold, is only a symbolic medium of exchange based on the mutual faith and good will of those who participate in a deal. It has no more intrinsic value than a stock certificate."

"Did you offer him any explanations on his own level?"

"Certainly. At least I tried. When I told him that a loaf of bread cost millions of marks in Germany during the worst of the inflationary period after the First World War, he just laughed and said we're so rich that Abu Bakr would never go hungry, no matter how much bread might cost."

Ahmed cupped his snifter in his hands, held it to his face, and inhaled. "History creates its own inevitability."

"To put it another way," Habib said, sipping his Cognac, "there are men in places of high responsibility who insist on digging their own graves. Nothing will turn them aside."

They glanced at each other, their expressions bleak, then looked away again. "You and I," Ahmed said, "have been happy with our own places in the hierarchy. We've never imbibed the poison of great ambition."

"You're the elder," Habib said. "So you know I'll support you without reservation in whatever you decide to do."

"Any decision we make must be joint. I've hoped affairs would straighten out, and that the policies of the previous regime would be adopted gradually as their sensible, practical nature became obvious. But the blind, as the Koran tells us, are those who cover their own eyes."

"From the day of the coup," Habib said, "I have felt certain in my own mind of what would happen. I know of no way to avoid it."

Again they were silent for a time, and when they drained the last of their Cognac Ahmed splashed more into their snifters. "It would be suicidal to act prematurely."

"I become impatient," his brother admitted, "but my ardor cools when I remember that his first act after taking the throne was to bind the army and air force to him by doubling their pay. A shrewd move, of course. He has inherited his mother's craftiness but none of our father's nobility."

"Do you remember the games he played when we were children living in the harem?"

"I still have nightmares from time to time."

"Some nightmares become real," the Foreign Minister said. "Just two days ago he boasted to me that he is reopening and strengthening the dungeons beneath the palace that our great-grandfather built."

"How he would love to hold members of the family there as the dungeons' first tenants. It would serve as a warning to all of the other relatives, and no one would plot against him for many years to come."

Ahmed rose abruptly. "I've wondered whether we might persuade one of our half brothers to take the lead and accept the throne, but I know of no one who has the strength. Young Muhammad would be eager to try, I'm sure, but we'd be signing his death warrant if we brought him home from Yale. Besides, it would be obvious that others were behind him, and the palace would know in which direction to look."

"That leaves you," Habib said.

The Foreign Minister sighed. "I know. I've forced myself to accept the principle that there is no one else."

Habib went through the ritual of sniffing his Cognac. "When?"

"Not yet."

"When, then?"

"We shall have to wait until he commits an overt act that will convince not only members of the family and the outside world that he needs to be replaced, but will also make the army and the air force eager to overthrow him too."

"I realize we can't succeed in this by ourselves," Habib said, "but it galls me to do nothing."

"A premature coup is certain to fail. We must wait until our natural allies turn to us. Which they will do, because they'll have nowhere else to go."

"There's a risk," Habib said. "He knows where the obvious threat is, and he might try to neutralize us before we can act."

"I've already thought of that possibility, and I've found a way to remove the risk."

For the first time Habib laughed. "I had an idea you would. Our mother was crafty too."

"There is one other possible source of danger to him. Muhammad, who spends his days looking at the snow on the Alps and wishing he could bask in the insufferable sun of El Ain."

"Muhammad would have no part in any coup, Ahmed! He's secretly delighted to have escaped from the rats' nest, and you know it. He'll spend the rest of his days clipping coupons and collecting young girls. He can drink his Dom Perignon in the open now, instead of hiding it in that re-frigerator-safe he had built in his palace bedroom. When I think about it, I'm almost willing to change places with him."

"You and I may know that Muhammad is harmless now," the Foreign Minister said. "That's because we were closer to him than others were, and we understand him. But the palace can't imagine he doesn't yearn for a return to power. The man who has swallowed the poison of great ambition sees everyone else in his own image, as the Koran tells us. So the very thought of Muhammad causes the palace to lose sleep. We shall encourage his insomnia. Mysterious visitors, including high-ranking European officers in uniform, will call on Muhammad at his home in exile. The agents of the palace will report these comings and goings, and attention will be diverted from us."

"Perfect!"

"We won't celebrate just yet. The road is full of potholes, and the curves aren't graded," Ahmed said.

The first wife was bossy and interfering, a nuisance who regarded everything that took place in the harem as her business. She didn't allow Leila to tan herself, but made her sit under a beach umbrella at the side of the pool to protect her pale skin from the sun's rays. Leila was not permitted to swim because the water would dilute the odors of the perfume smeared on her. Leila could not wear a bikini, but was required to dress in the harem outfit so she would be ready at a moment's notice to respond to a call from Suleiman.

So Lee had been stretched out on a chaise beneath an umbrella for hours at a time, scented and wearing as much makeup as a chorus girl. She had exhausted every subject on which the concubines were able to talk, no reading matter of any kind was available, and she had nothing to occupy her except soft drinks, cigarettes, and naps. She wondered how the permanent residents of the harem kept their sanity.

Suddenly, the lull came to an end. The first wife appeared at the pool and announced, "In a quarter of an hour His Highness will receive Leila."

The concubines swarmed around Lee, freshening the henna on her nipples, palms, and soles, touching up her makeup, and daubing her with additional perfume. Then she walked off alone down the tiled walks, open on one side, that led to the suite maintained in the harem by the ruler of Abu Bakr. The Arabs' idea of what made a woman physically attractive struck her as so absurdly juvenile that she laughed aloud. But she could hear a tremor of nervousness in her laugh and her heart was pounding. She was vulnerable in a way she had never before been, and it didn't help to remind herself that Suleiman was just another man. He was an absolute monarch whose whim was law in Abu Bakr, and here, in the inner core of his private domain, his power over others had no limits.

She paused at the entrance to the suite, automatically smoothing her blonde hair and moistening her lips. Then she raised her hand to the bell rope and was annoyed with herself when she saw her fingers were trembling.

A deep baritone voice invited her to enter.

Lee walked into the reception chamber and saw the

Shaikh sitting on a mound of cushions at the far end of the room. She prostrated herself, as he expected her to do, and touched her forehead to the tiled floor. There she remained for what felt like hours.

"Leila may rise," Suleiman said.

She drew herself to her feet.

"Come closer."

Her hips swayed slightly as she advanced toward him on bare feet.

The master of Abu Bakr inspected her closely, his expression unfathomable.

The girl felt her skin crawl.

"Leila may sit." He extended a hand and helped her to a place beside him on the cushions.

She forced a smile, reminding herself that he would take all of the initiatives.

The Shaikh continued to study her. "Is it true that you came to Abu Bakr of your own will?"

"It is true, Your Highness."

"Why?" His voice became rasping.

She assumed no flattery would be too obvious. "I admired Your Highness's boldness when you took the throne, and I wanted to meet a man of such courage."

If Suleiman enjoyed the compliment he did not show it. "You are being paid for this excursion by the Aapco people?"

It would be silly to deny the truth. "Of course."

"So you also like gold."

"Only a fool, a small child, or a camel fails to appreciate its worth," she replied, citing an old Arab saying.

His thin lips turned upward for an instant, indicating his amusement. Reaching into a satin-lined wicker basket beside him, he removed a thick gold bracelet and handed it to her.

If its weight was any criterion, she thought as she slipped

it over her wrist, it was worth a small fortune. "My gratitude to Your Highness knows no bounds."

"Leila will have the opportunity to demonstrate her appreciation." Once again he inspected her. "You are thin."

"Not too thin, I hope, to please Your Highness."

"It doesn't matter. Your hair is as lovely as gold." He reached for her head.

She thought he was trying to pull a handful of hair from her scalp, but managed to curb a gasp. His other hand grasped one of her near-nude breasts, and he squeezed it so roughly that she winced.

"Leila is not too thin," he said, and unexpectedly released her.

His breath was so foul that Lee almost gagged, and she struggled to regain her composure.

He continued to study her. "You have known other men?"

It was pointless to dissemble when he would soon discover she was lying. "Yes, Your Highness."

"You will find that Suleiman ben Yosef is a man among men," he said.

Even under these circumstances, she thought, an Arab could not resist boasting, but she lowered her head in a humble gesture. "I am eager to learn, Your Highness."

"Would you like some hashish?"

The question was totally unexpected, and Lee shook her head.

"You may change your mind," Suleiman said. "Come with me."

The girl followed him at the prescribed three paces, relieved that the ordeal soon would end. Instead of taking her to his bedchamber, however, he surprised her by leading her to a courtyard she had never before seen, an area fifty feet long and surrounded by high, windowless walls.

"Leila enjoys adventure," the Shaikh said, "or she would not have come here."

She nodded, something in his tone making her uneasy.

He reached behind him to what had looked like a box, and from a wooden cage he removed a hooded falcon, which perched on his hand.

When he removed the hood the bird peered at Lee without blinking; his small, hard eyes looked like Suleiman's.

"I make you a sporting offer," the Shaikh said. "Do you see that stone column at the far end of the court?"

"Yes, Your Highness."

"Run to it when I give you the word, and if you reach it before my friend touches you, I will pay you double the fee the Aapco people gave you."

"And if I lose?" She could not catch her breath.

His smile broadened. "My friend will return you to me, and then you will learn why Suleiman ben Yosef stands alone among men."

Lee looked at the hawk's razor-sharp talons and beak, and understood the meaning of the ugly scars that marred the bodies of the concubines. This man was a sadist.

"I am told," he said, "that hashish will minimize Leila's slight discomfort."

The girl shrank from him.

The hawk raised its wings slightly.

Suleiman stroked the bird. "I will treble your fee. Think of the gold."

"I can't," she said. "I'd bear the marks for the rest of my life."

"They would be stripes of honor."

"Other men," Lee said desperately, "wouldn't find them very attractive. Please, Your Highness, remember that my physical appearance is my principal asset."

"Then stay here, with one who will appreciate those stripes. You will be my favorite, and when you retire you will be wealthy."

Her nails dug into her henna-painted palms. "No, Your Highness. I am only a woman, so I am weak, and I lack both courage and the spirit of adventure you mentioned." At any moment, she thought, he would order the falcon to attack.

But Suleiman surprised her again by slipping the hood over the hawk's head and returning the creature to its cage.

The sun was beating down on the airless courtyard, and Lee was afraid she would faint.

"You infidel women are as empty of spirit as your men," Suleiman said harshly. "If you were one of my subjects, I would force you to do my will."

There appeared to be a chance, if she didn't anger him too much, that she would escape without harm. "It is not the fault of Your Highness that I am a coward." It took no effort on her part to weep.

His manner changed, and he tugged first at one side of his *burnoose,* then the other. "I must keep face in my own household," he muttered. "My women know my ways, and they will lose respect for me when they learn you scorned me."

The way out of the maze suddenly became clear. "Your Highness does me an injustice. I won't tell them."

Suleiman looked at the girl in surprise. "How can you avoid it?"

"Easily." There was a hint of hysteria in her laugh. "I'll tell them you're a man among men."

"But you will not bear the stripes of my friend."

"That doesn't matter." Lee improvised swiftly. "I'll just tell them I have my own way, that my way is a secret I won't reveal to anyone."

The Shaikh tugged at his beard. "What you say to me now may not be the same as that which you will tell my women."

"I'll be protecting my interests, too," she said. "Don't you see? It will harm me in my business if word should spread that I've failed."

He pondered, and at last he smiled. "It is agreed. Leila will live under my roof for another week. I will send for her again, and yet again, and only we two will know what has really taken place between us."

Her relief was so great that she wanted to collapse. He was displaying strength on the surface, but was more concerned with the impression he created than with substance. Happily she prostrated herself on the courtyard tiles, indifferent to their heat. She had been spared a horror, and a few minor burns didn't matter.

Turk Kenyon yawned, stretched, and slapped the plump buttocks of the girl beside him. "We can't spend the whole day here," he said. "I've got to get out to the Great Wadi this morning."

By the time he had showered, shaved, and dressed, Farima was preparing breakfast in the kitchen.

Turk joined her, and as he stood in the entrance he was reminded of the morning Bobbie had fixed breakfast for him, the day before she had helped him at Aapco. He could imagine what Bobbie would say if she saw him now. Maybe, after he made his pile, he'd persuade her to marry him again. She was ambitious and loved money, and he had to admit she was smart. She would help a man on his way to the top.

Arab bread wasn't too appetizing when it was toasted because it was too chewy, so they spread butter on plain chunks, which they tore from the loaf. Farima had learned to make American-style coffee, and liked it herself; sipping from an oversized cup, she leaned back in her kitchen chair.

"Before you leave this morning," she said, "there is something we must discuss."

Turk nodded absently as he glanced at his watch. The helicopter pilot was meeting him in twenty minutes at the pad behind the guest house complex.

"You have enjoyed our time together these past days," Farima said. "Now it is my turn."

His attention no longer diverted, he looked hard at her. "What's that supposed to mean?"

"I want money."

Turk realized he should have guessed, and laughed. Taking a twenty dollar bill from his pocket, he handed it to her across the table.

She tore it into pieces. "I want fifty thousand dollars," she said.

"Not even the girl visiting Shaikh Suleiman is making that much!"

Farima's jaw jutted forward. "She is not in my position, and the Shaikh is not in yours."

"You have a pretty high opinion of yourself, baby. Even if I had fifty thousand—which I don't—what makes you think I'd rustle it up for you?"

She couldn't understand his slang, but his meaning was clear. "Aapco is rich, and you have many friends there," she said calmly. "You will get the money from them."

For the first time he began to regard her demand as serious. "Suppose I refuse. Suppose I tell you to go to hell. What then?"

"I will go to Mr. Hamilton and tell him you seduced an Arab virgin. I will submit to an examination by your company physician. I know something about the oil people. Aapco will discharge you, and none of the other oil companies will hire you."

Turk's chair toppled with a crash as he leaped to his feet. "You don't have the brains to dream up this little blackmail scheme by yourself," he said, advancing toward her. "Who put you up to it?"

Farima stood too, and a tiny Arab knife appeared in her hand.

He grasped her wrist as she struck, and when the knife fell to the floor he slapped her hard across the face. "Don't ever try that stunt again. Now, answer me!"

She backed toward the far wall, looking like a trapped animal.

Turk slapped her again, then placed both hands around her throat. "Talk," he said, and began to squeeze.

Farima clawed in vain at his hands, and her frantic kicks had no effect on him.

"Talk!"

She was barely able to nod.

Turk released her. "Well?"

The girl rubbed her bruised throat. "Soon I would have been dead."

"The loss wouldn't have been mine. Talk!"

"The idea was my own," she said, unable to meet his gaze. "I need the money."

"What for? You've never seen fifty dollars in your life, much less fifty thousand."

"I must have it!"

Her desperation, he decided, was not feigned, and he waved her back to the table. "Five thousand," he said, "would buy you a home of your own in El Ain, a place with electricity and running water. You'd move up so far in the social order that some rich merchant would marry you."

"I would never marry a running dog of the imperialists! I would rather starve!"

Her slip told him all he needed to know. "What would the Communist party of Abu Bakr do with fifty thousand— hire an assassin to kill Suleiman? He has a dozen half brothers, all of them qualified to take his place. You'd gain nothing, and you and your pals would end on a gallows in the square in front of the *suq*."

Farima was frightened. "You have been spying on me!"

"Not at all." Turk was in command of the situation now, and could afford to be a trifle patronizing. "I have my sources of information, that's all."

"So you will denounce me to Mr. Hamilton, and he will

notify the Ministry of Public Order. But I'll kill myself before I'll let them torture me in their dungeons."

"Nobody is going to denounce you, and nobody is going to torture you. Drink your coffee."

The girl's dark eyes widened as she obeyed. "What will you do?"

"For the present, nothing at all." His mind was galloping, and he realized he had stumbled on a way of ingratiating himself with Suleiman. He could provide the girl with enough funds to gain her confidence, and through her he could learn more about her associates. The very color of red frightened the entire Husayn family, and Suleiman, whose phobia was even greater than that of his relatives, would become the friend for life of someone who could reveal to him the actual presence of a genuine Communist party apparatus in Abu Bakr.

"You are tricking me," Farima said.

He crooked a finger, led her into his bedroom, and, taking his wallet from a jacket pocket, counted out one thousand dollars, then thrust the crisp bills into her hands.

She was bewildered.

"No strings attached," he said. "That's just the first payment, and there will be more where that came from. Do what you like with it."

Farima slowly folded the money, then stuffed it inside the front of her low-cut dress. "You are an agent of the party!"

Turk's laugh was boisterous. "Hardly. The good comrades would throw me into Lubyanka Prison if I showed up in Moscow. They've hated me ever since I beat them to a lease. Behind their Iron Curtain, too, in Rumania."

"Then why do you give me money?" The girl had not yet recovered from the shock.

"I have my own reasons, and you'll find out about them at the right time. Maybe, before I make a quick trip to the States, you can arrange a meeting for me with some of your friends. I'll make you another payment then, and when I get back from America you'll be swimming in money."

Farima could scarcely believe her good fortune and, throwing her arms around his neck, she pressed close to him.

His caress was light but convincing. "Not now," he said. "There will be plenty of time after I get back from the Great Wadi. Why don't you take a few hours off, and get Judy to give you a lift into El Ain? Maybe you can set up a date for me by the time I get back this afternoon."

Her suspicions were somewhat diminished, and in any event it paid to be compliant. "I will. And forgive me for trying to hurt you with a knife."

"Forget it," he said, donning his sunglasses and moving toward the front door. "That was just a lovers' misunderstanding."

The pilot was just starting to warm up the helicopter when Turk reached the pad and climbed into his seat.

The chopper rose vertically to an altitude of fifteen hundred feet, then continued its climb to a ceiling of thirty-five hundred feet as it headed westward. It was a small aircraft, with room for only six persons, and since it was one of the older models it lacked a number of conveniences. The air conditioning was feeble, so the vents were left open, admitting streams of dry, hot air, and the absence of soundproofing made it impossible to converse at any level below a shout.

Turk, the only passenger, contented himself with staring out of the window at the desert. They flew over the Roosevelt oil field, then began the long crossing of the wasteland. Resisting the urge to defy the *No Smoking* sign, he looked out at terrain he and Suleiman had covered on their hunting trip, the helicopter reaching the farthest limits in minutes.

Mirages appeared on the shimmering horizon, and Turk realized anew how influential the desert had been in shaping the character of the Arab. Nowhere else on the globe was the environment more hostile to human life. Natural springs or wells provided a few, scattered patches of green where nomads could find pasturage for their flocks and water for themselves. The sun was merciless, the heat reflected by the barren ground was stifling, and when the wind blew, stirring up a dreaded *shamal,* the world was enveloped in a brown, grit-laden darkness.

A psychological factor was even more important than the desert's physical characteristics. As anyone who had traveled on the surface knew, it created in man a feeling of loneliness that turned him inward. He was forced to live on his daydreams, producing in him a concept of heaven on earth that was a cool place where water, food, and women were plentiful. The nomad needed stamina as well as obstinate courage in order to survive, but above all he had to be endowed with the will to live and the ability to find satisfaction in what he did.

The Oasis of Qar appeared on the horizon as the helicopter reached the halfway point in its flight. Dates, pineapples, and figs grew here in abundance, as did tomatoes, green peppers, and a thick-skinned vegetable that resembled an eggplant. The permanent population numbered almost four thousand, the residents living on the sale of their produce as well as that of cooking utensils, firearms, and blankets to the nomads, who came to Qar in large groups, an entire tribe of fifty to a hundred and fifty persons often arriving simultaneously.

The smoke from a dozen or more cooking fires drifted upward in the still air, and Turk could see men filling containers with water at one of the twenty-seven wells the oasis boasted. At one end of the settlement stood a row of huts that housed a number of hardy prostitutes. So Qar was proof to the nomad that his daydreams of heaven on earth were more than wishful thinking and could be realized.

As they left the oasis behind, Turk took a nap and slept for an hour and a half. The jolting of the chopper awakened him as it began to drop, so he donned a burnoose and a *galabia*, a less voluminous townsman's version of the *agal*. Since he intended to spend only a few hours at the Great Wadi he had no need for more cumbersome attire.

The landing pad was a natural shelf of bare rock and, as Turk had anticipated, was located at a considerable distance from the steel towers that had been erected over the test wells. The fear of fire was always present in the oil fields, and strict precautions were taken to prevent a catastrophe.

The presence of a high, barbed-wire fence extending toward the horizon in both directions was significant, as was the presence, at intervals, of armed guards whose tan *agals* identified them as Aapco employees. The pad was located a short distance from a gate manned by two guards who carried sub-machine guns. Turk made his way toward them.

"I am Kenyon." He gestured toward the field telephone near the entrance to their tent. "Will you send for transportation, please, and notify the director of the station that I'm here?"

The men made no reply. One of them went off to the telephone, his companion continuing to eye the visitor while he held his weapon ready for immediate use.

Turk knew he would not be invited to wait inside the tent, nor would he be offered a soft drink from the cooler that rested in the shade. Arabs, who made a fetish of offering hospitality, could be merciless toward their enemies, and the guards had been trained to regard all outsiders as potential foes.

After a long wait the other guard returned. "Someone comes," he said.

There were no clouds and the sun caused heat waves to shimmer everywhere. Turk wished he had worn a *ghutra* instead of the townsman's *burnoose*, but he was pleased to discover he was only perspiring slightly and felt little discomfort.

An open-sided jeep approached from the interior of the

Great Wadi. Two men were riding in it, and when the passenger alighted Turk did not recognize him from a distance. He wore an *agal, ghutra,* and sunglasses, his face was deeply tanned, and only the absence of a beard identified him as an American.

When he came nearer, Turk shouted. "Cal!"

They shook hands, and Calvin Hodges looked embarrassed.

"I was intending to look you up at Roosevelt," Turk said. "I didn't know you were out here."

"I'm on temporary assignment."

"Well, we'll have to have our beer-drinking contest in the Great Wadi, then. I hope you've got plenty of it."

"No, I won't be here long enough. I didn't bring any with me."

"Can't win 'em all. Anyway, we can catch up on old times while you take me sightseeing." Turk started to enter the gate.

But Hodges blocked his path. "I don't know how else to tell you this," he said, "but I can't let you in."

Turk stared at him. "What's the gag?"

"It's no joke, Turk. I have strict orders to admit no one except authorized personnel, and your name isn't on the list."

Turk laughed. "There's as much Aapco red tape in the field as there is at the home office. Some idiot in administration back at Roosevelt forgot to include me. Give them a ring and straighten it out, Cal, so we can get rolling. I've got to be back in El Ain by nightfall."

Hodges made no move. "Sorry. It can't be done, Turk."

"What the hell are you saying?"

"Mr. Hamilton gave me the authorized list himself, and there are no exceptions. If old Dugald McIntosh himself showed up I couldn't let him in."

Turk was exasperated. "I've spent three and a half hours in that chopper, and I have another three-and-a-half-hour ride ahead of me. I didn't come out here for the fun of it, Cal, and I have instructions from New York to follow."

"You know I'd escort you around the place with a brass band if it was up to me, Turk," Hodges said. "But I have my orders."

Turk pointed toward the telephone. "Hook that line into short wave for me, and put through a call to Red Hamilton."

"It wouldn't do any good." Hodges looked miserable. "I asked Mr. Hamilton specifically about you, and he said you aren't on the authorized list."

"I think I'm still sane, but the sun is driving some people nuts. Will you do as I ask and make that call?"

Hodges shook his head.

"Then I'll do it myself." Turk started forward, but found himself looking into the muzzles of the sub-machine guns. "You really do mean it, Cal, don't you?"

"Not through my own doing. We can still have our beer-drinking contest back at the base."

"Yeah." Turk looked at the rigs, and saw there were at least twenty of them. "What's so hush-hush here that a representative of company headquarters can't see it for himself?"

"I don't know, Turk. A guy on my level does what he's told and asks no questions. You know that. I take my orders from one man and nobody else."

The sentries still held their weapons at the ready.

Turk realized this was one argument he couldn't win. "Do me a simple favor, Cal." It was not a request.

"You know I'll do anything I can."

"Call Red Hamilton and tell him I've been here and that I'm on my way back to the coast. Tell him he's going to need a tremendous excuse for wasting my entire day!" Turk was so angry he did not shake hands again as he stomped back to the chopper.

The flight back seemed endless. Turk ignored the admonition against smoking and went through the better part of a package of cigarettes, his rage so obvious that the pilot decided not to protest.

A *shamal* blew up, seemingly out of nowhere, and the helicopter had to climb to an altitude of six thousand feet to escape the blinding sandstorm. The headwinds were still strong, however, so the chopper fell an hour and a half behind schedule, and it was late afternoon before the pilot put down on the pad behind the guest houses in Eisenhower.

Turk was so angry he forgot he had eaten nothing since breakfast. Once in his house, he downed a stiff drink, then telephoned Hamilton's office, only to be told that the general manager had gone home for the day.

It was a short walk to the Hamilton house, and Red answered the door himself.

"You're just in time for a drink," he said.

"Shove your drink. I want to know why you sent me off on a real wild goose chase today."

"I'm sorry you had a frustrating time," Red said. "If you had told me you intended to go to the Great Wadi I could have saved you the effort. But you ordered the helicopter direct."

Turk stared at Red. "Okay. You didn't send me off on a joy ride. But you sure as hell gave the order that kept me out of the test field."

Red met his gaze. "I accept full responsibility."

"How come?"

"In my best judgment it would have been unwise to place your name on the list of those authorized to inspect the field."

"I know you have reasons, good reasons, to hate my guts," Turk said. "And if you want to take a poke at me, go ahead. But this is no personal matter, Red. I had orders from old McIntosh himself to make a thorough inspection of the Great Wadi test field."

114

"I can only repeat that I accept full responsibility." Red was unruffled. "You're right when you say that you're not my favorite human being, but you'll have to take my word for it that my decision in this matter wasn't personal."

"What else could it be? I've got to protect myself, you know, which means I'll have to send McIntosh a cable telling him exactly what happened."

"Go right ahead," Red said. "I won't make any attempt to stop you, and I'd probably do the same thing if I were in your shoes."

"If this is a declaration of war, Hamilton, I warn you—I'll fight you to a finish. And in a war like this nobody raises a white flag."

Six

Bobbie Kenyon waited for a signal from Dugald McIntosh before seating herself in a chair beside his desk. By unspoken consent they observed different amenities in the office from those in their mutual social life.

"This cable makes no goddam sense," he said. "Even if Kenyon and Red Hamilton are feuding, and I accept your word that they are, I can't for the life of me see why Hamilton would use the threat of force to prevent a legitimate representative of this office from visiting the Great Wadi. What's your opinion?"

Bobbie placed her stenographer's notebook on the edge of the desk. "Dale can double-talk better than anyone I've ever known," she said. "It might be that the facts he's presented in the cable are true enough as far as they go, but he may be holding back elements of the story that would make Hamilton's actions plain."

"Then we've got to learn what Hamilton's side of it is."

"Yesterday," she said, "when you were in the Texas fields and I couldn't reach you, I sent Hamilton a cable in your name. His answer has just been decoded." She handed him a slip of paper that read:

FACTS AS PRESENTED BY KENYON ARE CORRECT STOP REASONS WILL BECOME SELF-EVIDENT IN DUE COURSE STOP PROTECTION OF AAPCO INTERESTS SOLE CAUSE STOP REMEMBER ME TO SPINDLETOP STOP REGARDS LYMAN HAMILTON

McIntosh read the message twice, then began to laugh softly. "Sounds pretty good to me. You know what he's trying to say?"

"Well, the Spindletop gusher in east Texas was the biggest this country has ever known. It may be he's hinting the Great Wadi field is in the same class."

"That's the way I read it." McIntosh sobered. "But if that's the case, why doesn't he notify us in so many words? Why doesn't he let Kenyon see the field so he can bring word back to us?"

"I'm just guessing, of course," Bobbie said, "but there must be complications he can't discuss right now."

"Get him on the phone!" the president of Aapco ordered.

His secretary made no move. "That wouldn't be wise. There's always interference on the line to El Ain, and you can never hear half of what they're saying at the other end. Which means your lunch will give you acute indigestion. What's more, a scrambler would make the conversation almost completely inaudible, so you'd have to talk in the clear. You know some Abu Bakrian government flunky will be monitoring the call, so Hamilton probably wouldn't even mention whatever it is that's on his mind."

"What would I do without you, Bobbie?"

Her situation required a display of modesty. "You'd make out just fine."

"The hell I would," McIntosh protested, and turned to

117

stare out at a sea of Manhattan skyscraper tops. "What this boils down to is a very simple question. Do we trust Hamilton or Kenyon?"

"Are you asking me?"

"I am."

"Then you already know my answer. Hamilton has been a reliable employee for a long time. He's no ball of fire, but he's steady, and there isn't a black mark on his record. I had personnel send me his confidential data card so I could check it. There was no need to send for Dale's card, of course."

"Okay, so far so good. The next question is what we do about Hamilton's Spindletop hint, and the answer is that you and I keep the information strictly to ourselves."

"I've already sent for the communications copy, and have it locked in my safe. A great many people have access to their confidential files, and I want to take no chances."

"What did I tell you? You're tremendous."

"It was just routine," she said.

"That's nonsense, as I'll tell you why in greater detail at dinner tonight. Now, where do we go from here?"

"I don't know," Bobbie said. "I've tried to figure that one out, and I'm stymied."

"I'm reluctant to bring Hamilton home when affairs in Abu Bakr are in a state of flux," McIntosh said. "So—if we trust him—then we've got to go all the way with him. We'll have to wait until he's ready to pass along information in his own way. When is Kenyon due to return?"

"Either the end of this week or the beginning of next."

"Fine. We may glean more from him, and in any case we'll learn his impressions of the new Shaikh. What will be difficult for you and me, Bobbie, is to keep what little we know to ourselves."

"I don't discuss what happens in this office with anyone in the company, and my friends outside the company really aren't interested," she said. "The whole burden is going to rest on you. The directors are bugging you, and Mr. Bell of ICO has been calling you daily. To mention just a few."

"They may be mad as hell at me for the moment," McIntosh said. "But if Red Hamilton means what we think he means, the champagne corks will be popping. And you'll have yourself a new coat. Mink."

Bobbie stiffened. "I don't think that would be appropriate," she said.

"Rubbish! I know what you're thinking, and you're wrong. You've already earned it as a special bonus. This has nothing whatever to do with the fact that you and I are seeing each other after hours. There's no connection."

"In that case, I'll accept." A mink coat, Bobbie thought, was a sign of what lay ahead if she continued to play her cards very close to her chest.

The sun was scorching, but Lee jumped into the harem pool at least once every half hour, protecting her hair with a bathing cap, and she spent the better part of each day acquiring a tan. To that extent, at least, she was in charge of her own destiny, and the first wife, accepting Shaikh Suleiman's seeming partiality to the visitor, could not complain. All the same, it was necessary to put up a front, and Lee continued to allow the women to daub her with henna, freshen her makeup, and dress her whenever she was called to Suleiman's quarters.

His mere proximity continued to send chills up and down her spine, but she had to concede that, so far, he had abided by the terms of their bargain. When she went to his suite he offered her coffee and Turkish cigarettes, questioned her at some length about the details of her way of life, and then released her without as much as touching her.

But she mistrusted him, and was afraid he might change his mind about taking her in his own way before she could leave the palace. And each night she dreamed about the hawk with the long claws and narrow beak.

Late one afternoon, the summons came as she was making her way from the pool to her own room. The concubines rendered their usual services, and even the second and third wives smiled at her companionably. Their lord appeared to be in a consistently good mood, and they believed they had the blonde to thank for it.

Lee took the now-familiar walk to the Shaikh's suite, once again warning herself to show no apprehension. She followed the customary routine of prostrating herself in Suleiman's presence, and he told her to rise. Then, instead of seating her on one of the lower steps of his dais, he directed her to join him.

She remembered, all too vividly, what had happened at their first meeting, and her heart began to pound.

His eyes were mere slits. "Leila has kept her word," he said.

"Of course." Her heart was hammering so loudly she felt sure he could hear it.

"My women believe what I want them to believe. But soon you will return to your world, and there you may be tempted to talk about Suleiman of Abu Bakr."

"Never!" the girl protested. "I always keep my word!"

"I do not doubt you," the Shaikh said, "but I have learned there are two ways to reinforce an agreement. One is in the dungeons."

For a moment her heart seemed to stop beating.

"This is the other." He reached into his wicker basket and handed her a diamond ring so enormous she could only gape at it. As nearly as she could tell it weighed seven or eight carats, and had to be worth more thousands than she had ever imagined owning. "I am overwhelmed, Your Highness," she said, bowing her head.

Suleiman's laugh was his usual, rasping sound. "If we do not meet again, Leila will not forget me, just as I shall remember her."

Lee raised her eyes to his. "Suppose I want to return to Abu Bakr some day. Will you allow me to enter the country?"

"Of course."

"And Your Highness would receive me here?"

He looked startled by the question.

She swallowed hard, then moistened her lips. "I mean, if I was willing—to agree—to your terms. If I wanted to—accept your challenge—and see if I could outrun the falcon."

His chuckle became louder. "I know of nothing that would give me greater joy!" He peered hard at her. "You will do that?"

She glanced at the huge diamond gleaming on her finger. "I—I don't know. I want to think about it—and see if there isn't a way I can summon my courage."

"Leila will find the courage," Suleiman said, reaching out to squeeze her breasts and then running a rough hand up the inside of her thigh.

She had to blink back her tears. His sadistic streak ran so deep, she thought, that he sometimes wasn't even aware of his cruelty. "I'll try hard," she said, "and I'll often think of Your Highness."

The hard-packed dirt lanes in the old town section of El Ain were so narrow that only thin shafts of sunlight pierced them. No foreigner ever entered this part of the city after dark, and even in daylight hours the residents resented the presence of tourists. But Turk Kenyon, in his *burnoose* and *galabia,* a pistol and long-handled knife protruding from his broad belt of raw leather, looked far more like an Arab than many of the natives.

His step was confident as he followed directions, taking two turns to the left, one to the right, and another to the left. The dilapidated wall was directly ahead now, just as he had been told, and behind it stood the house of dried mud that resembled scores of others. He was able to identify it because an American garbage can stood just outside the wall.

Still doing as he had been instructed, he began to whistle an Arabian air that dated back to the thirteenth century.

A woman shrouded in a black *yashmak* and *feredezah* was half hidden in an opening at one end of the wall; she raised a hand to her veil.

Turk did not directly acknowledge the gesture, but moved toward the opening, then followed the woman into the house. Neither spoke.

At last they reached a room with closed shutters, so dark the visitor could barely make out the bulk of an unidentifiable figure in a far corner.

"This is the one called Ali," Farima said. "This is the one called Kenyon."

Turk acknowledged the introduction, but the man in the corner remained silent.

The girl began to remove her robe and veil.

"Are you insane, woman?" Ali Nasar Jalal asked. "That man is not a member of our family."

Farima laughed. "I don't wear these ugly things when I work in his house. He has seen me in Western dress."

"I promised Farima I would make you another gift of cash before I leave Abu Bakr," Turk said. "I have it here for you." He took ten hundred dollar bills from his pocket.

Ali made no move.

Farima accepted the money, and went to the shutters, where a thin streak of light slanted into the room. She counted the money.

Farima remembered to express her thanks, then took the money to the corner, where the man snatched it from her and mumbled something in a low tone.

"Ali," the girl said, "wants to know why you are helping us when you are not a member of the party and do not share our aims."

122

Turk had to improvise. "I'm a capitalist, of course. I happen to believe strongly in freedom of speech." He was counting on their ignorance. "I believe your party has the right to operate openly, and I believe the climate in Abu Bakr will soon improve sufficiently so this will become possible."

The man muttered again, and Turk, although unable to make out his words, could hear his tone of incredulity.

"Ali," Farima said, "cannot accept your answer. No capitalist gives money to anyone unless he hopes to be given a far larger sum in return."

Turk had expected the reaction, and was confident he could allay their suspicions. "Ali is right," he said. "The princes who rule Abu Bakr make life very difficult for my employers. When democracy comes to this nation there will be fewer rules, fewer laws, and the American-Arabian Petroleum Company will earn a far larger share of the profits that it makes now. The greedy shaikhs take too much. So my company will become much wealthier if I give you money now. By helping your cause I help my own."

Ali forgot to mumble. "At last you speak the truth!" he declared. "I would not believe all that Farima told me about you, but I can accept what you have told me. Americans will do anything for money."

"You're a wise man," Turk said, and suddenly thought of a way to see the man's face. "I realize this isn't a social occasion, but I'd like to smoke a cigarette before I leave."

"By all means, smoke," Ali said.

"Will you join me in an American cigarette?" Turk asked, baiting the hook. Arabs, like most people throughout the world, preferred American brands to any other.

"I will take two," Farima said, "one for Ali and one for me."

Turk gave them to her and, before she could stop him, flicked on his lighter. In the time it took him to light the two cigarettes he had a glimpse of the man's face. Certainly he would recognize Ali if he saw him again, and believed he could offer a fairly accurate description of the man.

Ali turned his back toward the center of the room as he smoked.

"May I ask you any questions about the party?" Turk wanted to know.

"You may ask, but that doesn't mean you'll be given answers," Farima said.

"Does Abu Bakr have many members?"

"Very many," Ali replied.

The man was a liar, Communism having made few inroads in Islam, but Turk felt he had gone through the necessary motions that someone in his position normally would make. "I'm sure our arrangement will be of benefit to all of us," he said.

"You will see what happens in Abu Bakr," Farima said.

"Yes, it will be interesting." Turk stubbed out his cigarette on the dirt floor. "When I return from America I'll bring you additional funds."

Farima donned her robes and veil so she could lead him back to the opening in the wall. "Can you find your way to the new town?"

"I got here, didn't I? I always keep my lines of communication wide open." The expression in her eyes told him she didn't know what he meant.

"I will awaken you in the morning," she said. "In the usual way."

"Great. I'm going to miss you while I'm away." It would do no harm, he thought, if she believed he was developing a romantic interest in her. Certainly this little trip into the old town had been well worth the effort. He knew he could lead Suleiman's troops to the house, he could identify Ali, and he had already learned, through a slip, that the man was related to Farima.

He held all the cards, and when he returned to Abu Bakr he would play them. Then he would stand closer to the ruling Shaikh than any other foreigner, and it wouldn't be long before he would replace the double-crossing Red Hamilton as the Aapco general manager in the country. His cash gifts to the pathetic Communists would prove to be one of the best investments he'd ever made.

The message from the palace chamberlain arrived the next evening just as Turk was about to leave his quarters for dinner at the bachelor mess. He learned from the transportation department that a regularly scheduled commercial flight would stop at El Ain in two hours, so he ordered two seats booked, and after requesting the immediate use of a sedan from the car pool, he picked up the telephone again.

"Get me Mr. Hamilton," he told the compound operator, and felt a grim sense of pleasure.

In a few moments Hamilton came on the line, his manner so pleasantly calm that someone who didn't know better couldn't have guessed the two men were at odds. "What can I do for you, Turk?"

"Not a thing. I just want to let you know I've had the green light from the palace. I'm picking up the blonde, and we're catching the seven fifty-three flight to Beirut."

"Oh. Then we won't be seeing you again before you leave." Red was polite but reserved.

"It doesn't look that way. But I'll be back, and sooner than you think."

"We'll be seeing you eventually, then. By the way, I assume you'll let me know anything of significance that your traveling companion may tell you."

"You assume wrong," Turk said. "If New York wants you to know something, they'll tell you about it. I'll start cooperating with you, Hamilton, when you do the same with me."

"I wish you a safe journey," Red said, refusing to be drawn into an argument.

Turk laughed cynically and said an abrupt goodbye. He

hurriedly packed his belongings, which he threw into the back seat of the waiting car.

When he arrived at the palace the sentries waved his car into the main courtyard. Soon after he parked a shrouded figure in a *feredezah* and *yashmak* emerged through an arch and joined him. He wasted no time turning the car around and leaving the grounds.

"Are you okay?"

"Never better," Lee said.

"Then you got along with Suleiman?"

"We were able to reach an understanding."

"I'd like to hear what you think of him," Turk said.

"That wasn't part of our agreement."

Turk couldn't blame her for milking Aapco. "I think we can work out an extra payment that will satisfy you."

"How much?"

"That will depend on the value of the information."

"Five thousand, regardless of what you think my impressions are worth, and ten if I hit the jackpot for you. In cash by the time I leave Beirut."

"Fair enough," Turk said.

"We'll wait until we're on the airplane," Lee said. "I hope I'll have time to change in the ladies' room at the airport. My makeup is bad enough, but they just told me I was leaving, and I'm carrying my own clothes. They've got me dressed in a harem outfit that would get me arrested in any civilized society."

"I'd like to see it," he said, and chuckled.

"I'm sure you would."

Turk stepped on the accelerator, using his horn to clear pedestrians and donkeys from his path, and when he reached the open road to the airport he pressed the gas pedal to the floor. "You have exactly ten minutes to change," he told her as he deposited her at the airport entrance.

By the time he had parked the car, presented their tickets

at the counter, and checked their luggage to the flight's terminal point, Beirut, Lee emerged from the ladies' room wearing her own clothes beneath the Arab robes. The airplane was already on the runway, so they boarded it, taking their seats in the first class section.

As soon as they were aloft Lee removed her *feredezah* and *yashmak*. "Order me a double martini, please. I can use it."

Turk summoned the stewardess, then studied the girl beside him. "I see what you mean about the makeup."

"Garish but passable. I can't do much to tone it down before we reach Beirut because I'll have to strip all of it off and start again."

Their drinks arrived, and Turk raised his glass. "Here's to sin and corruption."

Lee lifted her own glass and took a large swallow. "This is probably the best I've ever had."

"Hey, that's some fancy ring!"

"I'm rather fond of it myself."

He examined the diamond, then saw her gold bracelet. "Gifts from our friend?"

She nodded. "When he's in a good mood he hands out trinkets like popcorn."

"Rather expensive popcorn. You've done all right for a nine-day jaunt."

"Not bad—so far," Lee said. "Which reminds me, you owe me the final payment of my fee."

Turk handed her an envelope, telling himself she was the first woman he had ever known whose mind never strayed from business.

She counted the money before placing the envelope in a zippered compartment of her shoulderbag.

"Now for the bonus."

"Our friend," she said, "would have been at home back in the eighth century. Particularly in the eighth century, when the Arabs had conquered the known world. He doesn't trust Christians, he hates Jews. He suspects all foreigners, and he takes it for granted that his word is final in Abu Bakr."

"I'd say that's accurate, based on my own acquaintance with him," Turk said. "What about his personality?"

"He's flaky."

"Be specific."

"The details aren't relevant." She intended to keep her promise to Suleiman—for reasons of her own. "But I can tell you this much. He has a cruel streak that goes far beyond the Arab norm. He's a sadistic man, and he enjoys inflicting real pain on others. That's how he gets his sex kicks."

Turk remembered the dismemberment of the living *dalu* birds. "You confirm something I suspected." He paused. "Would you trust him in a business deal?"

The girl was silent, and gazed out of the window at the clouds gathering over the Persian Gulf. "That's hard to say. If he thought he had something to gain, he'd keep a contractual agreement. Provided you had him at a disadvantage. If he thought he had the upper hand, though, you'd be wise to watch your step. He'd slit your throat without giving it another thought."

He made no reply, but instead handed her another wad of bills. "Ten thousand, on the barrel head."

Again she counted the money with care. "Thank you. You keep your bargains."

"That's good business. We may be working together some other time." He asked the stewardess for another round before dinner, and suddenly he noticed Lee's palms. "Are your hands bleeding?"

"This is henna, unfortunately," she said with a slight laugh. "It will take days of scrubbing to get rid of it."

"You really got the works at the palace."

"I don't believe I missed anything."

"I hope," Turk said, "he didn't treat *you* sadistically."

"I take care of myself."

He looked at her, and was convinced she did. She was tough and resourceful. "Just so you weren't hurt."

"Not this trip."

He raised an eyebrow.

"I have a standing invitation to come back. Any time."

"That's good to know. It could be useful."

"The circumstances and the pay would have to be enormous." Lee shuddered. "And even then I'm not certain I could do it."

Turk sipped his fresh drink. "Don't think about it now. We're due to land at 11:00 P.M., Beirut time, and the night spots stay open until dawn. I'm going on to New York in the morning, and I'll get you a ticket to London, or anywhere else you may want to go. I do think we owe ourselves a celebration tonight."

Her smile was enigmatic. "It's a possibility."

"I've reserved a suite for us at one of the best hotels in town."

"That's cozy."

"The degree of coziness will depend on you. The suite has two bedrooms." Turk spoke lightly, taking care not to press. He was not losing sight of the fact that she earned her living by selling her favors, but she had made a real killing in Abu Bakr, and she might want to express her gratitude to the man who had made her diamond ring and gold bracelet possible.

"Why don't we see how the night develops?" She smiled more broadly.

"It's a deal." He told himself he was in luck. She was showing all the signs of acquiescence, and if he continued to play it cool there was a reasonable certainty he would score.

They drank champagne with their dinner, following it with Cognac, and Turk imbibed freely, relaxing after the tensions of his visit to Abu Bakr. The girl kept pace with him, but didn't appear to feel her drinks. She was remark-

129

able, and he wanted to know more about her. He realized that she had told him literally nothing about herself, that he knew only her first name and could identify her only by her appearance.

"How will I get in touch with you again? Next month or next year. Or whenever."

"That might be difficult," Lee said.

"I suppose I could make contact the same way we hooked up this time."

She shrugged.

"In my work, I often need help from somebody in your line," Turk said.

"Perhaps our paths will cross again—at the right moment," she said.

It was impossible for him to determine whether she meant it or was just being polite.

They landed in Beirut, and as they made their way through the airport, the busiest in the Middle East, men and women of many nationalities paused to stare at Lee. She seemed unaware of the interest she created, and Turk knew that more than her heavy makeup was responsible for the stir she created. She was so accustomed to attention that she took it for granted.

A heavy, early summer rain was falling, making it difficult for them to see out of the windows of their taxi.

"Too bad the view is spoiled," Turk said. "The natives like to call this town the Paris of the East, and they aren't far wrong. I'll try to order some sunshine for you tomorrow."

"Thank you," Lee said, "but I know Beirut."

When they reached their hotel an assistant manager conducted them to their suite, which consisted of a living room and two bedrooms, each with its own bath. A basket of flowers and a huge bowl of fruit rested on living room tables.

"You really rate here," Lee said.

"It's the magic name of Aapco," he told her. "In this part of the world an oil company representative gets as much fuss made over him as a shaikh. Help yourself to the flowers."

She carried the basket into one of the bedrooms and closed the door behind her.

Turk went into the other bedroom and sent a cable to Dugald McIntosh, saying he was flying back to New York the next day. Then he shaved for the second time since morning, changed into a pressed suit, and wandered into the living room to wait for Lee.

The door of her room was open and he could hear no sound, so he looked inside. The girl was gone, and her luggage gone with her.

The mission was one of the most delicate that Red Hamilton had ever undertaken. Shaikh Suleiman had insisted on making an inspection tour of the Great Wadi, and no excuse had persuaded him to delay it. So Hamilton had been forced to agree, and they flew to the test field in the largest of the Aapco helicopters, accompanied by Shaikh Ahmed al-Husayn and three of the ruling prince's bodyguards.

The sentries at the gate saluted, as did an honor guard drawn up inside the entrance. A jeep was waiting, and as Hamilton climbed behind the wheel he exchanged a brief glance with Husayn. By unspoken agreement they were partners in a conspiracy to prevent the emir of Abu Bakr from learning prematurely that a major oil field had been discovered.

Two incidents marred the start of the tour. Suleiman protested when he learned there was no room in the vehicle for his bodyguards, who would be obliged to follow in another jeep. And when he lit a cigarette it was necessary for Hamilton to inform him that smoking was prohibited on the property to reduce the danger of fire. So Suleiman was in a sour mood.

Red drove at a crawl. "When the oil industry was born, the better part of a century ago, a strike was a matter of sheer luck. A prospector, usually a man of few resources, would sink an experimental well, and if he found oil the area soon was teeming with others like him, each staking a claim. Today the finding of oil is a science. Man hasn't yet been able to X-ray the interior of the earth, but we've come closer to it than the layman imagines. Oil companies have scoured the globe, so it isn't very often that we find natural seepages indicating the presence of oil below the surface. However, a trained geologist can tell by studying rock formations whether there's a possibility or even a probability of discovering a well."

Suleiman continued to sulk behind his dark glasses.

Maybe the imagined slights he had suffered would be beneficial, Red thought. If he refused to listen or look at his surroundings, it would be far easier to conceal the truth from him.

Ahmed al-Husayn played his part with grace. "Your geologists believe there is oil in the Great Wadi?" he asked, pretending ignorance.

"They've given us the opinion that there *may* be oil here," Red said. "They photographed the area from the air, and then made a much closer ground inspection. The geophysical survey proved to their satisfaction that rock structures suitable for oil traps exist here, and the geological surveys told them that reservoir, source, and cap rocks do exist in the area."

Suleiman returned to the present. "Then they have already found oil here?"

Red didn't want to tell an outright lie, so he replied obliquely. "We're drilling test wells to find out. And since there's never been any previous exploration in the Great Wadi, such a well serves a number of purposes." He drew to a halt near a fifty-foot rig, and invited the Shaikh to accompany him on foot.

As they started to walk toward the structure the second

jeep stopped, and Suleiman's bodyguards ran forward to surround him, their sub-machine guns ready for use.

"We are alone here," Husayn said. "There is no need for close protection."

Suleiman bared his teeth as he smiled at his half brother. "My troops are devoted to me."

Red behaved as though the guards weren't present. "This well," he said, "is testing the fluid content of the various rock strata through which it passes. It tells our geologists the nature and the thickness of the underground rock formations, and it takes measurements that tell us the pressures and temperatures of the rocks under the surface."

"How will you know if there is oil here?" Suleiman demanded.

"We won't need an expert for that, Your Highness," Red said. "The pressures will send it to the surface, and we'll have a geyser." He refrained from mentioning that twenty-five test wells had already produced oil, and that all were securely capped. "The beauty of a well such as this is that it can be transformed into a permanent installation by adding casing tubing and valves. That's the simplest and easiest part of the job."

Husayn stood between his half brother and the well, even though Suleiman wouldn't recognize the steel and concrete cap already in place there. "Do I understand correctly that one of the reasons this field is promising is because the geological formations are not very complicated?"

"Speaking in broad generalities," Red said, "the more complicated the field, the smaller the oil accumulations found in it. I'd like to stress that there's only one way to make certain there's oil in a field. You've got to drill for it." He led the way back to the jeep. "And that's a job for experts these days."

The bodyguards again abandoned their master with obvious reluctance.

Red started the jeep. "When necessary," he said, "we can sink test wells to a depth of ten thousand feet, and in some instances tests have even been made at fifteen thousand."

"In Abu Bakr?" Suleiman wanted to know.

"No, Your Highness. One of the qualities that makes this country so attractive is that it—like the rest of the Middle East—has its oil close to the surface. "Most of our wells here are no more than one to two thousand feet deep. But, to finish, in the first phase of exploration we don't necessarily depend on core samples that ground geologists take. For the past thirty years the industry has been making what's known as magnetic surveys, usually from the air. The earth's magnetic force—in general—is very weak, while that of an oil field is strong, so its presence can be detected by an instrument called a magnetometer. It has great sensitivity, and usually is mounted in the tail of an airplane or helicopter, preferably the latter."

"What do these surveys show here?"

"That the prospects are good," Red said, again becoming evasive. "I must repeat that only by drilling can you find out for sure. There are other types of surveys we're prepared to make too. Gravity surveys, seismic surveys, and the like. But we don't require such sophisticated tests in the Arabian peninsula."

"Allah," Suleiman said, "has been good to those whose faith in Him is strong."

Red nodded politely, but preferred not to discuss the Almighty with a rigidly devout Muslim. "As you'll see at our next stop, all oil wells are drilled by means of what we call a bit, which is any tool that bites into the ground and progressively deepens the well. In the old days we used what was called the percussion system. A chisel-shaped bit traveled up and down at the end of a rope and literally pounded the hole deeper. Now we use what's known as the rotary system."

"Allow me," Husayn contributed from the back seat,

"to show off what I know about the oil industry. In this system a different type of bit rotates at the end of a pipe, crushing the rock at the bottom of the hole, and fluid forced into the hole brings these cuttings to the surface. This leaves the hole free, ready to be cemented, if oil is found."

"Not so fast," Suleiman said, and waved in the direction of the many towers off to his right. "How many of these holes must you dig before you know whether you have found oil?"

"Your Highness is wise," Red said. "You've asked the most important question in the industry. In some of the Saudi fields there was a strike with the first well, but in others it took many tries. The companies working the rich Iranian fields had to try dozens of times. Everything depends on the skill of the drillers, the conviction of the geologists, and the determination of the men who pay the bills. No two fields have identical physical characteristics. So I can't answer your question categorically."

"But you've been trying for more than three months in the Great Wadi," the Shaikh said. "Surely you should know by now whether there is oil here!"

"Three months is a very short time," Red said. "Some fields have needed a year or two for initial development. Not that I think that will happen in the Great Wadi," he added in response to the Shaikh's sudden frown.

The jeep halted near a derrick, where several men were awaiting the royal party. Suleiman did not leave his seat until his bodyguards arrived and surrounded him.

Hamilton had arranged a special test for his guest. After carefully checking a detailed map of the Great Wadi made by the geologists, he had selected an area of solid rock at least five hundred to seven hundred feet deep. Therefore it was unlikely that the demonstration would produce a gusher.

"We've arranged to sink a well for Your Highness," Red said. "You'll note that we're using a sharp bit that is twenty-four inches in diameter, which is large enough to dig a ten thousand foot well. This pump will send fluid—water mixed with chemicals, and called mud, a slang term in the industry —into the well. As the mud brings up cuttings the rock pieces will land on the top of this large screen, and will be removed for analysis."

"How long should the operation take?" Suleiman asked.

"We're using electricity for power, supplied by a field generator, and our equipment is the most modern that's made. So we can achieve a maximum speed." Red already knew the answer to the Shaikh's question, but turned to his field superintendent. "What's your estimate, Cal?"

"We can drill about five hundred feet per day through soft rock," Calvin Hodges said. "A surface analysis indicates we're dealing with a resistant rock here, so we're using one of our sharpest bits. I'd say we'll average three hundred and fifty feet a day."

Husayn translated the reply into Arabic.

"That is all?" Suleiman was disappointed.

"If the well seems promising, Your Highness, we can always fly back here from El Ain so you can be on hand when we actually strike oil."

"I would enjoy that," Suleiman said.

At Hamilton's signal the operation began. The bit was lowered at the end of a pipe that extended downward from the top of the derrick, and several men steadied it until it made a hole sufficiently deep to support itself in the ground. The pump was started, cooling the bit as it hit the rock surface, and the drilling began.

A high-pitched, screaming sound startled the bodyguards, and Suleiman clapped his hands over his ears.

At the same time, he was observing the operation with care, Red noted, and it was clear he was beginning to realize that drilling was not as simple as it might seem. The screeching of the drill made it impossible to converse, and Red allowed the bit to continue its work for a quarter of an hour, by which time it had bored a sufficient distance into the ground to support itself.

At his signal Hodges threw two switches, and silence descended on the area.

"Ordinarily," Hamilton said, "we don't stop until the bit wears out, and even then we can replace it with another, never removing the pipe from the ground." He reached for one of the cuttings, which was approximately the size of an American half dollar. "Your Highness might want this as a souvenir," he said. "If I may, I'll have it attached to a key chain for you."

"Find two that are alike," Suleiman said, "polish them and make them into cufflinks. Then, if I travel abroad, I'll be able to take a little of Abu Bakr's soil with me."

"Nothing will give me greater pleasure," Red said, meaning it. Suleiman was no longer inquisitive, the immediate danger was ended, and it might be possible to keep the secret of the Great Wadi strike a little longer.

Seven

Bobbie Kenyon went to the theater with Dugald McIntosh, ate a light supper with him after the performance, and returned home by midnight, saying good night to him at the door. She hadn't remembered leaving her living room lights burning, but it didn't occur to her that anything was wrong until she entered her bedroom and saw a man reading a newspaper in the easy chair. She gasped.

Turk lowered the paper. "Don't scream, baby. It's the prodigal. In person."

"This is outrageous, Dale!" She recovered her breath.

"Not at all," he said calmly. "I landed at Kennedy a little while ago, and came here instead of going to a hotel."

"How did you get in?" Bobbie demanded.

"Didn't I tell you? I had your door key copied the last time I was in town."

"Well, you can turn it over to me right now, and then you can get out!"

"Don't be that way, baby. I wanted to have a little preliminary chat with you before I report to Mac tomorrow morning. And am I glad I came here! Damned if I didn't hear the unmistakable voice of McIntosh himself at the door just now. Seeing something of him socially these days, are you?"

"None of your business."

Turk laughed. "You ought to know by now that I wish you the best of everything. Just make sure he pays through the nose for his fun. He can afford it."

Bobbie discovered she was trembling. "If you don't leave —right now—I'll call the police!"

"You wouldn't do that," Turk said. "Too embarrassing, and too many complications. I'm having a drink, and I'll be glad to fix one for you, too."

"What colossal nerve you have!"

"Cool it," he said. "Maybe this will help." He thrust a small box into her hand.

She looked at it.

"Word of honor, it won't explode. Open it! Go on."

Bobbie opened the box and saw a pair of enormous Turkish earrings.

"I didn't have much time in Beirut, but I thought you'd like a little souvenir."

She laughed helplessly. "You're not only a bastard, you're incorrigible."

"Much more civilized. I'll make you a drink." He sauntered toward the kitchen, leaving her free to make good her threat to telephone the police.

Instead Bobbie followed him. "Just a weak nightcap, and then you go. And thank you for thinking of me." She knew he would find some way to hide in his expense account what he had spent on the earrings.

"I always think of you," Turk said as he finished making the drink and handed it to her. "Now let's have a little chat.

But it isn't very comfortable in here, so let's go back to the bedroom."

"No. Thanks all the same." She led him to the living room, waved him to a chair, and sat down on the sofa. "We'll talk for a few minutes, and then you'll go to a hotel. I've got to be on time at the office tomorrow."

"Me too. We'll go in together. I told McIntosh in my cable that I'll report to him promptly at nine, and so I will."

Bobbie had no intention of arguing with him. "What is it you want?"

"What's the reaction to my report?"

"You haven't told us anything of substance yet. Mr. Mc-Intosh is eager to hear whatever you intend to tell him."

"Plenty. Except for the state of development in the Great Wadi field. Hamilton deliberately froze me out, and I hope the front office burns his tail. But good."

"Mr. McIntosh will discuss that situation with you—if he wishes."

"Aren't we being grand! Come off it, baby, and give me the lowdown on his reaction to my cable."

"He expressed no opinion to me."

"You lie," Turk said. "You know when the old man is breathing through both nostrils or just out of one."

"You're entitled to believe what you please. I'm not a spokesman for Aapco or for the office of the president. I don't make policies, I don't hire anybody and I don't fire anybody. Please finish your drink and get out."

He lit a cigarette and leaned back in his chair. "I realize you have some fish of your own sizzling in the pan. But get with it. In the long run you'll make out best if you play along with me. You know what Dug McIntosh wants from you, but where will you stand after you give it to him?"

"Your conclusions are unwarranted," she said, striving to maintain her dignity.

Turk realized he hadn't broken through, and shifted

ground slightly. "One of these days you're going to marry me again, and we'll pick up where we left off."

"Never!"

"That's a big word, baby. Almost as big as 'if'." He stood, strolled to the sofa, and loomed above her.

Bobbie was alarmed. "Stay away from me!"

"You know I'd never slug you. Why are you so scared?"

"I'm not!" she cried, her manner defiant.

"That's what I like to hear." He reached down and took hold of her shoulders.

His touch made her shudder.

Turk was aware of her reaction, and slowly drew her to her feet, his smile broadening.

"Leave me alone!"

He ignored her protests, his hands running up and down her body, and then he silenced her with a long, demanding kiss.

"No," she moaned when he drew back.

Laughing aloud now, he caressed her buttocks, concentrated on her breasts, and then released her abruptly, raising his hands above his head. "Okay, is this what you want?"

Bobbie swayed dizzily, and tried to regain her balance. "I—I don't know."

He was not smiling now, and only his eyes reflected his triumph as he lifted her into his arms and carried her into the bedroom.

"You're a louse," she murmured. "A real louse."

"You want me as much as I want you, so save your breath, baby. You're going to need it." He began to undress her, and his touch was unexpectedly gentle.

Bobbie made no attempt to halt him, but her agony was plain. She wanted him now, but at the same time hated him and loathed herself for her weakness.

Turk relished his power over her, and he incited her with cool deliberation; he knew what aroused her, and his hands and mouth were busy.

141

She began to thrash on the bed, her eyes half closed.

"Send me away," he said.

She could not reply, but her ceaseless writhing gave him the reply he wanted.

Still fondling and caressing her, he managed to remove his own clothes. "Do I go or stay?"

Bobbie pulled him to her, her nails raking his back.

His triumph was complete, and he took her swiftly, his own satisfaction enhanced by the completeness of her surrender.

Bobbie cried out as she achieved a climax.

Turk kissed her, released her, and hoisted himself onto one elbow so he could study her.

Bobbie remained limp, her eyes closed.

"Well?" he demanded.

He had destroyed her dignity. "What do you want me to do, admit that you won a round? Okay, lover boy, you won."

"What you've got to admit to yourself," he said, "is that I'm your kismet."

"You're in the United States now, not in one of the Arab states."

"You and I," he said, "are destined to spend the rest of our lives together."

Bobbie struggled to a sitting position. "All you've proved is that you spark me physically, which is something both of us have known for years. When you back me into a corner you can make me go to bed with you, but that doesn't mean I want anything more to do with you."

Turk reached for her.

She eluded his grasp, leaped from the bed, and went to the closet for a dressing gown.

He made no attempt to follow her. "You'll give in again whenever I blow the whistle."

"I wish I could deny it," Bobbie said. "I can't."

"That's got to mean something to you."

"Only that our chemistry is right. You're a physical animal, Dale. When you're hungry you eat, when you're thirsty you drink, when you want a woman you take her. Then you attach all sorts of significance to what you've done, and you seem incapable of understanding that physicality for its own sake has no meaning. That's your big mistake in life."

"Nuts. I could walk out of your life right now. I could come back in ten years, and find you with a husband and a pack of kids. Even then, you'd come running if I crooked a finger."

"I can only hope I'll never be put in that position." Her hand shook as she lit a cigarette.

"Doesn't that prove something to you?"

"Only that you're a stinker who will grab any advantage."

"I prefer to grab you," Turk said.

Bobbie straightened, tugging at the sash of her robe. "If you had the sensitivity, it would be very easy to despise you. You won't be able to comprehend this, but I have just one feeling toward you. Pity."

He saw she was serious, that she was speaking with a minimum of emotion, and it began to dawn on him that he might have taken the wrong approach. "Hasn't it occurred to you," he asked, his manner suddenly subdued, "that maybe I have a strong yen for you, too? That maybe I go ape when I'm near you?"

Her voice became stronger. "Of course you do. I'm not bad looking, and you know how beautifully we hit it off together. But that doesn't mean anything to you. I was the wife who saw her billy goat of a husband through one affair after another, until I couldn't stand it any more. Sure, Dale. When you're with me, you want me. Just as you want any other attractive woman when you're near *her*."

"What can I say?" He was becoming conscious of his nudity, and reached for his clothes.

"Contrary to my conduct when you force yourself on me, I'm not one of the cheap little chippies you have listed in your address book."

He raised a hand to silence her. "Okay, baby, I goofed. But only because I wanted you so much. That's the truth, no matter what you think." He dressed rapidly, knotting his necktie without bothering to look in a mirror.

Her world was righting itself. "I recommended you for the job you've got with Aapco. I'm the one who got you into Mr. McIntosh's office. And although you don't know it, I even spoke up for you when I was taking notes at an executive committee meeting."

"I didn't know about that part, it's true. But I haven't forgotten all the rest. Why do you suppose I brought you those earrings from Beirut? They cost me the better part of a week's salary."

"I'm tempted to give them back to you, but I won't. I intend to keep them as a reminder of the night you and I said a final goodbye to each other."

"You won't get me out of your system that easily, baby. I'll go to a hotel for the night, sure. And I'll be careful not to let on to your new boyfriend that you and I hit the hay tonight—"

"If you thought it would do you any good, you'd tell him. Luckily for me and unfortunately for you, he wouldn't believe you."

He shrugged into his jacket. "I wish you'd trust me."

"I don't. And won't. From now on you and I will have a strictly business relationship. You're an overseas troubleshooter on the staff of American-Arabian Petroleum, and you report to the office of the president. I happen to be his executive secretary. I'll see you in the office when you're in town, and I'll handle Mr. McIntosh's correspondence with you. Period."

"Do I detect an unspoken threat?"

"If you want to find one, it's there," Bobbie said. "You're swinging on a trapeze hundreds of feet above a chasm. Make one slip and I'll cut your lifeline. You may think I

144

can't do it, Dale, but for the sake of your own neck, I'd advise you not to try me."

The office of the ruling prince had been stripped of the personal mementos that had made it a warm room during the reign of the deposed Muhammad. The desk was bare, there were no photographs on display, and a prayer rug had replaced a divan. Only one chair remained, behind the desk, and visitors were required to sit on cushions piled on the floor, in the ancient, traditional manner.

Ahmed al-Husayn tried to make himself comfortable on the silken mound, but had to admit that it was impossible to feel at ease in the presence of his half brother.

Suleiman ben Yosef looked at him harshly. "Why was it so urgent that you see me this morning?"

"The United States Minister has been pressing me for a renewal of the American-Arabian Petroleum Company lease on the new terms, and Red Hamilton calls me at least once each day. I've exhausted my repertoire of excuses for putting them off."

"Tell them the truth, Ahmed. Merely say that you've presented their pleas to me, and that I have them under consideration."

"I've already done precisely that. Now they keep asking me how the wind is blowing."

"At this time of the year," the ruling Shaikh said with a faint smile, "few *shamals* blow in Abu Bakr."

Husayn realized he was accomplishing nothing. "At least give me a final date for your answer."

"When Allah wills it, I will make His decision—and mine —known to the Americans."

His arrogance was becoming more pronounced each day, Husayn thought.

Suleiman saw his half brother's expression. "You have given me no cause to doubt your loyalty, Ahmed, and of all members of the family, you have the greatest experience in dealing with the infidels. But that does not mean it is impossible to replace you."

"If you lack confidence in me, Suleiman, I will submit my resignation to you."

The ruling Shaikh raised a hand in benign protest. "There is no need for dramatic gestures. Besides, I am prepared to test your willingness to abide by my wishes."

The Foreign Minister lowered his head in a gesture of submission.

"I have decided to make a gift of twenty-five million dollars to the Committee for the Establishment of an Arabian Palestine. You will announce this gift to the world."

"I must obey your commands, Suleiman, but it is my duty to offer you my advice."

"I shall listen." The older half brother was amused.

"The moderate Arabian nations are admitting the permanent existence of Israel—"

"Islam cannot make any such admission." Suleiman's voice became sharp. "We cannot rest until the last Jew is driven from Palestine!"

"But the Committee for the Establishment of an Arabian Palestine has been totally discredited."

"Because its members refuse to compromise, no doubt."

"No, because it is controlled by irresponsible radicals."

"Their chiefs assure me they are not Communists. I believe them. No man can worship both Allah and Marx."

"They are nihilists," Husayn said. "They want to tear down the existing order, not only in Israel, but throughout Islam. They have no positive program to replace their policy of destruction. The moderates of North Africa—Egypt, Morocco, Tunisia, even Algeria—have disowned them."

"Islam," Husayn said, "will unite and recover her strength only when all Arabs obey to the letter the instructions of the Koran. The moderates everywhere must be replaced, and our destiny will be fulfilled through men like the members of the Committee."

Husayn knew he would be forced to settle for half, perhaps even less. "You are free to dispose of your money as you see fit. You are my brother as well as my Shaikh, and I will give out your funds as you direct. But I urge you to make no announcement of this gift. Tread softly, so the world does not identify you as the sponsor of the most irresponsible group in all Islam."

"I seek that identification," Suleiman said. "And why should I care what the infidels think of me?"

"The Americans will refuse us arms and won't build the new petrochemical plants we want. The French will retract their offer to sell us aircraft, and the British will be afraid to trade us tanks in return for oil." Husayn was exaggerating, but thought Suleiman was too inexperienced in foreign relations to realize it.

Suleiman weighed the advice. "It may be that for a little longer Allah will grant me the gift of patience. Do you remember the old saying? When one lies in a nest of serpents, one must be as cunning as a serpent. But woe to him who forgets that his heart is that of the lion. I will give the money to the Committee, as I have promised, and I will supply them with the automatic rifles of the Americans. But I will keep silent for a little longer about my part in their enterprise. Allah will grant me the ability to wait. Then, at the right moment, I will take my rightful place as the leader of the *jihad* that will restore the glory of Islam."

Judy Hamilton followed her friend through the opening in the garden wall, and was relieved that the street odors of the old town were less pronounced here. Since early childhood the native quarter of El Ain had been off limits to her, and at the outset she had been excited by this adventure, but the stench and the heat had cooled her ardor. The sun's rays could not reach the interior of this mud building, however, and her spirits revived.

Not waiting for her companion to take the lead, she stripped off her *yashmak* and *feredezah*.

Farima was concerned. "You would be wise not to reveal yourself," she said.

"Don't be silly," Judy told her. "I'd have stifled in those robes if I'd worn them another minute."

She was wearing a halter top and a mini skirt, and Farima didn't quite know how to tell her an Arab man would be stunned by her near-nudity. "My brother will be here soon."

"What of it?"

Farima shrugged as she took off her own outer garments. She had tried to warn the American, and what happened later was no longer her responsibility.

Judy looked around in wonder. "Is this really where you live?"

The Arab girl showed her an adjoining cell, which was bare except for some cushions. "That is my room. Ali has another like it on the other side of the main room."

"Where's your kitchen?"

Farima pointed in the direction of an ancient stove outside. "When we can buy it, we use wood. Otherwise we burn camel dung and dried seaweed."

"I don't see a bathroom," Judy said in a small voice.

Her friend laughed harshly. "The sand in the desert is endless, and Allah has favored us with the ownership of two buckets. We are like our ancestors, so that is all we need."

The American girl sank to a mound of cushions, letting her skirt ride high on her thighs. "No wonder you've sworn to improve the lot of your people. In all the years I've been coming back to Abu Bakr from school, I never knew this kind of poverty existed in the country."

"Poverty? Ali sails with the fishing fleet, and I have my position in the house of your father. Together we earn enough to provide ourselves with many luxuries. Twice

148

each week we eat lamb. Once each month we buy fowl, and three or four times a year we buy beef."

"What do you eat the rest of the time?" Judy sounded meek.

"Sometimes fish. And always barley, seminola, and tomatoes."

"No one has a right to keep you on a diet like that!" Judy became indignant.

Farima laughed. "Ali and I enjoy the blessings of Allah. Many of our neighbors are less fortunate. Whole families— six or eight people—live in one room, and eat only fish and grains. During the month of Ramadan they break their day's fast after sundown, perhaps, with a handful of dates."

"But that's barbaric. I don't understand it. My father is proud that this is one of the wealthiest countries in the world for its size."

"The oil profits go into the treasury of the Shaikh and the vaults of your father's company. When starvation causes us to fall ill, we are restored to health in a hospital built by oil money, and when we are well again we have the privilege of starving once more."

Ali Nasar Jalal came into the room, and stopped short when he saw the scantily clad Western girl.

"Judy, this is my brother," Farima said. "Ali, my friend is shocked by the way people must live in the old town."

"Hi." Judy extended her hand.

Ali was startled by her informality, but recovered sufficiently to grasp her hand and hold it.

Farima signaled to him angrily.

At last he released the American girl's hand. "I am told," he said, "that you have a wish to join our movement."

"Well, I wasn't sure," Judy said. "But after the things Farima has been telling me and what I've seen for myself, I don't have much choice. I think of myself as being as much of an Abu Bakrian as I am an American, so I have a right to help the poor people of this country, too."

149

Ali wrapped himself in his *agal* as he sat, then flicked his *burnoose* out of his face. "We are pleased to welcome into our ranks those who share our ideals. But I must be fair to you, and ask you to heed my warning. Those who join our band of comrades share our risks."

Judy's clear laugh was innocent, and indicated a total lack of fear. "What risks?"

"If the agents of Suleiman ben Yosef learn what we hope to accomplish—and the danger is always present—we will be taken either to the headquarters of the secret police or to the dungeons the Shaikh has reopened in the cellars of his palace. There the men will be tortured before they die, and other things will be done to the women before they, too, are put to death."

It was impossible for the daughter of Lyman Hamilton to imagine that she would be raped, tortured, or molested by the legally appointed representatives of Abu Bakr. "The Minister of Public Order has visited our house. If you ask me, he's a very stupid fellow. By the time he learns what we're doing he'll be locked up in his own prison."

"I will conduct a ceremony this very week, and you shall take the oath of secrecy in the presence of three witnesses." Ali stared at her bare legs and thighs.

"Any time," Judy said.

"Now we must celebrate your conversion to our cause. Have you smoked hashish?"

"Only pot, up at school, and not much of that. Hash is like it, but stronger, right?"

Farima had been silent, but decided to intervene. There would be trouble if Judy's parents learned of their close relationship. "My friend," she said, "must return to the house of her father by sundown. If she smokes hashish, she might not be able to drive."

Ali's smile was condescending as he reached inside his *agal* and produced a small bag of unbleached muslin. "In this container are the finest of dried leaves and flowers from the Indian hemp plant. I bought this hashish from a sailor who arrived here this morning on a tanker from Calcutta. He is a true believer from Pakistan, and he swore in the name of the Prophet that this is pure hashish."

"Then it must be very strong," Farima said.

Her brother glared at her. "You have an errand to perform. Attend to it while we celebrate."

"Don't smoke too much, Judy," the Arab girl said. "If you should be too high when you return home your parents will know something is wrong, and your father will not rest until you have told him everything. Our movement must not be exposed at the very time we are beginning our most important work."

"Don't worry about me," Judy said. "I'll know when to stop."

Farima glanced at her wristwatch. "I shall return in two hours," she said and, after glowering at her brother, she left.

Ali was alone with the semi-clad American. He rolled a cigarette of hashish, packing it tightly and taking care not to spill a single crumb. Then he lit and tested it. "The Pakistani was telling the truth. The hemp has not been diluted."

Judy took the joint and drew on it. "Pretty good," she said. "But it doesn't feel any stronger than marijuana."

"It will." He continued to stare at her legs and thighs, but occasionally flicked a glance in the direction of her skimpy halter top.

She pretended to be unaware of his scrutiny. "How long before this stuff grabs you?" She saw he didn't understand the question, and rephrased it in simple Arabic.

The young Arab's face cleared. "One cannot say. No two people are the same, and I do not know you well, but that is something I hope to change."

Judy smiled as he slid closer on the cushions; she took the joint from him and again inhaled.

He watched her closely.

"If you're waiting for me to get high so you can make a

pass at me, you're wasting time. Farima will be back in a couple of hours, remember." It was her turn to move closer.

As a boy he had been taught the Arab cliché that all women were aggressive when alone in the company of a man, that they could not resist the lure of the sensual. She was living up to the reputation of her sex. Even though he had rejected most of the precepts that had been pounded into him in his youth there were certain verities that couldn't be denied.

"I've never made it with an Arab," Judy said, "but I've heard from the older girls who have lived in Abu Bakr that you're pretty great. So I'm curious."

He took another drag on the joint, then handed it back to her for a final puff. The situation called for some response, but nothing in his experience had prepared him for this moment, and he didn't know quite what to say or do.

"The best way to learn is to find out things for myself." Judy reached inside his *agal*, fumbled for a moment, and then found what she sought. "That answers my curiosity—the next couple of hours are going to be terrific!"

Hector Bell paced the length of his friend's office, pausing just long enough to accept a Scotch and water from the bar that had appeared from behind a paneled wall. "I don't like it worth a damn, Dug," he said. "The situation in Abu Bakr gets more complicated every day."

Dugald McIntosh ordinarily would have retreated behind his desk with his own drink, but as a courtesy to a peer he lowered himself into a leather easy chair. "I've never known anything in the Arabian peninsula to work out simply. The Arabs were under the rule of the Ottoman Turks for so many hundreds of years that their thinking is invariably Byzantine. Come to think of it, they probably taught the Turks a few fancy tricks."

Bobbie came into the office with a folder, which she

placed on the desk. "Here's the file you wanted, Mr. Mc-Intosh. Oh, good afternoon, Mr. Bell." She was the perfect secretary, and nothing in her manner indicated that she and the head of ICO had met socially.

"Young lady," Bell said in a booming voice, "you're the real reason I came over here today. Any time you want to escape from this doddering old wreck, just mosey down the road to my office. I'll always have a crackerjack job for you."

Her smile was polite and restrained. "Thank you, Mr. Bell, but nothing would persuade me to leave Mr. McIntosh." She left without waiting for a reply.

Bell looked at the door that closed behind her. "How do you inspire that kind of loyalty?"

"Trade secret," McIntosh said. "One of these days, real soon, I want you and Dolores to have dinner with us."

His colleague whistled softly. "So that's the way it is."

"Well, that's how it's getting to be, Hector." He opened a humidor and offered his guest a cigar.

Bell selected one, removed it from its metal container and clipped it, then sniffed it before lighting a match. "There's nothing I'd like better, but you ought to think twice before you include Dolores. What with her lunches and teas and fashion shows and all the other muck that's taken up her time ever since we left Houston, she's been on a merry-go-round with every other expatriate from Texas who happens to be in New York. And you know Dolores—she can't keep her mouth shut. Even if she never finds out this girl works for you, it'll be all over the industry that you're courting a woman half your age."

"The story will make the rounds sooner or later," McIntosh said, "so we may as well break ground for the test well and end the agony. The first few days will be the worst, and pretty soon everybody will get used to the idea."

"Does the girl know about this little dinner you're planning?"

"Not on your life, Hector. She looks pretty self-confident and all, and you'd think she'd know the score after being married to Turk Kenyon. But she's shy, and I've got to go slow so she doesn't bolt over the corral fence."

Bell chuckled.

"Now, where were we?"

"Abu Bakr."

"I've already told you Turk's impression of Suleiman, which isn't promising. He says he's found a way to get even closer to the Shaikh—and put him in our debt. He said it was best if I don't know any details until he's clinched his deal, but he's confident he can bind Suleiman closer to us."

"What'll it cost?"

"Just a few thousand for this caper, whatever it is. Pocket money. I honestly don't think Kenyon is trying to line his own wallet. He knows he's on a spot and has to deliver."

"For everyone's sake I hope he does. I lie awake nights when I think of the money that's riding on Suleiman's good will. And if he should ever cut us off, the energy crisis in this country will be catastrophic. We'll have to raise prices again, no matter how much Washington howls, and you and I and all the rest of the oil company executives will have to wear disguises so the American public won't lynch us."

"I'm counting on Kenyon, but we also have a solid bullet in the other barrel of the shotgun. Hamilton doesn't get rattled."

"What does he tell you about the Great Wadi tests?"

Lighting a cigar, McIntosh averted his face so his friend couldn't read his expression. "He's still drilling, and he's sinking at least one new well every week. Not even a magician could move faster than that, Hector!"

"Oh, I have no complaints about Hamilton, even if I do suspect he's been in Arabia a mite too long. What gets under my skin is the rumor that you've struck some big gushers in the Great Wadi. No matter how hard you deny it, the story won't die a natural death."

"The industry lives on rumors, Hector, and there hasn't been a major find in the Arabian peninsula for several years. The Great Wadi is one of the last virgin territories out there, so the industry can't help speculating, with ninety percent of them hoping we come up with a kettle full of brine."

"You'll keep me informed of any hard developments?"

"You have my word that I will," McIntosh said.

"That brings us to the French situation. You told me on the phone that the French Minister to Abu Bakr has been called home for so-called consultations. What's behind that?"

"Ten days ago," McIntosh said, reaching for the folder on the desk behind him, "Hamilton sent a coded cable telling us he's learned the French are offering Abu Bakr several squadrons of their new Mirage fighter-bombers if Suleiman will cut into our supplies and provide them with plenty of oil."

"How does Hamilton know all this?"

McIntosh handed him a sheet of paper.

Bell read it, then studied it a second time. "He doesn't say, Dug."

"That's all right. He has first-rate connections, and he doesn't go off half cocked. You'll notice he says in the cable that it was a firm offer from the French. According to Hamilton this wasn't hearsay, or a rumor floating around the foreign community in El Ain. Plain fact."

"Could be."

"Has to be. Red is pretty friendly, I know, with some of the Abu Bakr government Ministers, half brothers of both Muhammad and Suleiman who are holdovers from the previous regime. And some of them are on our side."

"Your experience in Arabia is greater than mine, so I'll defer to your judgment."

"As to the French situation, I'm inclined to guess that Gautier, their Minister, got a cold shoulder treatment from Suleiman. So he's gone back to Paris for some intensive discussions. The French are going to debate how many more chips they'll have to throw onto the poker table, and you know how they hate to part with francs."

"We'd better get on the ball, soon. Turn your Paris office loose, and I'll see if our people there can't come up with something too."

"That's a waste of time, Hector." McIntosh took their glasses to the bar and refilled them.

Bell was annoyed. "What the hell are you talking about?"

"I never let myself forget that France and Italy are the only countries in western Europe where their oil companies are state-owned monopolies. They'll do anything to protect their own interests, naturally, and they can play cute." He returned with their drinks.

"Meaning?"

"There are too many French in our Parisian office. Your place too. The top guys are American and are trustworthy, of course. But the secretaries, the messengers, the people in the cable rooms, even the telephone operators who might eavesdrop on transatlantic calls are all French. They'd report back to their government that we're snooping, and the French government would be doubly careful."

"Then we're stuck, Dug?"

"Hell, no! We're going to conduct our investigation outside normal channels. Turk Kenyon is on his way to Paris right now, with orders to stay there as long as necessary to clean this thing up before he returns to Abu Bakr."

"Kenyon again." Bell took a large swallow of his drink.

"A natural for the assignment. He knows everybody there, just as he does all over, and he has no scruples. He'll dig out the information for us, no matter how many rules he has to break, no matter how many people he has to flatten. This is the biggest poker game in years, and we need a player on our side who knows how to hide a few aces up his sleeve."

"Do you suppose the French know something we don't?"

McIntosh shrugged. "That's possible, of course, although I doubt it."

"I assume," Bell said, "that you've made contingency plans in the event Suleiman tries to give Aapco a hard time."

"Naturally. First, we'll try to put pressure on Abu Bakr through Arab states that are friendly to us. If that doesn't work we'll take a more direct approach. I fully expect Suleiman to demand a larger share of the profits, but that becomes a matter of bazaar haggling, and eventually we'll work out an accommodation. It might not be perfect, but I'll be satisfied if we can live with it."

"I suspect he'll hold a gun to your head."

"Well, it won't be the first time that's happened in our dealings with the oil-producing nations." McIntosh sounded resigned if not cheerful.

"Their threats are more genuine since they've discovered they have the power to create chaos by turning off the oil tap."

"My point," McIntosh said, "is that they never really turn it all the way off. They've threatened. They've talked about protecting their own future by leaving oil in the ground and simultaneously increasing prices so they earn just as much or more while producing less. All the same, they do continue to produce. And they haven't thrown us out, either, because they're in no position to refine, transport, and distribute the finished product. The West goes into a panic when the Arabs bluster, but the truth of the matter is that the oil producers need the industry as much as we need them. They know it and we know it, so it doesn't much matter if the public hasn't caught up with the facts of life."

"You're right as far as you go, Dug. It's true enough we've had to give bigger slices of the pie to Saudi, Kuwait, Bahrein, Dubai, Abu Dhabi—you name the country. Even Libya left us with a healthy minority interest when the government there made itself the majority stockholder. My nightmare is that some misguided shaikh or emir will demand the whole pie and send us away empty-handed. Then what do we do?"

157

"I can't imagine that kind of a catastrophe," McIntosh said. "So I think we ought to wait until it happens before we push the total disaster button."

Eight

✦✦✦✦✦✦✦✦✦✦✦✦✦✦✦✦✦✦✦✦✦✦✦

According to a saying that had been popular for half a century, all good Americans went to Paris when they died. Turk Kenyon didn't know whether Hemingway, Fitzgerald, or, for that matter, George Gershwin had been the author of the observation, but as far as he was concerned it was true. He checked into the little Hotel Vendôme, near the Ritz, overlooking the Place Vendôme, and after making a few telephone calls he took a nap.

Enjoying physical exercise for its own sake, he loved Paris, where walking was one of life's greatest pleasures, even in summer, when the city was teeming with American, Japanese, and German tourists. He strolled down the Rue de Rivoli to the Place de la Concorde, then made his way along a tree-lined path to the Champs Elysées, where girl watching was a fine art and window shopping a secondary joy. Eventually he reached the corner of the Avenue George

V, where he dined heartily and well at the Restaurant Fouquet, his favorite in Paris. He drank two half bottles of wine with his meal, a mellow white and a superb red, and was in good spirits by the time he emerged and seated himself at a table in the restaurant's sidewalk café, one of the most popular meeting places in the city.

There, in a quarter of an hour, he would meet the man who would tell him all he needed to know about the recall of the French Minister to Abu Bakr. Jacques Fauchon was a former diplomatic correspondent for *Le Monde,* a reporter who had gone into freelance writing and, over the years, had become an intermediary for those who were willing to pay handsomely for difficult-to-obtain information.

Knowing the right people, Turk thought as he ordered a Cognac and eyed a passing redhead, was all important in life. The man who reached the top wasn't necessarily brighter or more alert than the executive who never rose above the middle level, but he had learned where to turn for assistance when the crunch was on. He also had an instinct for rewarding his sources: sometimes it was money, sometimes a favor, sometimes merely an exchange of information. In Fauchon's case it was strictly cash on the line, but the Frenchman still liked to think of himself as a newspaperman, and had to be treated accordingly.

"There you are, my friend!" The middle-aged, impeccably tailored Jacques Fauchon spoke in English. "You're on time, as always. "

Turk rose to shake hands, and froze. Accompanying Fauchon was a blonde who had impressed herself on his memory: on her right hand she wore the diamond Suleiman ben Yosef had given her.

"Miss Lee," Fauchon said, "permit me to present Mr. Kenyon. I have taken the liberty of bringing Mademoiselle Lee with me, Turk, because she is far better prepared than I to tell you what you want to know."

There was no sign of recognition in the girl's green eyes. "How do you do, Mr. Kenyon?" She held out her hand in the French manner, her grasp light.

"I think we may have met," Turk said.

"I believe not," she replied. "I'm sure I would have remembered you."

Turk decided to play the game according to her rules, at least for the moment.

A waiter appeared, and Fauchon ordered a Cognac.

"What will you have?" Turk asked the girl.

"Orange juice only," she said.

"She doesn't touch liquor," Fauchon said, "not even wine."

Turk caught her eye.

Lee returned his gaze impassively.

"Ordinarily," Fauchon said, "I would split my fee with Mademoiselle Lee, but I am afraid that cannot be done in this instance."

"Quite right," she said. "I prefer to make my own arrangements with Mr. Kenyon."

"So," Fauchon said, "what you are giving me is a finder's fee. If you are not satisfied with what you learn from Mademoiselle Lee, or if her information proves inaccurate, I will gladly refund my fee."

"That's reasonable enough," Turk said, "but I'd like assurance about Miss Lee's credentials."

Fauchon, it appeared, was acting as her spokesman. "Like me, she is a freelance journalist."

"Oh? To whom do you sell your wares, Miss Lee?"

"The *Telegraph* and the *Guardian* have bought my articles on the Middle East in recent months," she said, reaching into her shoulderbag for the articles from the London newspapers. "And I have the tearsheets of a piece that will appear next month in the *New York Times* Sunday Magazine."

Turk examined the material, which seemed legitimate,

and saw that she wrote under the name of Beatrice Lee. "How unusual," he said, "that a girl with your beauty should be so talented, too."

"She is the envy of the profession," Fauchon said, drinking his pony of Cognac in a few quick sips.

Turk handed him an envelope.

The Frenchman took it, knowing it contained five hundred dollar bills. As if he knew what Turk was thinking, he said, "Her information is absolutely reliable."

"I'm sure it is. You've never yet failed me."

Fauchon rose, kissed the girl's hand, and shook Turk's. "You will forgive me, I'm sure, but I must keep another appointment. You know where to reach me tomorrow morning if you wish to get in touch with me."

Turk waited until he was out of earshot. "Okay, baby, what's the gag?"

"I'm afraid I don't understand, Mr. Kenyon."

He reached for her hand, turned it upward, and saw that a few faint streaks of henna had not yet been removed. "You're so flashy that every pedestrian is staring at you. We'll go where you won't create so much of a sensation. I suggest the bar of my hotel, which is usually deserted at this hour."

"As you will." She seemed indifferent.

He paid the bill, then hailed a cruising taxi.

The girl sat in a far corner, looking out of the window and ignoring her companion.

He was tempted to blast her, but decided to say nothing until they reached the bar. Both were silent on the ten-minute drive.

Only two small tables were occupied, and Turk chose a far corner, where no one was within earshot.

Again the girl ordered a small glass of orange juice.

"All right, drop the pretense," Turk said.

"In Paris," she told him, "I am known as a teetotaler. I have an image to maintain."

He stared at her. "Your image, it seems, depends on where you happen to be from one minute to the next. When we met in London—and judging on what happened after that—you were a hooker."

She smiled, accepted a light for her cigarette, and sat back in her chair. "You jumped to conclusions during our previous association, Turk. At no time did I tell you I was a call girl. You simply assumed it."

"Even though that's how you behaved?"

"Another assumption. You don't actually know what my relationship with Suleiman may have been."

He touched her diamond ring lightly. "It doesn't take a genius to guess."

"All the same, you don't *know*." For the first time a gleam of humor appeared in her eyes, and she flicked back a strand of her blond hair.

"Now we're bickering. You know what you know, and I know what I think I know. We'll let it go at that." Their drinks arrived, and he raised his glass to her. "Here's to Beatrice Lee, freelance newspaper reporter who specializes in the Middle East."

"I hope," Lee said, "you'll keep in mind that it was Jacques who called me a newspaperwoman. I made no such claim."

He was irritated. "More games. Are you denying you wrote the pieces you showed me?"

"I deny nothing."

"Did you write them?"

"In France, Great Britain, and the United States I'm recognized as their author."

"Obviously," Turk said, "you're an operator of some sort."

"If you say so."

"Is your real name Beatrice Lee?"

"That's what a number of editors and other people have been calling me. Does it really matter if the name is my own or just a pseudonym?"

Turk was so annoyed that he failed to feel his Cognac and ordered another, even though he knew he should stay sober. "No," he said, "I have no desire to see your birth certificate or any other credentials."

"I appreciate your undying trust."

"To hell with that. I have a job to do, and Jacques Fauchon was positive you can help me. Can you?"

"Of course. For a fee."

"How much?" No matter what her identity or profession, he thought, she was greedy for money.

"A thousand now, another thousand five minutes from now, after I've told you what I know. Satisfaction guaranteed."

"How do I know you won't vanish again?"

"I came through for you in El Ain, and I will again. If my information proves phony, you'll get double your money back."

"Sounds good, but I still don't know where to find you."

"That's unimportant," Lee said. Only two things matter. *I* know where to find *you*. And my sources are impeccable."

"You make it sound good, but I'd like to know more about you before I start shelling out."

She seemed to be enjoying her orange juice. "Do you require all of your informants to provide you with autobiographies?"

"You win," Turk said, and took a thousand dollars from his wallet.

Once again she placed the money in a zippered compartment of her bag. "The French," she said, "offered Shaikh Suleiman a squadron of fighter-bombers in return for a substantial quantity of oil."

"We knew *that* ten days ago."

Turk's reaction made Lee bristle. "Of course you did," she said sarcastically. "Do you want me to tell you exactly how Aapco acquired the information, the precise route it took in getting to New York? I can—even if it's not particularly relevant. What is relevant is the whole story. Which is why I started at the beginning."

Turk grinned. "Okay," he said. "You pass that test. Now, how would the French get the oil?"

"Abu Bakr would be obliged to terminate her contract with American-Arabian, and would take over operations. Then she could sell to anyone she pleased."

Turk whistled softly. "It's that drastic?"

"Yes and no. Suleiman hasn't taken anyone in his confidence, not even his cabinet ministers, but he couldn't be listening to French proposals unless he was thinking in terms of expropriation."

"Did he tell you this himself?"

There was amusement in her voice, although her expression remained unchanged. "You know better than that. Women perform only one function in the life of His Highness. He doesn't discuss affairs of state with them. Or business of any kind."

"My home office," Turk said, "will want to know why I believe expropriation is even possible. They're so afraid of the idea they don't mention the subject out loud, and they'll insist I cite some authority of stature. I can't quote an anonymous source."

"You may want to tell them the information came direct from French Deputy Premier Wieland."

He didn't try to conceal his surprise. "Claude Wieland is a monk. An ascetic. I knew him when he was French Ambassador to Israel, and again when he toured the Arabian peninsula on a special mission. He's so woman-shy he wouldn't even wish the old maids on his office staff a good morning for fear of entanglements with them."

"I know nothing of his relations with old maids," Lee said, "but I can assure you he is not reticent in his dealings with all women."

"You do get around."

"I have a number of good friends."

"In high places."

She looked bored. "I enjoy their company and they like mine. I don't care if they're prominent."

"Would you classify me as a friend?"

"You are a business acquaintance."

His vanity demanded greater fulfillment. "But the potential of friendship is there, wouldn't you say?"

Lee gave him no encouragement. "Anything is possible when two people deal with each other."

Turk grinned at her. "Especially when one is a man and the other is a woman."

"Now you speak in terms of sex, which is another matter altogether."

She would stop mocking him, he thought, if he could persuade her to spend an hour with him behind a locked door. But he couldn't afford to offend her, because, it seemed, he always was in need of her cooperation and good will. "What else did you find out from Wieland?"

"Suleiman made no response to the French bid, which was his way of rejecting it. So they intend to make him a bigger offer, and the government is currently working out the terms. Perhaps two squadrons of Mirages. Perhaps a cash gift as well as the airplanes. They are also debating whether to close their embassy in Israel if His Highness demands it."

"Stiff terms."

"The French lack of oil is almost as great as Japan's, although few people realize it. So she lays claim to what she calls a special relationship with Islam. In practical terms this means she submits to any Arab demand in order to get the oil she needs. The French, on a per capita basis, need as much as you Americans."

"When will the next French offer go to Abu Bakr?"

"As soon as the cabinet agrees on terms, Minister Gautier will return to El Ain. Suleiman has proved he is no fool, and this country's need for oil is so desperate that you can be certain the offer will be generous. French pride is at stake here, and so is her hidden desire to thumb her national nose at the United States, so she may even offer more than the oil is worth."

Turk felt certain she was no call girl. Yet she had voluntarily assumed the role of a prostitute when she had gone to Abu Bakr, and he had no idea why she would have submitted to such degradation. It was his job to do business with people of substance, power brokers and their hangers-on, but in all the years of his dealings with them he had known no one like Lee, and could not place her in any familiar category. His ignorance about her was dangerous.

"Once the final terms are determined, I'd like to know them," he said.

"That will mean another fee."

"You have the compassion of a Swiss banker," Turk said. "Don't you ever pass along data or do a favor?"

"Only for my friends. Everyone else, as you say in the States, must pay cash."

"I take the hint." He handed her an additional thousand.

"You are becoming a valuable client," Lee said.

"Close business associates don't keep each other at arm's length."

"So I've been told." She leaned toward him, lowering her voice. "There *is* something I'll tell you about myself. I take my appearance for granted. I use it as a weapon. But I can't help wishing, sometimes, that people would accept me for other reasons. And you needn't pretend you don't understand, Turk, because you're the same way. Your charm and appearance are weapons too, and you use them to gain your own ends."

She had turned personal with a vengeance, and he found it disconcerting that she could see through him so easily. Only Bobbie had a similar perception, and she had known him for years. Unwilling to tolerate the girl's criticism, he reacted instinctively by counterattacking. "How can any-

167

one appreciate you for what you are when you won't let him look inside you? If you want someone to develop a deeper appreciation, you've got to give him the opportunity."

"The same to you," Lee said. "You'll be staying in Paris until the question of the French bid is settled?"

"I'll telephone your information to New York. I have no doubt the head office will order me to sit tight until I get the full story."

"Then I'll call you here as soon as a decision is made." She applied fresh lipstick, gathered her belongings, and thrust them into her bag. "Meanwhile, be patient. I may need several days."

"Why leave in such a hurry?" Turk asked. "The night is still young."

Lee's full lips parted in a silent laugh. "One of your most impressive qualities is that you never stop trying. Neither do I, when I have my heart set on a goal. I can imagine situations in which you and I would become full-fledged partners, and what a team we'd make. Nothing could stand in our way—provided we didn't murder each other before we accomplished anything."

Turk watched her as she left, and felt certain her hips were swaying for his benefit. Lee was challenging him again, but there was no way, short of using brute force, that he could take her on any terms other than her own.

The work day began soon after dawn in the oil fields, partly because the old-timers had never lost the habits they had acquired in the days of exploration, but, more important, because so much more could be accomplished before the heat became unbearable. It was still dark when Red Hamilton arose, and the first streaks of light were appearing in the sky above the desert when he left the house after eating a full breakfast.

Ruth had made it her own custom since the first days of their marriage to join him at the breakfast table, even though she confined herself to fruit juice and coffee. Then, carrying a second mug of coffee with her, she retired to their bedroom and listened to a BBC regional newscast before shedding her negligee and taking a shower.

The newscast ended and she switched off the radio, then lit a cigarette and wandered out to the sundeck at the far end of the room. Ordinarily, in this brief period before sunrise, before the air conditioners began to purr, she enjoyed sitting outdoors. Certainly it was the only time of day she appreciated the desert, which she otherwise regarded as the enemy that prevented her and her family from living a normal life.

She had no more settled herself than Judy appeared, barefoot, in a bra top and short shorts.

"Morning, Mom." Judy poured herself coffee from a thermos she was carrying.

Ruth wasted no time launching her attack. "What time did you get home last night?"

"It wasn't late," the girl hedged.

"Don't lie to me, Judy Hamilton! It was after three this morning!"

"If you know, don't ask me."

"Where were you?"

"Nowhere in particular." Judy's gesture was vague. "We just rode around, mostly."

"Who is 'we'?"

"Oh, boy. Another inquisition. Just some of the other kids."

Ruth controlled her fury. "Don't lie to me. You weren't with anyone from Aapco."

"What makes you say that?"

"Because I checked with the sentry at the Eisenhower main gate when you weren't home at a reasonable hour, and he read me the log. You checked out when you gave the new servant girl a lift into El Ain, and you didn't come back."

Judy's sigh sounded martyred.

"I covered for you with your father," Ruth said, "and you needn't thank me. It wasn't for your sake; it was for his. I didn't want him worrying about you when he had so much on his mind. Which you seem to forget."

"What you and Daddy won't remember is that I'm of age."

"It would be hard to forget, since you remind me every day. In my opinion you still aren't an adult, and won't be until you act like one."

"Knock it off, Mom. I've got a headache."

"Too much to drink, dear?" There was malice in Ruth's voice.

"I avoid the curse of the desert, and you know it. I've seen what booze can do to American females out here."

Her mother bristled. "Was that personal?"

The girl was wide-eyed. "How could it be? You keep your drinking under control."

"There was a time when I didn't, and I'm trying to help you avoid my mistakes."

"You won't believe me," Judy said, "but I didn't touch a drop of anything yesterday or last night. Not even beer." But she was exhausted, and she gulped her coffee, then poured herself another cup. "I think I'll go back to bed for a couple of hours. I'm beat."

"Stay right where you are," Ruth commanded.

"Now what?"

"I have a right to an accounting of your activities last night."

"I don't see what difference it makes."

"You were with a man," Ruth said.

"That sounds as though I'm supposed to plead guilty. I refuse. I'm an adult—even if you won't admit it, and I don't see why I've got to report to you on my dates!"

"You weren't with anyone from Aapco." Ruth looked at her daughter over the rim of her coffee cup. "The counselor of the British Legation is in Cairo this week, the German military attaché went home on leave, and that good-looking second secretary of the French legation was having dinner next door."

"You could make a fortune writing murder mysteries. Your mind works that way."

Ruth ignored the interruption. "Unless you were with a married man, you spent the evening with an Arab."

"Part of the afternoon, too," Judy said with a giggle. "I didn't intend to spend that much time with him. But as the song goes—a rock number, so you wouldn't know it—one things leads to another."

Her mother sat upright. "Judith, if you listen to nothing else I ever say to you, listen to me now. Abu Bakr isn't the United States. It isn't Switzerland. It isn't even Beirut or Cairo. People here, including the highest-born shaikhs, live according to the social standards of a thousand years ago. Any Arab girl who went out with a man on a date would be disgraced for the rest of her life. A foreign woman who dates an Arab is in an even more dangerous position—"

"Except for one thing. The foreign girl may not give a hoot what the natives think. Because she doesn't intend to rot here for the rest of her life."

"Don't interrupt me," Ruth said. "Our kind of social life is totally unknown in a country like Abu Bakr. The only reason an Arab would see a foreign woman is because he intended to take her to bed."

"What makes him different from Americans—or any of the Europeans I got to know in Switzerland?"

"Tell a civilized man you're not interested, and he'll respect your decision. But the Arab—who regards the woman as inferior, as a chattel, remember—can't accept your 'no.' He'd think his masculinity was being questioned, and he'd persist, even if he had to rape you!" Ruth lit another cigarette.

"The Arabs," Judy said, "were civilized when our ancestors were roaming naked through the forests of the British

Isles and the Continent. In England they even painted themselves blue. Read George Bernard Shaw on the subject if you want a laugh."

"I'm not laughing. I'm concerned about your chastity, your well-being, and your reputation."

Judy became earnest. "Mom, my reputation is safe, Brownie honor. He won't say anything. He isn't the type, and anyway, he doesn't know anyone at Aapco, so who could he tell? You're the only one who knows."

"Who is this man?"

"A friend. You don't know him."

"I know everyone in Abu Bakr."

"Not him."

Ruth discovered her coffee had grown cold. The sun was rising and the heat soon would become unbearable, Judy was making her miserable, and she wanted to end the argument. "Judy, there are so many things you can do right here. I've asked you again and again to help me with my garden—"

"I don't have your green thumb."

"Daddy pays you by the hour for any work you do at the office, but you don't spend much time there."

"He's just trying to keep me occupied, that's all."

Ruth felt increasingly desperate. "The Drama Group is casting *My Fair Lady*. With your voice you'd be a marvelous Eliza Doolittle."

"Anywhere but Abu Bakr, I'd stink. I'd be laughed off the stage."

Ruth studied her daughter. "You're having an affair with this—Arab."

Judy lifted her chin. "Okay, Mom. I'm tired of denying things. Girls of my generation don't wear white to their weddings. I lost my precious virginity a long time ago—in Switzerland with the captain of an English skiing team. He was the captain, and that's why I snagged him. Just so you don't bombard me with any more of your district attorney's tactics, I haven't kept a scorecard of the others. Okay?"

172

Ruth steadied herself. "If your father learns about this, he'll kill this Arab, and—"

"I know. He'll chain me to the hot water heater in the cellar. I'm still Daddy's little girl. I don't mean to be flip. I love both of you, but I'm entitled to live my own life in my own way."

"Not by having an affair with an Arab in Abu Bakr. Everyone in Eisenhower and Truman will hear about it eventually, and word will follow you back home. We don't live in as much of a vacuum here as you seem to think."

"Mom, you've asked for it. Will your fling a few years ago with Turk Kenyon ruin your reputation forever back in the States? People here had to keep their whispers pretty low because Daddy is the big boss in these parts. But they talk about you, too, when they go home."

Ruth paled.

"I realize Daddy knows all the Kenyon affair. My second year in Switzerland, when I came here for vacations, I could hear you arguing when you thought I was asleep. But I'll bet Daddy doesn't know about the others. That creep from the legal department who was out here for a couple of months. That was a year or two before I went to Switzerland. And there was another one, when I was smaller. I don't remember much about him except he had a big mustache, and from the way he dressed, I'd guess he was one of the company's field superintendents."

Ruth clutched her throat.

"So don't preach morality to me, please."

"I don't want you to repeat my mistakes," Ruth said hoarsely. "I've paid for them, God knows, and because I failed in my moral obligations is no reason for you to do the same."

The sun was rising higher, but neither seemed aware of its blinding glare. "Like mother, like daughter," Judy said.

"That settles it." In the harsh sunlight Ruth's face looked haggard. "I agreed—reluctantly—when you persuaded your father to let you spend a full year in Abu Bakr. Life here is wearing enough for an adult, but it becomes impossible for a girl who lacks a depth of judgment and has little insight."

"Trying to get rid of me because I know too much, Mom?"

"How dare you." Ruth's voice sank to a near whisper. "For your information, your father knows of all my mistakes. He's not only a big man, he's a wonderful man, and I'm not going to let you hurt him, too."

Judy realized she had gone too far. "I wasn't trying to blackmail you, Mom. You didn't understand what I—"

"It doesn't matter. I won't waste my breath forbidding you to see this Arab again. I know you'll do what you please. If there were somewhere to send you, I'd pack you off today. But I can tell you one thing. You're starting college in California this September, and that's final!"

The girl watched her as she swept into the house, and had to admit that, in some way she didn't comprehend, her mother had regained her dignity. But that wasn't her concern.

No matter what plans her parents made for her, she intended to stay in Abu Bakr. Ali was not only different, he also made love like a maniac, and the rest of the summer promised to be magnificent. Besides, Ali and his followers were going to topple the throne. No other place on earth could offer that excitement.

Nine

✦✦✦✦✦✦✦✦✦✦✦✦✦✦✦✦✦✦✦✦✦✦✦✦

The Great Mosque, at the northeastern end of the old town, stood between the *suq* and the government buildings, and overlooked the Persian Gulf. According to tradition it was the soul and heart of Abu Bakr, and officially it was called *al-masjid al jami'*, or the place where man prostrated himself to God. The huge, domed structure was simple in design, and had been constructed seven hundred years earlier in the purest Islamic tradition. In essence it was a vast open place with a roof and sides.

There were no seats or benches of any kind inside the building, no statues, pictures, or other decorations. In accordance with Muslim law, only verses from the Koran and the names of Mohammed and his companions were inscribed on the walls in Arabic. The floor was carpeted with thick Persian rugs, which overlapped so there were no bare places. Men removed their sandals or shoes before entering the building, and the truly devout also took off their socks.

Women were permitted to pray there, also taking off their footgear first, but were required to use a special portion of the place, which was surrounded by a railing of polished wood. Small children were not allowed to set foot inside the mosque, but their attendance became compulsory when they reached puberty.

Only two objects stood out in the interior. One was the *mihrab,* a semicircular niche that was reserved for the use of the *imam,* who led the faithful in prayer. It pointed in the direction of the *qibla,* the holiest of holy places, the *Ka'ba* in Mecca. At the right of the *mihrab* was the *mimbar,* a seat at the top of a steep flight of steps, which was reserved for the exclusive use of the *khatib,* or preacher. Abu Bakr, clinging tenaciously to the old ways, was one of the only Islamic countries in which the ruling Shaikh was permitted by custom to address his subjects from the *mimbar.*

At either end of the Great Mosque stood a slender tower with a bulbous top. Rising high above the dome, these structures, known as *minarets,* were used by the *muezzin,* or criers, to announce the *azan,* the call to the faithful to gather for worship. No fewer than five such calls were issued daily.

No music or singing was incorporated into the service, which consisted of chants read from sections of the Koran. All worshipers joined in these prayers, prostrating themselves behind the *imam* and facing toward Mecca. They were led by *muqri',* members of the Great Mosque staff who learned their profession at a special school in El Ain.

Only in the mosque was there no discrimination of any kind. All men were equal in the sight of Allah, and the richest aristocrats and poverty-stricken town dwellers lowered themselves to the prayer rug side by side. Not even the ruling shaikh worshipped apart; literally as well as figuratively, he rubbed shoulders with the meanest of his subjects.

Along the north and west walls on the outside of the

Great Mosque stood a series of cold water faucets, with a trough of cement beneath them. Here the faithful washed their hands and feet before entering the building, and although this practice was not prescribed by the Koran, custom enforced it, and no one was exempt.

Under no circumstances was the collection of money permitted inside the mosque. All houses of worship were supported and maintained by the government, and the Ministry of *Wafq*, or endowment, paid the salaries of those who served there. No bells pealed in a mosque, but Abu Bakr clung to a custom that had been abolished in all but the most traditionalist of Islamic countries. A number of holy men were buried in the Great Mosque in defiance of the law, passed centuries after the lifetime of Mohammed, that required cemeteries to be located a considerable distance from the place.

The wail of the *muezzin* for the sundown service brought worshipers to the Great Mosque from every section of El Ain. This service had become the most important of the day because it was almost invariably attended by Shaikh Suleiman ben Yosef. Men waited patiently in line at the faucets, and women in *feredezah* and *yashmaks* used the two isolated faucets reserved for them. There was almost no conversation, and one by one the worshippers slipped inside the enormous flap of layered camel hide that served as a main door.

Three American-built limousines pulled to a halt in the street beyond the small garden of citrus trees, palms, and shrubs, but no one even looked in their direction. No man stood above his brethren in the holy place. The bodyguards in royal blue and white did not profane the mosque by carrying rifles or sub-machine guns here, but everyone knew they carried practical rather than ornamental scimitars, and it was taken for granted that automatic pistols were hidden beneath their *agals*.

Six soldiers who had been riding in the first limousine formed a vanguard, and after Suleiman descended from the middle car the six guards from the last vehicle fell in behind him. They would make it their business to surround him while they all prayed, and if their minds were elsewhere than on the teachings of the Koran it was because they were charged with keeping His Highness from harm. It was true, of course, that on occasion they allowed a very old man to slip inside their cordon and prostrate himself at the side of the Shaikh. This was a wise precaution, approved by the Grand *Imam* of Abu Bakr, a man noted for his secular as well as spiritual acumen, who had observed that no prudent ruler or the members of his entourage would want to arouse the ire of Allah.

Suleiman moved slowly, giving his subjects time to become aware of his presence and remove themselves from the first faucet on the right side of the entrance, which he habitually used. He had mounted no more than three or four of the stone steps when the line in front of that faucet vanished.

A man in a tattered *agal,* his face hidden behind a torn *ghutra,* dared to approach the Shaikh, his filthy right hand outstretched.

Two soldiers went into action, one grasping the man by his arms while the other made ready to kick him down the stairs.

But Suleiman intervened, wanting no violence at the entrance to the holy place. "Let him approach."

The man crouched in a semblance of a salaam and again extended his hand. "Alms, in Allah's holy name," he said.

Suleiman was amused. "You rogue, didn't I give you alms only two weeks ago?"

"You did, greatest and most noble Shaikh. Your generosity has provided food for my family and me all these days. But prices are high in El Ain now, and even barley and fish are dear. Help me again, I beg you, so my sons do not starve."

Suleiman knew that several hundred worshippers were memorizing the scene, and he saw, as he had a fortnight earlier, that Allah had provided a way to show his subjects that he was a compassionate and generous ruler. His smile benign, he reached inside his *agal*, then held a coin aloft for an instant before dropping it into the beggar's hand. He took care to grasp it by the edges with thumb and forefinger so the many witnesses would be sure to see it was gold.

Having dispensed alms, as the Koran instructed, he washed his feet and went into the Great Mosque.

No one paid any further attention to the beggar, who descended the stairs to the street, then turned into a narrow alley. There two women in black *feredezah* and *yashmaks* awaited him. He took no notice of them, but they dutifully fell in behind him as he made his way down the alley and walked into the old town. All three kept silent until they reached a drab little building surrounded by a wall.

"You saw and heard everything?" Ali Nasar Jalal asked when they were in the house.

"Everything." Judy did not say she had been reminded of tales from the *Arabian Nights*.

"Let me see the coin," Farima said.

"You may look at it, but I want it returned," her brother told her.

She bit it to make certain it was real. "Judy," she said, "this is a ten-*rial* piece. It is worth almost one hundred American dollars."

Judy took the coin and turned it over in her hand.

"It will buy the finest hashish on the market," Ali said.

Farima shook her head. "It should go into the party treasury. We will have many expenses in the weeks ahead."

"This is mine!" Ali's temper flared, and he snatched the coin from Judy. "When your rich friend returns from America we'll have plenty of money to complete our mission. I take the greatest risks, so I'm entitled to a small reward."

"A ten-*rial* gold piece," Farima said sarcastically, "is no small reward."

He ignored her as he turned to the American girl. "Now you understand," he said. "Suleiman already knows me as a beggar. Soon he will think of me as his very own beggar, and his soldiers will no longer even try to stop me when I approach him. Every two weeks he will give me a coin. On the day we strike I will carry a pistol under my *agal*, and at a distance of only a foot or two it will be impossible for me to miss my target!"

"But the guards will kill you," Judy said.

"I don't intend to be killed," Ali replied. "My plan is not yet completely formed, it is true, but I will think of some way to get away from the soldiers. Perhaps I'll join you in the alley and disguise myself as a woman. I don't really know, but it doesn't matter. What is important is that I've won Suleiman's confidence. All I must do is work out a few little details."

It occurred to Judy that his life would depend on these "little details." She said nothing, however, having learned that he resented feminine interference. Besides, another aspect of the situation required clarification. "Farima, who is your rich American friend?"

Sister and brother exchanged a quick glance.

"It is best not to reveal too much," Ali said. "If he becomes frightened he may halt his payments."

"I know every American in Abu Bakr," Judy said.

"You know him," Farima told her.

"Enough!" Ali became livid. "Your good name must be protected at any cost! And she already knows too much." Ali's concern deepened.

He had no idea, Judy thought, that he was making his private opinion of her all too clear. But she suffered no illusions that he respected her, so she wasn't hurt.

"You are stupid," Farima told her brother. "Judy can help

us evaluate the motives of this man. She has become our partner, and we must trust her."

Ali sighed. "Very well, but you must swear, Judy, on whatever you call holy, never to mention to any other living person that which you will hear."

Judy knew Arabs thrived on secrecy. "I swear it."

"It is Kenyon, the man who stayed in the guest house," Farima said.

Judy's laugh was explosive. "I should have guessed! He would have been my first choice." She looked at the other girl and laughed again. "He didn't waste much time, I've got to say that much for him."

Farima drew herself erect. "It was I," she said, "who made certain he would help us."

"Enough!" the outraged Ali roared.

Both girls ignored him. "Well," Judy said, "I'm sure you didn't have to try too hard. He makes a play for anyone who's attractive."

"You too?"

The American girl shook her head. "No, because of my father—who'd carve out his heart." An unexpected sense of family loyalty caused her not to mention her mother's affair, which was no outsider's concern. "But Kenyon isn't rich. He must get the money from Aapco. Offhand I don't know why he'd do it."

"First," Farima said, "I told him I would report to his superiors that he raped me. This made him very angry. Later he said that our activities would bring democracy to Abu Bakr, and that this would be good for American-Arabian Petroleum. This may be true, but I believe he gives us money because he is afraid I will say too much to your father."

"Daddy would love to hang him, and Kenyon must know it. On the other hand, even though I don't know him all that well, mostly because he treats me like a child, I've been told he isn't afraid of anyone or anything on earth."

"Then," Ali said, "it is true he assists us because his company will gain?"

"Kenyon is no company man," Judy said. "He would do nothing for Aapco unless he himself stood to gain. Apparently he believes his support of you will win him credit of some kind with the company. In my opinion, Farima, you're wrong when you say he's afraid of you. He might have an unpleasant half hour with my father, but he'd brazen it out, and that would be the end of it."

"The chiefs of the company wouldn't discharge him?" Farima asked.

"I'm not all that familiar with the top brass, but I'd be inclined to doubt it. I've heard of employees getting into trouble over women, but they don't lose their jobs."

Ali again became indignant. "The rich Americans exploit Arabs. And they do not care!"

It would be useless, Judy reflected, to remind him that he was exploiting her, so the situation was reversed. "I've told you all I can," she said.

"When Kenyon returns," Farima suggested, "perhaps you can learn more about his motives."

Judy considered the idea. "I'm willing to try, but it might be dangerous. There's no logical way I could find out he's making contributions to us."

"Nothing can be allowed to jeopardize the liberty of Abu Bakrians!" Ali declared.

Farima remained calm. "I'll take care of this. Kenyon will tell me his motives."

Judy envied anyone who showed that much self-confidence.

The bistro was located at the edge of the Latin Quarter on the Left Bank, but there was little of Paris in the atmosphere, and the place could have been transported to the back streets of Cairo. Several students from the Sorbonne, all but one of them Algerian, were playing the pinball machines at the rear of the long, narrow room, and four or five men in laborers' clothes sat at the bar. There was no air conditioning, and the odor of stale tobacco clung to the walls and furnishings. The blinds were drawn to keep out the summer sunlight. A half dozen booths lined the inner wall, but only one was occupied.

Turk Kenyon sipped beer from a bottle and watched the door. This was not the kind of place Lee frequented, so he thought it strange that she had asked to meet him here. She had given him no reason to mistrust her, but a man in his position stayed healthy by taking no needless risks, and he reached inside his jacket to loosen his .32 automatic in its shoulder holster. He was still bothered by his inability to establish a clear-cut identity for the girl, and while he waited he kept mulling over the same few, contradictory things she had told him about herself.

He ordered another beer, stubbed out his cigarette, and lit another. Lee was already more than a half hour late, and he wouldn't wait much longer for her, even though he had no idea where to get in touch with her. Presumably she wanted still more money from him, so she would call him at his hotel.

Lee came in through the swinging door, wearing huge sunglasses that hid the better part of her face, a turban that concealed her blond hair, and a loose-fitting tunic that neutralized her figure. Only her scarlet lipstick called attention to her.

"You're late," Turk said as she slipped into place beside him on the banquette.

"It couldn't be helped," Lee said, her manner nonapologetic. "I was being followed, and they were persistent devils, so it took me time to give them the slip."

"Why should anyone follow you?" he demanded.

Her expression remained unchanged. "Order me a white Dubonnet on the rocks, please."

"No orange juice?" His tone was mocking.

"Not here. The liquor will be just strong enough to kill the germs."

Turk went to the bar to place her order, then waited for the drink, the interlude enabling him to weigh what she had told him. There had to be some solid reason she was under surveillance, and apparently she was more involved in the affairs of Abu Bakr than he had imagined.

Lee's smile of thanks was fleeting when he placed the drink in front of her and sat next to her on the banquette.

"Well?"

"The French government has decided to double its offer. Four squadrons of Mirage fighter-bombers, six batteries of their new anti-aircraft gun, which they claim is better than anything the Swedes make, and a cash subsidy of forty million U.S. dollars."

"That makes no sense," Turk said. "Abu Bakr makes more than that from Aapco."

"This particular subsidy will be deposited in Swiss banks privately. Under any name or names Suleiman wants to assume."

"I see." He absently lit two cigarettes, handing her one. "Will Suleiman accept?"

"They don't know, and neither does anyone else." Her tone changed. "Put your arm around me, Kenyon. Two men at the pinball machines have been watching me. I don't think they're on to me, but I don't want trouble. Pretend we're lovers."

"Happy to oblige." He slid his arm around her.

Lee's manner remained casual. "There's a difference between friendliness and intimacy." She moved his hand, her gesture as swift as it was unobtrusive.

"What do the French want in return?"

"Only what they requested when they made their last offer. They're smart. What they're really seeking is a foothold."

184

Turk thought a moment. "Damn smart." His hand began to slide up the inside of her thigh.

Lee's eyes were hidden, but her smile was pleasant. "I may break this glass and jab it into the vein in your wrist. I can do it faster than you can get away."

Turk removed his hand.

"When I go to bed with you, it won't be in a fourth-rate hotel over a third-rate bistro."

He looked hard at her, wishing he could see the expression behind her sunglasses. "You said when, not if."

"Did I?" She laughed.

Turk knew better than to press the issue. "When will the French make their offer?"

"They don't know it, but there's a chance to kill their deal in advance. If Paul-Pierre Gautier were an American, he'd take the first airplane to El Ain. Instead he's going on a ten-day furlough with his mistress. She's out of sorts because she isn't allowed to go to Abu Bakr, and he needs to pacify her."

"You manage to keep informed."

Lee's smile became enigmatic and she did not reply.

"I believe I can derail the French," Turk said. "I've been developing a little plan of my own, and I think I can accomplish two aims at the same time. When I'm finished Suleiman won't even listen to the French."

"How will you do it?"

"Do you tell me everything?" he countered.

Lee shrugged. "It does no harm to ask."

Turk thought it remarkable that they had achieved such a complete mutual understanding.

"I hope you realize," she said, "that I've mentioned no fee for this new information."

"I was aware of it." He was on his guard. "How much?"

She shook her head. "This time," she said, "I'm not interested in cash."

"What, then?"

"You and I are working the same side of the fence, but there's just so much that can be done here. The real action will be in Abu Bakr." Anyone looking at them would think she was murmuring endearments in his ear. "The French deal must be killed in ten days, no more. That means there isn't much room for maneuver. If your scheme fails, I'll try one of my own. So I want you to take me to El Ain with you."

He concealed his surprise. "Back to the palace, huh?"

"Not this time. I don't want Suleiman to know I'm in Abu Bakr. He'll jump to conclusions I'm not ready to face."

Turk shook his head. "I'll need more of an explanation."

"We'll travel together. I'll go to your Aapco guest house with you. Neither Suleiman nor the people who work for him will know I'm there."

"You're not exactly inconspicuous. How will you manage that?" he demanded.

"Leave it to me."

"Okay, but what will I tell the Aapco crowd in Abu Bakr?"

Again she became mocking. "I didn't know it was necessary for Turk Kenyon to offer excuses because he's traveling with a woman. With your reputation, honey, they'll expect it of you."

"You've gone to a lot of trouble looking into my background," he said.

"No trouble at all. If you insist on saying something, tell them I'm important to the business you hope to accomplish in Abu Bakr. It happens to be true."

"Give me a minute." He drummed on the table. "There's one hitch. My plan hinges on a young woman at Aapco headquarters there."

Lee was unconcerned. "What else is new?"

"You don't understand. She's an Arab girl, and she may be assigned to keep house for me, as she was on my last trip.

186

If you're with me, well—you know Arabs. She's likely to tear the roof off the guest house."

She remained complacent. "I have every confidence that you'll find some way to handle that situation."

"I'll have to. But I've got to know how you can conceal yourself from Suleiman. The name of every foreigner who comes to Abu Bakr is reported to him."

"I'll be carrying an Egyptian passport. Really, Kenyon, don't worry about me. I can take care of myself."

"So I'm discovering. But there's one more angle that needs to be settled. You're asking a favor, and you're not asking Aapco for a fee. But I'll be subjected to personal inconvenience, not to mention certain risks. What's in this for me?"

"I thought that was implicit in our understanding," Lee said. "Accept my terms, and after we reach Abu Bakr I'll sleep with you."

Dugald McIntosh was closeted with several of his vice-presidents for an hour, and as soon as they left his office he buzzed for Bobbie.

She knew he was upset, and wanted to talk, so she took a chair without waiting for his invitation to sit.

"We've been hashing over Kenyon's messages from Paris," he said, "and if he's right we're in for real trouble in Abu Bakr. There's only one way Shaikh Suleiman could make a major deal with the French government. He'd have to reduce our share of Aapco to a minority holding, which would give him the power to work out contracts with anyone he pleases. He may not have learned much about the oil industry yet, but certainly he realizes we'll veto the proposal he's entertaining."

"If he's actually entertaining it," Bobbie said. "Turk made it very plain that the French won't be approaching Suleiman until late next week, and he may show no interest in anything they propose to him."

"I'm not panicking," McIntosh said, "but I've got to admit all of us are jittery. The French may have picked up some information we don't know. I can't help feeling they've found out that Abu Bakr is planning some degree of nationalization of its oil interests."

"Guesswork is dangerous."

"It would be even more of a risk to force Suleiman into the open. We've just been discussing whether to threaten him with a cancellation of our plan to go into partnership with him in the construction of a refinery in El Ain. Or to explore the idea of building a fertilizer plant there. But a threat without teeth is useless. He doesn't need our money, and he can get technical advice elsewhere. Anywhere. The French, the British, the Germans, the Belgians, and a half dozen others would be delighted to step into any vacuum we might create. The industrialized nations need oil so desperately that they won't take a common stand when the crunch is on, no matter how much lip service they may pay to the cause of consumer-nation cooperation."

"Is there some other way to smoke out the Abu Bakrians?" Bobbie asked.

McIntosh shrugged. "Hamilton tells us we've got to sit tight and wait for developments. Kenyon insists we're to leave everything to him."

"My personal prejudices aside," she said, "I have full confidence in Turk. His record is rather extraordinary—he has a strange genius for handling the Arabs, and I'm afraid we'll have to let him take care of the problem in his own way."

"Whatever that is. I don't even want to know what he has in mind. Every time we operate outside the law I worry about it. I've got to safeguard myself—and so do the vice-presidents—by pleading ignorance."

Bobbie felt a surge of sympathy for him. He was one of the most powerful industrialists in America, but he was

188

vulnerable, thanks to the vagaries of the oil business and his necessary dependence on someone as ruthless as Turk.

"Kenyon is too shrewd to talk, of course. All he'd tell me on the phone was that I'm going to be inundated with complaints about him from Abu Bakr after he flies there tomorrow, and he asked me to ignore the gripes."

"What kind of complaints?"

"That's the hell of it. He didn't say, and I didn't want specifics." McIntosh reached for a cigar. "Has it ever occurred to you that this is an insane business, Bobbie? Men who are in steel, automobiles, banks, whatever, work from a solid base. They have rules that everyone obeys, nationally and internationally, and if some maverick breaks loose, they can punish him accordingly. But oil is different. Colonel Drake, who discovered oil in Pennsylvania a hundred years ago and founded the industry, was a maverick. So were most of the old-timers who came up with gushers in Texas. And now—until we can complete the Alaska pipeline, find more offshore wells, and speed up the process of converting shale into oil—we're at the mercy of the most unpredictable mavericks of all. A handful of desert chiefs who don't think as we do, who hate the West and who are determined to assert what they regard as Arab supremacy over the whole world. Their whims rule us, and they can destroy the underpinnings of our society."

She wanted to soothe him, but had to remind herself that in the office she was a secretary.

"I have obligations to the directors, the stockholders—and when you get down to basics—to the American public. Most people think of the active heads of the major oil companies as robber barons. They're outraged by the high price of oil, and they've got to blame somebody. Television has taught them a simple approach to life, so they're quick to point a finger at us. Our public relations departments haven't been able to convince the public that we're caught in a vise too."

"You're doing everything you can to keep the oil flowing," Bobbie said. "Nothing more than that can be expected of you."

"There's been a clamor that our profits are too high, but the people who scream at us don't realize we're a high-risk industry, probably the highest on earth. Sometimes I think we aren't really in business at all, that we're players in the biggest crap game on earth."

Bobbie regarded him steadily. "It seems to me you ought to get away for a little vacation."

"Impossible! How can I leave now—when all hell may start popping in the Middle East?"

"It was just a suggestion," she said.

McIntosh stood and walked around the desk. "I have an even better idea. I'll grant you I'm wound up too tight. I'm not sleeping, I'm not eating, and I'm drinking more than is good for me. I've got to get myself back into line, but I can't do it alone."

She felt the color rise in her face.

"I haven't had much practice at this sort of thing. In fact, I've only done it once before in my life. I was going to wait for a more appropriate occasion, but this is as good a time as any." He paused, groped for words, and then spoke. "How long would it take you to break in a new secretary for me?"

"I think Miss Jeffers could take over in a week, two at the most. She's worked for you in the past, she knows our filing system, and she has an idea of who you'll talk to on the phone. It shouldn't take too long." Bobbie was cautious.

"That settles it. Break her in." He was decisive, acting as though the matter were settled.

She hated to prod him, but if he thought she would become his mistress she had to disillusion him. "What department do you have in mind for me? I never make a move unless I know where I'm going."

McIntosh grinned at her. "That's all settled too. You're

taking charge of Dugald McIntosh department, full time."

"I am?"

"Damn it, woman, at my age you can't expect me to get down on my knees to propose marriage to you!"

"I wouldn't dream of it," Bobbie said, and laughed.

He glowered. "What's so funny?"

"Nothing, Dugald. We'll arrange the details at dinner tonight."

When Ruth Hamilton saw her husband's car pull up to the house she hurriedly left the side of the pool and went indoors. She found Red in his study and wasted no time on small talk.

"I've been thinking about Judy lately. I think we should enter her in college this September instead of a year from now. And I'd like to send her to my cousin in Denver for the rest of the summer."

Red's face fell. "We promised her a year with us, Ruthie. Besides, this may be the last time we'll ever have her with us for any length of time."

"Our little girl," Ruth said, "isn't all that little any more."

"Is she unhappy here? She hasn't indicated it to me."

"She wouldn't. But she's spending almost no time at your office—"

"That doesn't mean much. I can't blame a kid for not wanting to get involved in oil."

Ruth was patient. "She's bored, and that can be dangerous."

He put his pen on the desk and went to her. "Stop living your own past over again. All that is behind us."

She shook her head. "This isn't a case of my guilts working overtime, Lyman. Perhaps I'm more sensitive to the symptoms than some people, but I've seen all the signs in Judy."

"I haven't," Red said. "She won't even touch a glass of wine with her dinner, and her friendships with the young people of the compound are harmless. I've been keeping my eyes open. She has no real interest in any of the boys here."

"Judy may be forming other relationships that are complicated and dangerous. Won't you take my word for it that the best thing we can do is send her off to Denver?"

"Not when I don't know what you're talking about."

"I hoped I could avoid giving you chapter and verse. You'll have to promise you won't tell her that I've told you anything."

Red nodded, reluctantly. "Okay, you have my promise. Now what?"

"Judy has been seeing someone on the sly."

He was puzzled. "Why should she bother? All the people from the legations come here sooner or later—"

"This man," Ruth said, "is an Arab."

Red stared at her, his face flushing. "Who is he?"

Ruth's gesture indicated that she had no idea.

"If he's a member of the Husayn family I'll have him hauled into line in a hurry. The shaikhs don't want their sons messing around with Western girls, not in Abu Bakr. Any more than we want it the other way around."

"From the little Judy has let slip to me he's neither a Husayn nor a member of any other noble family."

He was incredulous. "Judy has been seeing some ordinary Arab? The kind of Arab I hire as an unskilled laborer?"

"Exactly." She placed a protective hand on his bare forearm.

He was too shaken to become aware of the gesture. "I can't imagine why Judy would do a goddam fool thing like that!"

"She wants excitement. Adventure. This may be her idea of romance, but I don't think so. When I went off the deep end I did it with our own kind, but she's too young to be discriminating."

Red covered his face with his hands.

"Before you go after this man with a pistol, you'd better hear the rest. He isn't the first."

"Other Arabs?" he asked in a choked voice.

"I don't think so. People she knew casually while she was at school in Switzerland." Ruth became firm. "You can't go barging in like an aircraft carrier with its guns blazing, Lyman. Judy is a young woman now, not a child, and we'll alienate her permanently if we aren't careful."

"What am I supposed to do, pretend I don't know?"

"Correct. Work with me to find some logical excuse to ship her off to Denver, and send her on to college from there. I'm not saying she'll become a candidate for canonization. Her generation has its own standards, or lack of them. But at least she won't be creating an explosive situation by sneaking off afternoons to visit a man in El Ain."

"I could kill her as well as the man!"

"That won't accomplish anything constructive, either."

"I've spent most of my life earning the respect of these people," Red said. "I know how they react, and I know what they'll think of Judy. I suppose I'm not all that surprised to discover she knows the score. I realized it by the way she was handling Turk Kenyon the night he came here for dinner. But it never occurred to me she'd cross the line that separates us from the Arabs. They're our friends, but we don't sleep with them. They don't want it and we don't want it!"

"Youngsters like Judy are second-generation Americans out here," Ruth said, still trying to calm him. "When you look at it that way, I think, it seems natural that the barriers break down."

"Only on our side!" Red said. "The true believer who lives by the word of the Koran hasn't changed and won't change. He refuses to change. Do you realize Judy could wind up as one of several wives in a polygamous household, cut off forever from the outside world?"

"That's just one of many charming ideas that's crossed my mind, Lyman."

In his bewilderment he reached out to her. "What will we do, Ruthie?"

"We'll send her back to our own world. But we'll do it so carefully that we'll give her no reason to hate us and rebel even harder. We've got to set up an airtight plan, Lyman, and then act accordingly."

Ten

They had arranged to meet at Orly Airport, at Pan American counter number 1, an hour before the direct flight took off for Abu Bakr. Simplicity was the key to the success of any deception, Turk had said, so he had ruled out any stops en route to their final destination. He was a quarter of an hour early, so when Lee hadn't arrived by ten minutes after the scheduled time, he was annoyed and nervous.

A handsome young woman in a pantsuit of pale linen approached him. "Waiting for someone, or will I do?"

Turk stared at her. She spoke with Lee's voice, but otherwise was unrecognizable. Her skin was stained a dark shade, her makeup was circumspect, and she wore no polish on her long fingernails. What he found astonishing was that her long hair was black and her eyes were a deep brown.

He took care to speak in a low tone. "You didn't tell me you're a sorceress. Even a simpleton can figure out the wig, but how did you change your eyes?"

"Contact lenses," she said. "Let's go through, shall we? I'm dying for a drink or two before takeoff."

Still recovering from his surprise, he admired her as he followed her to the counter. Her small earrings were Egyptian, he noted, and her walk was unobtrusive. She was still exceptionally pretty, but she no longer called attention to herself and could melt into a crowd.

The passport Lee presented to the clerk was Egyptian.

Turk wondered if it was forged, but made no comment.

They checked their luggage through to El Ain, then went through customs and passport controls, and as the girl took Turk's arm he saw she was not wearing either the diamond ring or the bracelet Suleiman had given her.

He ordered two glasses of Dubonnet on the rocks at the outward-bound passengers' bar, then carried their drinks to a nearby table, where a smiling, self-assured Lee awaited him. An opened pack of Egyptian cigarettes rested on the table near her elbow.

"Don't look now," she said, making it appear that she was murmuring an intimacy, "but we're under observation."

"Where?"

"Third table to your left. A young Arab with a short beard and sunglasses."

He took his time, waiting until they silently toasted each other before sitting back to light a cigarette and casually glancing through the lounge. "I've never seen the guy before."

"Oh, he knows you. You're well known in his part of the world," Lee said, and rested her hand on his. "Our friend knows you're heading back to El Ain, where others will be following you so he'll soon lose interest, particularly since he doesn't recognize your girlfriend." Lee looked pleased.

"How do you know?"

"He'd be on the nearest telephone, and before we could finish these drinks one of his chums would book a seat on our flight."

"You're of that much importance to the Palestine liberation groups?"

"I don't think so, but they do." She sounded bored.

"Who the hell are you?"

"Let me enjoy myself," she said. "It isn't every day of the week I can fool an Arab surveillance expert by passing myself off as an Egyptian. My disguise must be good."

"You don't need me to tell you it's perfect. Now, how about leveling with me?"

"Our friend over there must be convinced by now that I'm a member of the limitless legion known as Turk Kenyon's women."

"Your flattery overwhelms me." He refused to be deflected. "You must be on somebody's payroll."

"Not necessarily," Lee said. "I kept the full amount of what you paid me."

"And hocked Suleiman's jewelry?"

"Don't be silly. It went into a safety deposit box."

"Fair enough. But you're still on somebody's payroll. Which of the oil companies is it?"

Her lips brushed his cheek. "You may be right, or you may be wrong. If and when the time comes I'll tell you anything I think you ought to know."

"Look, if we're working together—"

"I'll produce results, never fear." Her bantering manner vanished. "We have an agreement. I'll stand on the sidelines until you have a chance to kill the French deal with Suleiman. If you fail I'll step in and take care of things in my own way. Who I am and who pays me is irrelevant to our partnership. We have a job to do, and we'll be doing it together."

"At close range."

"I haven't forgotten our bargain."

"I've been turning a few wheels myself," Turk said. "I've tamped down the New York office in advance, so they'll pay no attention to the outraged morality of our people in

Abu Bakr. And I've notified our El Ain office that a companion is making the trip with me."

"An unidentified companion, I hope."

"Of course. Although I'll have to say something to Red Hamilton. I'll probably tell him you're a business associate."

"Will he believe you?"

"Not when he sees you, but at least I'll have gone on the record."

"I find it odd and rather sad," Lee said, "that in our work we must spend as much time protecting ourselves from our own bureaucracies as we do from our enemies."

Her tacit admission that she was engaged in work similar to his gave him small comfort.

The routine at the Foreign Ministry never varied. Red Hamilton sat on a pile of cushions, exchanged endless compliments with Ahmed al-Husayn and drank so many tiny cups of coffee that he invariably suffered an attack of indigestion that lasted into the next day. But he was resigned to the inevitability of observing the ritual, even though he knew his host was bored by it too. An Arab would be regarded as inhospitable, one of the worst sins he could commit, if he failed to abide by the traditions of his ancestors. Red counted a pile of eighteen little cups and saucers on the floor beside him, and knew they would soon tackle the business at hand.

The Arab boy in loose-fitting shirt and trousers, with a broad sash around his middle, appeared with two more steaming cups, managing the difficult feat of bowing low to his master, then to the guest, without spilling a drop.

"May Allah smile on all of your endeavors," Ahmed al-Husayn said.

"May you continue to bask in His favor," Red replied.

They raised their cups simultaneously, taking small sips of the thick, heavily sweetened brew.

Ahmed sat back on his cushions. "What brings you here when the sun is high overhead, my friend?"

"At our last meeting," Red said, "you and I reached an informal agreement to keep certain information to ourselves. I'm looking out for the interests of Aapco, and you're trying to protect your country."

Ahmed cut him off before he could proceed. "Let us be sure you do understand my position. I favor working with you Americans because I am convinced that only you can and will help accomplish what I believe best for Abu Bakr's future. I'm not being disloyal to my nation or Suleiman by saying nothing at present about the Great Wadi oil field discovery."

"I know, and I salute your patriotism." Red sympathized with his defensive attitude. "But now we have a new complication on a matter that New York has given Kenyon authority to handle. Unfortunately, he'll go straight to Suleiman, which means an adventurer will be bargaining with an eccentric."

Ahmed sighed. "Reasonable men are so seldom given the opportunity to prove they can come to sensible agreements for the benefit of all parties. I sometimes think the education of my sons is a waste."

Red pursued the matter at hand. "This new situation concerns me because Suleiman is unpredictable."

"For that very reason my influence at the palace is limited." Ahmed sat erect. "I'm bracing myself."

"It has come to our attention that the government of France has made Abu Bakr one offer of a deal for oil, and is going to make another that is even more attractive."

"I congratulate your company," Ahmed said. "I don't know how you do it, but you often hear of affairs of state before we know of them."

"We try to keep reasonably well informed."

"Thanks to your foresight, I won't be overly surprised if the French should approach our government."

199

The tacit admission that a potential deal was brewing was all Red could ask. "I'm sure you realize," he said, "that American-Arabian Petroleum exercises the greatest restraint at all times so we don't in any way impinge on the sovereignty of Abu Bakr."

The Foreign Minister's cynical smile said far more than his nod of agreement.

"At the same time, however, I would like to remind Your Excellency that a nation, like those with whom it does business, is obligated to observe the terms of a firm contract. Therefore any offer made directly to you by the government of France should be referred to us."

"We have no control over the activities of the French government," Ahmed said. "If they seek to make an agreement with His Highness's administration, we of Abu Bakr are in no position to quarrel with them."

"My company," Red said, "deplores all quarrels between good friends who have worked together for their mutual benefit. For that reason I hope Your Excellency will refer the French to me if they come to you before Kenyon sees Suleiman. I'm hoping you and I can deal with this crisis before unpredictable elements enter the picture and create insoluble complications."

"In my limited experience," Ahmed said, "I have found that governments tend to deal with other governments, not with corporations. Speaking for myself, I regard this proclivity as a demonstration of the herd instinct."

Red refused to digress. "France must know that in dealing with matters relating to Aapco she must negotiate with Aapco. It would do her no good, for example, to approach my government. The United States, as a nation, is not involved. There are only two parties to our contract, Abu Bakr and Aapco."

The Foreign Minister saw that his oblique attempt to blunt the impact of the American's attack was ineffective, so he tried another approach. "As you've undoubtedly come to know after the many years you've spent in my country, our system of government is based on an ancient Islamic tradition. All that comprises Abu Bakr belongs to His Highness, who has inherited it from his predecessor and will pass it to his successor. He is the guardian of our heritage, and he may do as he pleases with our land, provided he does not sell it. He may allow the people to use it free of charge, as he does at the Oasis of Qar. He may allow his subjects to lease it from him, as he does in the old town of El Ain. He may, as in the case of Aapco, rent tracts of land to foreigners who develop it for the good of Abu Bakr as well as their own enrichment."

"I'm familiar with the principles," Red said. "What concerns me is the day to day practice."

"It is the inviolable right of His Highness to make any arrangements that he believes will be of the greatest benefit to the greatest number of his subjects."

"Even if a new agreement violates a contract that Abu Bakr has observed for years?"

"It would be an unusual procedure," the Foreign Minister said, "but he has that right."

"Then you're saying that a contract with your government is worthless?"

"Not at all. Both sides must adhere to their written promises. But that doesn't prevent His Highness from canceling a contract, if that is his desire."

"Unilaterally?"

"Of course, since the land is his."

"As you know, Your Excellency," Red said, "it's my duty to notify my New York headquarters of the substance of this conversation. Since you know how much American-Arabian Petroleum relies on the demonstrated willingness of Abu Bakr to observe the terms of its contracts, you won't be surprised that my superiors will take a grave view of this reminder of principles."

"I'm sure Mr. McIntosh and his associates will be upset. I

hope you'll convey my sympathies to them, and tell them I regret any inconveniences I may be causing them."

"I'll be happy to pass along your message," Red said. "Would it be presumptuous of me to notify my headquarters that Your Excellency is one who counsels moderation?"

"An official in my position performs two functions," Ahmed said. "When his advice is requested, he gives it. Even when his words are unheeded, however, he obeys the will of his royal master. He is an instrument for the implementation of that will."

Red had no difficulty in interpreting the other's comments. Husayn had tried in vain to persuade Suleiman not to conclude a separate agreement with the French government, but had failed. He was being compelled to carry out policies of which he disapproved, but he had no choice. So, unless Abu Bakr drew back from the new course she was beginning to pursue under the direction of a reckless ruler, there was no doubt about the future. Aapco was facing a major, imminent crisis.

The Joint Congressional Energy Committee was planning to hold a new series of public hearings on the continuing fuel crisis in the United States. Senator Herbert Watrous (D., Okla.), the Committee chairman, had been ducking the press for days, so he preferred not to be seen in public on his overnight trip to New York.

Dugald McIntosh hastily revised his plans. Instead of taking the Senator to one of his clubs or a restaurant for dinner, he arranged to entertain his guest at the suite Aapco maintained in the Waldorf Towers. Bobbie Kenyon, who was introduced as McIntosh's fiancée, acted as hostess and was present at the cocktail hour, then discreetly withdrew when the men went into the dining room. They got down to business over coffee and brandy.

"I hate to put in an S.O.S. when you're busy, Herb," McIntosh said, "but our situation in Abu Bakr is deteriorating rapidly, and we may need the help of the Administration."

"Suleiman is feeling his oats, is he? I'm not surprised. I warned the State Department not to recognize him in too almighty much of a hurry, but Foggy Bottom always knows best."

"A refusal to recognize him—or a delay—would have brought the crisis that much sooner, I think," McIntosh said. "But it wouldn't have made a difference in the long run."

"Even an Arab ignoramus is going to think twice before thumbing his nose at the U.S.A. Sometimes it pays to hold people like that at arm's length for a while."

Senatorial chauvinism was a problem that had to be skirted with delicacy. "Suleiman seems to be in a class by himself," McIntosh said. "We've been getting reports from our general manager in Abu Bakr that he may be on the verge of nationalizing the oil industry there. And France isn't helping matters any by coming up with juicy deals as inducements to him to break his ties with us. We're making an extracurricular attempt, you might call it, to neutralize the situation, but I can't evaluate its possible success, and I think it's something you don't want to know about. To what extent can we count on you—and on the President—if Suleiman pulls the rug out from under us, Herb?"

Watrous poured his Cognac into his coffee. "This isn't the first time we've faced this dilemma, and it won't be the last, Dug. These two-bit rulers take themselves pretty seriously nowadays, and they have the oil—and the cash reserves—to make us wonder if they aren't something more than two-bit wonders."

"From where I sit they're the most powerful men on earth."

"From where the American people sit, too. Unfortunately. We can't tell them to drink their oil, not until we can replace it."

"Aapco has quadrupled its allotment to our research department, and we'll double it again at our next budget review meeting. But you can't find a replacement for oil overnight, Herb, any more than you can develop additional oil resources with a snap of the fingers."

"Some Arab rulers are okay," the Senator said. "Oh, they line their pockets with solid gold, but I can't blame them for that. They're sincere about the welfare of their people, and they take a global view of the oil problem. They realize that shortages in the industrialized nations and exorbitant prices will ruin everybody, including themselves. Then there's the other type—the Suleimans, who were born hundreds of years after their time."

"No question about that," McIntosh said. "But Abu Bakr is a key to Aapco's overseas operations. We've tamped out the fires everywhere else, at least for now. But nothing spreads faster than a fire in an oil field. If Suleiman nationalizes, a lot of others are going to get itchy too. There will be international hell to pay. Again."

Watrous's smile was wry. "I didn't know how well off I was when I served on the Post Office and District of Columbia committees. Dug, the complexities are enough to drive a sane man nuts. The White House is sensitive to the problem, but we can't throw our weight around these days. Not that far from home, and in an area that produces sixty percent of the world's known oil reserves."

"What will Congress do if Suleiman tears up our contracts and expropriates our fields?"

"I could guarantee you a bill to cut off all trade with Abu Bakr. Spontaneous combustion will occur in both Houses, and the majority margin will be overwhelming. The President will let the bill become law without his signature, too. All very neat."

"And useless."

"A wasted gesture," the Senator agreed. "France and all the other European nations will be glad to supply Suleiman with arms, food imports, and anything else he needs. He won't even feel an American embargo, and he'll be a hero in the Arab world because he's David, heaving stones at the American Goliath."

"So there's nothing practical either the Senate or the House can do? Nothing your committee can do?"

"Well, if it looks as though the nationalization is for keeps, the right people can do something about getting Aapco a special tax rebate."

"If we're denied Abu Bakrian oil," McIntosh said, "we won't be paying enough taxes to make a rebate worth anybody's while."

"Your best bet," Watrous said, "is to improve your relations with Suleiman. Do whatever you have to do. Kiss his ass, and pray for another coup, one that will overthrow him and put someone with a little common sense on the honorable throne of the Husayn family."

"We're trying, Herb! We're shooting the works, and we'll know soon whether we're still in business or whether people will start papering bathroom walls with their Aapco stock."

The DC 10 landed at El Ain on schedule, eleven hours after it had left Paris. Lee, wearing the *feredezah* and *yashmak*, was admitted without question on the Egyptian passport she was carrying, and Turk, who had already gone through the customs and immigration line reserved for men, recovered their luggage. An air-conditioned sedan provided by Aapco awaited the couple, and within minutes they were driving on the highway to the Eisenhower compound.

An unexpected hitch developed when they reached the gate of the American reservation, where a sergeant of the guard halted the car. "I'm right sorry, Mr. Kenyon," he said, "but I have orders from Mr. Hamilton. He told me to notify him the minute you arrived, and you're to wait for him here."

"To hell with that," Turk said. "I'll see him at his house."

"I've got my orders, Mr. Kenyon." The sergeant went to

the telephone, and two sentries picked up their automatic rifles.

Turk was livid, but Lee found it amusing. "I'll bet this delay is connected with me. I didn't see how you could bring me to a place like this without a fuss being raised."

They waited a quarter of an hour before Red Hamilton appeared, and he barely glanced at the shrouded figure of the girl. "I want a private word with you, Kenyon," he said, and walked a short distance from the car.

Turk faced Red. "You have no right—"

"I have every right. This isn't the Riviera. Or Las Vegas. I don't know what makes you think you can bring one of your chorus girls to an isolated American community with middle-class standards!"

Turk feigned surprise, then laughed. "So that's what you think! I haven't come to Abu Bakr for a vacation, Hamilton, and the young lady happens to be a valuable associate. I've already had clearance for bringing her here," he added, exaggerating slightly.

"From whom?"

"Dugald McIntosh himself. I discussed her with him on the phone from Paris, but I don't ask you to take my word for it. Check him yourself."

"I'll get a cable off to him right away."

Turk held his ground. "You've heard that France is trying to play international footsie with Suleiman."

"Yes, but don't change the subject."

"Believe me, brother, I'm not. The young lady in the car happens to be the person who came up with that information. All of it. She has the best connections in the business."

Red was intrigued in spite of himself. "If I've misjudged you it's the first time, but I'm willing to admit the possibility that I'm wrong. Who is she?"

Turk had no intention of revealing that the "Egyptian" was the blonde he had delivered to the palace several weeks earlier, and since he still didn't know who she was himself, he wanted to say as little as possible. "She's a member of an exclusive profession. She's an oil troubleshooter, and one of the best. See here, Hamilton. If I offend your midwestern sense of morality, put her up in one of the other guest houses."

"They're all full, as it happens."

"Then give us the benefit of the doubts, for Chrissake. This is no time to start acting like a prig."

Red realized he had been pushed onto the defensive. "If you think it's easy maintaining morale half a world away from Main Street—"

"I realize you have some damn nasty problems." Turk had won. He could afford to be generous. "What a debt we owe her for bringing us the inside on the French double-cross!"

"As a matter of fact, I had a session today with Ahmed al-Husayn. I was planning to tell you about it."

"Better tell the lady, too. She accomplishes more than I do. Come and meet her." Turk grasped Red's elbow and moved toward the car, indicating to Lee that he wanted her to lower her window.

She obliged.

"Sorry for the delay," Turk said, "but I was catching up on some confidential cables from New York. Leila, let me present Lyman Hamilton, our Abu Bakr general manager."

"How do you do. I've heard a great deal about you," she said.

Red glanced quickly at Turk, but did not reply.

"Shall we come to your office?" Turk asked.

Red glanced at his watch. "No, we'll be closing for the day. Why don't both of you come to the house in an hour?"

Turk silently gloated over the effortlessly gotten invitation as he slid behind the wheel and stepped on the accelerator. "You can get rid of the Hallowe'en outfit," he said. "We're inside the gates."

Lee struggled out of her robes. "Was I right?"

"You were dead wrong," Turk said. "He really did want to talk about from some cables from home. Besides, you heard his invitation. You don't think he'd ask a tramp to meet his wife and daughter?"

"No, I don't believe he would. You're clever, but not that clever."

"Hardly," he said. "But there is a problem I've got to solve. There are two bedrooms in the guest house. Bear right as you go through the living room, close the bedroom door behind you, and don't come out until I tell you."

She laughed. "Your personal servant problem?"

"Right, but I can handle it, provided you keep quiet until I give you the word."

"It will be fascinating," she said, "watching the one and only Turk Kenyon at work."

"See no evil and hear no evil, and you'll go to heaven." He waved at the rows of houses laid out on the neat, suburban streets. "How would you like living in one of these places?"

Lee became thoughtful. "With the right man," she said, "it might not be too bad."

"You'd blow your mind."

"Well," she admitted, "I've never met that man, and I don't believe I ever will."

"I can't see you pushing a supermarket cart, with a brood of little monsters hanging onto your skirt."

"It may seem funny to you, Turk, but there are moments when I yearn for just that sort of life." Lee jerked upright. "But not very often."

He turned onto the avenue graced by the largest houses. "Here you see the rewards of being a good boy. Play the company game and take no chances. Do what you're told and never step out of line. Earn a base salary of thirty thousand a year, plus fifteen percent for overseas duty. Plus a free house and a liberal food allowance. And when you retire you get two thirds of your base pay. By then, of course, you're housebroken and brainwashed, so you can't have any fun, no matter how much you get."

"Most people," Lee said, "would be satisfied."

"I wouldn't, and neither would you."

"I wonder. Respectability may be boring, but dullness may be a small price to pay for safety and comfort in a world that is greedy and corrupt and dangerous."

"Either I'll be rich enough not to care by the time I reach retirement age," Turk said, "or I'll be dead."

"We've had the same philosophy," she admitted, "but we may be wrong. It would be soothing to know that a house was my very own."

"You couldn't sit through one tea party of company wives," he replied. "You'd spend the rest of your days in a madhouse." He parked in front of Guest House Three. "Home again."

The door was unlocked, and Lee followed his instructions to the letter, walking swiftly through the living room and entering the bedroom on the right side. Before closing the door, however, she caught a glimpse of an attractive, buxom Arab girl. Turk's complications, she imagined, were never caused by homely women.

Farima remained motionless until Turk came into the house with the luggage. Then she cursed his ancestors and remarked at length on his resemblance to camel dung.

He waited until her diatribe ended, then motioned her toward the bedroom on the left, his exaggerated gestures mysterious. The Arab penchant for conspiracy, he hoped, would quiet her for the moment.

Farima followed him, but looked as though she intended to leap at him and claw his throat.

"Listen," Turk said, "before you make the worst mistake of your life. You are angry because I have brought a woman with me."

"An Egyptian, judging by her Western clothes!" She spat

on the floor. "They think they're superior, and they lord it over us. I don't believe they're real Arabs."

"She is here for a reason," he said, "so no one will ever know there is a connection between you and me. I've brought you the money to finance your revolution." He paused and waited.

In spite of her fury Farima's eyes lit up.

"I made you a promise, and I have kept my word. But how would it look if you fail? Aapco and Suleiman would learn that your funds were supplied by your good friend, and that would be the end of me. If the Abu Bakrians did not kill me, my own employers would discharge me. The Egyptian girl is my insurance, so no one will ever know what you and I have meant to each other." Turk gave her no chance to analyze too long. Reaching into his wallet, he handed her a wad of bills. "Here is a thousand dollars. I ask you to accept it as a token of my good faith."

Farima snatched the money from him.

"I shall make two more payments, both of them large," he said. "Tonight, at ten o'clock, I'll come to the house in El Ain, and tomorrow I'll give you the rest. All I ask in return is that you and Ali arrange for me to meet your principal lieutenants tonight."

The girl's suspicions flared.

"I have procured fifty thousand dollars for you," Turk said. "It wasn't easy for me to get that much money. For my own protection I need to be assured that your comrades share your dedication. How do I know they won't steal the money and squander it in Beirut? If they are afraid I'll trick them I won't object if they wear masks. But I must hear them tell me, themselves, that they uphold the cause you and Ali sponsor."

Farima was torn, and hesitated.

Turk's manner changed, and he became brusque. "Either you want the money or you don't. Either you plan to establish your own government in Abu Bakr or you're cousins of all the other Arabs who spray words like the waters of a fountain but never take action. I have no debt to you, much as I would like to see you do what you've sworn to do. Accept my conditions or I'll give you no more help. And I want your decision now, or the Egyptian will wonder why I am neglecting her."

Farima made up her mind. "I accept," she said, and left the house, heading in the direction of the bus that took the day workers of Eisenhower to El Ain.

Turk waited until she was out of earshot, made certain Lee's door was still closed, and then, closing his own door, put in a telephone call to the vizier at the palace. "This is Dale Kenyon," he said. "I returned to Abu Bakr a few moments ago, and I must see His Highness at once, without delay, on a matter of the gravest urgency. A matter," he added solemnly, "that concerns his personal safety, a matter so important I won't wait for you to confirm an audience. I'll drive into El Ain this minute in the hope that he'll grant me an audience."

As he hung up, he saw the bedroom door was open. Lee was lounging against the frame, her expression making it impossible for him to determine how much of his conversation she had overheard. "I'm going out for a while on an errand. If I'm late and Hamilton calls to ask why we haven't put in an appearance, tell him we'll be there soon, that I had to go back to the airport for a suitcase I left there."

"You cover your tracks well," Lee said. "I like that."

He decided she had overheard him, but there was no reason to believe she would talk. For the moment, at least, they were partners. "If you want something to do while I'm gone, you may want to change into something fancier. They take the cocktail hour as seriously here as they do in Providence, Atlanta, and Milwaukee."

Lee laughed as Turk went out the door.

He drove into the city at breakneck speed and kept his hand on the horn as he maneuvered the streets of El Ain.

The sentries at the palace gate detained him for no more than an instant, and he knew his plan was advancing as he hoped.

An attendant conducted the visitor to the audience chamber, where a number of courtiers and the always-present guards also were waiting.

As Turk bowed low he decided a frontal attack would be the most effective. "Speaking as one who lost a *dalu* shooting contest, I crave a favor. It is necessary that I speak to His Highness in private."

Shaikh Suleiman was startled by the unusual request, but concluded he would suffer no harm from one who had been his hunting companion. He cleared the room with a wave, then motioned his guest closer.

Turk dropped his verbal hand grenade. "Your Highness, I have discovered a group of Communist conspirators who threaten your rule."

Suleiman looked as though he had been punched in the stomach. "You're certain?"

"My evidence is conclusive."

The Shaikh moistened his lips. "I assume they are Palestinians."

The second hand grenade detonated. "They are Abu Bakrians, Your Highness."

Suleiman stared, incredulous. He took a few seconds to speak. "How do I know you speak the truth?"

"You will have the opportunity to capture and question their leaders yourself."

The Shaikh's long fingers closed over the ornamental handle of the dagger he wore in his belt. "When?"

The reply was unequivocal. "Tonight. At ten o'clock."

Turk thought he saw Suleiman's hands trembling.

"I ask only that no one be told of my part in bringing this information to you. Some members of your court may guess, particularly after this private meeting, but no one will actually know. To be of additional service to Your Highness

I need to keep my own sources of information confidential."

The secrecy of the American's role was the least of Suleiman's concerns. His hasty nod served as his agreement. "Where will I find these traitors?"

"Send for a map of El Ain, Your Highness."

The Shaikh pulled so hard at the bell rope that it tore.

When the map arrived Turk studied it, then asked to borrow the Shaikh's dagger.

Without hesitation Suleiman handed it to him.

Using the point as an indicator, Turk made a tiny hole in the paper. "This is the house, Your Highness," he said, and he described the place in detail, stressing the presence of the wall that surrounded it. "The leaders expect me there at ten tonight."

"You, Kenyon?"

"They think I intend to finance their attempt to depose you and establish their own government. I have been giving them small sums to win their confidence, and I have requested a meeting tonight with their leaders."

"Your cunning is that of an Arab."

Turk knew he could have been paid no greater compliment. "Their faith in me is shaky, Your Highness. Send no one in uniform into the area, and make certain your agents are men they won't recognize. They're clever, and if they think they may be betrayed, they'll vanish, and your men will break into an empty house."

"I shall do as you suggest," Suleiman said, "and I give you a guarantee I shall capture all of the traitors. Alive. Will they be armed?"

"I don't know."

"It does not matter. They shall have no chance to fire as much as a single shot."

"I hope you'll permit me to call on you again, so I may learn how well Your Highness fares on your fishing expedition."

"My face would be blackened, and my home would become a *bayt al-shan'a*—a house of degradation—if my doors were ever closed to you, Kenyon. You shall have *'assabiyya* here for all time."

As Turk well knew, *'assabiyya* was a state of kinship that an Arab regarded as sacred. One to whom it was granted was entitled to receive unlimited hospitality from the donor, so lavish that, as a rule, only close male relatives enjoyed its full privileges. A Persian Gulf monarch sometimes suffered from a faulty memory, but the American could claim the rights in the immediate future, at least, and for the present that was all he wanted. The government of France would never know why its offer was rejected.

"My men will not fail," the Shaikh said. "There is an old saying that the fisherman who catches the greatest number of *shanad* weaves a tight net."

The expression in Suleiman's eyes sent an unexpected chill up Turk's spine. He bowed again, backed toward the door, and halted. "May Allah favor your expedition, and may you catch many fish, Your Highness."

He was both elated and relieved when he left the palace behind him.

Lee was waiting for him, modestly dressed in a long skirt and turtleneck blouse. Only her brown-stained arms were bare, and she was wearing almost no makeup.

They walked the short distance to the Hamilton house, Turk making no comment about his drive into El Ain.

No matter what Lee might have overheard, she curbed her curiosity. Turk appreciated her silence. Her attitude and conduct met every professional standard.

Red came to the door himself and made an effort to be cordial; he studied the "Egyptian" girl briefly, and clearly approved of what he saw.

Ruth, who awaited the guests on the glass-enclosed terrace, was more reserved. Her husband had told her that Turk's companion was a business associate rather than a mistress, but she was dubious, and didn't mind if her attitude showed. The air of sensuality Leila exuded did not escape the older woman's attention.

Conversation was general while they sipped their first drink, but after Red poured refills Turk decided the time had come to demonstrate his companion's worth. "Leila," he said, "repeat to Red what you told me in Paris."

Lee's account of the offer the French intended to make to Abu Bakr was unchanged, but she added a few new details. "Two or three members of the French cabinet were in favor of making a chalet available to Suleiman and then presenting it as a gift to him if he should decide he liked it. That question hasn't yet been settled, but it isn't of much consequence. No one in France, including their minister, realizes Suleiman would only be interested in a chalet in Abu Bakr. He's so afraid of plots to dethrone him that nothing could persuade him to leave the country."

"You speak of Suleiman with authority," Red said. "Do you know him?"

"We've met."

Turk concealed a smile behind his hand.

"What do you think of him?" Red asked.

Lee seemed to consider the question as though it was being presented for the first time. "He's a barbarian. He can be viciously cruel, and he hides his cruelty behind the Koran. May Allah protect any Abu Bakrian who has the misfortune to displease him."

"I assume," Red said after absorbing her opinion, "that Turk has told you about Aapco's present situation here."

"I knew it without the telling," Lee said, and smiled.

"Well, what would you do if you were in our position?"

"I'd find someone trustworthy to replace Suleiman, and then I'd support your candidate's cause—secretly, of course—with every penny a wealthy oil company could scrape together."

"You think we're in that much trouble?"

"I know you are," Lee said. "I don't know when Suleiman will act, whether it will be tonight or two years from now. Eventually he's certain to believe that American-Arabian Petroleum is a threat to his throne. When that day comes he'll nationalize the oil industry here. Your lawyers will claim your contract is binding, and you'll fight in the courts, if it comes to the worst—"

"That's exactly what they've been doing," Red interrupted. "I've seen copies of the legal department's memos to the front office."

"No American lawyer who works in a Manhattan skyscraper can understand the mind of a traditionalist Persian Gulf Arab. Suleiman knows nothing about Western law, and cares less. His idea of law is simple. He issues a decree, and people obey it. And he's a victim of his own prejudices. I think it unlikely that he's ever met a Jew, for instance, but he has the Arab's ingrained hatreds. If he could, I think, he'd import some Jews so he'd have cause to step up his anti-Israeli campaign. It isn't easy to create hatreds for a nation neither he nor his subjects know."

Red was obviously impressed by her analysis. "I think Turk would agree with you."

"In the main," Turk said.

Lee appeared to be under no strain. "You must know we're right," she said to Red. "You've spent so many years here that you must understand the Arab better than anyone."

Ruth had made it a habit since the first days of her marriage never to interrupt a business discussion. But her interest in this intelligent and beautiful young woman was too keen for her to remain silent any longer. "You speak of the Arab as a breed apart. Don't you regard yourself as one?"

Lee laughed. "Indeed not. I'm Egyptian. Oh, we make our token obeisances to the ideal of pan-Arabism, but even our peasant farmers are light years more advanced than these poor desert creatures. Surely you've noticed significant

216

differences between Cairo and El Ain. Or Mecca and Alexandria. Memphis, our ancient capital, was a sophisticated metropolis long before Moses led his people across the desert. But the Gulf cities are overgrown villages, nothing more." She accepted a partial refill from Red, thanking him with a smile.

Ruth was not yet satisfied. "You live in Cairo, I gather."

The girl became vague. "I have no permanent home these days. I seem to spend most of my time traveling."

"How unpleasant for your family."

Lee shrugged.

Ruth became direct. "Do you work for the Egyptian government?"

"I'm afraid Cairo isn't all that advanced. The only positions open to women are secretarial. Even that is considered daring by the conservatives."

A telephone rang, but someone picked up an extension elsewhere in the house before Red could cross the room.

Ruth ignored the interruption. "I never worked. I had all sorts of plans, but I married early in life. So I suppose I envy career women. What do you call your job?"

"I don't," Lee said. "I've never put a label on it."

Judy Hamilton, barefoot and wearing jeans and a T-shirt, appeared in the archway that separated the terrace from the living room. "Sorry, Mom, and forgive me, Daddy," she said. "I've got to go out. I won't be late." She was in so much of a hurry that, as she raced off, she paid no attention to the guests.

Ruth and Red exchanged glances. "Excuse us for a minute," the latter said as he followed his wife out of the room. "And plan to stay for dinner. I know we're having asparagus, and that's a rare treat in this part of the world."

Lee's contact lenses could not hide the amusement in her eyes, but she waited until her host and hostess were out of earshot before she spoke. "You didn't tell me Mrs. Hamilton was one of your conquests," she said.

"There was no reason to mention it," Turk replied. "Does it show all that much?"

"It screams," Lee said. "I haven't been interrogated that thoroughly since the Syrian police stopped me for a traffic violation in Damascus. And watch the way she looks at me. With X-ray eyes that have a special, narrow squint. It's a look women reserve for other women. She's more perceptive than her husband—when it comes to you—and she doesn't buy the story that you and I are business associates."

"So far that's all we are," Turk said. "Besides, Ruth and I had our fling a long time ago. She doesn't want me these days."

"Maybe not, but she doesn't want anyone else to have you, either. In spite of all the women you've known, you really don't understand us."

The maze was too intricate for him. "If you find this irritating, we don't have to stay for dinner, you know."

"I'm loving every minute of it," Lee said. "It makes up for all the hazards of my work."

While the couple on the terrace chatted, husband and wife were holding a hurried consultation at the far end of the living room, where they spoke in low tones.

"We can't let Judy fly out like this," Red said. "Ten to one she's going to meet her Arab."

"I don't see how we can stop her without physical force. Or creating a scene."

"I like the Egyptian girl, but she's a stranger, and I don't give a hang what Kenyon thinks. I'm worried about Judy!"

"So am I," Ruth said, "but I'm trying to be sensible."

"This is the clincher. Put her on the next flight to the Continent. On Thursday."

"Thank God we agree," Ruth said. "Tonight will be her last chance to see that man."

Eleven

The dinner was surprisingly successful, thanks in large part to Lee. She not only held up the conversation whenever it threatened to sag, but she proved to be an able storyteller, and her listeners laughed so often that, before the meal ended, even Ruth grudgingly accepted her.

Turk was impressed by her performance. She spoke with such intimate knowledge of the geography and customs of Cairo that, if he hadn't known better, he would have sworn she was a native of the city.

They remained at the table for a long time, and just as Ruth suggested they go to the terrace for coffee, the telephone rang. Red went off to answer the call, muttering that he intended to rip the instrument off the wall if his subordinates didn't learn to keep normal office hours.

Ruth asked Turk to carry the coffee tray, and they moved to the terrace, where Lee offered the others Egyptian cigarettes.

Red appeared in the archway, his face pale, and when he spoke his voice was hoarse. "Judy has been arrested," he said, "in a government raid on supposed Communist headquarters in El Ain!"

Ruth leaped to her feet. "That's insane!"

"I'm telling you what I've been told, Ruthie!"

Turk felt as though a wall had crashed on his head. It didn't make sense. How could Judy Hamilton be involved with Farima and Ali?

"Where is she now?" Ruth's voice was faint.

"In custody at the palace," Red said. "Sorry to break up the party, but I've got to get her released."

Turk rose. "I'm coming with you."

Red eyed him coldly. "What the hell for?"

"I'm closer to Suleiman than you are. He might tell you to get lost, but there's at least a chance he'll listen to me. You don't want your kid spending the night in an El Ain jail, and the company will be in an uproar if there's a diplomatic incident when our relations with the Shaikh are so rocky. Maybe it'll be a wasted effort, but don't stand on pride when I might be able to help."

Red made a rapid judgment. "Come on."

"Thanks for the evening, Ruth," Turk said hurriedly. "See you later, Leila. Don't wait up for me if you're tired. I don't know how long this may take."

Red was snapping on the ignition by the time the other man joined him. He knew every inch of the road into El Ain and utilized that knowledge. The speedometer hit 115.

The two men exchanged no words on the highway.

When they reached the city, Red finally spoke. "Judy must have become involved in something way beyond her," he said. "If you're in this mess with me, I've got to lay it on the line. Her mother and I have reason to suspect she's been having an affair with an Abu Bakrian. All I can figure is that he may be a Communist, and that Judy didn't know it."

Everything fell into place. The Hamilton girl was involved

with Farima's brother, and had been caught in the trap that he himself had set. It was unlikely that Judy was as innocent as her father believed, and the phone call earlier had probably been a summons to the meeting. The fate of the Abu Bakrians was of little concern to him, but he didn't want the death of an American girl on his conscience.

"We'll get it all straightened out, Red," he said. "I'm sure I don't need to warn you—don't lose your cool. Those goons at the palace have a pretty high opinion of themselves."

"I'll try," Red said, "but I can't make any promises, not even to myself." He honked furiously at the driver of a donkey cart, almost crashing into a building as he squeezed past the creaking vehicle.

The car screamed to a halt at the entrance to the palace.

Turk saw that his companion was almost inarticulate, and took charge. "Inform the vizier," he said in his most authoritative manner, "that we must see him at once."

The sentries recognized both visitors, and one strolled to the telephone in the guard shack and made a brief call.

Red seemed on the verge of lunging forward, but Turk's hand on his arm steadied him.

The sentry made no comment as he returned to his post, but he did not send the visitors away. It appeared someone would receive them.

After a long wait the chamberlain who had been Turk's guide earlier in the evening walked across the courtyard. "The vizier can see no one tonight," he said.

"We want to see Shaikh Suleiman!" Red's voice was ragged.

"His Highness cannot be disturbed. He is engaged in urgent matters of state."

"This is urgent, too. My daughter—"

"Hold on, Red." Turk interrupted before the other American said too much. "Your Excellency, please inform His Highness that his brother, Kenyon, has a need to see him without delay."

221

No Arab used the word "brother" lightly; the visitor would not dare to call himself the Shaikh's brother without good reason. The chamberlain, obviously impressed, bowed and disappeared through one of the courtyard entrances.

In his fury Red seemed not to hear Turk describe himself as the Shaikh's brother. "The smaller the country," he muttered, "the worse the red tape!"

"Hang in there," Turk said, giving cigarettes to the guards before offering one to his companion and lighting one himself.

The cigarettes were stubs before the chamberlain reappeared. "His Highness," he said, "will grant an audience to his brother, Kenyon."

Both Americans started forward.

"Only Kenyon will be admitted," the chamberlain said.

The sentries raised their rifles.

"Sit tight, Red, and don't make any waves," Turk said. "I'll bring the kid back with me."

Red Hamilton subsided, but only because he had no alternative. "Don't waste time, Turk," he said. "Or I'll lose my mind waiting out here."

The chamberlain led the way down a long, outdoor path to the side of the palace facing the sea. Two sentries with sub-machine guns stood outside a bronze door, which one of them opened with difficulty.

Turk followed the chamberlain down a flight of narrow stone stairs. Oil lamps set in wall niches provided the only illumination. The sea wall was moist and smelled of salt, the air was fetid and the heat was so intense that Turk loosened his necktie. He realized he was being escorted to the ancient dungeons below the palace.

Two sentries at the foot of the steps raised lanterns, and did not allow Turk and his companion to pass until the chamberlain showed them a royal seal, stamped on a disc of gold.

They made their way down a long corridor lined with cells, each of them boasting a stone door held in place by bronze hinges.

The corridor opened onto a large, high-vaulted chamber cut out of the solid stone of the natural sea wall, whose rough-hewn walls made it look at first glance like a cave. Illumination was provided by torches set in wall sockets, and Turk was so blinded by the glare that he stumbled over something. As he glanced down he saw it was a thumb screw.

A tall man wearing a *burnoose,* with a brace of pistols in his broad belt, approached the newcomers. Turk swallowed hard when he recognized the emir of Abu Bakr. Suleiman's white shirt and breeches were spattered with blood, and in his hand he carried a heavy bullwhip, which he dropped to the floor as he embraced the American.

"May Allah grant you a long life!" he said. "Kenyon is truly the brother of Suleiman."

"The raid was successful?" Turk knew he had to proceed with care.

"Five were captured. I regret that two escaped, a brother and sister. They, too, will be captured."

So Farima and Ali were still at large.

Suleiman took the arm of his "brother" and led him around the chamber. "That one," he said, kicking a mangled body with a booted foot, "died before we finished questioning him. He was a student, as were those three, who still live."

Turk had to summon all his strength to look at the twisted bodies of three young Arabs. All were unconscious, and had been beaten so badly it was difficult to distinguish them as humans.

"Their heads," Suleiman said, "will be mounted on pikes in the square outside the *suq.* So others who may be thinking of treason will hesitate. We hope to arouse these vermin so they will learn their kismet before they expire. Perhaps you would like to stay, and even help."

Turk was beginning to feel queasy about the consequences of the arrangements he had made earlier in the evening. "I lack Your Highness's courage," he murmured.

Suleiman laughed, accepting the remark as a compliment, and was in high spirits as he led the visitor to the far side of the chamber. There, crumpled on the floor, was another figure. The girl was nude.

Turk barely recognized Judy Hamilton. Her entire body was crisscrossed with welts and raw wounds, her hands were bloody, and even though she was unconscious her puffy face was contorted.

"My God," Turk whispered.

"Not all of the schemers were Abu Bakrians," the Shaikh said.

"This girl is the daughter of Hamilton of Aapco." Turk's voice trembled.

"Well do I know it. She has made no confession yet, which is the reason she still lives. It may be she will implicate her father."

"Impossible." Turk was desperate, but his mind was functioning at top speed. "A frightful mistake has been made, Your Highness."

"My secret police make no mistakes." Suleiman's euphoria vanished.

"The daughter of Hamilton was working for me," Turk said. "It was she who infiltrated the ranks of the Communists on my behalf. It was she who told me of the plot against Your Highness. If it hadn't been for her, the plotters would all still be at large. She is a heroine, and deserves to be rewarded. Instead she has been punished like an enemy." He held his breath, hoping the Shaikh would accept the story.

Suleiman readily took the word of the man who had enabled him to smash the Communists. "It may be," he said,

224

"that one of my helpers was too zealous, and gave the girl no chance to explain herself. I will investigate this tragedy myself, and I give you my word, in Allah's name, that justice will be done in Abu Bakr."

Turk continued to stare down at the still figure of Judy, whose breathing was so shallow he was afraid she might die at any moment. "She needs medical help."

"She will be taken to the American hospital in one of my own cars," Suleiman said, his manner indicating that the honor more than compensated for the torture Judy had been forced to endure.

The night was cool and, as Lee strolled back to the guest house, she reflected that only Americans would use air conditioning in such weather. It was colder outdoors than it had been in the Hamilton house, and she rubbed her arms, wishing she had a sweater. But she didn't want to go indoors right away. The Persian Gulf was at its best after dark, and on a night like this, when there was no moon, the sky was filled with stars.

She stopped to watch a shooting star, and when it disappeared, she sighed. She lit a cigarette and stood quietly, hoping her mood would improve. It was absurd to feel depressed, and she knew it; rarely had she undertaken a less exacting assignment, so she'd be foolish not to take advantage of the opportunity to relax.

Her thoughts drifted to Turk. She could see readily enough why other women were attracted to him, but he failed to arouse her. Perhaps, she thought, she had known too many others who were cast in the same mold.

The truth was that she had become too cynical to develop a genuine interest in any man, and she sighed again, unconsciously.

As Lee entered the front door of the guest house she reached for the light switch in the hall.

The door slammed behind her, and at the same instant a thick arm looped around Lee's neck, choking her and pulling her backward.

She was stunned by the attack, but nevertheless reacted instantly, kicking backward into her assailant's knee, then bringing her heel down on a sandaled toe. The grip around her neck loosened, and she squirmed half free, twisting to face her unseen attacker.

A hand dug into Lee's hair, but, as her wig came free, she landed a karate chop on the side of the other's face, following it with a short punch, as direct and powerful as a man's, to the midriff.

She heard a low moan of pain as the other sank to the floor.

Lee snapped on the light, and was surprised to see the Arab servant girl stretched out in the hallway, the dark wig still clutched in her hand.

"Allah will destroy you!" Farima gasped.

Lee reached into her shoulderbag, and a tiny automatic appeared in her hand. "Save your breath for an explanation."

"You and Kenyon tricked us! You sent us into a trap!" For the first time Farima became aware of the wig, saw that her foe actually had blond hair, and was bewildered.

"That's mine, I believe." Lee scooped up the wig.

"You plotted against us—this proves it!" The Arab girl was screaming.

Lee slapped her hard across the face, then spoke slowly. "Walk into the living room," she said, snapping on additional lights. "One step at a time. And keep your hands over your head. That's right. Now stop and face me." She sat on the edge of a chair, her pistol unwavering and her eyes hard.

Farima turned slowly.

"If you attack every woman you suspect of being Turk Kenyon's mistress, you must be busy."

"Kenyon sent us to our death tonight. Our friends have

been killed. Ali and I have survived because it is Allah's will that we live long enough to avenge ourselves. And you are the partner of Kenyon. You pretend to be one person, but you are another."

"Many women wear wigs. It doesn't mean a thing in my part of the world," Lee said. "I'm not your enemy, and I don't know what you're talking about. But I do want to know. Talk. And tell me from the beginning."

"You are not the partner of Kenyon?"

"I do business with him, but you're welcome to him as a man."

"Allah is my witness that he shall die, as my friends have died tonight."

Lee was irritated. "Sit down before you collapse. All I know is that you tried to strangle me—for no reason I'm aware of."

Farima sank into a chair, covering her face with her hands. "You are not a member of Suleiman's secret police?"

The idea was so ridiculous that Lee laughed. "His Highness doesn't hire infidels."

"That is true." Farima stared at the other girl. "You know nothing of Kenyon's plot against us?"

"Nothing."

"When you came with him to this house," Farima said in a tremulous voice, "he gave me money for the party. It was not the first time."

Lee made a shrewd guess. "The Communist party," she said.

The Arab girl nodded. "He promised to pay much more tonight if all of our leaders were gathered. But Kenyon did not come. Instead the secret police arrived, and Ali and I escaped through a trap door known only to us. The others were captured, and by now they are dead."

"The daughter of Hamilton was there?"

"She was not a leader, but she wished to help us."

The Arab girl's revelations, combined with the telephone

227

conversation Lee had overheard, told her all she needed to know. Turk had mousetrapped a band of bumbling Abu Bakrian idealists who thought of themselves as Communists, arranging their capture to put Suleiman in his debt. And inadvertently catching Red Hamilton's daughter in the net. "What were you going to do after you killed me?"

"I would wait for Kenyon and kill him, too. Before the night ends Ali and I will be captured by the police, but it will no longer matter."

"Where is Ali now?"

The Arab girl was not going to say. "For the moment he is safe. You will not trick me."

"I don't intend to." Lee's mind was working rapidly. "Suppose I give you money so you and Ali can leave the country—"

"I have money, one thousand American dollars that Kenyon gave me today."

"If you try to pay for airplane tickets with dollars, the police will pick you up." Still holding the automatic with one hand, Lee reached into her bag with the other and took out a wad of Abu Bakr:an *rials*. "Here. Buy your tickets with these. The police won't be looking for you there. Most Abu Bakrians can't afford plane seats. The late flight to Cairo leaves at three in the morning. Can you reach the airport by then?"

Farima nodded, her eyes widening as she took the money. "It could be done."

Lee scribbled something unintelligible on a slip of paper. "Tell the stewardess to give this to the co-pilot. He'll give you and Ali passports that will get you into Egypt. They won't be perfect, but they'll work well enough in an emergency. Understand?"

Farima nodded again.

"At the Cairo airport," Lee said, "change some of your American dollars into Egyptian pounds. Then take a taxi to the Al Mokattam Hills, near the old city. Walk to the house of the breadmaker on the street of the Pasha Fuad. Tell those who will greet you there what has happened to you, and of the help Leila has given you. They will assist you, so that you and Ali will live to continue your fight."

"You are a comrade?" Farima asked in a whisper.

"No. And if you're caught before you get out of Abu Bakr, make no mention of me."

"I would die before I betray you!" Clenching her fists, Farima continued to stare at her benefactress. "Why does the woman of Kenyon help me?"

"I'm not his woman. I'm helping you because the day may come when you'll help me. Do the police know you and Ali when they see you?"

"We escaped before they came into the room."

"Good. Then you'll be coming back to Abu Bakr. I may need friends here."

"As Allah is my witness, I swear you eternal friendship." Forgetting the pointed gun, Farima jumped to her feet and kissed the other woman on both cheeks.

"If I were you, I'd leave before Kenyon shows up."

Farima quickly donned her *feredezah* and *yashmak*.

Lee watched through the window as Farima made her way past the other guest houses and disappeared. The chance that the pair could escape from the country was remote, but she had lost nothing except a little money making her gesture, and it might pay off.

It was possible that Turk might not be alone when he returned, and her disguise was imperfect, to say the least. Lee went to her bedroom, combed her wig and put it on again, then spent some time carefully repairing her makeup. She mixed a strong gin and tonic and went into the living room.

She was finishing her third drink when the front door opened and a haggard Turk Kenyon came in.

Lee glanced at her watch, saw that it was after two A.M., and bit back a flippant remark when she saw his eyes.

Turk went straight to the bar and poured himself a stiff Bourbon. "Suleiman was seeing Communists in his closet, and had a bunch of young kids picked up. The Hamiltons' daughter was one of them, the only one still alive when I left. They worked her over in the old dungeons under the palace." He gulped half his drink, and his hand was trembling so violently that he could not light a match.

Lee silently gave him a lighted cigarette.

"Suleiman himself was the chief butcher. He loved every minute of it. Holy God!" He drained his glass and poured a refill. "We rushed her to the hospital in Truman, and the doctors have been standing on their heads for the past couple of hours. They say she'll live."

"Will she recover?"

"Who the hell knows? She has some broken bones, but there's no way of telling the emotional effect on her."

"How did you persuade Suleiman to release her?"

"I convinced him she was a spy for Abu Bakr." He checked himself and stared at her. "That was a pretty good guess."

"I prefer facts to guesses, and the principal fact in which I'm interested is whether Suleiman has agreed to make no deal with the French government."

"I'll see him tomorrow. He'll come through for us." Turk was steadier now; his guard was raised and he continued to watch her.

"I should hope so, after what you've done for him."

"How do you know what I have or haven't done?" he demanded, his tone threatening.

"The same way you know things. I use this." She tapped her forehead.

"And you do a little eavesdropping too?"

"It helps," she said, without a bit of discomfort. "I'm in the information business, you know. You haven't objected to my methods before."

230

"Okay, so you've got the whole pitch. The idea was fool-proof—until that dumb kid stuck her nose in."

Lee moved closer to him. "If you wish," she said, "I'm prepared to abide by our private agreement."

Turk's laugh was harsh. "After what I've seen tonight I'm in no mood for it. For perhaps the first time in my life." He went off to his bedroom and closed the door behind him.

Lee added a splash of gin to her drink, allowed herself a small, satisfied smile, and went off to the bedroom on the right. This was one night the terrible Turk wouldn't live up to his reputation.

Farima could not rid herself of the feeling that she was naked, that the whole world was staring at her. Never before had she worn neither a *feredezah* nor a *yashmak* in public, and she clung to Ali, hugging his arm as they made their way down the broad boulevard to the address they had been given by the breadmaker. It didn't matter that the streets of Cairo were filled with women in Western clothing, women in short skirts and skimpy blouses, women in pants, women in dresses, or that most of them were Arabs who were indifferent to the men with whom they shared the sidewalks. They were enjoying their freedom, but the sudden realization of Farima's goal overwhelmed her.

Thanks to Ali's protective air the men who looked at her quickly averted their eyes. It was comforting to know that he felt as she did, that he glared at anyone who dared to let his gaze linger on her for more than an instant. But Ali was confused, too, and could not help gaping at the breasts and buttocks and legs being exhibited with such abandon. Brother and sister found it difficult to believe they were still in Islam, that the hurrying pedestrians and the occupants of the countless automobiles were devout worshippers of Allah.

So much had happened in so short a time that they were still dazed. Thanks to the bribe of a hundred dollars in

American money they had given the Abu Bakrian immigration inspector at the El Ain airport they had been permitted to leave their homeland without passports, and no record of their departure appeared on the airport logs. Their blonde benefactress had not played them false, and everything had happened as she had said it would: the co-pilot of the airplane had provided them with passports that had won them admission to Cairo, and the breadmaker had asked no questions, but had given them shelter for the night. This morning he had supplied them with the address of a small restaurant in the heart of the city, indicating they would be met there by someone who would offer additional help.

"Allah," the young man said, "is guiding our footsteps."

"Why did that girl at the guest house assist us? We are forever in her debt," Farima murmured.

The restaurant was small and crowded with men drinking Turkish coffee, but no one bothered to look at the brother and sister from Abu Bakr who hesitated at the entrance.

Farima was frightened, although her confidence was partly restored when she saw two young women chatting at a small table. The male patrons were not molesting them, and they appeared at ease, apparently confident that no harm would come to them.

Summoning his courage, Ali followed the instructions the breadmaker had given him, and he walked to a rear table. Farima followed so close behind him that she had to take care not to step on his heels. A shirtsleeved waiter brought them coffee, and they were so ravenous that they ordered patties filled with chopped meat like those they saw at an adjoining table. Ali felt slightly foolish because he didn't know what the dish was called.

A man in a Western suit sat down unbidden in the empty chair at their table, and they took what comfort they could from the fact that he was a dark-skinned Arab.

"When you leave this place," he said without preamble,

speaking an accentless Arabic that did not reveal his national origins, "buy yourselves clothes that will make you look like Egyptians. Anyone can tell you come from the Gulf states." He peered at them, his expression neither friendly nor disapproving. "How much money do you have?"

Ali was guarded. "Enough."

The man showed impatience. "How much?"

"Almost seven hundred American dollars, a little of it in Egyptian pounds."

"Enough for three or four months, if you're careful, but you will need some of it for your return fare to Abu Bakr and other expenses. So, after we find you a little apartment, we'll need to get work for both of you. Can you read and write?"

Ali was proud of his accomplishments. "Of course."

The man turned to Farima, raising an eyebrow.

Too shy to speak, she could only shake her head. For the first time in her life she was ashamed of being illiterate.

"We'll get you a position as a clerk," the man told Ali. "It will not be easy to find something for the girl, but we may be able to place her as a cigarette seller in a nightclub."

Ali stiffened. "What would be expected of her in such a place?"

"She will wear a costume that will show off her legs, and she will go from table to table selling cigarettes. And you needn't frown. This is an expensive city, so you'll need work, and you're in no position to turn up your noses. Her body is an asset, so we'll use it."

Farima was mortified, and felt trapped.

"You will stay here," the man said, "until the authorities in Abu Bakr have forgotten you. Six months, perhaps, if you enjoy Allah's favor, or as long as a year."

Ali shook his head. "You don't understand. I have an important mission."

The man was amused. "I know more than you realize.

The party you represent is banned in Egypt, and if the police learn of your affiliation you'll be sent to prison."

"I have risked my life and my sister's for our beliefs! If you are a true comrade—"

"I'm not." The man cut him off. "I have no connection with your party, and I'm convinced you represent a cause that will never gain a foothold in Islam."

Brother and sister were puzzled. "I assumed you were one of us," Ali said. "If you are not, why do you help us?"

The man worded his reply with care. "Your enemy is my enemy," he said. "I have my own reasons for wanting to see him driven into exile. It is my hope that he'll be replaced by someone more moderate and intelligent."

"You're wrong," Ali said fiercely. "All members of his family are the same. It is the system that must be changed."

"Believe what you please," the man said. "What you will do when you return to Abu Bakr helps me, and that's all I ask."

Ali ate the last of his meat patty, sipped his coffee. "Very well," he said at last, "I will become your ally. And I will be patient for a personal reason. We also have a private mission."

Again the man raised an eyebrow.

Farima broke her silence. "We must avenge our honor," she said, "by killing the American who betrayed us. It doesn't matter if we must wait six months or a year. We will not rest until he dies."

Foreigners were never granted audiences in the private office of the ruling Shaikh, and Turk Kenyon was elated when the palace chamberlain took him there. His pleasure faded, however, when he saw that Suleiman ben Yosef al-Husayn was in a foul mood.

"My generals and colonels are fools," Suleiman said. "They claim they have searched every house in the old town and have sent patrols as far as the Oasis of Qar. But they cannot find the man and woman who escaped from our net last night. Abu Bakr is a small country, yet they insist the pair has disappeared."

Turk had his own reasons for hoping Farima and her brother would be found and executed. "Your army and your secret police are noted for their efficiency, Your Highness. I feel sure the Communists will be captured."

Suleiman shook his head. "Only this morning I learned that no watch was maintained at the airport or the docks. They could have escaped by air or sea."

"Well, good riddance to them if they're gone, Your Highness. You smashed their organization, and it will be a long time before they can establish another network in Abu Bakr."

The Shaikh allowed himself to be mollified. "By now," he said, "everyone in El Ain has seen the heads of the traitors in the square. And not an hour ago my air force reported that entire caravans of Bedouins are heading toward the city from every part of the desert to see the sight for themselves. The word has spread to the farthest reaches of the country."

"Those who plot against you won't dare raise their heads again."

"I intend to make certain of it," Suleiman said. "My secret police are making an investigation at the airport and the docks to find out if any man who wears my uniform accepted *baksheesh* from the man and woman in return for allowing them to flee. If we find such a man, his head will join those of the other traitors." He paused. "You are an exceptional man, my brother. You do not ask for a reward, but if it were not for you, the traitors would still be plotting against me."

"I do not seek personal gain, Your Highness." Turk tried to sound casual. "But there is one small favor I'd like to ask."

"Name it!"

"I hope Your Highness will reject the new offer the French soon will make to you."

The Shaikh was amused. "What would you gain if I were to send the French away with empty hands?"

"Nothing for myself," Turk said. "Aapco would be pleased, and would give me the credit."

"They would pay you higher wages?"

"I don't think so. I'd have greater prestige because they would believe I have the power to influence Your Highness."

Suleiman's sudden, loud laugh filled the small room. "Then you may consider it done. I will not entertain the offer of France, no matter what it might be." He laughed again.

Turk couldn't understand the reason for his laughter, but it was enough that he was agreeing to turn away the French. "I'm grateful to my brother."

"Allah would think me ungrateful if I failed to offer you some token of my love for you." Suleiman reached into his belt and drew a handsome double-edged knife with a hilt of solid gold.

Turk accepted it with a deep bow. "I'll carry your gift to the end of my days," he said, and bowed again as he left the room.

He drove from the palace to Truman and parked behind the three-story compound hospital. In its twenty-five years of existence it had become one of the best in the Middle East. While it served the American colony, most of its patients were Abu Bakrians who had overcome their suspicious hostility to Western medicine. Nine physicians and surgeons, three anesthetists, twenty-six registered nurses, and eleven technicians, all Americans, comprised the staff. They soon would be joined by four Abu Bakrian interns who had just been awarded medical degrees in the United States.

Dr. Abner Keating, the chief of staff, who had been the neighbor of the Hamiltons for more than twenty years, received his visitor in his office and carefully closed the door. "Suleiman," he said, "is a throwback to the barbarians of the Middle Ages. Judy has two broken ribs, a compound fracture of an ankle and more deep lacerations than we could count."

"How is she, Doctor?"

"Everything considered, in fairly good shape. She'll recover, thanks to her youth and basic good health, and the scars will fade. I'm concerned about her ankle, though; I'm afraid she may have a permanent limp."

"How long will it take until she's up and around?"

"That's hard to say, Mr. Kenyon. Ruth and Red want her sent to a hospital in the States for therapy, but I've treated her since she was a baby and want to keep an eye on her for a while."

"May I see her, Doctor?"

"I'd rather you wait a day or two."

"Well, I've just cleaned up my business here, so I may be heading back to Europe later in the day. And I'd very much like to look in on her for a minute."

The physician hesitated. "No more than a minute. Ordinarily I wouldn't allow anyone but immediate family into her room, but I understand you were responsible for her rescue, so you've more than earned the right. Just remember she's still under sedation, and don't say anything that might upset her. Room two fourteen."

Judy Hamilton, swathed in bandages, lay with her eyes closed as Turk came into her room. Then she opened one eye, recognized him, and smiled. "They tell me I'm indebted to you."

"No such thing," Turk assured her. "How are you?"

"Not very well."

"I can imagine. Judy, I want you to listen to me carefully. Besides your parents you and I are the only people who know about the friends you had. I got you released last night by telling Suleiman you were an undercover agent,

237

that your whole purpose in going to that house was to expose the Communist movement here. Stick to that story. Permanently. Suleiman would have you hauled out of here by force if he knew the truth, and your father would be in a bad jam, too, as would Aapco."

"I understand." She moistened her cracked, swollen lips. "But Ali and Farima know better."

"They escaped, and they haven't been found. My hunch is that they skipped the country, although I can't imagine how they could have managed it without professional help."

"Thank God," she said. "I've been worrying about them. How come you weren't picked up too?"

So she knew of his supposed intention of meeting the Abu Bakrian Communist leaders. "Your folks invited me to dinner. There was no way I could slip away."

Judy accepted his story at face value, perhaps because she was incapable of thinking clearly. "You're lucky. You can't imagine—how awful—it was."

"I'm afraid I can. I saw you in the dungeons just before I got you out."

A shudder shook the girl's torture-racked body.

"Don't think about it."

"I'll never think of anything else," Judy said.

Turk's conscience bothered him on the drive back to Eisenhower, but he consoled himself with the thought that the French deal was killed. He might not get a pay raise, but he was in a position to put the heat on old McIntosh for a long-term contract, and he had no intention of being shunted aside.

Turk found Lee in the living room of the guest house, drinking coffee and reading a day-old edition of the Paris *Herald Tribune*. "Mission accomplished," he told her. "Suleiman is going to kiss off the French."

Lee put aside her newspaper. "You're sure?"

"He gave me the pledge of a brother."

238

"Congratulations," Lee said, her expression echoing the admiration in her voice. "I've enjoyed watching you in action. Nicely done."

"I've also rounded off the corners. I've just come from the hospital, and Judy Hamilton is going to be okay."

"Which will prevent you from suffering a relapse. You were in rare shape last night."

"If you had seen the dungeons—"

"Spare me, please. Suleiman already causes me quite enough nightmares."

Turk had no desire to pursue the subject. "Hamilton ought to be home, so I'll tell him the news about France. Then I'll be back." He paused, then spoke with care. "We can take the early flight to Paris, and have the whole afternoon to ourselves. I'm in a mood to celebrate. I'll be back before you know it."

He walked the short distance to the Hamilton house, and found that, as he had thought, Red had just returned home. Haggard after a sleepless night, the Hamiltons showed little pleasure when he told them of Suleiman's promise to him.

"Are you trying to tell us she really was an undercover agent?" Red demanded.

Turk smiled. "Strictly between the three of us, I want Suleiman to keep believing it, so he doesn't take her into custody again."

"Over my dead body," Red said.

"He could arrange that, too, so keep your story straight. Judy was no more a secret agent than she was a member of the Abu Bakr Communist party. My own hunch is that she happened to be on hand when the government made its roundup. But I have Suleiman believing my tale, so Judy is partly responsible for his agreement to turn down the French."

"Fair enough," Red said. "But why perpetuate a lie by repeating it to Aapco?"

"You're a little slow today," Turk interjected. "It was your daughter's presence in the old town last night that convinced Suleiman he owes us a favor."

"Suppose there had been no raid." Red was puzzled. "What persuasion were you planning to use when you saw the Shaikh?"

Turk sidestepped. "It doesn't matter now."

"There's something in all this that doesn't hang together," Red said. "Ruth and I are grateful to you for stepping in the way you did, and for persuading the Shaikh to release Judy. But it was all so fortuitous I can't help wondering if you've left out a chunk of the puzzle."

Ruth was annoyed. "We hashed all this out this morning, Lyman. Unless Turk is clairvoyant he couldn't have known of the raid in advance, and he had no more idea than the rest of us where Judy was going when she raced off to El Ain."

"You could be right." Red's gaze was level as he measured the other man. "For his sake, I hope you are."

Turk was glad to escape, and put the Hamiltons out of his mind as he walked back to the guest house. He would send a victory cable to McIntosh and then he would devote the rest of the day to Lee. He'd open a bottle of champagne, and if they were too busy to eat they would have their next meal on the flight to Paris.

She wasn't in the living room, and he was immediately suspicious when he saw her bedroom door ajar. That room was empty too, but a note awaited him on the dressing table:

Turk:
    You did so well here that you made it unnecessary for me to stay any longer. I have urgent business elsewhere, so I'll say goodbye until our paths happen to cross again.
                                                                            L.
P.S. I was ready to fulfill my part of the bargain last night, but you, with reason, did not accept. Enough said.

Twelve

◆◆◆◆◆◆◆◆◆◆◆◆◆◆◆◆◆◆◆◆◆◆◆◆◆◆
◆◆◆◆◆◆◆◆◆◆◆◆◆◆◆◆◆◆◆◆◆◆◆◆◆

At sundown a brunette entered the house of the Cairo bread-maker; an hour later a green-eyed blonde emerged, with tags for New York on her baggage and a U.S. passport in her shoulderbag. She went by cab to the Nile Hilton, where a suite had been engaged in a name that matched the pass-port. She cashed an American traveler's check at the cashier's window, asked directions to a renowned restaurant, and had the doorman commandeer a taxi for her.

She dined alone. Pleading ignorance of Arabic, she re-quested a translation of the menu. Following the suggestions of the maitre d', she ordered *maza,* a plate of assorted hors d'oeuvres, followed by *hamama mishwi,* or grilled pigeon. She ended her meal with a cup of strong Turkish coffee, which she drank unsweetened. Still playing the role of a tourist, she took another taxi to a shopping street in the vicinity of the Citadel, Cairo's great fortress. Her timing exquisite, she arrived moments before the retail establishments closed for the night. She entered a jewelry store, whose proprietor, an elderly Arab, welcomed her. "*Ahlan wa sahlan,*" he said.

"Good evening," she replied. "I'm looking for a gold wrist-watch."

"We have many I can show you," the old man said.

The girl moved quickly to the rear of the store. As she parted the drapes and started up a flight of stairs, the proprietor locked the door, turned off the lights, then followed her.

She awaited him in a small office dominated by a heavy safe. "*Shalom,* Yacob," she said.

"*Shalom,* Leah," he replied, kissing her on the cheek. "I was a little surprised when I heard from Itzak that you had arrived. I wasn't expecting you for another few days. You had troubles in El Ain?"

Leah, sometimes known as Lee and other times as Leila, laughed. "You worry like a grandfather, Yacob. Everything went perfectly. Suleiman will reject any offer the French may make."

"Then you've done it again."

"Not this time," she said. "Kenyon handled the whole caper himself while I sat in the Aapco guest house and waited for him."

"Tell me."

Leah gave him a detailed account of what had taken place in Abu Bakr.

"I think," Yacob said, "that I'll give you full credit in my report to Jerusalem."

"That's very generous of you."

"I'm never generous," the old man said. "The General is submitting his budget request this week, and he's more likely to get the entire amount if he can tell the Cabinet you spoiled the French deal."

"I might have guessed."

"There is another reason, as well."

"This time I don't have to guess. The General is going back on his promise to let me go home to Israel on a full month's leave. You have another impossible assignment for me."

Yacob's manner became soothing. "A new assignment, yes. But so easy and so pleasant it's almost like a holiday."

"I can hardly wait to hear it."

"You go to America."

"Which is not going home on leave."

"Well, no," the old man said. "That much I must admit. But there's no danger, no problems. You're to meet the top echelon at American-Arabian Petroleum and find out what action they would take if Suleiman expropriates their holdings in Abu Bakr."

"So the General is borrowing trouble again."

"Not the General!" Yacob was horrified. "The Jerusalem bureaucrats. You know how they think."

"There's no risk, you say, but I think there is. Kenyon will be going to New York soon, and it won't be long before he figures out my identity and my employers."

"Kenyon I'm not worried about. He's proved useful to us."

"Yes," Leah said, "but he's creating personal problems now. I had to give him the slip today, or I'd have had to spend the whole afternoon in bed with him."

"For that," the old man replied, "you should get something solid in return."

"The same thoughts have occurred to both of us, Yacob. Suppose I tell Kenyon who I am before he works it out for himself, and swear him to secrecy. That will make him feel important, which he loves."

"But will he keep his mouth closed?"

"He'll have no choice." Leah's manner became cold. "He set up the raid in El Ain, and if Hamilton of Aapco ever learns Kenyon was responsible for his daughter's torture, that will be the end of Kenyon. Literally. If he talks, I'll talk."

243

Yacob nodded in approval. "I'm listening."

"The rest is obvious. When do I leave for New York?"

"Jerusalem allows you to settle the details yourself. But I have a quarrel of my own with you. Why did you send those naive Abu Bakrians to us through the underground? A boy who knows nothing but thinks the world of himself. And that girl! Good only for a tussle, if one likes them chubby. And don't tell me you felt sorry for them. In our business there is no place for such feelings!"

His indignation caused Leah to smile. "What's happened to your imagination, Yacob? That boy and girl are beholden to me for their lives. They'll do anything I want. Think of it—native Abu Bakrians who know every back alley in El Ain. When we're facing a fluid situation there and don't know what may happen from one day to the next, that boy and girl could be worth their weight in solid gold."

"If it will make you happy," Yacob said, "I'll grant your point."

"I should see them, preferably tonight, so I can leave for the new assignment tomorrow."

The old man smiled. "The girl has a job, a cigarette girl in a nightclub, the Pyramids. Her brother is so afraid of what will happen to her that he's spending the evening sitting at a table there, but he's so busy watching the belly dancers he doesn't see the customers pinching his sister's bottom. A classic case."

"There's nothing more natural than a visit to a nightclub by an American tourist. Where is this place?"

"Not so fast, Leah," the old man said. "To this dump you don't go alone. Not even a crazy American tourist would go there by herself!"

"Then provide me with a guide."

Yacob's smile was weary. "I put Moishe in charge of them, and these days he looks more like an Egyptian guide than any Egyptian. Wait until you see him, you won't believe it."

"I'll believe anything of Moishe. Tell him to pick me up at the Hilton in an hour." Leah kissed Yacob on the forehead. "Do you want me to report to the embassy in Washington?"

"Telephone them as a courtesy, nothing more, and don't go to Washington. There aren't many beautiful women there, and you'd attract too much attention."

"Give my love to the General, Yacob. But don't tell him I'll fly direct to Israel to make my next report in person—before the Jerusalem bureaucrats find still another assignment for me."

The Pyramids was one of the sleaziest clubs in a city renowned for low-class night spots, but Farima thought she was in heaven. The tiny stage was an enchantment, the trio that alternated between rock tunes and Arabian numbers played celestial music, and the patrons, half of them Egyptians and the others visiting tourists, were sleek, expensively dressed, and generous beyond belief.

She knew, of course, that she wasn't being given tips because of her efficiency as a cigarette seller. The patrons were drinking expensive Western drinks or Turkish *raki,* and the alcohol put them in an expansive frame of mind, particularly after they caressed her behind or her breasts. Ali would be furious if he saw what some of the patrons were doing to her in the darkened room, but Farima actually didn't mind being pawed. Men were finding her attractive, which she found flattering; they did her no harm. After spending her entire life being hidden beneath a *feredezah,* she enjoyed their attention.

Her costume was outrageous. The high-heeled pumps and black mesh stockings hurt her feet; the skirt, what there was of it, revealed her thighs, and her breasts almost popped into the open whenever she bent down to give a customer his change. *Bismi 'llah!* In a scant forty-eight hours her entire approach to life had been turned upside down, and the change made her almost deliriously happy. For the first time in her life, she was her own person, free of Muslim tradition and demands.

It did not occur to Farima that her own outlook on life had changed so appreciably that her goals were altered too. In Abu Bakr, where women were still condemned to the servitude imposed on them by traditionalist Muslim views, she had sought freedom for herself, her sex, all the oppressed. But now that she had unlimited personal freedom in Cairo, she had unthinkingly fallen under the spell of the teachings to which she had been subjected all her life. Women, the old-fashioned Muslims believed, could not curb their erotic desires. She was convinced that the way of life she had adopted was natural, not only for her but for all women like her.

Ali persisted in hovering over her, but she would not permit him to jeopardize her new freedom. Farima warned herself, however, not to borrow trouble. She could see that Ali was infatuated with one of the belly dancers, a scrawny creature with dyed red hair, and it was possible that his own new involvements would keep him too busy to maintain his traditional role of chaperone.

Farima completed her rounds of the tables, her smile unwavering as men groped and pinched and stroked her in the darkened room, and the approving nod the maitre d' gave her told her she was a natural whose attitude made her job secure.

She returned to her station near the cloakroom, where patrons could see her as they arrived. Wondering whether she dared to remove her shoes to relieve the agony in her feet, she straightened as the street door opened, and forgot her discomfort when she saw her Egyptian mentor, the man who had gotten her the job. Farima started to smile with delight when she saw, with him, the girl from the Aapco guest house who had saved her and Ali.

The blonde swept past her without a flicker of recognition,

and Farima froze, realizing the woman undoubtedly had reasons for ignoring her.

The beaming maitre d' approached the newly arrived couple.

"Madame," the Egyptian said, "has been told this is one of the naughtiest clubs in the city, and she wished to see it for herself. But she doesn't want to be any more conspicuous than necessary, so give us a table in the rear. Bring us champagne, and make certain it is French, not bottled gas from Beirut. Madame may be American, but she knows real champagne from the imitation."

A bottle of champagne resting in a tarnished ice bucket was served with ceremony, and a moment later Ali was called to the table. He bowed awkwardly over the hand the blonde extended to him, and Farima smiled. Her curiosity overwhelming, she remembered she had duties to perform, and she sauntered to the table herself.

The Egyptian paid her a pound for a pack of the cheapest local cigarettes, an exorbitant price, and then said, "Sit down, please."

Uncertain whether the maitre d' permitted such familiarity, Farima hesitated.

"The management has granted permission," the Egyptian said in a loud voice. "Madame knows no Arabs, and this gentleman has consented to answer some of her questions. She would like to speak with you, too."

Farima sat, surreptitiously wriggling out of her shoes.

"Since Madame speaks no Arabic," the Egyptian said, "I will translate for her."

The blonde looked straight at the other girl, and one heavily made-up eyelid fluttered in the suggestion of a wink. "Speak very softly," she murmured, "so no one will hear us."

Ali, who was just beginning to guess the blonde's identity, hunched forward in his chair.

Farima moved closer too. "I cannot tell you how grateful

I am to you," she said. "Only by looking into my heart will you know."

"I know," the blonde said.

Ali swallowed hard, then turned to his sister. "Is she the one who—"

"Yes," Farima replied hastily, cutting him off.

He blinked as he gazed at their benefactress. "What can I do to repay you?"

"Nothing," the blonde said.

Ali stared at her. "But you took risks for our sake, and you gave my sister a large sum of money. Surely you had a reason for helping us."

"You were in great danger, and I knew you would be tortured and beheaded if you were caught. Wasn't that reason enough?"

He nodded.

"It may be," the blonde said vaguely, "that some day you will be in a position to do me a favor."

"Anything!" Ali was fervent.

"There is a tie that binds us together," she said. "You believe, as I do, that your country will be a happier land if the man who sits on the throne is removed."

Ali smiled broadly at her. "I would give my life for that day!"

"Let us hope," the blonde replied, "that the goal can be achieved quietly, without shedding blood."

The Egyptian called for additional glasses, then poured champagne into them. "We will drink to our friendship," he said.

Ali was shocked, and could not conceal his feelings.

"You are in Cairo now," Farima told him, deep scorn in her voice. "Here we aren't stoned as infidels for drinking spirits." She lifted her glass, spilling some of the contents because her gesture was too vehement. She tasted the champagne, smiled, and drained her glass. "If Mohammed had tasted this," she said, "he would not have banned it."

248

Ali, not to be outdone, sipped his wine, then made a wry face. "It is rancid," he said. "Allah does not want me to drink spirits."

The blonde seemed to understand. "You must be true to yourself and your faith," she said.

The expression in the young man's eyes indicated he was already falling in love with her.

"Live as you would in your own land while you are in Cairo," she said. "Prepare yourself for the day when you will return to your home. I will know when the time is ripe for your next move, and if I don't get in touch with you myself, my friends will bring you a message on my behalf."

"I will wait forever!" Ali said.

"It won't be that long." The blonde turned to Farima. "You are making a new life for yourself here. That is good."

The Arab girl was elated. The woman understood her.

"When the time comes," the blonde asked, "will you be ready, too, to join hands with me?"

"May Allah curse me for all eternity if I fail you," Farima said.

The blonde looked at the Egyptian, who handed wads of paper money to brother and sister. "The American lady," he said loudly, "thanks you for your patience. She has learned much about Arab life from you."

Ali stood, bowed stiffly, and returned to his own table.

Farima jammed her protesting feet into her high-heeled shoes and picked up her cigarette tray. "No matter what you may ask of me," she whispered in parting, "I will do it. That is my sacred vow, and I swear it in Allah's name."

The sentries at the American compound were stunned when they saw the approaching limousines, all three flying royal pennants of blue and white. Soldiers filled the first and third cars, but a glance at the figure who sat alone in the rear of the center car was sufficient to identify the ruling Shaikh. The limousines were waved through the gate, and a quick telephone call alerted headquarters of the unprecedented honor. The word was given to every installation, and general manager Hamilton recessed the meeting over which he was presiding.

Because the driver of the first car stopped to ask directions, it was possible to learn the Shaikh's destination, and Dr. Keating stood at the entrance to the hospital when the cars halted in the driveway.

The soldiers leaped out, brandishing their sub-machine guns.

Suleiman took his time, and his men formed in a semicircle around him as he approached the physician.

Keating's bow was as perfunctory as his voice was dry. "Welcome, Your Highness."

"I am much in the debt of the daughter of Hamilton," Suleiman said, "I wish to express my thanks to her."

The doctor was afraid of the complications that a refusal might cause, but the health of his patient was his primary concern. "She is not allowed to see visitors as yet."

"I bring her a small gift." The Shaikh's attitude made it plain that he would not be denied in his own realm.

Keating realized the incident would be magnified beyond the limits of reasonable reality if he refused. "Very well," he said. "I'll take you to her. But she suffered a great shock, and I know you will not want to stay for more than a moment."

The soldiers moved forward in a body as their master started up the hospital steps.

Keating paused with his hand on the door. "I'm sorry, Your Highness, but I can't allow my hospital to be disrupted by your troops. They'll have to wait for you out here."

The officer in charge made a threatening gesture with his sub-machine gun.

The doctor held his ground. "This is a place where the sick are healed. It is not a military parade ground."

Suleiman was in a benevolent mood. "I am safe here," he

told the troop commander. "You will wait, as the physician has suggested."

The officer was unhappy, but had no choice.

Keating and the Shaikh went into the hospital alone.

"When I was last in London," Suleiman said, "some X-ray pictures of me were made on Harley Street. You have such machines here?"

"No equipment is more modern or complete than mine, Your Highness." The doctor led the way up a flight of stairs to the second floor.

"I am no longer able to travel to London," the Shaikh said, pleased by the discovery that the hospital might be of benefit to him. "One day, soon, I will allow you to take pictures of me with your X-ray machine."

Keating concealed his feelings beneath a professional demeanor. "Give me twenty-four hours' notice, and we'll be at your disposal."

A *No Visitors* sign was hanging on the door of Judy Hamilton's room. Keating turned the knob and entered, Suleiman close beside him.

The girl appeared to be sleeping, and the doctor raised a finger to his lips.

At that moment Judy opened her eyes and saw Suleiman standing at the foot of the bed. Her terror was so great she failed to see the doctor beside him, and she emitted a hoarse, piercing scream that echoed down the quiet corridor.

Keating unceremoniously pushed the Shaikh out of the room, pausing just long enough to tell an approaching nurse to administer a sedative.

Red Hamilton, who had tracked the Shaikh to the hospital, started to run down the corridor toward the two men.

"As I told you," Keating said, "the young lady is still in a state of shock."

Suleiman straightened his *agal*, and turned to Red. "It grieves me that your daughter is so ill," he said, and handed him a small box. "Give this to her for me when she begins to recover." Not waiting for a reply, he moved away and vanished down the stairs.

Red opened the box and saw a ruby and diamond bracelet worth a fortune. Tears of rage came to his eyes, and he had to resist the impulse to hurl the glittering toy at the wall.

A private three-minute ceremony, with a Maryland justice of the peace officiating, changed Bobbie's status from that of executive secretary to that of executive wife. However, she reflected, as she stretched out on a deck chair on board the Aapco yacht as it slowly cruised through the waters of the Chesapeake Bay, only the externals were changed.

She had been Mrs. Dugald McIntosh for seventy-two hours and, as she had anticipated, she had traded her freedom for security beyond her dreams. Her gains were staggering, but she was just beginning to appreciate the extent of her losses. In another day she and Dug would return to New York after an abbreviated honeymoon, taking up residence in a hotel suite until she had time to furnish the penthouse apartment he had bought for them.

In the past three days she had acquired a fur coat, jewelry, a parcel of real estate in her own name, and the undying hatred of Dug's sons and daughters-in-law. The ink was still fresh on the newspaper headlines announcing her marriage to one of America's more prominent tycoons, but only she knew that her second husband, thirty years her senior, was not the lover her first husband was.

That was the least of her worries, since she had learned there were plenty of compensations. What bothered her was the knowledge that she had exchanged an eight hour per day, five day per week job for one that knew no limits.

Dug joined her on the aft deck, dropping into a chair beside her after spending three quarters of an hour talking to Beirut. His frown indicated that he was concentrating on business.

"What time tomorrow does our flight get us to Kennedy?" he asked.

"One o'clock." Bobbie continued to face into the sun.

"If you take our luggage to the hotel, I could schedule an executive committee meeting at two."

"Easily, dear."

"Okay, call the meeting." He paused, as though he had forgotten himself, then spoke less brusquely. "I'll appreciate it, I should have said, if you'll notify the office and ask them to schedule the meeting. While you're at it, I'd like last week's production figures and an up-to-date chart on tanker movements. I've been out of touch these past few days."

"Detained by personal business," Bobbie said.

McIntosh placed a hand on her bare arm, and his tone was apologetic. "I'm not giving you much of a honeymoon."

"I disagree." Bobbie favored him with the smile he expected. "Am I complaining?"

"You wouldn't, but I can guess what you're thinking. I depended on you in the office, and I can't seem to break old habits overnight."

"I spoke to the office after lunch, while you were taking your nap," she said. "The Delaware refinery operated at ninety-three percent of capacity this past week. Hector Bell and his wife have invited us to Oyster Bay for the weekend. I've accepted. Senator Watrous has been trying to reach you, I don't know why, and I told his office you'd return his call after three. And I cabled Turk in Paris under your signature, telling him he's been celebrating in Paris long enough, and that you expect to see him in your office on Wednesday at ten."

"I shouldn't have taken you off the payroll."

She smiled. "You'll find I'm more expensive this way."

McIntosh hesitated. "Do you suppose Kenyon knows—about us?"

"He does if he reads the newspapers. Provided he's been

sober enough since he hit Paris." She yawned. "I really don't care what he's heard, and I hope you don't, either."

"I'm bothered, and I don't know why," he admitted.

"If you let him see how you feel, Turk will take advantage," Bobbie said. "He'll act like a member of the family unless you slap him into place."

"That won't be difficult."

"Just so you know, dear." She reached for her sandals. "I'll get busy on those calls so that the members of the executive committee can change their other appointments for tomorrow."

McIntosh watched her as she made her way forward on the deck, and told himself that his was the best of all possible worlds.

Turk buckled his seat belt, asked the stewardess for coffee laced with brandy for his hangover, and settled back for a lazy examination of the *Herald Tribune* and the London newspapers. He hadn't yet recovered from the discovery, thirty-six hours earlier, that his former wife had married Dugald McIntosh, but he had virtually convinced himself that his own standing at Aapco would not be affected. His success in persuading Shaikh Suleiman to make no deal with the French government spoke for itself, no matter what Bobbie might be telling McIntosh about him. The whole front office knew of the power he could exert in Abu Bakr, and to hell with Bobbie.

Someone took the seat adjacent to his, but he did not look up from his newspaper. It was a long flight from Paris to New York, and he was in no mood for idle conversation with a stranger.

"Good morning," Leah said.

She looked like a travel ad in her off-white pantsuit, but Turk regarded her sourly. "You again."

"I'm sorry."

"You make a habit of it." He returned to his newspaper.

Leah was not discouraged. "It isn't accidental that I'm sitting next to you. I had to go to considerable bother to make the arrangements, you know."

"I'm flattered to death." He gulped his coffee.

The 747 began to taxi toward the runway, and Leah handed his empty cup and saucer to the stewardess. "You won't accept my apology?"

"Sure, but nuts to that. You've made me feel like an idiot twice. Twice is enough."

As the airplane gathered speed before takeoff Leah took his face in both hands, drew him closer, and kissed him, her lips parting as she pressed a hand against the back of his head.

They were airborne when she released him. "Now you're talking my language," Turk said, lighting two cigarettes and handing her one, then asking the stewardess for two glasses of champagne.

But Leah saw he was still wary. "You've made reservations at the Plaza. So have I. Change that to a suite for both of us, and I'll spend the next three to four weeks with you. No conditions, no tricks."

He studied her at length. "There must be something you want."

"There is. An introduction to the top brass at Aapco. My employer wants some information from them."

Turk realized she was giving information. "Okay, who are you working for?"

"The government of Israel."

"That's the one possibility I hadn't figured. Stupid of me, Lee."

"Leah."

Their champagne was served, and, still studying the girl, he raised his glass to her. "Why are you coming clean with me all of a sudden?"

"You're Aapco's expert on Abu Bakr. I've been ordered to concentrate my efforts there too. We've proved we can achieve results when we work together, and I'm proposing a closer alliance. Also, as you might say, I'm making the stakes more attractive to you."

"To make my job easier," Turk said, "I've created some legends about myself. According to one of the more popular ones, no woman can resist me. But you've proved that one is phony. So what do you get out of a partnership?"

"First, the information my superiors want," Leah said. "Second, a continuing relationship that brings results." She smiled and raised her glass to him. "As to whether you're irresistible, I haven't found out yet. But that's the next step on the agenda."

"Well, it would seem I have nothing to lose." Turk weighed the various angles. "What is it your people want to know?"

"What Aapco will do if Suleiman nationalizes Abu Bakr oil."

"Brother! Do your people really think he'll go that far?"

"Our government doesn't confide in me," Leah said. "They give me instructions, and I do what I'm told."

"Suleiman is erratic, so no one can pin him down," Turk said, "but I don't believe he'll nationalize. Do you know what makes your bosses think he will?"

"I can guess," Leah said. "He's poured money into anti-Israeli organizations, and it isn't his fault that attempts to create an increased anti-Jewish spirit around the world have backfired. Like so many Arab leaders, he fails to realize that now the West is too busy hating Arabs to return to the old pastime of hating Jews. But if Suleiman trebles or quadruples his income, which is what expropriation will do, he'll have that much more cash for his pet projects."

He thought for a time, then shook his head. "I wouldn't want to go out on a limb. You know him better than I do. What's your reaction?"

"I wouldn't put anything past him," Leah said.

Turk thought of Judy Hamilton's battered body. "You could be right. And if he decides to nationalize, Aapco will panic, that's for sure. The company has billions at stake."

"They'll recover from their panic," she said. "What then?"

"Aside from turning the legal department loose—which will accomplish nothing—it's hard to say. Only Dugald McIntosh can provide the answers, if he's thought that far ahead. This much I know. He's tough, and he won't allow himself to be driven out of business without a hard fight."

"Then your Mr. McIntosh is my immediate target."

Turk's grin was sour. "You might do better to find an approach to him other than through me. He and my ex-wife got married this past weekend, so I may not be his favorite troubleshooter any more."

"That doesn't worry me at all," she said. "I've known she was after him for a long time, and wasn't surprised when the marriage was reported to me. I was wondering if *you'd* tell me." She laughed.

"I hate like hell to interrupt your honeymoon, Dug, but this is serious." Senator Herbert Watrous paced the length of the hotel living room.

"We were coming back today anyway," McIntosh told him. "What's wrong, Herb?"

"Nothing. Yet. But it will. The State Department showed me a confidential cable from Chris Trevenian in El Ain. Your boy—what's his name?—Kenyon—apparently pulled off a real coup when he persuaded Suleiman to make no deal with France. But the Shaikh has had time to do a little thinking, in true Arab style, and he's hungry."

McIntosh fingered an unlighted cigar. "Figures."

"He's listened to the French offer, and now he's come back to us in spades. He's demanding three squadrons of F-15's as a starter, and the rest of his hardware list is as long as your arm. He wants tanks, anti-aircraft guns, enough small arms for a brigade. And as a final payoff, two new frigates for his navy."

McIntosh whistled. "He's seen what we've turned over to

the Saudis and Iran, and he knows about the arms deals Britain and France have been making up and down the Persian Gulf."

"But we're not as desperate as Japan and some other countries. The President will get his back up, and the Senate will never agree to this kind of blackmail. I couldn't possibly put through a new treaty that would give Suleiman what he wants. The Senate would lynch me."

"Stall, Herb. That's the first step."

"How?"

"Suggest that the State Department bring Trevenian home for consultations."

"What'll that accomplish?" Watrous asked. "Chris Trevenian is a good guy who makes generous contributions in election years. But he's operating beyond his depth in Abu Bakr, and you know it."

"Sure, but if he comes home for a few weeks we'll buy time, and that's what I'll need to make an analysis of this situation. Kenyon is home, and I'm seeing him tomorrow, so I'll sound him out. He called me from the airport to say that he's brought one of the real experts on Abu Bakr in general and Suleiman in particular with him, and he's setting up a date for me. I want to get their opinions, and I may bring Hamilton home for talks—or meet him in Europe. I want Hector Bell's thinking, as well as the reactions of my own executive committee. Needless to say, I'll appreciate any contributions you may be able to make."

"What would happen," the Senator asked, "if you told Suleiman to fry in his own oil? Suppose you sell out your installations in Abu Bakr and get out of the country?"

"Impossible," McIntosh said. "We buy oil from four Persian Gulf countries other than Abu Bakr, but our stake there is bigger than all of the others combined. Our stockholders would panic. The executive committee and the board of trustees would panic. Hell, Herb, I'd go into a state of hysteria myself. Within six months we'd have to file for receivership. We couldn't hold off until our fields in Alaska and our experiments with Wyoming and Colorado shale pay off. Aapco would be finished."

"It's that bad." Watrous sat down. "So the little tin god sitting in his palace way off in El Ain has his hand around your throat, and there's no way you can pry him loose."

"If he has a weakness, we haven't found it yet, although Kenyon appears to have the best clues so far. He's the worst kind of crusading, traditionalist Arab. He'd probably make a pilgrimage of thanks to Mecca if he could create a depression in this country. And between us, we have proof that he's been contributing millions to fellow crackpots in the United States, the *Protocols of Zion* loonies. Very little anti-Semitism has developed here as the result of the oil crisis, which you well know, but it isn't because of any lack of enthusiasm on Suleiman's part. We've been keeping quiet about his activities because our own image is tied to Abu Bakr, unfortunately. But there's no way of telling what the man will do next."

Watrous's laugh was harsh. "You could always try to persuade Israeli intelligence to put a bullet through his head."

McIntosh was grim. "That's a possibility," he said. "At worst, we might even be forced to take on the assignment ourselves."

Thirteen

∗∗∗∗∗∗∗∗∗∗∗∗∗∗∗∗∗∗∗∗∗∗∗∗

The bellboys deposited the luggage, and Turk went to the windows that overlooked Central Park. "This," he said, "is the best view in New York."

Leah wasn't interested in scenery. "I see the suite has only one bedroom."

"Sure. I took you at your word. But it's still early. Do you want to go out?" He didn't want to appear too anxious to leap into bed, not after the way she had managed to avoid him twice.

"If that's what you'd like."

"Why not? Tomorrow we work, but tonight we play."

"If you don't mind," she said, "I'd like to unpack before we do anything else."

"Okay, I'll order a drink, and we can take our time deciding where to go. I think we'd better stick to champagne after all we drank on the airplane."

"I'll leave all that to you," Leah said, and went into the bedroom, closing the door behind her.

Turk called room service, and as he wandered around the living room he reflected that his luck wasn't just good; it was improving. Not only had he killed the French deal with Suleiman, but he would also introduce Leah to the top Aapco echelon as the most authoritative of experts on Abu Bakr, the person who could accurately predict the Shaikh's future course of action. Naturally, he would take full credit for bringing her to America. He had no doubt that she would make a good impression, so he might be able to win himself a salary raise as well as the long-term contract he wanted.

A waiter arrived with an ice bucket and poured two glasses of champagne.

After he departed Turk went to the bedroom door. "Don't take all night in there," he called, "or your champagne will get warm."

The door opened. "That would never do," Leah said.

He stared at her as she went to the coffee table and picked up her drink. She had changed into a short, sheer nightgown that left nothing to the imagination, but her manner was so casual that he felt compelled to try to match it. He was dismayed, however, when a shaking hand betrayed him as he raised his own glass.

"Here's to a successful stay in New York," she said.

"Right on." His voice was hoarse.

Leah's green eyes were mocking as she feigned surprise. "Is something wrong?"

"I'm flipping, and you know it."

"I do keep my word, you see."

He refrained from saying that she was reliable when it suited her purposes. As, she had pointed out, he was.

"I decided there was no reason to go out when we have all the comforts of home right here," she said.

"Always thinking. That's what I like about you." He gulped his champagne and refilled his glass.

She sat in a chair opposite his and lit a cigarette, her manner as matter of fact as if she were fully dressed. "You astonish me."

"How so?"

"Your reputation—and your behavior—have led me to believe you'd be Casanova reincarnate." She was enjoying teasing him.

"We have a long night ahead of us," Turk said, determined not to give her an advantage. She was more than a mere bedmate, he reminded himself.

"How civilized," Leah said.

He hoped his seeming calm was having its effect. "It seems to me that you feel the way you claim I do." He was beginning to enjoy the duel, even though the sight of her body beneath its flimsy covering was making it difficult for him to concentrate. "You believe *you're* irresistible."

She smothered a laugh. "Are you insinuating that I'm not?"

"I'm the last to make insinuations."

"Well, we'll soon find out. The question isn't academic." She deliberately sat upright, squaring her shoulders, so her breasts strained against the thin nylon.

"Would you like a little more champagne?"

"Not just now, thanks." She stood and slowly sauntered toward him. "You've stalled long enough. Now we're going to find out whether you live up to your reputation."

He smiled too, as he rose to his feet and removed his jacket and necktie. "Are you challenging me?"

"You've been indicating you're a civilized man."

"I don't believe in rape, if that's what you mean, even though you've given me enough provocation."

"I just wonder if you know there's no such thing as civilized behavior in bed."

"That's a half truth, baby." He reached for her.

Leah held him at arm's length, unbuttoned his shirt, and ran her hands over his bare chest.

"I should have known you'd turn lovemaking into a con-

test. If that's the way you want it, that's the way it'll be."
He brushed her hands aside, took her in his arms, and kissed
her.

Her lips parted and, as her teeth closed over his tongue,
she rubbed her body against him.

Turk, already aroused, was no longer in a mood for teasing, but knew she would win a victory of sorts if he rushed
her. He grasped her buttocks, drawing her closer, and his
probing tongue became more active.

Leah appeared to respond in earnest, her long fingernails
digging through his shirt.

With no preamble he picked her up and carried her into
the bedroom.

"At last," she said, her tone still mocking.

He deposited her on the bed, undressed quickly, and then
removed her nightgown. Only one small lamp was burning,
but it was enough for him to see the sardonic expression in
her eyes, and he became infuriated. "We've had enough
games," he said, and began to caress her in earnest.

"There is no such thing as enough games," she said, her
voice muffled, and her hands and mouth became active, too.

She was goading him, he realized, trying to arouse him
further while she remained detached, but he could not allow
her to gain such ascendancy over him, and he redoubled his
efforts.

By mutual, unspoken agreement, however, there were
limits to their game, and neither pressed too far, drawing
back instinctively when they appeared to be approaching
the brink.

"Ready?" Turk demanded at last.

"Why don't you find out for yourself?" Leah replied.

He took her, or thought he did, and not until later did it
occur to him that, perhaps, it was she who took him. Their
desire soared as their locked bodies heaved in unison, and
Turk made a supreme effort to retain a final measure of self-
control.

Leah was no longer pretending. Her eyes were closed, her nails raked his back and shoulders, and her convulsive, rhythmic movement became violent.

Turk could hold back no longer and, as nearly as he could tell in the moment of ecstatic release, the girl simultaneously reached a climax.

Leah's happy sigh broke the long silence. She propped herself on one elbow. "I refuse to compliment you. It isn't necessary."

"The same to you," he said, and grinned, unwilling to admit that she was the only woman he had ever known who was his equal, his full partner. He wouldn't want her permanently—she was too aggressive, too demanding—but for the present she offered a continuing challenge.

Leah seemed to share his feelings. "It's going to be an interesting two or three weeks," she said.

Turk nodded. "It won't be easy, but we'll have to find time for work."

Bobbie had a drink ready for Dugald McIntosh when he reached their hotel apartment precisely at 5:00 P.M. As she raised her face for his kiss it was obvious to her that he was preoccupied, but she didn't press him for an explanation, and for the next quarter of an hour she made small talk.

"I tried to reach you a couple of times today," he said at last, "but you were out."

She felt it would be unwise to remind him she was no longer a secretary waiting to pick up the telephone when he called. "I came in a few minutes before you did. I was buying furniture today. I spent a fortune."

McIntosh had no interest, at the moment, in the decoration of their permanent home. "I had a long session with Kenyon today. He came through in spades. The French deal with Suleiman is dead, and can't be revived, no matter what bait Paris offers."

"Turk delivers. I've always said that much for him. How did he do it?"

"He was a little vague on details, and I gathered there were angles it was better for me not to know."

"That's like him, too," Bobbie said.

"He's ingratiated himself with Suleiman, who calls him a brother. That much is certain."

"Very neat. Let me guess the rest. He wants a new contract."

McIntosh smiled. "Not just yet, although he hinted he'll bring up the subject. He seems to have pulled an even bigger stunt. He's brought an expert on Abu Bakr and Shaikh Suleiman with him, and he's going to arrange a dinner meeting for me."

"We can entertain them here, if you like," Bobbie said. "Who is he?"

"She."

Bobbie laughed. "Turk's at it again. Are you sure this expert isn't flim-flam?"

"He says she'll present her own credentials. Kenyon led me to believe—without saying it in so many words—that she operates as a private representative in certain Middle Eastern countries for the government of Israel."

"You mean she's a spy?" Bobbie was incredulous.

Her husband nodded. "I'm only repeating what he told me. He didn't say she's an espionage agent. All he said was that she knows Suleiman better than he does—"

"How could that be possible?"

McIntosh was uncomfortable. "Very much off the record, and not to be repeated in her presence, I think she's the girl Kenyon took to Abu Bakr for a week as a gift to Suleiman."

Bobbie couldn't resist. "Call her by her right name. She's a prostitute."

"Not necessarily. Labels are dangerous. In this case her motive may have been patriotism, which is no worse than having an affair for money or marrying for security. And it may be better."

Bobbie reached for his drink, as if to freshen it, making certain he couldn't see her face. She had seen too many people trapped by his seemingly impersonal remarks. "Have you set up a date?"

"I'm meeting them tomorrow night."

"We'll have them here," Bobbie said.

McIntosh raised an eyebrow. "Afraid she'll become the next Mrs. Kenyon?"

"That didn't enter my mind," she said, allowing her anger to show. "I can't imagine a woman like that not having an affair with Turk, which makes her the latest in a long series of conquests. My relationship with Turk has been casual for years, as I've told you; his private life means nothing to me. My only concern is for the future of Aapco, and if you're going to give any weight to what she tells you, I want to judge her for myself. Just because I don't work in the office any more doesn't mean I've lost interest in the company. We agreed that I'd continue to help you in every way I could, so we'll have them here. I won't tolerate any other arrangement."

The man whose orders were obeyed without question by a hundred thousand employees was secretly pleased by her ferocity, even though he realized she was sparked by the influence she felt she could exert. "As you wish, my dear," he said.

The Arabian sun was suffocating, and Ruth Hamilton, keeping an eye on the clock, insisted that her daughter return to the house after spending an hour at the side of the pool.

Judy protested, but made her way on crutches to the glass-enclosed terrace. "I don't see why I had to come in," she said. "You heard Uncle Abner Keating tell me the sun will help get rid of my scars."

"In moderation." Ruth placed a tall glass of fruit juice at the girl's elbow. "You've only been home for a day, so don't try to do everything at once."

Judy hated being treated like an invalid but knew her mother meant well.

Ruth handed her a letter bearing a French stamp and postmark.

The girl ripped open the envelope. "It's from Turk Kenyon."

"I recognized his handwriting."

Judy was too busy reading the letter to comment. "He knows about the bracelet."

"Your father won't approve. He wants you to return the jewelry."

"I earned anything I get. I loathe the monster, but—"

"Turk?"

"Really, Mother! Suleiman. Turk is wonderful."

"Your opinion isn't shared by everyone." Ruth's voice was dry.

"It wasn't so long ago that I looked down at you for what you did, Mother. But now I can understand why you fell for him."

"I didn't." Ruth knew she couldn't explain the bored desperation that had been responsible for her affair.

"Of course you did! Turk is dynamite! I told you and Daddy when you brought me home yesterday that I made a horrible mistake when I let myself become involved with Ali. And I've paid a pretty high price for it."

"Too high."

"If it weren't for Turk, I'd be dead. I don't think anybody else in this world would have been smart enough and quick enough and firm enough to get me out of that insane spot."

Ruth thought it best to let her husband deal with the

problem of gifts. She wanted to see the letter, but because of her own situation was reluctant to ask for it. "You're vulnerable right now, Judy, and Turk knows it. Be careful."

"He's my friend."

"He's almost twice your age."

"As if that mattered! Nobody can badmouth him to me, ever."

Ruth changed the subject. "Daddy and I are trying to decide whether to send you to the Mayo Clinic or to Johns Hopkins."

"I won't go to either," Judy said. "School is out of the question for another year. You and Daddy have agreed to that much. My ribs are healing, and there's no permanent damage to them. So that leaves only my ankle."

"Only."

"Don't be such a pessimist, Mother." Judy was impatient. "You heard Uncle Abner say that no doctor will be able to tell until the cast is removed whether I'll limp. So why go halfway around the world to some hospital if it isn't necessary? We'll know in six to eight weeks."

"We believe you'll enjoy greater peace of mind if you leave Abu Bakr."

"That's what I thought at first," Judy said. "But you and Daddy are here, so this is the only home I have. I'll be just fine, provided I don't go near the palace."

"You don't want to stay because of your father and me," Ruth said. "I can't believe that."

The girl ignored the pain in the ribs that laughter caused. "All right, Mother. I won't try to fool you. Turk is coming back in a few weeks, and I want to be here. So I can thank him the way he should be thanked for what he did."

"Your father won't tolerate it!"

"I'm of age, so I'll make my own decisions!"

The doctors had said that the girl shouldn't be allowed to become overwrought, so Ruth didn't press. But she couldn't help asking, "Just how are you intending to express your thanks?"

"That'll depend, Mother. I don't plan to follow in your path, if that's what you mean."

Ruth was unable to reply.

"When the time comes," Judy said, "I'll know what to do."

Finance Minister Habib al-Husayn was tired after his business trip to London, Frankfurt, and Zurich, so it was natural for him to relax after his return to El Ain by going off into the desert on a hunting trip with his brother, the Foreign Minister. They promised Shaikh Suleiman the first gazelle they shot in the highlands, and planned to leave before sunrise. Official business detained them, however, so it was mid-afternoon before they set out, and as it was too late to reach the Oasis of Qar that night, they pitched their camp in the open.

Their servants set up the tents and, building a fire, began to cook *couscous*. The brothers wrapped themselves in wool *agals* to ward off the night chill, then made themselves as comfortable as they could on camp stools that they carried to the far end of their camp, out of their retainers' earshot.

"I am convinced," Habib said, "that international bankers have the best espionage system on earth. I wish I knew how they do it."

"Their techniques are the same as anyone else's," Ahmed al-Husayn said. "They pay for information."

"However they find out what they want to know, my mission wasn't encouraging."

"They're reluctant to sponsor the float of an Abu Bakr bond?"

"They refused. Outright. I'll show you the list of eleven banks that turned me down."

"Later. I can't read unless I use an oil lamp, and I know the caravan leader and the assistant cook are devoted to

Suleiman. Besides, it isn't important that I see the list."

"I explained again and again," Habib said, "that Suleiman wants to keep the bulk of our state treasury intact, that he thinks of it as his personal fortune—"

"Which it is."

"In a manner of speaking. I made it clear that he wants to use the cash from bond issue to build a refinery, to buy tankers and set up some petrochemical plants. Without exception they wished me good luck elsewhere. They've been in touch with each other, I'm sure."

"With billions of *rials* in gold sitting in our vaults, not to mention many more billions in oil underground, I can't imagine that any country would have a better credit rating."

"Ordinarily," Habid said, "they'd be having a camel fight, with each of them offering us better terms for a loan. We'd write our own contracts, instead of being sent begging. *Bismi 'llah*, Ahmed, it was humiliating to be dismissed like a penniless Bedouin!"

The elder brother frowned. "It may be that some of the Jewish bankers in London and Paris intervened and persuaded their colleagues to send us away."

"I thought that too, initially. But Saudi and Kuwait get anything they want from the banks. So can Dubai and Bahrein and Abu Dhabi, all of them with oil production below ours. I finally wheedled the truth out of one of the Swiss. It's Suleiman."

"What about him?"

"They believe he's unstable."

"I wonder," Ahmed said, "if a certain deposed shaikh who lives in Switzerland has been whispering in the bankers' ears."

"That's possible, but their information on him was more up to date than anything he could tell them. They heard about the execution of the so-called Communists, naturally. And the rejection of the French government's proposals."

"The diplomatic community here knew the details of both

incidents," Ahmed said. "That sort of news always makes the rounds."

"The bankers," Habib said, "also have a file on his private life. They're familiar with many details we've kept secret for years."

"I see two distinct problems," Ahmed said. "The first is that of tracing the information leaks, and there's nothing anyone but the ruling shaikh can do about that. The other is how to persuade the banks to change their minds."

"We can't, and they won't. As long as Suleiman remains on the throne it will be impossible for Abu Bakr to obtain a substantial foreign loan. Much as I dislike making categorical statements, I can see nothing that will change that situation."

The wind that blew across the desert from the west lacked the strength of a *shamal*, but it was cold and brisk, and Ahmed, watching the cooking fire leap higher, wrapped his *ghutra* more securely around his neck. "Every government in the world lives on credit. In this matter I am forced to agree with Suleiman. I hate to see us spending our gold. It is like allowing our oil wells to leak and spill into the sand."

"The banks will not open their vaults until Suleiman is gone," Habib said, his voice becoming harsh. "I am convinced there is no alternative."

"Patience, little brother," Ahmed said, patting him on the knee. "Cultivate the Bedouin virtues."

"How long must we wait?"

Ahmed's eyes were gloomy as he stared at the fire. "Only Allah knows, and has not yet chosen to reveal the mystery to us. During your absence Suleiman has grown stronger day by day. He has given his regiments another pay increase; they swear their devotion to him. The heads of those poor students he exhibited in the square outside the *suq* convinced the people that the Communist threat is real, so they continue to support him, even though he does nothing for them."

"A revolution—"

"—would fail. Any attempt to trick him or force him into exile would fail. He is too shrewd to leave the country, even to make that two-day pilgrimage to Mecca he talks about so incessantly. He is like a fisherman who builds himself a *barastis* of reeds on another's property, and then refuses to leave, defending his home with a scimitar to drive off the actual owners of the land."

"We cannot wait forever," Habib said.

"Forever is too long," Ahmed agreed. "That is a luxury only Allah can afford. Surely you remember the tale about the pearl diver who opened one hundred oysters each day, from the time of his youth until he was old. He lived on the oysters, and at last Allah took pity on him, rewarding his patience by guiding him to an oyster that contained a pearl of great value. That pearl supported the fisherman for the rest of his life."

"I can't wait until I am old to be rid of Suleiman," Habib said, "and neither can you. One day he'll turn against us, and we won't enjoy the luxuries of exile. Our heads will look down on the *suq* from pikes, and the people will applaud because of the evidence he'll manufacture that proves we're traitors."

There was no humor in Ahmed's deep chuckle. "Allah gave you the gift of a vivid imagination, little brother. In this instance, I am afraid, you predict the future accurately."

Habib was so incensed he raised his voice. "Will you go to the slaughter like an aged camel that can no longer march across the desert?"

Ahmed quieted him with a gesture.

The Finance Minister mumbled an apology.

"My courage is as great as any man's," Ahmed said. "No one in Islam has greater valor. But it happens that I am allergic to the blade of a knife. It causes me to bleed."

His younger brother laughed politely.

272

"So I have no intention of waiting until I am sacrificed on the altar of another's madness."

"What will you do?"

"The Koran tells us there is a time to think and a time to strike boldly. I am thinking, and my thoughts fill every waking hour."

"There have been times in the history of our family," Habib said, fingering the hilt of his dagger, "when we have cleansed our honor with the blood of those who drag an ancient and honorable name into the sand."

"No," Ahmed said with an emphatic shake of his head. "We who are the hereditary leaders of Abu Bakr must not stain our own hands with blood, particularly fraternal blood. Think of the embarrassments we would cause our friends at Aapco. Think of your bankers in Zurich and Basel. No, little brother. We must find another way."

"Hired assassins are unreliable," Habib said, "and his enemies in the radical Arab states are our enemies."

The Foreign Minister was amused. "You begin to think too," he said. "That is a good sign."

"Where have your thoughts led, Ahmed?"

"I have not yet found the oasis I seek, but I know it exists somewhere in the desert. I shall continue my search, Habib, with your help, and because I must. The time grows shorter, our supplies of water are dwindling, and our thirst is great. So be cheerful! We shall achieve our goal because we have no choice."

Turk Kenyon neither felt nor displayed any sense of uneasiness when he arrived at the McIntosh hotel apartment with Leah and presented her to his former wife and her new husband. His attitude, which was genuine, indicated that his personal relations with the blonde were not the concern of any third party. He and Leah treated each other

273

with a cordial impersonality that seemed to say they were business associates, nothing more, and that they wanted to be accepted accordingly.

Dugald McIntosh sat back in his upholstered leather chair, saying little as the others chatted over cocktails. Turk, who had predicted that the Aapco president would reach his own conclusions, silently was not surprised, and Leah took the occasion in stride, talking about restaurants in Europe and the United States, and telling ordinary anecdotes about extraordinary people.

Bobbie, like Ruth, sensed that there was more to Turk's relationship with Leah than appeared on the surface, and found it difficult to conceal her curiosity. She had quickly sensed that, even though the blonde had supposedly spent a week with Shaikh Suleiman, she was no ordinary prostitute. And her jewelry was stunning, particularly an enormous diamond ring and a heavy gold bracelet.

"Do you know this country well?" Bobbie asked. "Your accent sounds American."

"I inherited a chameleon-like quality from my mother," Leah said. "When I am in England people think I'm British, and the French assume I am one of them."

Bobbie had learned nothing, but tried to cover her retreat. "You have a gift for languages, then."

"Oh, I take no credit for it," the other girl said. "It's like the color of my hair. I was lucky to be born with it."

A maid announced dinner, and they moved to the adjoining room, where Bobbie soon noted Leah's table manners were American too. She was clever, whoever she might be.

Aside from making an occasional, inconsequential comment, McIntosh remained silent until they returned to the living room for coffee and liqueur. "Let's talk about Abu Bakr," he said abruptly, dropping all pretense that the occasion was social.

Leah's reply was prompt. "I am sure there is much we can exchange," she said. Her signal was clear. She would divulge

274

what she knew on condition that the head of American-Arabian Petroleum did the same.

McIntosh's quick smile showed that he agreed to the deal. "We can help each other," he said, "but you haven't told me who your principals are."

"Certainly Turk has given you a few hints," she said.

This was no time for coyness, and Turk didn't want to remain on the periphery. "I have," he said. "Mr. McIntosh understands your situation, and he'll agree that anything we say here will be strictly confidential."

McIntosh needed no spokesman, and was irritated by Kenyon's brashness, but it was more important to learn what he needed to know than to rebuke a subordinate. "I've spent my whole life in the oil business. It goes without saying that I never reveal the sources of any data I receive."

The ground rules were set, and Leah nodded. "Abu Bakr," she said, "has an influence out of proportion to its size for several reasons. As you know, it has enormous wealth, which is concentrated in the hands of one man. And that man is more than rich. Because of the so-called purity of his religious beliefs he has already developed a following throughout Islam. The heads of other Arab governments are afraid of a backlash in their own countries if they adopt any policies he doesn't like."

McIntosh's expression indicated that her analysis coincided with his own.

Leah went on. "The importance of Abu Bakr is enhanced by other factors. All Arabs take an anti-Israeli stance because they think their people demand it, but Shaikh Suleiman pays more than lip service to the principle of destroying Israel. He wants to scatter or exterminate the Israelis and give their land to the Palestinian Arabs, and he spends large sums of money for that purpose. But his enmity toward Israel is only a symptom of far greater ambition. He thinks of himself as a successor to the Turkish sultans who ruled all of Islam, men like Mohammed the Conqueror and Suleiman

275

the Great. He believes the Arab dream of consolidating in one nation is more than a dream, and like Quaddafi of Libya, he sees himself as the natural ruler of that new empire. Islam will be purified by literal obedience to the Koran and the customs that were observed during the height of Islamic world power."

"You present a frightening picture," McIntosh said, "if it's true."

"It is true."

"How can you be so certain?" McIntosh asked. "Everything depends on it."

"I had an opportunity to become well acquainted with Shaikh Suleiman under specialized circumstances."

Turk silently applauded her delicacy, as did his employer. Only Bobbie felt a certain skepticism, and that she kept to herself.

"I observed him," Leah said. "Certain conclusions follow, as I have written in highly confidential reports to my own superiors. Suleiman will allow nothing to deter him from the achievement of his ultimate goals. Also, he is indifferent to the methods he uses, and he enjoys inflicting pain on others. He's a sadist, and he believes that people everywhere are conspiring against him."

"Leah's right," Turk said. "I've become closer to him than any other foreigner, with the exception of Leah, and I've seen it myself. Twice. He's naturally vicious, naturally cruel."

McIntosh drummed on the arm of his chair, then lit a cigar. "We'll assume both of you are right. Apply your character study in practical terms."

"On the surface," Leah said, "Suleiman is generous, at least in what he regards as small things." She glanced at her diamond ring and gold bracelet. "But on a broad scale he needs much more money than he now possesses. If he's to become the master of all Islam he requires more than he's accumulated. And right now the banks, for all his wealth, are not lending him what he wants."

"Now," McIntosh said, "we get to the core. How does he plan to get it?"

The girl had anticipated the question, and worded her reply with care. "I can only tell you my own opinion. I'm sure you realize Suleiman wouldn't confide in a woman, so I can only guess."

"An educated guess," Turk said.

She thanked him with a smile. "Examine his present financial position, Mr. McIntosh. It would be presumptuous of me to tell you what you know far better than I, that Suleiman has one, just one source of income. Oil."

"What about Abu Bakr's plans to expand into petrochemicals and other industries?" McIntosh wanted to know.

"Those plans were formulated during the reign of his predecessor, and grew out of the thinking of foreign-educated government officials. Suleiman hopes to benefit, of course, but there's no evidence that suggests he's giving those plans active support."

"It seems to me," Turk added, "that he'd be pleased if some new industries were established and brought him additional revenue. But I suspect he thinks only in terms of oil."

"I'm sure that's right," Leah said, "although I can't prove it. Suleiman's thinking is in no way similar to that of his better-educated relatives. He sits on the throne and they serve him for the simple reason that he holds power. He's primitive. That one word summarizes his personality."

McIntosh bit hard on his cigar. "You're suggesting he'll find some excuse to nationalize the Abu Bakrian oil industry?"

"He needs no excuse," Leah said. "He can expropriate your holdings by issuing a decree. He can do it without consulting anyone and by rejecting any advice others might give him."

"You think no one can influence him." McIntosh made a flat statement.

"I'd be inclined to qualify that conclusion," Leah said. "Turk influenced him to kill the French offer. But there *is* a limit to what any outsider can do. We can't allow ourselves to forget that Suleiman is one of the few absolute monarchs on earth."

"My concern," McIntosh said, "boils down to one basic question. Will Suleiman nationalize Aapco's holdings in Abu Bakr?"

"He will." Leah was equally forceful. "I believe expropriation is inevitable."

"When?"

She smiled. "I am not a soothsayer, Mr. McIntosh. Whenever he feels he needs additional money. Whenever the mood comes over him. Whenever he feels a need to demonstrate his power."

"You're not very encouraging."

"There's one other aspect I should mention," she said. "I'm certain he'll nationalize as soon as he learns you've discovered new oil fields in Abu Bakr."

Turk was astonished. "What new oil fields?"

McIntosh ignored his subordinate. "That is a closely held secret, young woman. How did you know about it?"

"I supply my superiors with important information. Nothing is more important in Abu Bakr today than the oil strike in the Great Wadi."

For the first time Turk understood why he hadn't been permitted to visit the exploratory fields in western Abu Bakr. "A great deal of effort was expended to keep me in ignorance," he said.

"There was no need for you to know," McIntosh said. "Now you'll keep your mouth shut."

"Sure." Turk was still annoyed as he turned to Leah. "You didn't tell me."

Her shrug was attractive. "The information didn't lie within the limits of our agreement."

At that moment McIntosh was called to the telephone, and Leah took advantage of his absence to pay a visit to the bathroom, leaving Turk alone with his former wife. He lost no time. "Congratulations on your marriage, Mrs. McIntosh. You've done all right for yourself."

"Is there any reason I shouldn't?" There was an undertone of savagery in her voice.

"Not at all. I'm delighted for you, baby. You'll have everything you've ever wanted."

"I think so." Her answer was smug.

"Including power," Turk said. "You've moved a few steps ahead of me, so you don't have to compete with me any more."

"I never competed with you!"

"I'm not arguing with you, Bobbie. I just hope you'll remember old times occasionally."

"Oh, I'll never forget them, you can be sure. Especially when I see you with your latest conquest."

"Leah and I have a business arrangement. That's all."

Bobbie's smile was tight. "Tell that to Dugald, not to me. I called the Plaza. Mr. and Mrs. Dale Kenyon are registered there."

"I'm unmasked," he said sarcastically but not defensively. "I'm flattered you went to the trouble of checking. But I have a business relationship with her, however you look at it."

McIntosh and Leah returned at almost the same moment and resumed their seats.

"I hope your predictions are wrong, young lady," he said.

"For everyone's sake, I hope I am, too. But there's no doubt in my mind. So it becomes my turn to ask a question, and I'll make it brief, Mr. McIntosh. If and when Suleiman nationalizes, what will American-Arabian Petroleum do?"

His eyes hardened behind his horn-rimmed glasses. "Our geologists tell me there are between five and seven trillion tons of oil in the ground under Abu Bakr. And for that kind of a reserve we'll do anything to protect our interests."

"What do you mean by anything?" Leah persisted.

"Exactly what you think," McIntosh said. "If we must, we'll find a way to get rid of Suleiman."

Fourteen

❖❖❖❖❖❖❖❖❖❖❖❖❖❖❖❖❖❖❖❖❖❖❖❖❖
❖❖❖❖❖❖❖❖❖❖❖❖❖❖❖❖❖❖❖❖❖❖❖❖❖

Ibrahim Hassan slept apart from the Bedouins. He had traveled with them from the Great Wadi to the Oasis of Qar, but had chosen a place away from their campfire. His *agal* was threadbare and his discomfort was great, but he could not impose on the hospitality of those who had given him food and transportation. The knowledge that Allah was watching over him was enough to sustain any man.

Watching the first smudged streaks of dawn appear in the eastern sky, Ibrahim found renewed resolution. For five years he had worked for Aapco, and for five years he had been treated as an inferior. It was true that he had received no formal education, that he could neither read nor write. It was also true that the Western physicians had cleansed his body of the parasites that had threatened to destroy him, but that cure had been his due after his long and faithful service. He was willing to grant, too, that he had acquired no technical skills, but that was the fault of the Westerners, who had trained others to work on the machines that pumped oil out of the ground.

Ibrahim Hassan had been neglected by his employers, and resented it. He had been a kitchen helper, and had scrubbed pots, swept kitchens, and performed other menial chores. In all that time his wages, which had started at a measly ten *rials* per week, had risen no higher than a niggardly fifteen *rials*. But others earned several times that sum each day, and Ibrahim knew the Westerners had lied to him. After giving him what they called aptitude tests, which had consisted of such childish feats as fitting blocks of wood into spaces on a board, they had mocked him by saying he was already in his right place.

The past few months had been even more galling than all of the earlier years. The field workers had received double pay for their efforts, but when Ibrahim had complained he had been told to count his blessings. Only Westerners would believe that a man with an independent spirit who prayed thrice daily to Allah and whose most precious possession was a dagger that had belonged to his father's father would bow his head in gratitude just because they gave him his meals and a place to sleep.

He faced Mecca, prostrated himself on the soft grass, and offered his morning prayers. After washing his right hand he joined the Bedouins, helping himself to a breakfast of mutton and seminola. He was disappointed when the leader of the caravan told him the Bedouins would remain in the Oasis of Qar for another day.

With nothing better to occupy him, Ibrahim Hassan strolled aimlessly through the oasis. He could buy little cakes of almonds and honey, whole tomatoes, and the white meat of fowl. Or he could buy the favors of a woman. But Allah was testing him, and he resisted the temptations of the flesh. He had a sacred duty to perform, and Allah, through his surrogate on earth, the great Shaikh Suleiman, would grant him an immediate reward.

A way toward his reward appeared when Ibrahim Hassan least expected it. Directly ahead, in a grove beyond a double row of palm trees, stood a helicopter. He had seen many of those machines, and had hated them because extra mouths to feed had meant additional work for him.

But this machine was different. It was blue and white, the colors of Abu Bakr. Beyond it stood the tents of a score of soldiers. Ibrahim's heart pounded as he approached the troops. He hesitated until he saw the man in charge, a burly soldier with a band of blue and white decorating his *ghutra*. Summoning his courage, Ibrahim moved forward again.

"Great pasha," he said, "you have come to the Oasis of Qar from El Ain?"

The sergeant's head still ached after his consumption of forbidden Algerian *arak* the previous night, and the taste of fermented grapes and anise was sour in his mouth. He barely nodded.

"You will return to El Ain?"

"What is it to you, son of a camel?" The sergeant's nerves were raw.

Ibrahim Hassan lowered his voice. "I seek to fly to El Ain with you. I carry news of importance to His Highness."

The sergeant laughed. "What news could you bring to Shaikh Suleiman, sheep dung?"

Ibrahim Hassan drew himself erect. "For five years I have labored in the kitchens of the Westerners who steal the oil of Abu Bakr. I know much about them."

The sergeant's interest was aroused. "What are you doing at the Oasis of Qar?"

"I am on the way to El Ain to beg the boon of an audience with His Highness. I came here from the Great Wadi."

"Wait," the sergeant commanded, and walked to a silk tent that stood apart from the others. Soon he reappeared and beckoned.

The bearded man who sat behind a small desk wore a band of gold on his *ghutra,* his dagger had a gold hilt, and his *agal* was made of the finest hand-woven linen.

Ibrahim Hassan, overcome, prostrated himself on the ground. "Noble pasha—"

"Stand up!" the annoyed colonel said. "No one can hear you when you mumble into the dirt."

Ibrahim pulled himself to his feet.

The colonel inspected him with cold, dark eyes. "What news could scum such as you have for Shaikh Suleiman?"

"I can tell no man except His Highness, but I crave the favor of a ride to El Ain so there will be no delay."

Picking up his riding crop, the colonel slashed his visitor across the face. "Stop quibbling. When I ask a question, I expect it to be answered."

Ibrahim Hassan wiped a trickle of blood from the corner of his mouth with the back of his hand. The chief cook in the kitchen of the Westerners had treated him even more miserably, and his resolution hardened. "You may drive your knife deep into my heart, great pasha, but my news is for the ears of His Highness alone."

The man's unexpected display of courage impressed the colonel. He had not cringed when the riding crop had cut into his flesh, and the colonel studied him more closely. "I hope you know that if you waste the time of Shaikh Suleiman you will die a thousand deaths in his dungeons."

"I know His Highness will reward me with gold," the stubborn Ibrahim said.

The colonel sighed and told himself the problem was one for the vizier to settle. He was paid to direct the household of the Shaikh, and he could decide whether this person brought information of value or was a sun-crazed nomad. "Very well," he said, "you may come with us to El Ain, but you will ride with the luggage at the rear of the helicopter. Do not come near me. I find your odor offensive."

Dugald McIntosh called an emergency meeting of Aapco managers in Amsterdam.

Most of the executives stayed at the Hotel Amstel, where McIntosh and his bride were in residence, but Turk Kenyon elected to take a suite at the Hotel de l'Europe, facing the Mint Tower. It was equally luxurious, and his colleagues gave him credit for a demonstration of surprising delicacy. He and the young blonde woman who, it was rumored, would address the gathering were traveling together, and it was assumed that he didn't want to embarrass her.

Turk's rationale was far simpler. "If we stay with the others," he said, "we'll have to hang around after working hours, which will mean sitting around the McIntosh suite every night. There are as many great clubs in this town as there are anywhere on the Continent, and I'm partial to genever-on-the-rocks. That's how we'll spend our evenings, and we'll keep an air cushion between us and the old man. And his court."

Leah insisted on what she called a solitary shopping trip immediately after she and Turk arrived in Amsterdam. Alternately taking taxis and walking, making certain she wasn't being followed, she eventually made her way to a small bookstore on one of the canals, a place known to bibliophiles for its rare books and antique maps.

After making a small purchase, she vanished into the rear, where she conferred at length with the manager. In the store again, she promised to return the next day for another seventeenth-century book. As she made her circuitous way back to the suite she shared with Turk, she knew her report to her superiors in Jerusalem was already being drafted in code.

The formal meetings were held in the soundproof directors' room of the Aapco-Europe headquarters, and before the talks began the chamber was searched by electronics experts, who were able to assure Dugald McIntosh that no microphones were hidden there.

The Aapco president opened the meeting with a brief statement about a critical situation that was threatening its entire future. He promised to make available all the facts already presented to the board of directors in New York.

Turk Kenyon was the principal speaker at the morning meeting, and explained in detail his reactions to Shaikh Suleiman. That afternoon Red Hamilton presented a secret report on the oil findings in the Great Wadi. His colleagues, after reading the statistics compiled by teams of geologists, agreed that the new field might be the richest in the Middle East.

Leah, who had been given a separate copy of the Hamilton report, took it to the bookstore for transmittal to Jerusalem. A message from the general awaited her, and she was angry when she left the bookstore, her request for a furlough in Israel having been denied. Instead she was ordered to return to Cairo for new instructions after the Aapco conference ended.

Turk had already returned to their suite, and greeted her boisterously. "The boys are primed for your little chat with them tomorrow," he said. "McIntosh has already paid me a bonus of ten thousand, and you'll get fifteen thousand in cash when we break up at noon. Tonight we'll have ourselves a champagne celebration."

"Do what you please," she said. "I won't be doing it with you."

"Hey, what's eating you?"

"I plan to spend the evening alone, that's all."

Turk approached her, arms extended. "I don't know what's bugging you, but you need a little soothing."

"If you come one step closer," Leah said, "you'll learn why I won a black belt."

He halted, his eyes narrowing.

She returned his glare. "I'm not like your other women, remember? That's because I'm not *your* woman."

"The time has come to part. Is that it?"

"More or less. I'm being sent on tomorrow."

"Ah, you're getting your furlough in Israel."

"No, but that's the breaks."

"You were born hard-boiled," Turk said.

"At least I have good reason to be. I've lived through more wars than I can remember. What's your reason?"

"Don't get nasty because your vacation has been postponed," Turk said.

"Okay, I'm a tough bitch. Satisfied?"

"Why not?" He matched her tone. "At least we hit it off in bed."

"I've known worse," Leah said.

"So have I." Turk filled a glass with ice and splashed genever over it. "I have no regrets."

"Neither have I. We may have to work together again some time. I wouldn't mind." Leah's spirits began to rise. "Sorry. I was a bit on the snappy side just now, but the idea of making the rounds of more nightclubs was too much for me. I'll have a Dutch gin, too, if you'll pour one for me."

"Anything to oblige." He prepared a drink and handed it to her.

She raised it in a toast. "No hard feelings?"

"Why should there be?" He returned her salute. "You know what's wrong with people like you and me? We can't tolerate domestication."

"Right. We were beginning to take each other for granted, like a married couple, and suddenly it was too much for me."

"One marriage was enough."

"I couldn't tolerate even one. Turk, I'll compromise with you," she said. "I'll go out for one of those Indonesian dinners. Then we'll come back here, drink ourselves silly on champagne, and have a long farewell session in bed. How does that strike you?"

"Wonderful," he said.

Shaikh Suleiman ben Yosef al-Husayn sat impassively on

287

the inlaid ivory throne of his ancestors as the members of his Cabinet, his half brothers, cousins, and two nephews filed into the formal audience chamber. One by one they prostrated themselves before him, then took their places according to rank, with the senior official, Foreign Minister Shaikh Ahmed al-Husayn, standing to the right of the prince.

The guards raised their scimitars in salute to their monarch, then backed out the chamber and closed the door behind them.

"This is the first full meeting I have called since I brought you here to tell you I had taken the throne," Suleiman said. "Today I have news of equally great importance. I have been preparing for the day when Abu Bakr would assume her place as the first nation among equals, the leader of all Islam. That day is at hand."

His relatives stirred, and Finance Minister Shaikh Habib al-Husayn caught the eye of his older full brother for an instant, then hastily looked away.

"In order to achieve that place," Suleiman said, "we need vast sums of money, some portion of which we must spend as *baksheesh* to win universal acceptance of our cause. We shall have that money, and much more." He paused, looking in triumph at each of his relatives in turn.

When it became evident that he was waiting to be questioned, one of the younger ministers murmured, "How is that possible, Suleiman?"

The ruling Shaikh struck the arm of his chair with his fist. "The Americans," he said, "have tried to conceal from me the fact that they have discovered a vast new oil field in the Great Wadi, the richest field in the entire Persian Gulf."

Ahmed al-Husayn was alarmed. If Suleiman knew about the strike, he might also know that his Foreign Minister had possessed the information for some time. If that was the case, he was already a dead man. "Surely Aapco would have revealed the discovery to us," he said, instinctively taking the boldest approach.

"No, you, my brother, would have told me."

Ahmed repressed a sigh of relief.

"The Americans will be punished for their treachery, as you will hear."

Habib wanted more details. "How do you know oil has been found in the Great Wadi, Suleiman?"

"A loyal subject who was in the employ of Aapco for years, and who arrived from the Great Wadi only today, brought me proof."

The Minister of Defense, who had been chosen for his key post because he was slow-witted and therefore harmless, shifted his feet. "I hope you'll present the man to us so we may question him ourselves."

"Unfortunately, he died under interrogation." A plaintive note crept into the ruling Shaikh's voice. "It was my duty to Abu Bakr and myself to make certain he was telling the truth and wasn't an agent sent by my enemies. I conducted his interrogation myself. You will rejoice with me because he was the most loyal of my subjects. I am sure that by now Allah has granted him a heavenly reward."

His relatives stood unmoving, and when one of them nervously cleared his throat the sound seemed to echo from wall to wall.

"Abu Bakr's earnings will increase," Ahmed said, "but I am not certain we can afford to assume the leadership of Islam. Every developing Arab nation will ask alms of us."

"We will turn away no brothers," Suleiman said, and his lips parted in a bloodless smile. "I shall seize the property of the American-Arabian Petroleum Company, and shall take possession of all oil fields in the name of our people. We shall operate them ourselves."

For a time the Cabinet members stood silently, until Habib at last stirred. "That might be dangerous, don't you think? I am not sure there are enough Abu Bakrian experts who can pump oil, separate it from gas, and send it out of the country."

Suleiman frowned at him. "There are many men we can hire to replace the Americans. Frenchmen, Englishmen, Dutchmen, Germans. All infidels will sell their souls for high wages."

Ahmed knew he was right, that there would be no lack of applicants experienced in the oil industry. "When do you propose to make this nationalization effective?"

"At once," Suleiman said.

"May I offer a slight amendment to your plan?" Ahmed asked. "I believe we'll need a fortnight to prepare."

"How so?" Suleiman bristled.

"I don't believe the Americans will offer armed resistance, but we can afford no risks. Our regiments on the northern and southwestern frontiers should be recalled, and strategically positioned so they can occupy all oil fields—including the Great Wadi—the moment your decree is read in the square in front of the *suq*."

"Allah has given you wisdom," Suleiman murmured. "This is a wise precaution."

"Also," the Foreign Minister continued, "while the troops are on the move, I can quietly assemble a fleet of commercial aircraft and ships to take all Americans out of the country without delay. I'll need to take care not to arouse Aapco's suspicions, so the airplanes and ships will have to be gathered one by one."

"It will be as you have suggested, Ahmed," Suleiman said, and terminated the meeting.

Ahmed and Habib left the palace together, and the former dismissed his chauffeur for the day, explaining that he wanted to clear his head by driving his Rolls Royce himself. The brothers did not speak until they could no longer see the palace behind them.

"You won two weeks," Habib said. "Very clever. But what do we do now? We'll be outcasts in the international community after nationalization. No nation will do business with us, and even the Arab moderates and conservatives will wash their hands of us. This is a catastrophe!"

Ahmed was surprisingly cheerful. "Do not despair, my brother," he said. "A fortnight is ample time."

"For what?"

"The deposition of Suleiman."

"We lack the strength to send him into exile. The troops will support him, and so will the people."

"Then he must be assassinated. There is no other way." Having reached his decision, Ahmed was calm.

"No man we might hire would be trustworthy. He'd give us away, thinking Suleiman would reward him. That's what the worker from Aapco must have thought."

"May Allah grant him peace now, and again on the day of the last judgment," Ahmed said piously.

Habib was upset. "We can't put the knife into Suleiman ourselves, Ahmed. Family tradition forbids it, and in a few months he would be avenged."

"True." The elder brother was still tranquil.

"If we can neither do the work ourselves nor hire an assassin, the two weeks you've won will pass, and Abu Bakr will be ruined by this insane nationalization. Once the oil fields have been expropriated, it will be almost impossible to arrange a new and viable deal with Aapco or anyone else. Remember the people think in simple terms, and will call us traitors."

"I hope to prevent nationalization."

"How?"

Ahmed's smile faded. "There are others whose stakes are as high as yours and mine. Jerusalem won't be happy when it learns that the man who has sworn to exterminate Israel will have new billions to pay for his campaign. And I can imagine what will happen in the board rooms of American-Arabian Petroleum when the company finds itself driven to bankruptcy."

The Finance Minister's expression was cautious but expectant. "You have a specific plan?"

"Of course. For years Rashid has been the source of accurate information, and the Israelis have learned to trust him. I'll notify our private representative in Athens, and instruct him to wire Rashid in Haifa. He will inform the Israeli government, and they will do the rest."

Habib sighed. "Brilliant!"

"That is just the beginning. Red Hamilton is meeting with Dugald McIntosh in Amsterdam at this very moment. I'll arrange for him to be notified—today—of what is in store, and McIntosh will do what he must if his company is to survive."

"These messages will be traced back to you."

"By whom? Suleiman, after he's dead? In all the years we've been building our private network there have been no leaks. I don't see why we should fear leaks now."

"Because the stakes are so high."

"That," Ahmed said, "is precisely the reason we must take a risk. A minimal risk, in my opinion."

"But a risk, all the same."

"There are two bullets in my gun. If one should misfire, the other will find its target."

The devout Finance Minister recited the *shahada*, the central creed of the Muslim: "*La ilaha illa-'llah wa Muhammadun rasulu-'llah*," he said. "There is no god but Allah, and Mohammed is His prophet."

The sound of the telephone joined the jangling of the other bells in Leah's head. Vaguely recalling that she and Turk had consumed far too much champagne, and smiling wryly when she saw their clothes scattered around the bedroom, she reached over his sleeping body and picked up the instrument.

"Yes?" She was surprised by the hoarseness of her own voice.

292

"Madame," the man at the other end of the line said, "I'm calling from the rare book store. I'm pleased to tell you we've located the sixteenth-century edition of Catullus's poetry that you wanted."

The girl cut through the fog of her hangover, and was wide awake. "I must examine it for myself. When may I come in?"

"Another customer is interested, Madame, so I would urge you to look at it as soon as it is convenient for you. This morning."

"Thank you." She hauled herself out of bed, rang for coffee, and began to dress. She was doing a hasty job on her makeup when Turk opened one eye.

"How can you be so energetic?" he demanded.

"I've just had a full alert from my contact, so I'll have to meet you at the Aapco office for the conference."

She was in such a rush, she left before the coffee arrived.

No customers were present when she entered the bookstore, but the proprietor nevertheless preserved security. "You'll be delighted with the book, Madame," he said. "The binding is eighteenth-century, but the book itself is one of the earliest reprints of Catullus in existence. I'm keeping it in my safe. Come to my office, if you don't mind."

Leah nodded, then followed him to a room at the rear. "What is it?" she asked as he closed the door.

"A message came in for you, direct from the General," he said. "The first time in the five years he's been head of the bureau that he's sent his own cable."

She became tense, but her feelings did not show.

"You're to go without delay to Cairo and report to Yacob."

"Why?"

"Look," he said, "I was told to give you the order, which I've done. I was also told to make reservations for you on the direct flight to Cairo, which wasn't easy, because it's the only flight of its kind out of Amsterdam. My son is picking up your ticket, so go back into the shop and browse until he gets here."

"When do I leave?"

"Noon."

"It will be very awkward to miss the conference this morning."

"Argue with the General, not me."

When the ticket arrived, Leah hurried back to the hotel to pack. Turk had already left for the meeting, so she followed him there, taking her luggage with her. She could spend an hour addressing the meeting before racing to the airport.

A wooden-faced Dutch receptionist in the executive office suite handed her an envelope, in which she found a hastily scribbled note: *"Conference canceled. Hell popping, but don't yet know what. Turk."*

Leah asked for another envelope, and wrote two words on the same sheet of paper: *"Nile Hilton."*

"Please see to it that Mr. Kenyon gets this message," she said. "It's important."

Bobbie poured coffee for the three men, but her husband and Turk were wandering restlessly around the suite, and only Red Hamilton picked up his cup. But even he was so upset he had no idea what he was drinking.

"The problem," Dugald McIntosh said, "boils down to a single question. Can we trust the word of the fellow who came to your room this morning?"

"I trust him," Red said. "Implicitly."

"Why?"

"Because I did business with him in Abu Bakr for years before he came to Europe. He's absolutely reliable, and I know Ahmed al-Husayn has great confidence in him. He's been acting as a troubleshooter for the Foreign Ministry, and he's highly regarded in every capital on the Continent."

"Is that why you believe it was Husayn who sent you the nationalization warning?"

"I'm sure of it, just as I'm positive this is authentic information," Red said.

McIntosh broke a cigar in his agitation. "What I can't understand is why Suleiman's half brother—the Abu Bakrian Foreign Minister at that—should try to dynamite his country's new policy."

Turk's expression was sour. "Appetite for power is contagious on the Persian Gulf. Suleiman has only been number one for a short time, and he's just beginning to consolidate his own position. Maybe Husayn likes the palace plumbing better than his own."

"I don't pretend to know Ahmed al-Husayn's personal ambitions," Red said. "But I've known him for fifteen years, ever since he returned to El Ain from Harvard and went to work for the government. He's a patriot who wants to bring his country out of the Dark Ages into the modern world. He's also a gentleman who keeps his word."

"Whatever his motives, we can't ask him about them," Turk said. "Not after he's chosen a roundabout way to tip us off."

McIntosh stopped pacing. "A long time ago I gave up trying to figure out what goes on in the minds of Arabs. That's why I have men like you two on the payroll. All I want to know is, where do we go from here?"

Red Hamilton was pained. "If Suleiman can't be dissuaded and goes through with the nationalization of the oil industry, we'll have to get out of the country. He might offer some of the boys, mostly our foremen, their same jobs at their present or even bigger salaries, the way the Libyans did when they expropriated American holdings. But for most of us, as well as for the company, it will be the end in Abu Bakr."

"Like hell it will," Turk said. "This expropriation is supposed to come off in two weeks, so we have fourteen days to put up a fight."

"You've already given him a Rolls Royce," Red said. "And

no gift, I don't care what it is, would change his mind—not when he's got billions of dollars at stake."

McIntosh looked at his subordinates in turn, pausing for an instant when his eyes met Turk's.

Bobbie saw them communicate, and guessed what they were thinking.

"Red," McIntosh asked, "when are you meeting your Arab friend?"

"In about ten or fifteen minutes. He'll want to know Aapco's reaction, other than shock. I don't know what to say to him."

"Tell him," McIntosh said, "that I'm flying home to consult our legal department and the board of directors. Tell him we'll go to court if we must to prevent Suleiman from carrying out his threat."

Red knew such measures would be ineffective. His mood was glum as he left.

Turk turned to Bobbie. "Coffee never cures my hangovers, and this is a day for thinking."

She made no comment, but went to the bar and made him a drink.

"Well, Turk?" McIntosh was impatient. "Obviously, something went through your mind a couple of minutes ago."

"We had the same thought, Mr. McIntosh, but the fewer people who know it, the better. Anyway, Red wouldn't approve."

"Are you proposing we offer the throne to Ahmed al-Husayn?"

"How could we make good a promise like that?" Turk countered.

"We could sign a blank check and hand it to him." McIntosh was fencing, not wanting to be the man who first verbalized what each was thinking.

"He has plenty of his own money, Mr. McIntosh. We'd be pouring cash down the drain. Besides, revolutions are always being concocted on the Persian Gulf. It's the Arabs' favorite sport, even though ninety-nine out of every hundred fall flat. The odds are too great that Ahmed al-Husayn would muff it, especially on such short notice. Don't forget that Arabs spend months—sometimes years—refining and talking about their plots before they're ready to do anything concrete."

"What then?"

"There's only one sure way," Turk said. He paused. "Assassination."

"That occurred to me, of course, but I rejected the idea for several reasons." McIntosh ticked them off on his fingers. "First, it won't be easy to hire a reliable killer."

"It can be done."

"Second, he'd have to gain admission to the palace, and an opportunity would have to be created for him to get a shot at Suleiman."

"More difficult, I'll grant you, but still possible."

"Third, some sort of escape would have to be planned so the killer wouldn't be gunned down on the spot by Suleiman's bodyguards."

"Harder still," Turk said, "but there's an outside chance it could be arranged."

"Fourth, Aapco's connection with the killing would have to be concealed for all time. And I don't see how that could be guaranteed. A hired gunman would realize we'd be ruined if the truth ever got out. So he could not only blackmail us, but he might also be persuaded to talk if someone else offered him still more money."

Turk scowled. "I don't know how to beat that problem," he said.

"Besides, we'd have to offer a killer a reasonably safe escape plan. A man with any brains would know we might want him shot down to prevent him from talking." McIntosh dropped into an easy chair and took a long time preparing and lighting a cigar.

Turk went to the window and looked out at the glass-enclosed tourist boats on the canals, their windows open to the summer air.

Bobbie broke the silence. "There's one person who could bring it off," she said.

Both men looked at her.

"You, Dale."

Turk knew her revenge against him was complete. Nationalization would destroy his usefulness to Aapco, he would be quietly discharged, and no other oil company would want to hire him because his name would be associated with American-Arabian Petroleum's total failure.

McIntosh watched him. "What do you say?"

"I don't know." Turk felt as though he had been kicked in the stomach.

"Bobbie is right. You're the one man who can bring it off, the one man who'd be reliable."

"I've done a lot of things since I've been in the oil business," Turk said, "but I've never been a gunman."

"Aapco," McIntosh said, "has never had this much to gain—or lose. We're dealing with a man who isn't rational, so we're forced to resort to extreme measures. Unless you can think of some other way."

"There isn't any." Turk's shirt was drenched with sweat.

Bobbie studiously examined an innocuous print on the wall.

Again there was a long, tense silence.

"Name your price," McIntosh said.

Turk knew Bobbie had trapped him, that there was no way out.

"One million dollars. In cash. And all expenses."

McIntosh wasn't surprised. "One angle needs to be covered," McIntosh said. "Regardless of whether you succeed or fail, the company can't appear to have any connection with you."

"That's reasonable," Turk said, "provided I can make use of Aapco facilities in Abu Bakr."

"Up to a point. I'm taking you off the payroll, effective immediately. Our records will reflect your dismissal. But I'll say nothing to our people in El Ain because, presumably, it wouldn't occur to me that you'd head back there and try to pass yourself off as an Aapco employee."

"Fair enough." With a cool million at stake, Turk had no intention of quibbling.

"We have a deal then," McIntosh said. "On one further condition. You will never reveal to anyone, under any circumstances, what we discussed in this room. I'd deny it, and you'd have a difficult time making anyone believe you," he added, twisting the knife. "My reputation for credibility is better than yours."

During rush hour Cairenes clung to the outsides of buses, their acrobatic agility astonishing visitors, and the little taxis careened through traffic so recklessly that most foreigners who rode in them were terrified. But Leah paid no attention to the antics of her driver or the surroundings, and sat calmly until she reached the jewelry store, which was just opening for the day.

The proprietor whisked her to his second-floor office at the rear. "Your stay in America did you good, Leah," he said. "You look relaxed."

The girl cut through the amenities. "My flight was late last night, too late to come here. What's the emergency?"

Yacob sighed. "The government in Jerusalem," he said, "has received definite information that Suleiman is going to nationalize the oil interests. In thirteen days."

She whistled softly.

"The General is very upset," the old man said. "This has been his nightmare. Suleiman will shower money on every Palestinian guerrilla organization that promises to make trouble for us. We can expect new commando raids on our frontier settlements, torrents of fresh propaganda, a major diplomatic campaign against us. Our neighbors will get so many fighter planes and tanks and guns that we'll have to revise our defense budget again."

"You don't have to tell me," Leah said. "It will be hell, and the worst of it is, we can do nothing to stop it."

"Ah, but we can." Yacob took a tea kettle from a hot plate and filled two glasses, adding lemon and sugar.

"The General has had another of his ideas?"

"Drink your tea before it gets cold."

Leah obediently picked up her glass, even though she disliked tea. "What is it this time?"

"The shaky peace of the Middle East must be maintained. At all costs. If the balance of power is disturbed there will be another war—which nobody on either side can afford. Except Abu Bakr, which wouldn't be directly involved. So Shaikh Suleiman must be executed."

"The pressures are too much for the General. He's lost his mind."

"That's what I thought at first. But he's right. There is no other way."

Leah's laugh was forlorn. "So we kill Suleiman, just like that. With you in charge and me helping you."

The old man shook his head. "The General," he said, "has put you in direct charge of the project. I've been ordered to give you logistical support."

"Does he know what he's asking?" she demanded angrily. "Suleiman leaves his palace only when he goes to the Great Mosque to pray, and then he rides in a bullet-proof car, surrounded by guards. Travel into Abu Bakr is strictly controlled. And even if we could sneak a killer into the country, how would we get him into the palace?"

Yacob's voice dropped to a whisper. "You have free entry to the palace. Any time you wish."

She stared at him.

"Nobody can order you to do it, of course. You would face the possible consequences alone; we could give you no help if you fail. All the same, the General hopes you'll agree to volunteer."

Leah thought of the falcon and the scars borne by Suleiman's women. Slowly her hand crept up to her shoulder. "Yacob," she said, "send the General my love."

Fifteen

Dugald McIntosh hoped for the best, but methodically prepared for the worst. Saying nothing to anyone about the planned assassination of Shaikh Suleiman, he nevertheless suggested to Senator Watrous that United States Minister to Abu Bakr Christopher Trevenian be called home for consultations. "All I can tell you, Herb, and you don't want to know more," he said, "is that we'll be saved potential headaches and embarrassments if Trevenian isn't in El Ain next week. In fact, it would be helpful if his arrival in Washington is publicized."

Watrous asked no questions. He called one of his close friends, the Undersecretary of State for Political Affairs. That same day a cablegram was sent to Minister Trevenian, summoning him to Washington.

McIntosh decided, however, that some semblance of normality had to be maintained in Abu Bakr, so his parting instructions to Red Hamilton in Amsterdam were succinct.

Giving his subordinate no hint of what he had in mind, he said, "Ordinarily, in a situation like this, we'd evacuate dependants. But I don't want Suleiman to think we're aware of the situation, and I don't want to force his hand prematurely. So keep your ears open, have a chat with Ahmed al-Husayn, and learn what you can."

"I think we're taking a hell of a risk," Red said. "The mobs in El Ain will go wild when nationalization is announced. They'll march by the hundreds to our compounds. They'll grab furniture, clothing, and everything else that isn't nailed down, and they'll take physical possession of our houses, the hospital, the commissaries, the works."

"Post a maximum-strength guard," McIntosh said, "and if nationalization actually goes through, demand protection for our complex and our people. We're entitled to that much, even if they throw us out."

"I'll do it your way even though I disagree with you," Red said. "But I reserve the right to send out women and children if Suleiman launches an anti-American campaign just before nationalization. I insist on using my own judgment."

McIntosh was forced to agree.

"One thing more," Red said. "My daughter still has a cast on her leg, and couldn't get out of the path of a mob. She's suffered enough in Abu Bakr, so I'll send her up to Rome by the end of this week, and my wife will go, too, to look after her."

McIntosh did not argue.

Red returned to Abu Bakr by way of Beirut, and the following afternoon he landed at El Ain International Airport. Ordinarily he would have preferred to drive his own sedan and would have dismissed the Aapco chauffeur who had come to the airport, but he had already decided to pay a visit to the Foreign Minister on his way home, and consequently needed to remind the Arabs that he, too, was a man of consequence.

He telephoned Ahmed al-Husayn from the airport, then had himself driven to the Foreign Office, where his host awaited him with the unalterable ritual of coffee drinking. They spent three quarters of an hour exchanging compliments as they sipped from tiny cups. Not until Ahmed waved away his servants and closed the door could either man speak of other matters.

"I saw one of your assistants in Amsterdam, Your Excellency," Red said. "Rashid al-Kauayi."

Ahmed was careful to correct him. "A former assistant. He lives in Europe as a private citizen."

Red bowed to indicate that he accepted the correction. "We had several interesting talks."

"Our friend," Ahmed said, "has a real gift for making conversation. When he lived in America, I'm told, his classmates at Yale thought him very witty."

"I enjoy his sense of humor," Red said, "but I like his company even more because he discusses matters of substance."

Ahmed's smile was faint. "In my experience," he said, "he has always kept himself abreast of news. Everywhere in the world. I might even call him remarkably well informed."

Red abandoned his last hope that nationalization of the oil industry could be avoided. "We were sorry you weren't there with us, Your Excellency. Your name frequently came into the conversation."

"I am flattered."

"Not at all," Red said. "He often cited you as a final authority in many matters."

"We have been good friends for many years. He knows me so well," Ahmed said, "that I sometimes think he creeps into my mind and speaks with my voice."

"I don't doubt it," Red said. "He spoke with such wisdom and learning that I found myself repeating much of what he said to Dugald McIntosh."

"I hope you extended my highest regards to the *Pasha* McIntosh."

"Indeed, Your Excellency. Thanks to our friend, your name often came into our conversations."

The Foreign Minister's anxiety almost overcame him. "What does McIntosh think of our joint future?"

"He views it through your eyes, Your Excellency. But I regret to say that Mr. McIntosh doesn't confide in me."

"I quite understand." Even if Hamilton knew how his superior intended to meet the coming crisis, Ahmed thought, he was wise to pretend ignorance. Assured that the president of Aapco, who had much to lose, was at least aware of the pending expropriation, the Foreign Minister was relieved. McIntosh was the kind of American he most admired, a man who took direct action to protect his interests. "Send him my greetings when you write him, and tell him I hope we shall meet in the near future, under circumstances in which Allah shows his favors to both of us."

On his way out to the Aapco complex, Red stopped at his office long enough to compose a cablegram to Dugald McIntosh corroborating the reality of the crisis. He took the message to the communications center himself, destroying the original after it was translated into code.

At home, he found Ruth awaiting him with a drink on the glass-enclosed terrace. Judy saw him from the side of the pool, where she was sunning herself, and came into the room on crutches.

Red listened as they brought him up to date on the local gossip, but his mind was on more important matters. He could not mention the impending nationalization even to his wife and daughter, however, so he had to proceed with caution. "Getting away for a few days was good for me," he said. "It gave me a new perspective."

Ruth knew he intended to issue an order.

"I had almost forgotten how invigorating Europe can be, even in the summer," he said. "So I want both of you to fly to Rome at the end of the week. You can go to Switzerland. Judy will recover far more quickly there."

"I hate Switzerland," Judy said.

Her father ignored the interruption. "I'll join you in St. Moritz or Davos."

Ruth raised an eyebrow. Never had he left Abu Bakr for a vacation during the dry season, when the wells were pumping twenty-four hours a day. She waited for an explanation.

None was forthcoming. "The three of us haven't been together in Europe for a long time."

"It will be wonderful for Judy, and for us, too," Ruth said.

The girl stared at her father. "When is Turk coming back?"

Red was startled. "I have no idea."

"He was in Amsterdam with you, wasn't he?"

"We attended the same conference, if that's what you mean," Red said.

"Then you must know when he's coming back to Abu Bakr!"

He was annoyed. "I have no idea if he's coming here again, much less when. We didn't discuss the matter, and he had already gone by the time I left."

"Where did he go?" the girl wanted to know.

"I don't keep tabs on Turk Kenyon." Red peered at his daughter. "Why all the interest in Kenyon?"

"Because I have no intention of leaving Abu Bakr until Turk comes back—and I see him again."

Red glanced at his wife.

Ruth's expression indicated this was not a new subject, and that she could not cope with it.

"I know of no reason," Red said, "why you should want to see Kenyon again."

Judy's temper flared. "How can you talk that way after he saved my life, Daddy?"

"We've thanked him for it. All three of us."

"Not the way I want to thank him. I was in the hospital, half out of my mind when he left. If we're off in Europe for the rest of the summer it might be years before I see him again. He'll make another trip out here soon, and I'm not going anywhere until I've seen him."

Red could think only of an Arab mob descending on the compound. "You're flying to Rome this weekend!" he said, his voice sharp.

Judy glared at him. "I'm not budging until I've seen Turk. The only way you'll get me out of here is to carry me, and I'll scream all the way to Italy."

Turk Kenyon checked into the Nile Hilton, found a message from Leah telling him the assumed name under which she had registered, called her, and went at once to her suite. The changes in her appearance since he had last seen her were striking: there were deep smudges under her eyes and she looked haggard, but even more significant was her lack of buoyancy. She greeted him with a wan smile, and he dropped wearily into a chair.

"You haven't had much sleep," he said.

"Neither have you."

"I've got a lot on my mind."

"Your situation couldn't be worse than mine," Leah said. "Tel Aviv has decided the only way to stop Suleiman is to execute him, and I've been volunteered to do the job. Because nobody else in the bureau can get into Abu Bakr."

His laugh was humorless.

"What's so funny?"

"One step at a time. Have you agreed to do it?"

"I'm trying to make up my mind. It would mean the end of my career as an agent, because word would get around in the agency, and my superiors wouldn't want someone vulnerable in a field job. I've known all along it would come eventually, but I'm not the kind to settle down in an office job, and I can't see myself living on a kibbutz."

"You could live anywhere on the bank account you've piled up."

"I haven't made all that much, and certainly not from my

government. We're supposed to be inspired by patriotism."

"Aren't you?"

"You want the truth? No. I lost my religion a long time ago, and my kind of work drains the patriotism out of you too. You keep going because of the momentum you've built up. And because you've lost your options. When you no longer believe in a cause, or in people, there isn't much left." She was annoyed with herself. "Why am I telling you all this?"

"Because I'm in the same bind," Turk said, "and more than you know. Aapco has asked me to take on the same assignment. I've accepted it."

Leah laughed, but her anger mounted. "They know we can't refuse challenges."

"Sure, but that wasn't my only reason for—"

"Governments and big corporations are the same everywhere," she continued, ignoring the interruption. "They need people, as they need guns and machinery, but people can be replaced, just as weapons and equipment can be replaced when they break down. People like us think we're cynical, but we're fooling ourselves. We're incurable romantics. The people who hire us know it, and exploit us. Not that we'd have it any other way, of course. We want them to take us in, to give us impossible jobs that we can pull off in spite of the odds. We live on excitement, and convince ourselves we're necessary, that we perform such valuable services we can't be replaced."

He raised a hand to halt the torrent. "I won't argue with you. I'll even agree you're right, as far as you go, but some of us aren't as stupid and romantic as you make us out to be. I've accepted the assignment because I've been offered one million dollars."

Leah was not impressed. "A billion won't do you much good if your head is stuck on a pike outside the *suq*."

"I don't intend to be caught."

Her manner changed, and she became professional. "You have a plan?"

"Not yet," Turk said. "I got your message in Amsterdam—"

"Oh, that. I didn't want you to think I was vanishing again."

"Well, you didn't, and here we are." His eyes hardened. "In the back of my mind, I guess, I hoped we might work this out together."

"The supreme challenge. A couple of tough experts who have spent their lives weaving through loopholes beat the odds."

"Something like that," Turk said.

"I can't do it. I don't mind dying. I've faced death so often that I've become more like the Arabs than I've realized. Not that I believe in kismet, but if my time comes I'm ready to go. But my vanity—if that's what it is—won't let me become disfigured and have to spend years and years living that way."

He was puzzled.

"It's simple," Leah said. "I can go back to Abu Bakr any time I want as Leila. But I'll have to do it on Suleiman's terms." For the first time, she explained about the falcons and the scars on the bodies of the Shaikh's concubines, and as she talked her hand gripped her shoulder. "I have nightmares. I can feel that damned hawk sinking its talons and beak into me."

Turk sat unmoving for a long time. "There must be a way we could protect you and still do the job."

"If we could find that way," Leah said, the sense of challenge beginning to overcome her fears, "I might be willing to try."

"I can't guarantee something that's one hundred percent foolproof."

"There is no such thing. But if we can figure out a reasonably sound way to do the job and escape without the falcon leaving his marks on me, I'll consider it. Provided the risks against us aren't too overwhelming." She smiled wanly.

He grinned back at her. "Let's go to work. As a starter, draw me a rough sketch of the palace interior. Include every detail you can remember."

Farima had her own following now, and had made a place for herself at the Pyramids. The management knew that some of her personal clients came to the nightclub and spent money while waiting to go off with her when she was finished with her work there, and others came to the place because they enjoyed watching her as she moved from table to table with her cigarette tray.

The Pyramids had become her home, and she was completely at ease as she joked with the customers and fended off the groping hands of those whom growing experience had taught her would neither run up a substantial bill nor pay generously for her after-hours favors. She was becoming increasingly expert in her treatment of her regulars, too, brushing up against them as she passed, her eyes and mouth evoking her delights. Only the girls who sat at the bar nightly, singly and in pairs, had disliked her, but they too, having learned that her presence encouraged their own business, had become her friends. After all, she could go off with only one man at the end of the evening.

Farima's one problem was Ali. Unable to find work in a city where mass unemployment was chronic, he had finally been hired by the Pyramids as a waiter, thanks to her intervention. He showed no gratitude, however, and felt it his duty to lecture her incessantly, reminding her that her conduct was reprehensible, that she was ruining their good name and tempting the wrath of Allah. But Farima no longer listened to him. She had found a nearby hotel where she could entertain her customers, and she avoided her brother as much as possible.

She had settled into the routines of a life that was both pleasant and profitable, far removed from the miserable existence she had known in Abu Bakr. So she was startled one night, shortly before closing time, when the man who had been her benefactor came into the Pyramids.

He gulped a drink at the bar, then beckoned to her and bought a pack of cigarettes. "The lady who saved your life has returned to Cairo and wants to see you. Tonight." As he paid for the cigarettes he handed her a slip of paper on which an address had been scribbled. "She will expect you and your brother as soon as you can leave here."

Even though she was fully aware of her debt to the woman, Farima wanted nothing to complicate the new life she had made for herself, and she pouted. "I have other plans tonight. The lady will have to wait until tomorrow."

He spoke very softly. "You have a short memory."

"My friend is waiting for me," she said petulantly, half pointing to a man who sat at a nearby table.

"Make other arrangements with him."

"What if I refuse?"

"You won't. You and your brother will be there in thirty minutes. Don't keep her waiting." He paid for his drink and departed.

Farima weighed her chances if she disregarded the request, and decided the risks were too great. Her benefactor was a man of influence. He had gotten her job for her, and he might be strong enough to have her discharged, no matter how much the management liked the business she brought in. The past she wanted to forget was intruding, but she would not return to Abu Bakr under any circumstances, she told herself.

Her customer was disappointed and angry when she postponed her date with him, but Ali was elated when he learned they had been summoned by the lady, and he paced up and down outside the Pyramid as he waited for her to change into street clothes.

His euphoria dissipated as they walked to the address they had been given. Men stared at the girl in tight-fitting Western attire who had not removed the heavy makeup she wore at the Pyramid, and Ali cringed when he saw their expressions. But he knew Farima no longer heard anything he said, so he muttered under his breath, swearing vengeance against the whole world.

The address proved to be a shop selling cotton fabrics. It was dark, its bamboo shutters lowered and securely held in place for the night. But the door opened as brother and sister approached, then closed after them.

Farima sucked in her breath.

Ali instinctively reached for the dagger he now carried on a chain inside his shirt.

The shadowy figure of a man made a chiding sound, then led them up a rickety, spiral staircase. The showroom was high-ceilinged; they had to mount thirty steep steps to reach another door, which the man opened before gliding off down a corridor.

Lights were burning inside, and for a moment Ali and Farima were blinded, but they looked again and could make out heavy drapes drawn to conceal the windows. "Come in," a woman called, and they recognized the voice of the woman who had helped them to escape from Abu Bakr.

Leah was seated behind the door, which she closed when they entered. "I hope I haven't frightened you," she said. "In my work I must take precautions." She waved them to a low divan opposite her chair, and, with a gesture, gave the young man permission to smoke.

"The time is at hand," Leah said, "for us to join hands again."

Ali sat forward, but his sister remained indifferent.

"We have the same goal now," Leah said, and silenced the young Arab when he would have blurted something about Suleiman. "There's no need for any of us to name it. We understand one another."

"Whatever you wish," Ali said, "will be done!"

His eagerness caused Leah to smile. "Very little will be required of you. You'll be subjected to few risks, and you'll be well paid."

"It is enough to strike at tyrants!" Ali exclaimed.

Farima was more practical. "What do you want, and how much will you pay for it?"

Leah looked at her, and saw at a glance how much she had changed. It was preferable to deal with her brother. "You were a fisherman. You still know how to sail a *dhow?*"

"Around the world, if you wish!"

"You'll make two shorter voyages. How large a crew will you need to sail a diesel-equipped *dhow?*"

The young man weighed the question. "I could sail such a ship alone, but I would like one helper. My sister, if she will remember the place of woman in Islam and do what she is told."

Farima laughed.

Leah remained serious. "You're familiar with diesel engines?"

Ali raised his head proudly. "For three months I went to the diesel school in El Ain. Many would have hired me, but I would not accept work from the running dogs of the imperialists."

Leah absently noted that he had used a phrase popular with Chinese Communists. The remark would be worth sending to the General. "Do you know the village of Kafr el-Haj, where the great dunes slope down to meet the sea?"

"I have gone there often for provisions, and I have anchored there during storms. The harbor is secure."

Leah nodded. "Then your task will be easy. You will be given tickets and new passports, and at dawn you will take the early flight to Kuwait. You will be met, and you will take possession of the *dhow*, which has enough fuel, food, and water to remain at sea for more than two weeks. How long will it take you to sail from Kuwait to Abu Bakr?"

313

"One day and two nights."

"Perfect. You will go direct to Abu Bakr, and you will fish off her coast. After four days you will go ashore at Kafr el-Haj and sell your catch. Then you will wait."

"For what?"

"A companion and I will join you. We'll go to sea together, and after you take us to another country, following the directions we give you, we will go ashore, and the *dhow* will belong to you."

Ali's eyes gleamed. "Such a prize is almost enough to make one a capitalist."

Leah bit back a smile. "Only at Kafr el-Haj will you face possible danger. You will hear wild stories about events in El Ain. Some will be true, others will not. Your ship's papers will be in order, so you needn't fear inspections by the harbor constabulary or Abu Bakrian patrol ships. But you may need cunning to smuggle my companion and me aboard."

"Allah gives the courageous the cunning of a serpent," Ali said. "You have nothing to fear. When will you come?"

"I'm not sure." For a moment Leah's green eyes became clouded. "Wait three days and nights. If we have not come by then, you'll be free to sail away, and you'll be obligated to no one."

"If you wish," Ali said, "I'll wait until the hour when Allah pronounces the last judgment on us all!"

"Three days will be long enough," Leah said.

Farima stirred. "I have dates every night this week. It would cost me too much to change my plans. If you had given me advance warning I might have considered your offer. But this way it's impossible. I can't go."

Her brother gaped at her. "Have you forgotten what this lady has done for us?"

"No, but I won't go."

Leah had anticipated her reaction, and afraid that Ali would create a scene by striking his sister, she intervened. "How much would you earn in two weeks?"

Farima made a rapid calculation. "Five hundred Egyptian pounds."

Only the most expensive call girls in Cairo could make that much in a fortnight, but Leah pretended to be deceived. "Very well," she said. "You will be paid double that sum. And," she added, reading the other girl's mind, "you can use the extra money to buy the new wardrobe you've wanted."

Farima had expected the usual bargaining, and was dazzled. She couldn't earn one thousand Egyptian pounds in a year, but a new wardrobe would enable her to frequent clubs far more expensive than the Pyramid, where she would have the opportunity to meet men who afford higher prices. "When will I be paid?"

"On board the *dhow*, after we've left Abu Bakrian waters."

"I would like some portion of it now," Farima said.

The outraged Ali could remain silent no longer. "Enough! You shame me in the presence of this generous lady who gives much and asks little in return. Your greed makes me sick. No wonder woman holds an inferior place in Islam. The more I see of the world the more convinced I become that the old ways are the best."

There, Leah thought, sat a future *dhow* owner who would become a stolid member of the conservative majority in Abu Bakr. Other ideologies could not take root in a society where men interpreted every facet of life according to rigid Muslim precepts.

Ali stood and bowed. "Great lady," he said, "it is a joy to serve you. May Allah bless your venture."

Dugald McIntosh refilled his glass of Scotch throughout dinner, but had no appetite for the jumbo shrimp, filet mignon, baked potato, and salad that made up his customary menu. Bobbie knew what was troubling him, but tried to avoid the subject by talking at length about some paintings, rugs, and vases she had purchased that day.

"I wish we had some way of knowing that Kenyon will do the job for us," McIntosh said when she paused for breath. "I wouldn't blame him for getting cold feet."

"He always boasts that he likes the tough jobs best," Bobbie replied, realizing she had to give in. "And I think he really does."

"He's never had one this tough." McIntosh drained his glass, reached for the decanter, and then thought better of it. "It's this sitting around and waiting that I can't stand. The outfit I've spent my whole life building into a major oil company may collapse. And what do I do? I worry."

"What more can you do?"

"Well, I discussed it with Hector Bell today. He was saying that nationalization in Abu Bakr needn't necessarily be one hundred percent. I'm wondering whether I ought to fly over myself and tackle Suleiman. If he listens to reason I might persuade him to let us keep forty percent, plus our usual transportation and refining rights."

"Profits would drop badly, of course," Bobbie said.

"But we'd still be in the black. Oh, he'll offer us some kind of compensation if he expropriates, but there's a whale of a difference between promise and performance in the Middle East."

"If you're asking my advice," Bobbie said, "I'd leave well enough alone. From everything that's been reported from the time Suleiman seized the throne, he isn't reasonable. We heard story after story in Amsterdam proving it. That's why you decided on the plan in progress now."

"But—"

"A trip to visit Suleiman might complicate everything. You don't know when Turk is going to act, exactly, and you could get there at the wrong time. And with Trevenian called home by the State Department, there might be all kinds of embarrassments for you."

"I might be more optimistic if I knew what the hell he's

planning," McIntosh said. "When is he going to do the job? How will he go about it? Who else is involved with him, and how reliable are they?"

"Trusting Turk Kenyon isn't the easiest thing in the world, but there was no alternative."

"I may have moved too fast. Not that this is an excuse, but Aapco has never faced the possibility of bankruptcy before, not since the day we founded the company. I should have told Kenyon to stay in touch with me."

Bobbie realized his concern was affecting his objectivity. "That's just what he shouldn't do. If anything spectacular happens in Abu Bakr during the next few days, you've got to be the most surprised man on earth."

"Oh, I know." McIntosh's smile was feeble. "The public relations boys will prepare a statement saying how grieved and shocked I am. I'll even offer a reward for information about the killers. That ought to go over big in Abu Bakr."

"I like that idea."

"Suppose I go over for the funeral. Too much?"

"And too grisly." She thought of herself as hard-bitten, but her cynicism had limits. "Either let Hamilton represent you, or send one of the younger front office people. Someone like Chet Baker, who makes a good appearance and can speak Arabic to the Abu Bakrian press and radio people."

"Your ideas are always good, although in this case I'm not sure I agree. They'd expect me to appear," he said, taking a cigar case from his pocket. "But now we're assuming that Kenyon will succeed."

"It's the only assumption we can make, Dug." She rose from her place, went to him, and put her hands on his shoulders. "I never dreamed our whole future would depend on Dale Kenyon's success or failure. But that's the way things are happening. We'll just have to sweat it out."

They leaned over the table in Leah's suite, studying the

map they had drawn of the royal palace. Turk used the gold-hilted dagger Shaikh Suleiman had given him, and lightly drew the point down a line on the map. "Here's the courtyard he uses for his fun and games. What I like is that it's located only a few feet from the outer wall of the palace itself. You have no idea whether sentries patrol the passageway between the two walls, I suppose."

"I never caught more than a quick glimpse of the passageway," Leah said. "I've only been on the inside of the inner wall, in the women's section."

"Okay." He placed the dagger on the table and made notes on a sheet of hotel stationery. "Add to the list of imponderables. Possibility of sentries in the outer passageway."

"Assuming the worst, as always," Leah said, "we'll have to get rid of them."

"By eliminating the element of surprise," Turk said, "we also get rid of potential dangers. You're sure you can get me the Colt .32's I want? Two of them, with silencers. I know American small arms, and this is no time to experiment with foreign makes."

"We'll have both guns no later than ten tomorrow morning. Two hours before we leave for the airport."

"Then here's the scenario. After I drop you off at the palace, giving Suleiman our agreed line, I dispose of the man who'll be taking me back to my car. That's the greatest danger, but he'll complicate everything if he isn't knocked out. I'll slug him when we're heading down the corridor between the inner and outer courtyards, where there are no sentries, and I'll leave him behind that huge Chinese urn at the end of the corridor. Check?"

"We've already covered that ground. I'm worrying about possible sentries in the passageway."

"The space between the inner and outer walls can't be more than four feet wide, so there won't be much traffic there. If any sentries are patrolling the walk, I'll have to take care of them, which is one reason I'll be carrying two pistols."

"It's riskier than I'd like," Leah said, "but I see no way to overcome it. Take five percent off our chance of getting away."

"No more than two percent," he said, "and I'm looking at the dark side. I'll carry the rope ladder under my *agal*, and after I've used it to climb the inner wall to get Suleiman, I'll lower it for you. The next question is whether we ought to scale the outer palace wall too. We won't have too much time when we leave."

"We might save three to five minutes. The car will be outside?"

"On the street, next to the outer wall of the palace. At the exact spot where we'll scale the wall. Call it ten minutes saved in our escape."

Leah ran a hand through her hair. "It won't do. They'll think it very strange that we're arriving at the palace on foot."

Turk smiled at her. "I've worked out something for that problem. The car will happen to break down. It'll stall. I'll get one of the sentries to keep an eye on it for me, and I'll give him the biggest tip he's ever seen."

She nodded. "He'll want a great deal more *baksheesh* when we climb down the outer wall."

"And he'll get it. Either that or a bullet, depending on whether he cooperates or acts tough."

"We'll come back to that, but something else may be a much bigger problem. We're basing our whole plan of action on the belief that Suleiman will take me to the court-yard again."

"Right."

"Suppose he doesn't. Suppose he picks some other area of the palace. The place is enormous, and that falcon could tear me apart in the time it would take you to find me. He

319

could stay safe and sound, and I'd be a freak for the rest of my life. Unless we can make it foolproof, I won't do it," Leah said.

Turk fished for a cigarette. "It seems to me that this is a place where feminine psychology is needed."

"Whatever that means."

"Dream up a reason that you'll go along with him only in the courtyard, no other place. You know him well enough to figure out some seemingly valid-sounding excuse that will make sense to him."

Leah reached for a cigarette too. "I might manage it. What am I saying? I'll have to. Give me a few minutes, and I'll try it out on you."

"You'll think of something," Turk said. "Everything depends on it."

She sat back in her chair, and as she concentrated she idly picked up the dagger. "Handsome," she said.

"I've got to hand Suleiman this much," Turk said. "He's an Arab gentleman of the old school when it comes to handing out trinkets. I'll have it priced and insured when I get back to New York. If I get there, I should say."

"Not only decorative," Leah said, testing the blade with her thumb, "but very sharp. And just the right size."

He knew she had something in mind, and looked at her.

"What frightens me more than anything," she said, "is that I'll be helpless. I'll be dressed like a chorus girl under my *feredezah*. Let me borrow the knife. For good luck."

"What will you do with it?"

"If anything happens to delay or prevent you from climbing that inner wall," Leah said, "I want to improve my odds against the falcon. I'll have some protection if I'm carrying it."

Turk was skeptical. "Where would you hide it? There isn't a square inch to hide anything under that harem outfit."

"Watch." Leah slid the blade of the dagger under the gold bracelet Suleiman had given her. The band held the knife in

320

place on the inner side of her wrist, with the palm of her hand concealing the hilt when she curved her fingers. Then, with a sharp shake of her forearm the hilt fell into her hand and the blade was free.

"Pretty good," he said, "provided you aren't searched."

"I wasn't last time, that's all I know, and I'd rather lose your knife than my shoulder."

"If you think you can sneak it into the palace, take it. And may you not be forced to carve a trained hawk with it."

Sixteen

The direct flight from Cairo was late, and Red Hamilton was too tense to wait in the air-conditioned airport building. Instead, he roamed the grounds inside the barbed wire fence until the arrival of the airplane was announced in Arabic, English, and French. Then he stationed himself a short distance from the immigration officials, and waited until the inspection of the passengers was completed.

"This is quite an honor," Turk Kenyon said. "The general manager himself is picking me up."

Turk took Leah's luggage when the girl, hidden by the customary *yashmak* and *feredezah*, came through the women's line.

"I had no idea you were making another trip here until I got your cable a few hours ago," Red said. "What brings you here this time?"

"We hope we can put a damper on Suleiman's nationalization scheme," Turk replied. He did not elaborate.

322

When Red realized that no explanation would be forth-coming he refrained from further questions. He suspected he wouldn't approve of any plans Kenyon and his blonde companion might be making, and his situation was already complicated enough.

"Anything new at this end?" Turk wanted to know.

"Not really. Production is normal. There's been no hint of expropriation from the palace. I saw Ahmed al-Husayn the day I came back from Amsterdam, though, and he confirmed —obliquely, of course—that nationalization is in the works. There's no doubt it's coming."

"If we can," Turk said, "we'll stop it."

"I came to the airport myself because I wanted a few words with you in private before we reach the compound," Red said. "I assumed you'd be alone, so I hope the lady will forgive me for bringing up a personal matter."

"Naturally," Leah said.

"Your return can clear up one problem for me, at the very least," Red said. "I've been trying to send my wife and daughter off to Switzerland. Judy can't get around very well on crutches, and I don't want her in Abu Bakr if fireworks start. But she's refused to leave until she sees you."

Turk was surprised. "Why me?"

"Because she's young and impressionable." Red's voice became harsh. "She can't put the palace dungeons out of her mind, and she regards you as her savior. She's insisted on staying to thank you. I've got to get her out of here before Suleiman expropriates," Red continued. "I'm afraid of mobs marching on Eisenhower and Truman."

Turk knew how difficult it was for Hamilton to request a favor from him. "I'll try to talk her into leaving."

"That's all I ask. Thanks."

"I had to cancel their plane reservations," Red said, "but after we'd learned you were returning today, Ruth ordered tickets for the day after tomorrow."

"In that case," Turk said, "you can relax. I'll try to talk

Judy into clearing out, and I'll do my damnedest to convince her. But your worries may be over by the day after tomorrow. I have reason to believe the crisis may be ended by then."

Ahmed al-Husayn handed his brother the carbon copy of the day's list prepared by the immigration department. "See for yourself," he said. "I've underlined the names."

"Dale Kenyon, of American-Arabian Petroleum, and a woman named Leila Smith, who has a British passport." Habib al-Husayn was puzzled. "Why should this be important?"

"She is the girl Kenyon brought when he made Suleiman a gift of the new Rolls."

The Finance Minister was shocked. "Is this how Aapco hopes to prevent nationalization? Can they really believe a woman will change Suleiman's mind?"

"So it would seem." Ahmed smoothed his mustache. "I gave McIntosh too much credit, I fear."

"But Kenyon is a realist. Surely he must know that this girl can't prevent expropriation."

The Foreign Minister sighed. "The arrivals list speaks for itself."

"Then we must find some way to notify Hamilton—or Kenyon, if he has influence with McIntosh—that this is a futile and foolish gesture."

"We can't," Ahmed replied. "I took a great risk by indicating to Hamilton, as clearly as I did, that Suleiman will seize the Aapco properties in a few days. We cannot allow ourselves to become directly involved."

"Then Hamilton is as stupid as all the others in his company." Habib was glum.

"My faith in them was too great," Ahmed said.

"If Aapco has failed us, we can only hope Israel will act. Have you had any sign—"

"The government of Israel and I do not communicate with each other," Ahmed said acidly.

"Then what can we—"

"Nothing. We wait for the sword to fall, either on Suleiman or on us."

Within minutes of the newcomers' arrival Judy Hamilton, walking slowly with the aid of her crutches, made her way to the guest house. Leah tactfully withdrew into a bedroom when the younger girl approached the threshold.

"Well! Look who's as good as new!" Turk thought Judy had aged ten years, and that realization, plus the sight of the scars that had not yet faded, made it difficult for him to be jovial.

Judy accepted a soft drink, but was so nervous she could barely say hello.

He made a greater effort. "Your father told me you were eager to see me."

"I can never repay you for what you've done for me," she said, sounding like a small child who had memorized a speech.

"That isn't why I helped you." In his embarrassment, and aware that Leah might be listening from the adjoining room, he tried to change the subject. "What happened to your friends who escaped?"

"I no longer think of them as my friends," Judy said with a new, mature dignity. "They used me. But I have no grudge against them, and I did what I could to help them. When the security police came to the hospital to question me, I purposely gave them false descriptions."

"And they haven't been caught?"

"Not yet, and I doubt that they'll ever be found. A reward was offered for them, but nothing more has happened. My own theory is that they're still in the El Ain old town."

"What about you, Judy? When do you get rid of the cast?"

"The doctors are going to take new X-rays in another two or three weeks."

"I understand your parents want to take you to Switzerland. You might think about going, you know. The medical facilities are much better there." Turk was doing his duty, and congratulated himself.

"I'll think about it, but not yet. May I be honest, Turk? It wasn't so long ago that I hated you. Because of you and my mother. Maybe I was just jealous—I don't know what it was. Anyway, I don't hate you any more, not after what you did for me."

"That's good to know." He began to feel uncomfortable, and wished she weren't looking at him so intently.

"I've been thinking a lot about you, and I believe I know you pretty well. Better than most."

"I guess you do." Her hero-worship was obvious.

"There's something more I want to say. I just hope you won't laugh at me."

"Never."

"If you go off on a vacation one of these days, I'd be willing to go with you."

He was flattered, even though he could forget neither her condition nor the fact that she was Ruth Hamilton's daughter. "That's the best offer I've had in a long time. Ever since you've grown up I've thought you're pretty cool."

"I was sure of it!" Judy exclaimed. "I really do know what's happening inside you."

"First," he said, rising and helping her to her feet, "we both have jobs to do. Mine is here for the present, and yours is in Switzerland. Get rid of that cast, make sure your leg is okay. Then we'll make plans."

She moved beside him to the front door. "Where will you be in another three weeks?"

That, he thought, was a question no one could answer. "I'll know where to get in touch with you." He saw she expected to be kissed, so he obliged, finding her eagerness pleasing.

Judy looked back repeatedly as she hobbled down the path.

When Turk finally closed the door he discovered that, in spite of the air conditioning, his shirt was soaked.

Leah came in from the bedroom, and refrained from sarcasm when she saw his expression. This was no time to remind him he was more sentimental than he believed, that under duress he was capable of making a decent gesture, so she merely patted his arm in a sign of approval.

"Let's go to work," he said, and called the palace to notify Suleiman that Leila had returned to Abu Bakr with him.

A palace chamberlain carried his master's messages to and from the telephone, complicating and prolonging the call, and a quarter of an hour passed before Turk put down the instrument. "Suleiman can't receive you at sundown tomorrow. He's going to the Great Mosque then, and he won't change his plans. But he did agree to move around some of his other appointments, and he expects us at five."

"That will give us two hours," Leah said.

"But without the benefit of dusk. Our first setback."

"It can't be helped," she said. "We've started, and it's too late to stop."

"We'll draw another map, and then go over the whole plan again to see if we've left any loopholes."

"A friend of mine who was a tank officer in the force that crossed the Suez Canal in the 1973 war told me he felt all right after the fighting started," Leah said. "What bothered him was the waiting for the battle to begin. I know what he meant."

The day dawned like any other in Abu Bakr. The shrill calls of the *muezzins* summoned the faithful of El Ain to prayer soon after daybreak. Fishermen who had spent the night in the Gulf were returning to port, and other *dhows* were just putting out to sea. Long lines of natives employed by Aapco filed into buses that would transport them to the

327

oil fields. The *suq* came to life—the proprietors of shops and booths unlocking their doors, while those who owned no property spread their jewelry and kitchenware, hand-tooled leather, and beaten-copper trays in open-air displays. There was more of a bustle in the old town than would be seen at any later hour, and members of the growing professional and middle classes, secure in their new homes on bluffs overlooking the sea, were stirring too. Porters opened government offices, clerks and bailiffs began to straggle into the law courts, and Shaikh Suleiman ben Yosef al-Husayn left the women's quarters of his palace for his own section, thereby signaling his retainers that he was ready for breakfast and work. Only the foreign businessmen staying in the two modern hotels behind the city were still sleeping, and soon the rising sun would slash through the bamboo blinds in their rooms and awaken them.

Most people in the American compound were busy too. Housewives had already prepared the morning meal, and men were driving from their homes in Eisenhower and Truman to the oil fields in Roosevelt. Children gulped their breakfasts and raced to their school bus stops; classes would begin promptly at 7:00 A.M., before the day became too hot, and would be dismissed at 1:00 P.M. Executives who had already taken quick dips in their pools enjoyed the luxury of lingering at home over second cups of coffee, but their assistants had already reached headquarters and were decoding the cables from New York and the telegrams from branches.

Ruth and Red Hamilton were relieved when Judy cheerfully told them at breakfast she was willing to leave for Switzerland the next day. There was no doubt that Turk Kenyon was responsible for her abrupt change of mind, and Red, though still hating the man, was grateful to him.

Nets were hauled aboard a forty-foot *dhow* that stood off the coast near the fishing village of Kafr el-Haj, and, after the catch had been dumped into a huge, modern freezer, the vessel moved slowly toward the port.

A Bedouin camel caravan left El Ain and started across the open desert, heading toward the Oasis of Qar.

The night flight from Beirut, which had been delayed while refueling in Kuwait, arrived at the airport, and a handful of weary travelers subjected themselves to the red tape that would admit them to Abu Bakr.

Ahmed al-Husayn paid no attention to the censored edition of the local morning newspaper. Instead, as he sipped a tiny cup of sweetened Turkish coffee, he tuned in his radio to an overseas B.B.C. newscast, hoping to hear some hint that might indicate Israel was aware of the heightened menace Suleiman represented. But the news was bland, and the disappointed Foreign Minister dressed for the day, considering and then rejecting several possible courses of action.

Only in Guest House Three of the American compound were heavy drapes drawn to keep out the sun, and the occupants, who had rehearsed until the small hours of the morning, slept late and fitfully. They roused themselves shortly before noon, went for a swim, and then ate a light meal delivered to their living room. Both wanted a drink but abstained as they made their preparations for the afternoon.

Leah bathed, then spent a long time at her dressing table, where she made up in the Arabian manner, even smearing henna on her soles and palms. Occasionally her fingers crept to her left shoulder, but she could not allow herself to touch it, and she tried as hard as she could to avoid thinking about the danger that awaited her.

Turk cleaned and loaded the pistols, and, after carefully attaching Maxim silencers to them, dropped two dozen rounds of ammunition into a pouch attached to the specially designed belt he had made several years earlier. This was his action belt, fitted with pockets containing emergency equipment of various kinds, and he checked the contents of each section before donning it.

He paid special attention to his high, laced boots, testing

their two-inch crepe soles, which he smeared with a sticky substance that made them semi-adhesive. He had purchased a small phial of the liquid in Alexandria many years earlier, and had never before used it on an assignment.

He examined his rope ladder carefully, and as a final precaution he dropped iodine and a small roll of gauze into one of the pockets of his belt. When everything was ready he stretched out on the divan in the living room, and soon dropped off to sleep again.

Leah awakened him when she completed her dressing, and he sat up to look at her.

"Only the Arabs," he said, "could dream up a costume like that. You look like a model of everything women's lib is protesting."

"Watch," Leah said, and jerking her right arm downward, produced the gold-handled knife. "I've been practicing. I can do it in half a second."

"Unless we foul up badly, you won't need any time at all." Turk went to the telephone and ordered a car delivered from the motor pool.

The automobile arrived, and Turk made certain it was filled with gasoline. He had already obtained two special passes from Hamilton that entitled the bearers to enter the American compound at any hour, and he offered one to Leah.

"Where would you suggest I carry it?"

"That's a problem. But I thought you should have it if we become separated."

"I'll have to take my chances. Carry it for me, please."

They fell silent, and spent their last hour at the guest house smoking and staring at the clock. At 4:15 P.M. they stood and clasped hands for a moment.

"We'll celebrate in London, Paris, New York—you name the town," Turk said.

"First we'll get the job done." Leah carefully donned her outer Arab attire.

330

Turk put on his *agal* and *ghutra* after winding the rope ladder around his middle and stuffing the pistols into his belt. Suleiman, he hoped, would regard his wearing of Arab dress as a compliment.

They said nothing as they drove into El Ain. Turk had timed the journey with care, so they reached the palace at 4:55 P.M. He began to circle the perimeter, and glanced at Leah as they approached the place he had marked on their map.

"Not yet, but slow down," she said. "Another ten yards. Now."

He cut the engine, turned it on long enough to pull to the narrow curb, then gunned it and again cut it. "Let's go."

As they had anticipated, a sentry carrying a sub-machine gun approached.

Turk said that something had happened to his engine, and handed the man a 5-*rial* coin. "We have business in the palace," he said. "If you will keep watch on the car for me, I'll pay you again when we return."

The sentry was pleased, his half salute indicating that he accepted the offer.

Leah fell in behind her companion as they walked to the main gate.

The guards on duty there apparently did not think it strange that foreign visitors to the ruling Shaikh were arriving on foot, and they called a chamberlain to escort them across the courtyard and into the palace. As they neared the urn behind which Turk intended to conceal the body of the chamberlain on his retreat he asked, "Has His Highness consented to grant the boon requested by his brother?"

"You will be received in private," the man said.

Turk glanced at Leah. Her face hidden, but the sheen in her eyes told him that, with their mission underway, she was sharing his tenseness.

Shaikh Suleiman ben Yosef al-Husayn was seated on a mound of cushions, a low table with a pile of documents on it drawn up in front of him. He held a thick wax pencil over a small flame emanating from an oil lamp, smudged a portion onto a paper and stamped it with his royal seal. Then he looked up.

Leah's stomach churned as her eyes met his, and she quickly prostrated herself on the floor.

As Turk bowed he wondered if they should have utilized an alternate plan they had considered, that of shooting the Shaikh here and now. But he was glad they had rejected the notion. The door was still open, a possibility they had weighed, and he could see two armed guards in the corridor.

"You again place me in your debt," Suleiman said. "You will always be welcome under my roof."

Turk expressed his gratitude at length and in flowery Arabic before coming to the business at hand. "Leila has told me she does not yet know how long she will remain here as Your Highness's guest, as that is a matter you and she will decide. So I will await word from you before I return to take her away."

Suleiman's eyes gleamed.

"She has also given me a message I do not understand, but which I have sworn to repeat to Your Highness in her own words." Turk spoke very slowly, enunciating with care. The entire scheme depended on the Shaikh's willingness to listen and act accordingly. "She begs Your Highness not to delay because, if you do, she will lose her courage."

Suleiman's expression remained unchanged as he nodded, then signaled that the brief audience was ended.

As Turk withdrew, he saw that Leah was still stretched out on the floor, her forehead pressing against the tile.

The door closed, and Leah was alone with Suleiman.

He took his time sealing another paper, and did not speak.

Time dragged, and she was afraid perspiration would ruin her makeup. Nothing could be allowed to go wrong, since the smallest slip could be fatal.

"You may rise," the Shaikh said, and sealed two more documents before he glanced at her. "You have changed your mind."

"Yes, Your Highness." Somewhat to her surprise her voice was strong and clear.

"I have found I have been awaiting this day."

"So have I," she said.

"What reward do you seek from me?"

"I've thought about it for many weeks." Every word had been planned, which made it easier for her to speak with apparent confidence. "I've had many ideas, but none seemed right to me. Your Highness has already been so generous in your dealings with me that I am content to let you decide the size and nature of my reward." She could see he was pleased, precisely as she had hoped.

He chuckled. "You make a mockery of the old Arab saying that women and children are foolish and only men are wise."

Leah was straining to listen, but she could hear no commotion in the corridor outside or the area beyond it. By now, if their plans were working, Turk would be hiding the body of the chamberlain and would be heading toward the passageway between the inner and outer walls. If something unexpected had happened, she felt reasonably certain, she would be hearing the bursts of sub-machine guns. As nearly as she could judge, this chamber was not soundproof.

"You will not regret the decision."

Leah snapped back to the present.

"I am sure of it."

"Allah may open your eyes to the joys of the experience, and you may wish to remain here to repeat it, as others have done before you. You will be rewarded accordingly."

By now Turk would be making his way around the palace, and Leah's head swam. "My only request, Your Highness, is that we don't tarry here. Soon weakness will betray me, and I'll draw back."

"I have no wish to delay any longer." He reached behind the cushions for a large wooden cage.

She could not look at the creature that had haunted her.

Suleiman rose, carrying the hawk, and Leah fell in behind him.

They walked slowly down the corridor toward the women's wing. The guards stood at attention until the Shaikh passed. After he went by, their eyes moved to the falcon, and they grinned at the shrouded figure of the woman who brought up the rear.

The walk seemed endless, as Leah had known it would, and her dread increased.

Two sentries raised their sub-machine guns in salute as the Shaikh unlocked the door of the women's quarters and went into the world that no other man could enter.

The door closed, and the girl heard a metal bolt grating into place. There was no escape.

Suleiman took a route unfamiliar to her, and her fear became so great she thought she would faint.

At last he halted. "You may undress," he said.

She forced herself to focus, and saw she was standing under the roof on the inner side of the courtyard so familiar to her in her nightmares. Stealing a glance at the wall, she saw no sign of Turk. The quiet doubly disturbed her. Surely, if he had encountered sentries, she would have heard the noises of a scuffle.

Suleiman took the falcon from its cage.

The sight of the creature galvanized Leah. She removed her *yashmak*, then her *feredezah*, her back turned to the Shaikh so he wouldn't see the dagger that her bracelet held in place on the inner side of her right forearm. Carefully folding the garments, she steadied herself and turned to face the demented master of Abu Bakr.

He studied the face and figure of the fair-haired girl who stood before him. He moistened his lips.

334

Leah felt compelled to look at the hawk, and was mesmerized by its talons and beak.

"You are ready?" Suleiman asked.

Leah was still staring at the bird.

"I'm ready," she said, praying that Turk could hear her.

"You will walk to the pillar at the far end of the courtyard. As soon as you turn I will release my friend, and the race will begin."

Waves of panic washed over her. This was not what she and Turk had planned. If she ran toward the Shaikh she would come between him and Turk, whose aim would be spoiled because he could not fire at the man without striking her.

"I—I thought I would run from this spot to the pillar at the other end," she said, her voice almost failing.

Suleiman's face hardened. "You will do as I have ordered. You may begin."

Leah commanded her legs to move, and to her surprise they obeyed her. She searched the lip of the wall for the prongs that would tell her the scaling ladder was in place. But the top of the wall was bare, and as she drew nearer to the pillar, she knew she would be playing Suleiman's mad game in earnest.

She could avoid being disfigured only if she could reach the haven offered by the man she detested above all others.

She was only a few short paces from the pillar, and knew that if she slowed her step she wouldn't have the strength to run.

A protective haze settled over her, but just before she reached the pillar she shook her arm in the motion she had practiced, and the dagger fell neatly into her hand. She wasn't completely helpless, but couldn't permit herself to think of the damage the hawk could do to her before she disposed of it. And this was no time to dwell on what Suleiman's reaction might be.

Leah touched the pillar, turned and sprinted toward the man who stood at the far end of the courtyard.

She caught a glimpse of a blurred streak moving skyward, but devoted all her strength to her goal, the security of Suleiman's arms.

The falcon circled overhead, gauging the speed of its victim.

Leah's heart pounded in her ears until she thought they would burst.

A grinning Suleiman awaited her, his arms outstretched.

The falcon swooped in a headlong dive that no living being could escape.

Leah knew she could not reach Suleiman in time.

She didn't know why, but the hawk did not touch her. It crashed into the tiled floor, grazing her as it fell.

There was no time now to find out what had happened. Suleiman loomed directly ahead, and as he grew larger in front of her she knew what had to be done. Raising the dagger that had been his, she plunged it with all her strength into his unresisting body.

At the same instant a bullet tore into his brain, and he fell, dead before he hit the ground.

Leah snatched her *feredezah* and *yashmak,* and not taking time to remove the blade from the body of the dead Shaikh, she ran to the rope ladder that awaited her.

Her legs were trembling so violently that it was an agony to climb.

Turk's hands appeared from the far side to pull her up. He threw the ladder over the other side of the wall and they both climbed down to the passageway between the walls.

The girl donned her outer garb with shaking hands.

"I would have killed him sooner," Turk whispered as he jolted the ladder free and lowered it, "but I had to get the falcon first."

Leah had no idea whether his bullet or her knife had killed Suleiman; neither of them would ever know.

"I've killed one sentry and knocked another out. The chamberlain, too." He threw the weighted end of the ladder to the top of the outer wall, but the prongs failed to take hold. "They patrol this passageway in pairs. Every five minutes." Before making another attempt to raise the ladder he handed her one of the pistols.

As Leah's hand closed over the cool metal she grew calmer, and for the first time allowed herself to exult. Whatever else might happen, Suleiman was dead.

Turk succeeded in hooking the prongs to the lip of the outer wall, and climbed to the top. A moment later he descended again, his face anxious. "There are four or five soldiers out there now, all of them looking at the engine of our car—and expecting *baksheesh* if they can get it running again. We'll have to leave the way we came in."

Leah followed him down the passageway as he headed back toward the palace. She had to run in order to keep up with him, and she almost crashed into him when he halted abruptly.

He signaled silently that two sentries were approaching, and they crowded close together into a niche in the inner wall that was scarcely big enough for one.

The two sentries were having an amiable argument about the reasons for their sergeant's recent dyspepsia.

Leah knew what had to be done, and needed no instructions. As the pair came into sight Turk fired at the farther soldier, leaving the closer one to her. Her hand was steady as she fired, her pistol making a sound no louder than the popping of a champagne cork, and the sentry dropped to the ground, a bullet hole in his temple.

Turk took knives from the bodies of both soldiers. He handed one to Leah and resumed his rapid walk.

The death toll was already so high that it was certain an alarm would be given at any moment, but Leah obeyed Turk's urgent signal and concealed her pistol and knife beneath her *feredezah* as they came to an arched opening and entered the palace. This was the way she had come with Suleiman, and she realized a misstep now well might prove fatal. "Turn left, then right," she said.

He obeyed without indicating he had heard, and when they saw a pair of guards ahead they slowed their pace to a saunter. The bored soldiers ignored the couple, and Turk, having found his bearings, moved confidently toward the courtyard.

The better part of five minutes had passed since the killing of the sentries in the passageway, and Leah knew that another pair making their rounds would discover the bodies and give the alarm. Then Suleiman would be found, and the entire palace would be sealed. She wanted to break into a run, but instead she maintained a steady pace as she continued to walk behind Turk across the open courtyard. The main gate was directly ahead, and in seconds they would be free.

The guards stationed at the gate glanced at the departing pair, checked their visitors' list, and waved them into the square beyond the wall. Leah's relief made her feel light, almost giddy. But Turk neither paused nor offered her any explanation as to where he was going, and she was bewildered when she saw he was heading toward the *suq*, one of the most crowded bazaars in the Middle East.

A chill shot up her spine when she heard whistles blowing in the palace behind them, followed by the piercing wail of a siren.

All at once, Leah understood Turk's purpose. Hundreds were shopping in the *suq*, and few paid any attention to the commotion on the palace grounds. Abu Bakrians knew the wisdom of minding their own business, and customers continued to haggle with merchants.

Turk did not pause as he made his way past the permanent shops. He seemed to be looking for something, however, and glanced at leather goods, kitchenware, and ornamental trays as he walked past them. At last he halted long enough to buy a large melon, which he thrust into Leah's arms, and she knew what he had in mind. They looked like a local couple, the burdened wife dutifully followed her husband, and the girl kept her head lowered so no passerby would see her green eyes peering out of her *yashmak*. The *suq* had two entrances, one opposite the palace and the other opening onto its own square, and Turk marched the entire length of the bazaar as he headed toward the latter.

Additional sirens were screaming as the couple emerged into the open, and the people around them, finally realizing that something very serious had happened, were pausing and looking around. A new spasm of fright shook Leah when two tanks, their turrets closed and their guns elevated, rumbled through the square toward the palace.

By now, she reasoned, the officers in charge of the sentries would have managed to force open the bolted door and would have realized that she and Turk were responsible for the assassination of Suleiman and the deaths of several soldiers. It was just a matter of time before traffic was halted and every pedestrian searched.

But Turk did not falter, and for an instant Leah wondered if he intended to hail a passing taxi, which was beyond the means of the ordinary Abu Bakrian. He paid no attention to it, however, and she caught her breath when she saw his destination. He was walking toward an American-Arabian Petroleum Company bus standing at the far side of the square.

The only passengers on board were night porters going to work in the American compound, and Leah told herself that in all probability, it was the last bus of the day that would go to the American compound.

Turk showed the passes Hamilton had given him, and the driver barely glanced at them. Leah headed toward the empty women's section at the rear, holding the melon in her lap when she sat down, and Turk remained in the front with the other men, craning his neck as he, too, looked out of the window.

The driver seemed to be afraid he would be delayed beyond his usual quitting time if he waited any longer, so he slammed the bus into gear, and jolted it across the cobblestones.

Leah reached inside her *feredezah* to grasp the butt of her pistol, and held the melon in place with her other hand. One of Turk's hands, she noted, had crept inside his *agal*.

A troop of elite cavalry thundered past the bus, the cavalrymen riding with drawn scimitars. A police car roared off down the same road, its siren screaming, and when Leah looked out of the rear window she could see additional tanks coming into view from the direction of the army base.

The bus driver, who had no intention of being delayed by traffic, took the sea road as he headed northward, and soon left El Ain behind. Sirens could still be heard in the distance, but it was quiet in the desert, and Turk turned casually in his seat to look at the girl who sat alone a dozen rows behind him. His face was expressionless, but one eyelid fluttered in the suggestion of a wink.

Leah lowered her head.

Three fighter planes flying in close formation streaked northward, and for a few moments their shrieks drowned the rattling noises made by the decrepit bus. They quickly vanished into the twilight, leaving long vapor trails behind.

An army staff car shot past the bus, a blue and white flag fluttering from the radiator front.

Leah knew the danger had not yet ended, and remained tense.

Turk appeared to be at ease, however, and chatted in Arabic with the porter across the aisle. When the bus drew to a temporary halt at the gate of the American compound he followed the example of the other passengers and held his passes against the window pane so the Aapco sentries could see them.

The guard in charge waved, and the bus headed toward the residential district of Eisenhower.

Turk moved to the rear door, and Leah, still playing the role of an Arab woman, dutifully rose and stood behind him. When they left the bus he allowed her to struggle to the ground alone, the melon still clutched in her arms.

Not until the bus turned a corner did he take the melon from her and drop it into a garbage can. "We've done it!" he said. "We've brought it off!"

They had reached the relative safety of Aapco property, but Leah knew it was premature to rejoice. They were still on Abu Bakrian soil. They were not yet in the clear. And they knew that while the local authorities would not pursue them into the compound, they knew also that they could not consider it a haven for long.

Seventeen

Shaikh Ahmed al-Husayn was the first member of the Cabinet to reach the royal palace. He was met by a delegation of high-ranking officers, two of them his cousins and a third a nephew, and they escorted him to the inner courtyard to see the body of the slain Suleiman ben Yosef. He listened to the reports of the officers, briefly interviewed the vizier and several chamberlains, then acted with a firmness that the various officials found comforting.

Summoning the assembled heads of the armed services, he swore to them that Suleiman's killers would be found and prosecuted. Almost as an afterthought, he directed them to inform all soldiers, sailors, and airmen that armed service wages would be increased fifteen percent, effective immediately. The grateful generals and admirals responded by providing him with an honor guard of household troops.

Guards armed with sub-machine guns were very much in evidence when other government Ministers arrived and were scorted to the smaller of the palace audience chambers. When they were admitted, they found Ahmed al-Husayn seated on the throne of his ancestors.

He opened the meeting by telling them of the murder of Suleiman, and added what they could see for themselves— that, for the sake of peace and continuity of rule, he had mounted the throne.

One by one the Cabinet members swore to support and serve him. He asked each in turn to remain in his post until he could promote each of them. He began that process by naming his full brother, Habib al-Husayn, as his Prime Minister and temporary Foreign Minister.

The preservation of order was the first business of the government, and each Minister was accompanied by a platoon of armed soldiers as he left for his own headquarters.

Shaikh Ahmed al-Husayn went to the office that had been his predecessor's, and signed a number of decrees prepared by the palace staff. In one he announced his assumption of the throne, and in another he formally raised the pay of the armed forces. Yet another set the date for Suleiman ben Yosef's state funeral. A special decree sent Suleiman's widows into retirement in a villa overlooking the sea (and in the meantime Ahmed took the murdered Shaikh's sons under his personal protection), but Suleiman's concubines would remain in the harem until the new Shaikh decided whether he wanted to incorporate them into his own household.

These immediate matters having been attended to, Ahmed used a private line to call the Aapco general manager.

Red Hamilton was shocked by the Shaikh's news, but recovered sufficiently to wish His Highness a successful reign, then inquired whether the assassins had been caught.

"Not yet," Ahmed said, "but you can be of great help to us, and to your own interests."

"I can?" Red was startled.

"We believe the murderers were the man named Kenyon —who may have been in the employ of Aapco at one time,"

Ahmed said, pausing delicately to let the full import sink in. "And a blonde woman using the name of Leila Smith on a British passport. We have begun a search for them, and we won't rest until they are placed under arrest."

"I'm stunned," Red said, and meant it.

"The reason I'm calling you myself," Ahmed said, "is to clear the air. I'm sure you know how my people would react if they thought the killers were on the American-Arabian Petroleum payroll. Public indignation would be so great it would be impossible for me to arrange an agreement favorable both to Abu Bakr and your company."

There was a pause before Red said, "I quite understand. I'll take immediate steps to find out if Kenyon is still employed by the company. As for the young woman," he added, glancing in the direction of the guest houses, "I know of no one named Smith."

"We have reason to believe she is the same person Kenyon brought here on a previous visit to Suleiman."

"In that case, I assure you she doesn't work for Aapco, Your Highness."

"I was certain of it," Ahmed said. "I needn't tell you that my subjects will expect me to prosecute this matter with vigor. The martyred Suleiman was loved by all of us, not only as a man, but as a symbol of Islam."

"If you'll be good enough to provide me with an official overseas telephone line, I'll call New York right now and find out Kenyon's status with the company," Red said.

"Certainly," Ahmed said, "and I know I can rely on you to help bring the killers to justice."

Turk sat on the edge of the guest house bed, sipping a Bourbon and water as he watched Leah apply the body dye, then don the black wig and contact lenses that were again transforming her into an Egyptian. "If your *dhow* is waiting at Kafr el-Haj," he said, "we'll be out of trouble before the

344

night ends. We've been lucky every step of the way." Turk laughed. "The only time I almost lost control was when that falcon went into his dive. He was moving so fast I wasn't sure I could pick him off."

"No talk about falcons, please."

"Okay, let's go over the last lap of this race. There are sure to be armed patrols on the roads tonight, but our car has desert tires, so we can drive across country to Kafr el-Haj, if necessary. Suppose we need four hours instead of three to get there. We'll still board the *dhow* no later than midnight. An hour later we'll be in international waters, and tomorrow we can slip ashore up north somewhere."

"You make it sound easy," Leah said as she worked on her makeup.

"After what we've been through, baby, anything is easy," he said, but his smile faded as they heard the front door open and close. He reached for his pistol.

He was on his feet when Judy Hamilton limped into the bedroom. "You've got to get out of here!" she cried. "Right now!"

Leah glanced at the younger girl in the dressing table mirror, but methodically continued to apply eye make-up.

"Sit down," Turk said. "Don't get hysterical."

"You don't know!" Judy was pale beneath her tan. "Shaikh Ahmed, who is the new ruler of Abu Bakr, called Daddy a little while ago—"

"Good for our side," Turk said, and grinned at Leah.

"I hope so," she replied. "Let her finish."

"Anyway," Judy continued, "Daddy has just been talking to Mr. McIntosh in New York. Mr. McIntosh said to be sure Shaikh Ahmed understands you don't work for Aapco any more—"

"Ah," Turk interrupted. "Sold down the river. No need to explain, Judy. We understand. Perfectly."

345

"I was afraid of this," Leah said.

Judy stared at them. "I'm so happy Suleiman is dead I could do cartwheels, in spite of my bad leg. Did you actually kill him?"

Turk and Leah looked at each other.

Neither answered.

"You'll be handed over to the government," Judy said. "Daddy knows you're here and he knows about the car with desert tires. He's going to wait until you drive off, and then he'll notify Ahmed, so you'll be picked up outside the compound. That way Aapco won't be embarrassed. I—I've been listening on the telephone extension in my room for the past hour. I heard the whole thing being planned."

"Damn McIntosh, damn Hamilton, and damn Ahmed," Turk said. "We were stupid to rely on others."

Turk's expression was grim. "I deserve to be shot, but that's the least that'll happen to us."

"I'm too tired to think," Leah said, getting up from the mirror and turning into the room.

Both had virtually forgotten Judy's presence. "I have an idea," she said in a small voice.

They stared at her.

"Do you know the camel corral at the western edge of the compound? You could—"

"She's right," Turk said, and his face cleared. "We'll borrow a couple of camels. It'll take longer to reach Kafr el-Haj, but no one will think we're traveling that way. By the time anyone discovers we've gone, we'll be at sea."

"You mustn't go to the coast," Judy said. "They're pretty sure that's how you intend to escape, and every little port on the Persian Gulf is being watched."

Turk began to curse.

Leah stopped him. "Suppose we go by camel to the Oasis of Qar, and then double back to Kafr el-Haj. If we leave now we should be able to make the whole journey in the three days our *dhow* will wait."

"We might be able to make it," Turk said, "but what's the advantage of the extra travel? A camel ride across the desert isn't my idea of fun."

Leah's smile was tight. "We're dealing with Arabs, remember," she said. "After seventy-two hours they'll have grown careless, and it will be easier to board our boat and slip away."

"We'll have to try," Turk said, and looked at Judy.

"Don't you dare thank me," she said. "I've paid off my debt. And I hope we can still meet in Switzerland."

"I don't know of a date I'd rather keep," Turk said. "Now get back home before they realize you've come over here."

Judy picked up her crutches, moved to the door, and hesitated, tears appearing in her eyes as she looked at Leah. "Take care of him," she said, and left the guest house without looking back.

Turk put Judy out of his mind as he hurried to the kitchen and began to collect the supplies he found there.

Leah followed him with the saddlebags she had insisted they bring with them, even though she had envisaged no need for them. She opened the small refrigerator, and showed him the contents. "Some cold meat we'll have to eat for breakfast. Before it spoils."

He looked at the cartons he had piled on the kitchen table, and his laugh was harsh. "Three cans of assorted nuts, some bags of potato chips, four boxes of breakfast cereal, a container of sugar."

"And some oranges," Leah said, beginning to dump the food into the saddlebags. "As well as a case of carbonated water, which is really precious."

"The very things any traveler needs in the desert of Abu Bakr," Turk said. "Let's go, and start praying for more miracles."

Dugald McIntosh led a large contingent of American-Arabian Petroleum Company executives to Abu Bakr for the funeral of Suleiman ben Yosef, the party arriving in a chartered Boeing 707 less than twenty-four hours after the Shaikh's murder. It did not escape the attention of foreign diplomats stationed in El Ain that the group included the head of the Aapco legal department and two of his senior associates.

McIntosh and his resident general manager, Red Hamilton, immediately paid a condolence call on the new ruling Shaikh, Ahmed al-Husayn. The trio apparently found grounds for conversation. After being joined by Premier and acting Foreign Minister Habib al-Husayn, they conferred for several hours.

The president of Aapco went directly to the office space made available for him at his local headquarters, and summoned a number of his associates, the lawyers included, to a meeting.

The housing facilities in the American compound were strained. All the guest houses were utilized, and senior officials of the resident staff took some of the visitors into their own homes. McIntosh was given a seldom-used suite at the Hamiltons, but he had not yet put in an appearance there, and was still tied up at the office long past the normal dinner hour.

Red Hamilton left the meeting at 7:30 P.M., arriving home a short time later, and was pouring himself a much-appreciated drink when Ruth came through the living room, several dresses draped over her arm. "They didn't need me any more tonight," he said, "but it looks as though the meeting will last until midnight. I had food sent in, so we won't have to worry about dinner for any of them. That McIntosh is incredible. The way he keeps slugging, you wouldn't know he'd spent all last night on an airplane."

"Yes, he's remarkable," Ruth said, and left the room.

Red, drink in hand, followed her to their bedroom, where a number of open, partly packed suitcases were spread. "What's all this?"

Ruth busied herself placing the dresses in a folding case that was hanging on the back of the door. "I'm sticking around while the brass is here," she said. "I couldn't walk out and leave you to entertain McIntosh alone. But as soon as he leaves, I'm taking Judy to St. Moritz."

"Oh?" His drink was forgotten.

"Judy and I are beginning to understand each other, and she wants to go. So do I, Lyman."

He regarded her in silence for a long time. "Is this your way of telling me we've had it?"

She turned to face him. "Is that what you think?"

"Sure. The way you and Judy hopped all over me yesterday when I refused to find some way to sneak Kenyon and his blonde friend out of the country, you made me think it was the end of the world."

"I expected you to act exactly as you did," she said. "I wasn't in the least surprised. Judy had an eye opener, but in the long run it will be good for her."

Red became defensive. "As you damn well know, Ahmed put the heat on me. How the hell could I have flown Kenyon out of the country in a company plane?"

"You couldn't," Ruth said, "without jeopardizing the new contract with Abu Bakr that you and McIntosh have been working on since the minute he arrived!"

"Do you know how much oil is in the new Great Wadi field?"

"Yes," she said. "You've told me."

"You act as though I've handed Kenyon and the girl over to Shaikh Ahmed for execution, which I haven't. Oh, I've dreamed of revenge. But I've done everything possible for him within the limits of the options that were open to me. I haven't reported the disappearance of two camels from the corral, for example. As far as the Abu Bakrians know, Kenyon and the blonde sneaked out of the compound on foot. Ahmed is convinced they're somewhere in the vicinity of El Ain, waiting for a chance to escape by ship or airplane.

I told him I'd let him know when they left the compound, but I've even fudged that. God knows where they are, but they sure aren't in these parts. Thanks to me."

"It was the least you could do." Ruth was still remote. "He and the girl prevented nationalization and made it possible for McIntosh to work out his fancy deal with Shaikh Ahmed. It seems to me, strictly as an outsider, that Turk Kenyon and his girlfriend have saved Aapco's neck."

"What else could I have done," he demanded, "with Ahmed putting pressure on me?"

"Nothing."

"Then what's your objection? I know you're still not soft on Kenyon."

She gestured angrily. "Sometimes you make me sick! I don't care whether Turk is alive or dead."

Red sank into a chair. "I guess," he said, "I'm too damn stupid to understand."

Ruth faced him angrily. "Then I'll put it in plain language. I have oil in my nostrils, oil in my lungs, oil in my blood-stream, and oil all over my hands. I just can't take any more of it!"

"I'm a little old," he said, "to look for some other kind of work."

She softened, drawing up a hassock beside his chair and placing her hand over his. "I'm not asking you to do the impossible, Lyman. I'm thinking of Judy, not you and me. She'll carry her scars for the rest of her life, and she's had more than enough. We'll stay in St. Moritz until she's completely recovered, and then we'll go to New York. Judy can go on to college somewhere on the Eastern seaboard, and she'll have a home, a real home she can come to."

"Where do I fit into all this, or do I?"

"If I can't get the oil out of my system, I can't expect you to, either," she said. "And I can't tell you what to do. You've told me Aapco will give you an office job at headquarters any time you want it, so you can sit it out there until you retire. When you grow tired of Abu Bakr, you'll accept. And however long it takes, I'll be waiting for you."

"I won't keep you waiting," Red said, "as long as you think."

The desert was endless, but Leah's stamina matched Turk's, and she made no complaint. Her camel's swaying motion reminded her of a ship, and she found its stench almost unbearable, but after thirty-six hours she no longer felt queasy. It was far too easy, however, to let her mind drift as she viewed the unlimited expanses of sand and rock from the protective shield of her sunglasses. The sun made her drowsy, but one part of her mind remained constantly alert. She saw a Bedouin family in the distance, the men and boys driving a flock of sheep across the sands, the women bringing up the rear. She was conscious of the airplanes and helicopters that crisscrossed the cloudless sky overhead, and she realized their frequent reappearance meant there was no lessening of the manhunt being conducted by the new ruling Shaikh of Abu Bakr.

A *shamal* had blown up out of the southwest, and she and Turk were hours behind schedule. They had pressed close to hard rocks during the worst of the storm, and she could still taste the sand as well as feel it in her eyes, her hair, her skin itself. Her eyes smarted and she itched everywhere, perspiration adding to her discomfort, but still the discomfort was minor.

What mattered was that they could spend only three to four hours at the Oasis of Qar before heading back to Kafr el-Haj on the Persian Gulf. She didn't need Turk to tell her what problems they would face if the *dhow* that awaited them put out to sea without them.

Saudi Arabia to the west, Kuwait to the north and even radical Yemen far to the southwest were undoubtedly maintaining a sharp watch for the fugitives who had assassinated Suleiman ben Yosef, so it was too much to hope that they could escape across their borders, and another long overland journey by camel would be almost impossible. However, escape by sea would have to be ruled out if the *dhow* was gone, so there was literally no choice.

Leah knew what was in store if she and Turk should be captured by Ahmed al-Husayn. With Suleiman dead they might escape the worst torture, but what they would be forced to undergo, though lenient by traditional Arab standards, would be bad enough. Wearily, she imagined their fate. She knew they would both be subjected to sexual assault in the palace dungeons before being dragged to the square in front of the *suq* for a public spectacle that would culminate in their execution by decapitation. Fear was a language well understood by the people of all primitive nations, and the new ruling Shaikh could do no less than kill his half brother's assassins if he himself hoped to survive. The law of desert kingdoms had remained unchanged for centuries; those who lived by the sword had to accept the consequences.

The sun sank and the dinner hour passed, but Leah put food out of her mind. Their supplies of sparkling water were exhausted, and it was dangerous to eat their only remaining provisions, salted nuts and potato chips, which would increase their thirst. The night air of late summer turned cold, and she shivered beneath her *feredezah,* telling herself it was astonishing that any people could survive in this most inhospitable of climates.

At last they saw the towering royal palms of the Oasis of Qar ahead. Turk increased their pace. Bedouins and other travelers were bedding down for the night by the time the newcomers found an empty patch of green, but 'there was much still to be done before the couple could take brief naps.

They followed the Arab customs, Turk taking the camels to be watered and fed, while Leah went to the bazaar for food. Only a few stalls were open, but she was able to buy several round loaves of Arab bread, a few skins of water, a handful of dates, and another of figs. With that she had to be content, and she consoled herself with the thought that even if she had been able to purchase some mutton there would not have been time to cook it.

Turk had returned from his own errands, and having erected their tent, was sitting cross-legged before it when she approached. Leah sat opposite him, silently gave him a loaf of bread, and waited until he tore off a chunk before helping herself. If anyone happened to be watching, they were conforming to Arab ways.

She waited until they ate the better part of their meal before she spoke. "In the clearing at the far side of the oasis, beyond the bazaar," she said in a low tone, deliberately addressing him in English so any Bedouin who happened to overhear her would not understand, "there is a sedan belonging to Aapco."

Turk paused, a fig still in his hand.

"The passengers are sleeping in a large tent, and the driver is asleep on the ground near the car."

He knew what she had in mind. "Why the hell didn't you tell me right away?"

"Let them fall into a deeper sleep," she said. "Besides, we were too hungry to leave before we ate."

Turk grinned and consumed the fig.

"The sedan has desert tires. Since they must plan to leave early in the morning, I hope it has a full gas tank, too."

"That doesn't matter," he said. "When Aapco sends a car across the desert, there are always cans of gasoline, oil, and water in the trunk."

Leah smiled. "You haven't thanked me."

"Wait until we're on our way," he said, and his fatigue seemed to vanish.

She felt stronger, too, and ate more heartily. Two loaves of bread were left at the end of the meal. She dropped them into a saddlebag, along with the filled water skins.

Turk went into the tent, where he checked their pistols. He handed her one when she joined him. "The driver may have left the keys in the car. It's an Arab habit that Aapco has had a tough time breaking," he said. "If he hasn't, I'll have to knock him out and take the keys from him. In fact, I ought to knock him out no matter what."

"Why should that be necessary?"

"Because there may be other cars parked overnight here. Or a helicopter or two. And we'll have hell's own time if he gives an alarm. We won't be invisible out there on the desert, you know."

She nodded as she placed the pistol beneath her *feredezah*. "We'd better leave the tent standing so our neighbors will think we're asleep."

"Fair enough. The Bedouins will take everything, including the camels, when they discover we've gone."

He started across the Oasis of Qar, with the girl walking the customary three paces behind him. Not until they passed the bazaar did she move up beside him, and when they approached the grass clearing that faced the desert she nodded in the direction of the car.

The Arab driver was snoring gently in a sleeping bag near the car. There was no sound from the nearby canvas tent, and no light showed from the interior.

Turk led Leah to the far side of the car, peered inside and laughed in silent triumph when he saw the key in the ignition lock. Then he indicated, in pantomime, the role he wanted her to play.

Leah carefully opened the door on the passengers' side, leaving it ajar as she slid behind the wheel and pumped once on the gas pedal. Through the open window she heard a thud as a pistol butt struck the head of the sleeping chauffeur. She switched on the engine, but it coughed and died, the sound seemingly echoing across the silent oasis.

Again she turned the ignition key, and this time the engine began to function. Turk joined her, and she put the

354

car into gear, starting forward before he closed his door. She drove slowly, her foot barely touching the accelerator, and maneuvered the car between two majestic royal palms at the edge of the grass.

Reaching the open desert, she pushed her foot to the floorboard, and the sedan leaped forward. She consulted the compass on the dashboard, and headed toward the northeast. The full moon was bright, so there was no need for the headlights.

Turk chuckled. "It didn't even occur to me to ask whether you could drive."

"I love American cars, they have so much power." Sighing happily, she accepted a cigarette from him. "By the time the Aapco travelers wake up, we'll be at sea, I hope. Anyway, this is better than riding by camel. Why don't you sleep while I drive for an hour or two?"

He started to protest, but changed his mind when he realized her advice was sound, and paid her the compliment of respecting her professionalism by dropping off in a matter of moments.

Leah soon found that the car responded best on its wide desert tires at a speed of eighty miles per hour, and the needle didn't move as she cut across the rolling hills of sand and rock. There was almost three quarters of a tank full of gas, more than enough to take them to the coast, so she relaxed for the first time since they had left Egypt for Abu Bakr.

After Turk had slept for an hour she awakened him.

"Where are we?"

"My guess is about halfway to the Gulf, but I'm not sure we'll locate Kafr el-Haj all that easily."

"Your turn to sleep. Stop the car and move over."

She obeyed and, as he took the wheel, she had no difficulty in drifting off. Exhaustion was an enemy as dangerous as Ahmed al-Husayn's troops, and she knew it.

An hour and a quarter later Turk was shaking her, and she

awakened to discover the car was only creeping. Suddenly alarmed, she sat upright.

"Take it easy," Turk said. "I just saw the water from the crest of that dune. We're only a couple of miles from the Gulf, and Kafr el-Haj is directly ahead."

"Shouldn't we leave the car and walk the rest of the way?"

"I've been thinking about that, and I've decided against it. I'll grant you that not too many automobiles come to the village, so a few people may wake up and become curious. But we'll make far better time by driving to the waterfront. And if the *dhow* isn't waiting for us, for some reason, we'll have a better chance of crossing the border if we have the car."

She weighed his proposal. "All right, even though it is risky."

Turk reached into his belt for his pistol and handed it to her. "Remove the safety catch, please, and do the same to yours."

Leah complied in silence.

The winding main street of Kafr el-Haj was barely wide enough for the sedan, and Turk drove with care until they reached the waterfront.

"When the car is traced here the Abu Bakrians will know we've gone by sea," he said, "but it'll be too late. I can't believe there's a wireless set in Kafr el-Haj, and I've never heard of a village this size on the Gulf with a telephone."

"Turn right," Leah said, a sudden lilt in her voice. "There's our ship."

A *dhow* was tied to a crumbling stone jetty, rising and falling gently as tiny waves slapped its hull.

Turk parked the car and walked slowly toward the jetty, with Leah beside him. The vessel was dark. At first glance no one appeared to be on board.

Suddenly the voice of a man cut through the night. "Who is there?"

"A good friend," Leah replied. "Your wait is ended."

A young man who looked vaguely familiar to Turk helped Leah aboard, then turned to stare for a long moment at her companion.

The only member of the crew, a woman in a *yashmak* and *feredezah,* roused herself and cast off, the man starting the diesel engine and lighting oil lamps that he displayed from the prow and stern.

Turk accompanied Leah into the cabin and, as they watched the coast of Abu Bakr growing smaller behind them, they shed their Arab outer garments. "I've always said there's nothing healthier than a salt water cruise."

Leah pointed toward a gunboat anchored outside the harbor, its lights extinguished. "We won't open the bon voyage champagne just yet."

They continued to watch the gunboat as they glided past. No one on the warship stirred. "I'd hate to think of what a modern navy would be doing," Turk said. "We'd be boarded in no time."

"We couldn't have planned a smoother departure if we'd bought seats on a scheduled flight."

They remained in the cabin for the better part of a half hour, waiting until they were certain the *dhow* had reached international waters and was far enough from the gunboat.

The night air was cool and sweet when they went on deck. The young man stood at the wheel, but the woman was nowhere to be seen.

"We should head for Bandu Abu Shehr in Iran at the nothern end of the Gulf," Turk said, "and from there we can go by a domestic flight to Teheran. If we had to, of course, we could land at one of the smaller Iranian ports like Gada or Hissar, and somehow we could find overland transportation to Bandu."

Instinct caused him to duck and jump aside as the young man, abandoning the wheel, leaped at him.

"Prepare to die, betrayer!" Ali Nasar Jalal shouted as he brandished a long knife.

The stunned Turk first thought the young man was mad. By the time he realized who his attacker was, Ali lunged at him again.

This time Turk was ready. Dodging and weaving, he repeatedly sidestepped the other's lunges. The knife cut harmlessly through the air.

Ali cursed the man he held responsible for his misfortunes.

Turk shut out the sound of the voice, and awaiting his chance, kicked the knife out of the younger man's hand. He smiled as he heard the blade clatter across the open deck; the odds had suddenly improved.

Ali, who had never fought with his fists, was at distinct disadvantage, and could not protect himself from the blows that jarred his head and body. Clawing and kicking in vain, he retreated toward the fantail.

Turk followed, measuring him for a left to the pit of the stomach and, when he doubled over, a hard right to the cheekbone that straightened him for an instant, then caused him to topple over backward into the black waters of the Gulf.

The water foamed, then thrashed, first turning white and then a deep red in the moonlight as sharks attacked their helpless victim.

Turk turned away, and at that instant heard the silencer-muffled sound of a pistol shot.

Farima was crumpled on the deck, a bullet through her head. Leah stood a short distance away, her pistol still in her hand. Ali's knife was still clutched in his sister's hand.

"I hated to do it, just when she could have lived her own kind of life in the way she loved. I'm afraid she gave me no alternative," Leah said. "But I honestly hadn't thought either of them would try to carry out their threat against you, especially the girl."

For a moment Turk looked down at the face of the Arab girl with whom he had enjoyed a brief affair. Then he rolled her body overboard too. Realizing for the first time that the *dhow* was sailing erratically and without guidance, although her engine was still running at full speed, he quickly took the wheel. When he spoke his voice was toneless and calm. "If our luck holds," he said, "we'll reach Iran by late morning."

"No later than noon," Leah said. Her composure matched his.

The state funeral of Suleiman ben Yosef al-Husayn was the most impressive ever held in the memory of even the oldest Abu Bakrians. A cavalry contingent formed the vanguard, and was followed by infantry and dismounted tankmen. The kings and emirs, presidents and shaikhs of the many nations that comprised Islam rode in the long procession through the streets of El Ain, and although members of the diplomatic corps also participated, they were crowded together in several older limousines at the rear of the line.

Military jets screamed overhead in formation, and the navy put on a maneuver of its own in the waters just outside the harbor, the frigates and gunboats firing salvo after salvo. Suleiman's actual burial was private, in accordance with tradition, but the spirits of the people were not dampened. Thousands stood in line waiting to be admitted to the square outside the *suq* for the distribution of funeral meats, rice, millet, and seminola that the new ruling Shaikh had ordered distributed, and they cheered him for the better part of the day.

Suleiman's wives went into retirement, and various of his relatives offered their protection to the concubines, who were happy to accept.

Ahmed al-Husayn had already moved his own family into the palace, and in a daring move that departed from Abu Bakrian custom, he allowed both of his wives to observe the banquet he gave for the visiting heads of state and other dignitaries. The ladies had little opportunity to watch, however, since they were too busy supervising the serving of the many courses to more than two hundred guests who sat at long tables set up in the larger audience chamber.

Among those present at the banquet were Dugald McIntosh and several of his associates, who had watched the funeral procession from the palace roof, where they had been able to see without calling themselves to the attention of the volatile Abu Bakrians. Westerners were not popular in the country at the moment.

Ahmed al-Husayn was sensitive to the mood of his subjects, too, and for that reason he delayed the announcement of the signing of a new, long-term contract with the American-Arabian Petroleum Company. Later, when passions cooled and the escaped assassins were forgotten, the people of Abu Bakr would begin to enjoy their increased wealth, as well as the opportunity to find employment in the petrochemical plant, the oil refinery, the steel plant, and the shipyard that the nation soon would build with the aid and advice of Aapco.

The company's resident general manager, Red Hamilton, was busy seeing his wife and daughter off to Switzerland on a late morning flight, and consequently did not attend the funeral banquet.

The jewelry store was busy, with foreign visitors as well as expensively dressed Cairenes shopping, so Leah took her time. Looking at watches, then at rings, she gradually worked toward the rear. Making certain she was not under surveillance, she slipped through the curtain and climbed the stairs to the second-floor office.

Yacob, who was waiting for her, greeted her with the usual kiss on the cheek. "You're thinner," he said, "and you don't look as good with less weight."

"You'd be thinner, too, if you'd spent three weeks going from one miserable Iranian village to another—and then hiding out in Teheran for days."

"I've known you and the American haven't had an easy time."

"Easy?" She was almost shaking with anger. "It's been miserable! I hate being hounded like a common criminal, and I'm so tired of this wig and body dye I could scream."

"Scream, Leah, if it will make you feel better."

"It won't. The passports our bureau in Teheran gave us were such poor imitations we had to use the last of our money to pay *baksheesh* or we'd have been picked up at the Cairo airport when we landed. And I can't understand why I was told to come here instead of going straight to Jerusalem. What's going on, Yacob?"

The old man looked unhappy. "You and Kenyon are notorious all over the world, and it hasn't helped that the press has been calling you the 'blonde mystery woman.' You're perceptive; you should realize there are complications that can't be waved away."

She stared at him. "Such as?"

"The government has established an unofficial detente with Abu Bakr. Nobody has said anything official, but Ahmed al-Husayn has stopped the payments to the guerrilla organizations, and although it may be years before we set up diplomatic relations, nobody is crusading against anybody."

"So the assassination of Suleiman wasn't the crime of the century."

"It suited everyone." Yacob spread his hands in a gesture of appeal. "Try to understand, Leah. Suppose it came out in the open that the mysterious blonde killer was an Israeli agent. Not only Abu Bakr, but all the rest of Islam would start a new anti-Israeli campaign. It's much better if the world thinks Kenyon was a disgruntled former employee of Aapco, and that you're the mistress who helped him. A very tidy story, and the new balance of power has a chance to stabilize."

"Tidy for everybody except Kenyon and me."

"The General appreciates all you've done, believe me. He wants you to know how he feels."

"His gratitude overwhelms me." She lit a cigarette.

"I've been instructed to make certain you're safely transported to Israel, if that's what you want."

"What then?"

Yacob shrugged. "You'll retire, of course, just as so many other agents have done. The General will help you to find a job in private industry—"

Leah's savage laugh cut him off. "Can you see me working as a secretary somewhere, or as an office assistant in an import–export company? Be sensible, Yacob!"

"You could do worse, and some day you'll settle down—"

"After the way I've lived for seven years?"

The old man ignored her interruption. "The General wants you to know his offer of help is conditional. Once you reach Israel, you'll stay home. For a number of years. Until even the Abu Bakrians forget the assassination of Suleiman."

She sat back in her chair, looking haggard. "What happens if I refuse the General's condition?"

Yacob smiled wearily. "I've been sure you would. The General is prepared to deny you've ever worked for him. You know the ground rules."

"I do." She was fighting for her existence, and had nothing to lose by speaking bluntly. "But no matter what the General claims, he'd be embarrassed, and so would the government, if Kenyon and I were picked up by the police—here, in London, Paris, or even the United States, which has signed a new extradition treaty with Abu Bakr."

"If you know where you want to go, Leah, I've been authorized to offer you the bureau's help in getting there. But this will be the last we'll do. Don't come to us again for anything."

"All right. If you'll help Kenyon too."

The old man was surprised. "Why Kenyon?"

"Because he can't go back to America under his own name. He'd be arrested and shipped off to Abu Bakr. And I need leverage in my bargaining with him."

Yacob studied her. "You want to go to America?"

"I have private business there."

"Two years ago, when I sent you to Iraq, you looked good as a redhead." His voice was so low he seemed to be talking to himself. "Dye your hair red, and keep it that way. It changes your appearance so much you won't need plastic surgery to go with your new personality and life."

Judy Hamilton's cast had been taken off and she no longer needed a cane as she walked from the center of St. Moritz to the Suvretta House, a half hour stroll from the village. She joined her mother for tea in the spacious lobby, and her limp had become so imperceptible that the hotel's other guests, looking at her in admiration, were unaware of her slight disability.

Ruth had been quiet in recent days as she had waited for a letter that had not arrived, but her daughter kept up a steady stream of conversation. Judy described a dress she had seen in a boutique, the pastries she had bought, and casually mentioned that she had accepted a date for the following night with a tennis instructor.

But no subject interested Ruth, and she replied in monosyllables, her mind elsewhere. She had so little appetite it was useless to urge her to eat, and the dark circles under her eyes indicated that she hadn't been sleeping.

Judy ran out of small talk, and fell silent. Absently looking around the lobby, she caught sight of a familiar, heavily tanned figure, who raised a finger to his lips to caution her.

Red Hamilton bent to kiss his wife, and she clung to him so fiercely that others in the lobby stared. Then Judy jumped to her feet to greet her father, and he enveloped her in a bear hug.

"I was going to write to you tonight," Ruth said when she

grew calmer, "and tell you I've decided—in spite of all I've said—that I'm ready to go back to Abu Bakr."

"That won't be necessary," he said, and helped himself to one of the little sandwiches on her plate. "I've left El Ain. Permanently."

"You're being transferred to the New York office?" Ruth's eyes widened.

Red shook his head. "Guess again."

"I can't."

"I've resigned."

She was too stunned to speak.

Judy grinned at her father.

"I'm eating my words, too," Red said. "I was wrong when I told you I'm too old to find a job in some other line of work. And I can prove it."

"You've given up your pension rights?" Ruth asked. "Everything?"

"I accepted twenty-four months' terminal pay, plus a bonus, because I earned that money. But that's it. I've severed all connections with Aapco."

Ruth took his hand. "It doesn't matter. We'll make out."

"Oh, we'll do fine." With his free hand he took a sheaf of letters from an inner jacket pocket. "There's a new interest in Islam, particularly the Arabian countries, back home," he said. "I sent off letters to a number of universities, and I have a half dozen teaching leads."

"That's great, Daddy," Judy said. "Maybe I can enroll wherever you go, and I can save money by living at home."

"We won't be all that broke," Red said. "First we'll take a little holiday together, and then we'll choose our university. We'll have to reduce our scale of living a little, but nobody in this family is going to suffer."

The young tennis instructor started across the far side of the lobby, caught sight of Judy, and waved.

She had the perfect excuse to give her parents a little privacy, and jumped to her feet. "I'll be right back."

Ruth still didn't trust her voice, but she looked at her husband, and her smile was tremulous.

He held her hand more tightly, and they lost sight of everyone else in the crowded hotel lobby.

Eighteen

✦✦✦✦✦✦✦✦✦✦✦✦✦✦✦✦✦✦✦✦

Turk perched on the foot of the bed in the shabby Cairo hotel room and stroked his three-week growth of beard. "I went out long enough to buy the Paris *Herald-Tribune*," he said, "and the first thing I learned is that the reward for any information that leads to our capture has been increased. Ahmed al-Husayn is putting up twenty-five thousand dollars, and Aapco is matching it. So I came straight back here, and I've been waiting for you."

"I haven't wasted the afternoon, believe me," Leah said, and her voice was tart.

They looked at each other, their hostility undisguised, and all the strains they had undergone were apparent. They shared too many guilts, and their memories, combined with the continuing, enforced intimacy they had endured had created a mutual contempt.

"When will you be spirited off to Jerusalem?" Turk finally asked.

"I won't." She explained, briefly, that she could not accept the conditions imposed on her return to Israel.

"So we turn ourselves in to some friendly Egyptian who'll claim the reward."

"There's a way out," Leah said, "but it will be expensive for you."

Turk's eyes narrowed.

"There's a million dollars waiting for you in New York, if you can reach the United States safely. Share it with me, and I'll not only get you a plane ticket and a little spending money, but you'll also have a passport—for one-time use only—that will get you through U.S. Customs."

He weighed the offer. "After I'm paid, I suppose, I meet you somewhere and split with you."

She shook her head. "I'm not letting you out of my sight, Turk, and not only because of the money."

He realized she was right: they knew too much about each other, and were obliged to stay together for their mutual, long-range safety.

The following day a young woman with red hair and a man with a neatly trimmed beard, both wearing sunglasses and both painfully thin, flew from Cairo to Rome, where they picked up a direct flight to New York. U.S. Immigration officials found their Latin American passports in order, and they were admitted on one-month visitors' visas.

They stopped speaking Spanish by the time they reached Manhattan, and checked into an inexpensive midtown hotel under assumed Anglo-Saxon names. They had made their plans with their customary care, and having decided to wait until evening so they could reach Dugald McIntosh at home, spent the better part of the day sleeping fitfully.

At last nightfall came, and Turk placed the call, asking for Bobbie because he knew she would recognize his voice without making it necessary for him to identify himself.

"Believe it or not," he told her, "I'm here."

"I'm not surprised," Bobbie said. "Thanks for helping me win a bet that you'd show up."

"There's a little unfinished business that needs attending."

"I'll expect you in an hour," she said.

Turk and Leah dressed with care in the best of the second-rate clothes they had managed to accumulate in Teheran and Cairo, and the girl's diamond ring and heavy gold bracelet looked incongruous on her. Thanks to the irony of their situation the money each had put aside for emergencies couldn't be touched. Approximately a hundred thousand dollars awaited Leah in a London safe deposit box, but the efficiency of Scotland Yard made it impossible for her to claim her property, at least for years. Turk's money rested in a New York savings account, but he had taken it out in his own name, so he had to avoid his bank too.

They took a taxi to an apartment building in the Sixties overlooking Central Park, and Turk told the lobby attendant that "Mr. and Mrs. Brown" were expected.

Bobbie greeted them at the door in a sable-trimmed hostess gown, and led them through a handsomely furnished living room to a leather-and-oak library. "You really are clever," she said. "I'm not sure I'd have recognized either of you."

Turk had no patience with the social amenities. "Where's McIntosh?"

"He had to go out unexpectedly, so he delegated me to act for him."

That was a lie, as both visitors well understood. McIntosh didn't want to be compromised by dealing with a couple for whose apprehension he had offered a substantial reward.

Bobbie went to a wall safe and withdrew an attaché case, which she placed on the desk. "I'm dying to know how you escaped from Abu Bakr and got all the way over here when thousands of people have been searching for you."

"It's too long a story," Leah said, her weariness evident.

Turk was harsh. "Some other time."

Bobbie's manner changed, and she became brusque. "The bulk is in negotiable bonds and stocks, with fifty thousand in cash. We thought the cash would be useful in setting yourselves up in new identities somewhere."

"Very considerate of you and Mr. McIntosh," Leah said.

"Mind if I count this?" Turk stood and removed the contents of the case. He counted them with care, then demanded, "Where's the rest?"

"This is it," Bobbie said, and smiled.

"There's only four hundred and fifty thousand here!"

"I'm sure you two can live for a long time on that amount —if you aren't too extravagant."

Turk was livid. "The agreement was for one million!"

Bobbie's shrug looked as though she had practiced it in front of a mirror.

It was impossible to determine whether she had appropriated the rest herself or was acting in collusion with her husband. But Turk was so aroused he didn't care, and took a step toward her.

Leah placed a restraining hand on his arm, well aware that he was in no position to threaten anyone. "We'll manage on it," she said, resignation in her voice as she closed the case. "You're welcome to the half million."

Turk stood silent, then absently picked up the case.

Bobbie looked at him, then at the other woman. "You're welcome to *him*."

"Thanks," Leah said in the same, dry tone, and it was obvious that both his future and past wives knew him all too well.

A joint announcement made by Shaikh Ahmed al-Husayn and the American-Arabian Petroleum Company indicated that Abu Bakr, after the new Great Wadi fields were fully developed, would produce more than four million barrels of crude oil per day. The experts agreed that this would constitute a significant step in the alleviation of the worldwide energy crisis.